Catherine Siska was born and raised in Midland, Texas. She holds a Bachelor and Master's Degree from Texas Tech University and is periodically a University Tutor for the English Language Centre at the University of Liverpool. She currently spends time in Horwich and Slovakia with her husband Peter and their children.

Dedication

To my Lord who makes all things possible, to my husband Peter who has always helped me be the best I can be, and my loving children who have been so supportive.

Catherine Siska

UNLOCKING THE IRON GATE

AUSTIN MACAULEY PUBLISHERS™

LONDON · CAMBRIDGE · NEW YORK · SHARJAH

A CIP catalogue record for this title is available from the British Library.

ISBN 9781786938800 (Paperback)
ISBN 9781786938817 (E-Book)

www.austinmacauley.com

First Published (2018)
Austin Macauley Publishers Ltd.
25 Canada Square
Canary Wharf
London
E14 5LQ

Prologue

Honza was busy repairing the exit sign above one of the platforms at the Prague train station. As he carefully mounted his ladder, a young couple caught his eye. They were standing near the newspaper kiosk looking intently at one another. This was nothing unusual; during the past several years, Honza had seen many young lovers saying good-bye, but he noticed something different about these two.

The young man looked to be in his late twenties. He had a fine handsome face that was quite intense, yet, at the same time, sensitive and rather artistic. Definitely Slavic – probably one of theirs. The young woman was tall and had a mass of reddish brown hair that seemed to distract her at the moment. Judging by the way she was dressed, she looked like someone from the West. *Who are they*, he wondered. Curious, he moved his ladder a bit nearer to where they were standing. They did not pay him any attention. Hearing them speaking English, Honza could not help but feel a trifle disappointed, but he listened anyway.

"It's so hard to go," the woman murmured. The dark-haired man pulled her closer to him.

"I know," he said shutting his eyes and squeezing her. "But you will come back soon. You will come back, won't you?" He looked at her a bit fearfully as if afraid to hear her answer.

She beamed and sniffed as a tear rolled down her cheek. "Of course, I am coming back. We are getting married! I wish it were tomorrow."

The train slowly rumbled up to the platform. The young man sighed and turned her face towards his. He leaned in and kissed her. Then stepping back, he released her and tried to smile.

"Texas is so far away. It's like you are going to the moon."

She tried to laugh, but the tears began to flow in earnest.

"Don't cry, Katka. Please don't cry," he said softly stroking her face. "We will write. I enjoy our letters."

She nodded as she struggled to control her emotions. Having a good view of her face, Honza was amazed to see that her eyes were a bright translucent green color, any dullness washed away by her tears.

The young man picked up her suitcases and helped her onto the train. Honza could see that she settled herself into an empty compartment. *She probably wants to be alone*, he reflected sympathetically. He saw them embrace one last time and then saw the young man reluctantly disembark the train. The curly-haired woman pulled down the window and they held hands until the conductor blew the whistle and the doors closed.

"Please give your parents my best regards. Your sister and brother, too!"

"Yes, I will. Tell your mother and father thank you for me. They were so good to me. Goodbye, Pavol. I love you."

The young man looked flustered and fervently kissed her hand one last time. She blew him a kiss as the train began to pull out.

Honza stood at the top of the ladder mesmerized. There was something special about these two. What was going on? As the train disappeared around the bend, the young man's shoulders sagged as if under a heavy burden. He turned around and slowly descended the stairs, staring at the ground.

"I wonder what their story is," Honza mused as he tightened the last screw in the sign. Shrugging, he descended the ladder and packed up his tools.

Unexpected News

Zuzana Tesarova sighed as she cut the hard dry roll into her milk coffee. Stirring the thick grounds, she looked absentmindedly out the window at the distant mountains. At forty-six years of age, her face was weather-beaten and lined with worry. She stretched her calloused hands over her stomach and felt as if she were carrying a heavy weight indeed. The real weight would grow heavier in about nine months. It was the fall of 1950, and life was in transition in their little village in Czechoslovakia.

"Mama, how could this happen?"

Zuzana looked up to see her daughter Helena standing in the doorway with the afternoon light streaming behind her. Her hands were on her hips, and the light lit up her auburn colored hair. The expression on her face reminded Zuzana of a stern schoolteacher who had just caught a mischievous student in the act. With a slight grunt, the young woman slipped off her shoes, sat down at the wobbly oak table, and glared at her mother, who remained silent.

"Mama!" she said demanding an explanation.

Her mother looked at her wryly and asked simply, "You don't know?"

"You know what I mean! You have already given birth to four children! Martin and I are already over twenty, and Ondrej is only ten. I don't even want to mention poor Maria." Helena hung her head sadly but quickly snapped it up again. "Now, at your age, you're going to have another baby? What were you thinking?" Helena slapped the table.

"Do you think I planned this? Is that what you think?" Zuzana asked wearily looking over at the peeling plaster on the kitchen wall.

The two women sat silently together. The wood cook stove heated the small room on that cool October afternoon. Without another word, Helena got up from the table, pulled on her mother's faded blue *vertucha*[1], and

---

1 Apron

glanced out the window at the blue, hazy mountains behind the river. She grabbed the broom and began to energetically sweep the wooden floors.

"What did Apa say when you told him the news?" Helena asked more quietly after a few minutes.

"Nothing. He pretended not hear me and went out into the garden," shrugged Zuzana. She got up from her wooden chair and emptied the coffee grounds into the compost can.

Staring at the can, she reflected on the previous day when she had gone to the doctor. Clinics and hospitals were not at all to her liking, but she had no choice as she had been feeling so ill and nauseated. Helena, who worked in town, had arranged the appointment through her colleague. Zuzana's stomach churned as the steam train chugged and pulled those fifteen kilometers to Topolcany. After the doctor had examined her, she waited restlessly on the hard bench outside of his office. The smell of antiseptic burned her nostrils and the white tiled walls made her feel dizzy. Finally, the doctor came out of his office with a grave look on his face. Zuzana felt her heart drop as she waited for him to deliver his diagnosis.

"Well, Pani Tesarova, you may not believe this, but you are pregnant," he said seriously looking at her over his black-rimmed glasses.

Zuzana gasped and stared at him.

"The point is that babies born to women of your age are at a high risk of"—he paused and cleared his throat a little nervously— "well, of not being normal. You may want to consider having an abortion. In fact, I would strongly advise it. We can schedule it as soon as next week."

Shocked, Zuzana looked at him with wide-open eyes and then shut them again feeling faint.

She left the doctor's office that afternoon and walked several blocks to the church in the middle of the town's square. Pushing the heavy doors open, she walked inside the chilly, dark sanctuary. Kneeling down on the hard tile floor, she buried her face in her hands. After several minutes, she took a deep breath and tried to clear her head; she had to consider everything that had just happened. A baby! She was expecting a baby! For a moment, a thrill of joy coursed through her veins. A baby!

But no – the doctor said there might be something wrong. She was too old to have a healthy and normal child. He told her to get rid of it!

Rocking back and forth, she felt a panic attack coming on; her heart began to race.

Losing track of the time, she prayed and rested her head on the massive, wooden pew in front of her. Elderly *babkas*[2] in their colorful scarves and petticoats shuffled by her, their rosaries swinging.

Zuzana's shoulders began to shake as she was no longer able to hold back the tears. One of the *babkas* noticed her and drew closer to her. Pressing a prayer card into her hand, she looked at her with concern and then shuffled off. Zuzana slowly raised her head and squinted through her tears at the picture on the card. In the dim light she perceived that it was a wrinkled, faded picture depicting the Visitation. Her tension slowly eased away as she looked at the smiling images of the blessed mother greeting her elderly cousin Alzbeta. Zuzana stared at the artist's rendition of the elderly lady's swollen abdomen. Then she turned the card over thoughtfully. She sat back on the hard wooden pew and began to breathe a little easier.

"Mama."

Her daughter's pensive voice brought her back to the present. Zuzana looked in her eyes and saw that her daughter's expression was a little more relenting.

"You must promise me that you will rest and take care of yourself. Please. You are not so young anymore," Helena pleaded earnestly.

Zuzana could not help smiling. It was ironic how their roles had suddenly reversed.

"Of course, *moja Zlata*[3], of course," Zuzana said stroking her daughter's worried face. Then she rose to fetch the laundry hanging outside in the crisp autumn air.

---

2 Grandmothers

3 My dearest; literally, "my gold"

11

Collecting

Ludo Sykora lit a cigarette as he watched his brothers and the other workers load the wagons. The stars were bright that night, but he was unaware of their brilliancy as he mentally counted the boxes of eggs. They had made a good haul that day; one hundred sacks of grain, seventy-five sacks of corn, and innumerable boxes of eggs. He pulled out his clipboard and looked at the list of names. He sighed. *This is not going to be a picnic*, he thought as he glared at the next one on the list. Most of the village farmers had already signed over their fields since the new socialist government had promised them high positions of leadership in the new cooperatives. However, some of the farmers were more resistant.

"All right, *chlapsi⁴*, let's go. We have one more stop to make tonight," he said as he climbed in the wagon.

The horses strained as the driver flicked the reins. The wheels slowly turned and the wagons lumbered down the village street past the church. Sykora spat contemptuously in front of the statue of the Blessed Virgin as they drove by. The spittle froze before it hit the ground. The wagon driver looked at him out of the corners of his eyes but said nothing.

"Stop!"

The driver pulled back on the reins several meters before Bolek Skalicky's house. Sykora threw away his cigarette and nervously slicked back his black greasy hair under his cap.

"Jano! Come with me!" he ordered one of the larger men in the wagon. The two men walked to the tall iron-gate and banged on it.

"Who is there?" a voice demanded on the other side.

Sykora cleared his throat and said loudly, "Sykora! Ludovit Sykora – the secretary of the communist party in Čerešňa!"

---

4 Boys

12

He could hear the key turning in the lock and the large iron door squeaked open. A very large peasant man loomed in the doorway and stared unsmilingly at them.

"So now you are the 'secretary of the communist party'! What an honor that you come to see me! What do you want, *Tuntulak*[5]? Do you know what time it is?" the muscular man asked angrily glaring at Sykora and his companions. The secretary and the other men unconsciously stepped back.

"Look, Bolek, you know why we are here. You did not pay your local taxes on the crops this season and the co-op has come to collect their share. Of course, if you sign your fields over to the co-op, we don't have to go through with any of this. As the head of the communist party in Čerešňa, I can assure you that everything will go smoothly," Sykora said trying to appear poised and confident in front of Bolek Skalicky who seemed to be growing menacingly larger in the darkness. The air felt frigid.

Bolek snorted like an angry bull and stomped off. Sykora beckoned the other men to follow him and they stepped cautiously inside the courtyard. The wooden barn was across the courtyard. Sykora signaled for them to go around behind the aging wooden edifice. As they approached it, the chickens began clucking anxiously, and the intense lowing of the cows filled the air. Suddenly, Bolek appeared in the door of the barn with a huge pitchfork in his massive hands. The steel prongs glinted in the moonlight.

"Take one more step and I will run you through – each and every one of you! Ludo Sykora! You and your miserable brothers! You – who have guzzled my wine and sat in my home as guests!" Bolek hissed angrily, "You! Have you no respect for your own relatives? And now you want to steal the fruit of my land! Shame on you! Get off my property, you *Lapaj*[6]!"

Bolek clutched the pitchfork firmly in his hands. Everyone froze to the spot. After what seemed like an eternity, the angry peasant giant let out a guttural roar and began running towards the group of men. The mob of men began to scatter like ants in all different directions. Bolek began pursuing them one by one. Lunging wildly across the courtyard, one unfortunate soul was not quite quick enough, and the seat of his trousers was pierced through.

---

5 Idiot

6 Thieves

"Yiiyyy!" the worker screamed in pain and fled through the gate.

"Now, look, Bolek, let's discuss this rationally," Sykora shouted trying to hide the quaver in his voice.

Bolek whirled around to face Ludo Sykora with his pitchfork. He braced himself there like a gladiator ready to attack his opponent when suddenly two of Sykora's brothers grabbed Bolek's arms from behind. The pitchfork fell to the ground as he wrestled with the two men. One of them went flying into the air, but the other one hung on to Bolek's thick neck like a bulldog. Bolek spun around in a circle trying to pull him off his back.

"Get off of him!" a high pitched female voice screamed.

With a big wooden rolling pin in her hand, Bolek's wife deftly smacked the man who was clutching her husband. Stunned, he slid like a limp rag doll onto the ground. Free once more, Bolek began swinging his massive fists into the faces of the remaining men. Drops of blood spattered against the barn wall.

"Enough!"

Sykora wiped the salty blood and dirt out of his mouth as he glared menancingly at Bolek. He then shakily raised his finger towards him and said, "We'll be back, Skalicky! You'll regret this!"

The other men picked themselves up and limped slowly backwards towards the gate. Sykora whistled for the driver and motioned for one of the men to help his brother who still lay unconscious on the ground. Bolek's wife stared back unflinching. As they left the property, she slammed the iron gate, bolted it, and ran back to her husband who was still panting.

There was no more need for a brave face. "Oh, Bolek, what are we going to do now? You know they will never forget this." She began weeping as she looked at her husband's ripped shirt and bleeding forehead. She ran to the pump and vigorously began pumping water in a bucket. Running back to him with the water sloshing in the bucket, she dipped her handkerchief into it and began wiping his face.

Bolek shook his head wearily pushing back her hand. "What is happening in this place? How can they steal a man's property? What have I ever done to them?"

He stared at his wife and then stared in amazement at his big, calloused fists. "Look at these hands! Every bit of this soil has been worked by them! These fields have been in our family for generations! The lazy bastards! They want everybody else's land because they

14

squandered their own!" He put his face in his hands while his wife sobbed.

Ludo Sykora and his companions ran swiftly to the wagon and nodded curtly to the driver. The driver briskly flicked the reins. The stocky workhorses strained against the heavy load. The secretary of the communist party leaned back in the seat and gingerly dabbed his bleeding mouth with his handkerchief.

"He will pay for this course of action! He will pay," the angry man muttered fiercely.

The old wagon driver glanced over at Sykora and a slight smile tugged at his face. *I think I'll stop by the pub on my way home*, he pondered to himself. *I have got a few stories to tell tonight…*

Waiting

It was a hard winter. The countryside was covered in a pure white blanket of snow, but the clouds in the gray sky loomed heavily above the red tiled rooftops and the misty Tribec Mountains.

The temperatures dropped drastically below zero and the river froze solid. This was cause for great delight among the children. Skates were hauled out of the cupboard and eagerly clapped on. Spontaneous games of ice hockey broke out; colorful stocking caps bobbed up and down as they played. Governments and wars had come and gone, but village life in Čerešňa went on pretty much as it always had for the last 700 years. Children still seemed to find pleasure even in the midst of oppression.

Ludo Sykora, the secretary and head of the communist party, had taken over the previous mayor's job. He and his brothers had recently returned to the village after a few years of manual labor in Bohemia. They had been forced to go there after spending all of their inheritance, losing their parents' fields in drunken card games. However, they had sensed that the winds of change were now more favorable to them, and they came back to the village to join the new "socialist" movement that had picked up momentum since the Second World War. They soon established themselves in the local government by intimidating the villagers and taking all advantages that came with their newfound power. Feeling particularly satisfied with the current situation, Sykora examined all of the agricultural items he had gathered; his prospects were finally looking up! Bolek Skalicky was still a thorn in his side, but he would deal with him in his own way.

There were several shortages in the stores, but the newspapers promised them a bright new future in their new socialist society. However, that month there was no milk, so every evening Zuzana Tesarova's oldest son took the light blue milk pail to their neighbor Milan Skalicky who had the best milk cow in the village. Milan was Bolek's brother; he was not as big and strong, but what he lacked in strength, he made up in cleverness.

Twenty-one year old Martin, Zuzana's eldest son, enjoyed being the one to fetch the milk. He leaned against the barn wall, ran his fingers through his wavy hair and quietly watched the big brown-eyed cow as she peacefully chewed her cud during the milking. The smell of hay permeated the air. It was peaceful. The cow's owners were happy to make a few crowns selling milk and homemade cottage cheese to any interested parties, and Mrs. Skalicka always greeted him warmly when he showed up at milking time. She brushed away the straw off her skirt with a big, callused hand. He noticed her shirt had a wet stain from nursing the corpulent baby on her hip.

"I heard about Sykora and your brother-in-law. Have you heard any news about him?" Martin asked with concern.

Mrs. Skalicka looked around to make sure they were alone and then answered him in a hushed tone, "Poor Bolek. We are not sure, but we think they took them to the jail in *Topolcany*[7]. After he refused to sign the papers and threw Sykora out, the police showed up the next day. They arrested Bolek and his wife! Their poor daughter is home alone with her *babka*." She shook her head. "I don't know what is happening anymore. I just don't understand. My Milan also refused to sign his fields over, but every time they come, we manage not to be home," she said winking sadly at Martin as she poured the milk into the can. "Of course, my Milan has a few good friends in the local government. Maybe they will work things out."

She continued chatting as she finished milking the cow. She related to Martin how she drank three liters of milk per day and another at night so that she would have plenty of milk to nurse the baby. As Martin was preparing to leave, Mrs. Skalicka gave him a little round of cottage cheese wrapped in a clean cloth for his mother. He tucked it in his pocket and thanked her gratefully. He walked home carefully balancing the milk pail between his gloves.

A soft haze of smoke hung over the roofs of the houses. The smell of burning brown coal was in the air.

"Martin! Wait!"

He stopped and turned around. He saw his friend Dano waving at him.

"Did you hear the news?" Dano asked breathlessly as he came sliding up on a patch of ice.

---

7 The nearest town – population 30,000

"What news?" Martin asked curiously.

"Mischo is the new foreman at the brick factory!" Dano blurted out, his breath forming an icy cloud.

"Mischo? Mischo? Mischo Kovac?" Martin asked astonished.

"Yes! I just met him at the pub and he was bragging about it to everyone!"

"How could such a young *soplak*[8] get that position? He knows absolutely nothing about the business, much less about bricks!" Martin sputtered out furiously.

"Well, he and his father joined the party – and his father does have some good connections with the local government, you know," Dano said. He looked somewhat resigned.

"First, Vlado becomes head of the co-op, then, Miro becomes supervisor at the dairy, and now this!" Martin shook his head with frustration. "All of the poorest students in our class are becoming our bosses and managers. This world is *blasny*[9]!"

Dano nodded his head with a wry smile and added, "Yes, and they are making good money while the rest of us have to scratch like chickens."

"Well, I am not going to sit around and watch these boys climb to the top while I end up sweeping the streets," said Martin with determination in his face. Shaking his head, he bid his friend farewell and stomped home to his mother.

***

Zuzana could no longer hide the fact that she was pregnant from her neighbors. She was showing, so she stayed at home as much as she could and sent ten-year old son Ondrej to the store for bread. People whispered to each other when she passed them in the streets. She hated the fact that she was now the main topic of conversation among the villagers. However, by gritting her teeth, she managed to go ahead with her daily routine as much as she could. In spite of the gossip, a surge of excitement would shoot through her each time she thought about the new baby; yet, she could not help but worry.

Six a.m. Mass was first on her daily social calendar. She woke up at five o'clock every morning and dressed herself by candlelight. One particularly frosty morning after church, she carefully stepped on to the

---

8 Snot-nosed kid

9 Crazy

icy dirt road and began guardedly making her way home. As she slipped and slid cautiously along, she noticed one middle-aged gentleman passing her along the way with his shopping bag. The unshaven man eyed her contemptuously and hollered at her, "*Daj si pozor, Pani Tesarova!*[10] I could take care of that for you, if you want!"

Zuzana stopped to look at him, shuddered and pulled her coat tighter across her bulging stomach. "*Debil!*[11]" she shouted at him. He snorted and turned away.

Her thoughts wandered back to another time when she was pregnant for the first time, and even her *own* pious mother had quietly offered to get her an abortion. Zuzana was young and unmarried, and she realized her distraught mother only wanted to protect her from the local gossip. However, it was still a shock when well-meaning friends and neighbors now took her quietly aside and recommended the old bastard to her to "help her out of this inconvenient situation." Pani Hantuchova at the butcher shop even warned her that the baby might be born an idiot! She told her, "You never know at your age. Babies born to older women are either geniuses or just the opposite." Zuzana shook her head as she also remembered what the doctor had told her – it often tormented her in the night, robbing her of much needed sleep.

She sighed. There were all kinds of people in this world. Observing people and their behavior patterns had always been one of her favorite pastimes, but she was still amazed at the depth and complexities of human nature. Quickening her pace, she soon arrived at her little wooden gate.

Zuzana's husband Jozef sat huddled by the wood cook stove. He checked the fire periodically and fed it with a few more pieces of kindling. His chair seemed to be a permanent fixture by the warm oven. Ten-year-old Ondrej burst through the door with his cheeks rosy and his bag full of warm, fresh *roshky*.

"What took you so long, *synchek moj*[12]?" she asked as she stirred the pan of cocoa for her young, robust son.

"Oh, nothing," he said breathlessly trying to look nonchalant.

His mother looked at him sharply.

"Well, I was just playing a little hockey on the river. Janko fell in – I saw him backing up toward the middle where the ice was a little thin, but I didn't bother to tell him," he said smiling mischievously. "Suddenly, all

---

10 Take care, Mrs. Siska!

11 Devil!

12 My little son

you could see were his legs going up in the air. His mother was so angry – you could hear her yelling clear across the village!" He dropped down on the wooden chair hungrily grabbing a roll.

"Ondrejko, that's terrible! You should have warned him – that's dangerous!"

"Oh, he just got a little wet – serves him right! He thinks he's so smart."

Zuzana tried to look stern, but had a hard time hiding her smile. She had never been too fond of little Janko or his mother for that matter. She busily started grinding the coffee beans for her old man and herself.

"Where's Martin?" she asked Jozef.

Her weather-beaten husband shrugged and scooted even closer to the stove. Zuzana narrowed her eyes and continued grinding. Suddenly the door flew open, freezing air rushed in, and Martin walked in with an armload of wood. He dropped the logs in front of the stove and put one of the larger logs on the fire.

"Now it will be warm," he said nodding to his mother.

"Do you want something hot? They finally got some coffee beans in stock. Thank God – I am so tired of drinking this brown water they call coffee."

"Thank you, but I have to go to Nitra today," he said avoiding her eyes.

Zuzana looked at him suspiciously. "Why?"

Martin swallowed nervously, glanced at his mother, and then sat down. "Well, on second thought, maybe I'll have a cup of coffee after all."

She fixed his coffee with milk and handed him the cup.

"Mama, you know when I was serving in the military in the Czech lands, they were pressuring us to join the party," he began still not daring to look at his mother. Zuzana faced him with her hands on her hips, giving her eldest son her full attention.

"Well, I am going to sign up today!" he blurted out looking up at her anxiously.

Zuzana said nothing. He waited for her reply, but she remained silent.

"What can I do, Mama? If I want to go forward, I must join the party! Am I going to work for nothing while my classmates are becoming directors and making big salaries?" Martin asked miserably.

Zuzana looked at her son sadly and then said, "You always have to be first, don't you? The biggest, the best, the strongest"—she paused and reflected for a moment—" but you are a good boy. You have always tried to help." She glanced over at her husband who was cleaning his nails with a knife. "Look at your father! Did his communist membership do our family any good? *Synchek moj*, you have done as much as you could. God will bless you for it. But my son, don't sell your soul. Money is not that important."

"Please understand, Mama," he said desperately looking in her eyes. "I can help our family even more. And now the baby is coming, it is crucial for us. Money is important!"

Zuzana got up abruptly from the table and gazed out the window for a few minutes. To young Martin it seemed like an eternity while he sat uneasily waiting. She turned slowly around and looked firmly at her son.

"God will always provide," she said and then she paused. "Martin, please – don't do this."

Her son looked down at his hands and then said quietly, "I have to go; I will miss the train if I don't hurry. Don't save lunch for me, I will get something in town."

Then he grabbed his hat and coat off the hook. He left quickly without another word.

Zuzana looked up at the brass crucifix above the door and her lips moved in silent prayer. She felt that heavy weight pressing on her again. Sighing, she started washing the dishes.

Recollections

Jozef Tesar's black hair was becoming gray and thin on top. He was a small, wiry man with angular features. He stared blankly at his middle-aged pregnant wife as she waddled across the floor to prepare his lunch. A scene from the past kept playing over and over in his mind.

"Pan Tesar, I need to talk to you." Mr. Petrikovic stood directly in front of his office desk.

"Yes?" Jozef asked carefully laying his pen down and looking up. He noticed the mayor's hands were trembling as he fingered some papers on the desk.

"Jozef, you have worked for me as a notary some thirty odd years," he began, clearing his throat and pulling off his glasses; he wiped them rather nervously.

Jozef nodded eyeing his boss warily.

"You and I have not always seen eye to eye, but we have worked things out, have we not?" Mr. Petrikovic looked anxiously down at him.

Jozef shrugged, feeling a little uncertain where this conversation was leading. Was the mayor referring to the time during the war when the Nazi army commissioned workers? The Nazis had demanded that trenches be dug in the fields. They had paid the local government a good sum of money for the worker's wages; however, the workers were never paid, and Jozef was the only one who knew the mayor had pocketed the money for himself. He simply could not tolerate this kind of dishonesty, and he had made the mayor's dealings known to the entire village.

However soon after, the mayor quietly paid Jozef's wife Zuzana a visit. He called her outside in their small courtyard and told her quietly, "Pani Tesarova, you know I have always had the highest respect for you. In fact, I don't even know how Jozef managed to get a good woman like you. However, if he doesn't keep his mouth shut, I will be forced to take action! I don't want to report your husband to the Gestapo! Please, for your sake and the children, do something about him!"

Jozef winced inwardly hoping that this particular incident was not going to be mentioned again.

The point is that I am going to retire," the mayor said abruptly, "and the new mayor, Sykora, wants to replace you. Then there is uh, ahem... uh, yesterday's incident. "

Jozef sat motionless. He stared blankly at Mr. Petrikovic. He had never seen the mayor looking so unsettled before.

"When Comrade Sykora asked you to remove the crucifix in your office, you should have done it."

Jozef snorted and replied, "Pan Petrikovic, I did not put that crucifix up on that wall, and I am certainly not going to take it down. He can do it himself!"

"I'm sorry, Jozef, but that's what it is. There have been several problems lately, and the new administration does not believe you are suitable for the position. Your nephew Vincent is going to take the job."

"Vincent! That good-for-nothing! He has never worked a day in his life! Besides, I am a member of the party! I joined before any of them even knew what it was! They can't get rid of me like that!" Jozef mustered angrily, "I have been working in this office for over thirty years!"

Mr. Petrikovic got up from his desk, walked towards Jozef, and repeated in a quiet tone of real remorse, "You had better start playing their games, Jozef. They will not tolerate that kind of insubordination."

Then stepping back, he looked carefully around and said loudly, "I am sorry, *Pan*[13] Tesar, but there is nothing more I can do for you."

He walked quickly out of the room.

Jozef sat on the edge of his chair trying to understand what had just taken place. He was out! Just like that! *Bande*[14]! He forced himself to stand up and went outside. He leaned against a tall oak tree and felt his chest tighten. That oak tree was just a little acorn when he planted it there thirty years ago. He moaned as he thought about what his wife Zuzana would say – a family and no job?

The *Krchma*[15] was busy that day. Jozef huddled in his usual corner staring at the pictures of President Gottwald and Comrade Stalin on the wall. He pulled out his communist membership book and laid it on the table. He was no stranger to their rhetoric: equality among the classes,

---

13 Mr.

14 Crooks!

15 Bar or pub

down with facism and imperialism! Work and food for everybody! He picked up his book and began tearing it apart deliberately, page by page. Stalin leered at him mockingly.

Suddenly, he stood up. The room spun around him and he clutched the table to steady himself. The bartender looked over at him and watched him closely. Jozef raised his glass and swayed there for a few seconds. Drunkenly, he flung his glass against the pictures of Comrades Gottwald and Stalin. Slivovitz dripped down from Stalin's moustache.

Jozef took a deep breath and started singing a patriotic song he had learned as a child. He sang more loudly with each verse. The entire pub became silent. The burly peasants stared at him with their mouths open and their cigarettes hanging. Kolar, the local policeman, rushed over to him with his big black moustache quivering; he grabbed Jozef by the neck.

"Shut up, you drunken fool! You know that song is forbidden! Don't be an idiot!"

Jozef pushed Kolar away and sang with even more gusto, beckoning his friends and neighbors to join in. Everyone looked down or away. Kolar shook his head, but a sadistic look of pleasure glittered in his eyes.

That night, Jozef made his way home in a stupor. After a fitful night's sleep, a telegram arrived the next morning at his house. Zuzana looked at him anxiously as he tore it open. The contents stated that he was expected in town at the courthouse – immediately. Hoping against hope that he might be able to talk to someone about his job, he didn't tell his wife where he was going or what it was about in spite of her questioning look. He showed up in the municipal building and saw Kolar leaning back in a chair with his hands behind his head, talking to another policeman. The other officer nodded at Kolar and left.

"Hallo, Jozef. How are you this morning? Your head aching? Come with me, I want to show you something!"

Jozef hesitated for a moment. Something inside was telling him to run, but shoving his nervousness down he followed Kolar down the tiled hall. Suddenly a barred door opened; someone pushed him from behind, and he fell hard on the floor of a small cell. The door slammed, and he heard the key turning in the lock. Kolar's hollow laugh echoed through the hall as he walked away.

Jozef shuddered involuntarily as he recalled those weeks he sat in jail, the interrogations, the beatings… his sentence was for three months due to disorderly conduct. His head jerked back to the present. His wife Zuzana was humming as she sprinkled salt in the bean soup.

"What's the matter with you?" Zuzana asked not bothering to glance over at him.

Jozef said nothing. After a few minutes of silence, he remarked, "You did not put enough salt in the *polievka*[16]."

"What are you talking about?" she replied impatiently. "I just salted it!"

His wife waited until he turned his head away and then cautiously tasted the soup again. *Hmm, the old man is right*, Zuzana thought with surprise.

The clock ticked on the shelf. *Well, it was high time that my children started taking care of me for a change*, Jozef told himself. He had done his duty, had he not? He had helped many people in his life and what good had it done? He had warned his friend Satchko, who was a helping to feed the partizans, when the Gestapo were after him during the war. Satchko heeded his words and ran for the hills. They never arrested him, and as a result, he was still alive and well. Satchko always took off his hat when he met Jozef in the streets, bowing respectfully. Jozef had tried to help another villager in the same way by quietly informing him that the Gestapo were planning to arrest him. However, that particular villager didn't heed his warning and stayed home. One night, they came and took him away. He was never seen again.

Jozef did not consider himself as very brave, but it made him angry when certain groups thought it was their right to step on others. Čerešňa had a large Jewish community until the Nazis started gathering them and deporting them by train – they even burned down their synagogue. Jozef never forgot the night he heard that soft knock on the door; Bernard Schwarz stood there holding his hat, his eyes full of desperation.

Jozef, along with a few other villagers, hid Bernard and his family in their cellars until they were able to escape to Israel. He even kept the Schwarz family's possessions and money for them while they were being moved secretly from house to house. It wasn't easy, especially when the German officers stopped by to eat lunch or collect food. Both Zuzana and he were immensely relieved when the officers would leave the premises.

When Bernard came back that last evening to Jozef's home, he was astounded to see that his gold pieces were all intact – not one was missing. He thanked Jozef profusely for all he had done and quietly slipped out into the night where his family was hiding in a covered wagon. A month later, Jozef received a postcard with an invitation to come to Israel, all

---

16 Soup

expenses paid – Bernard said he could make his home there, and he would help him. Jozef thought a little about it, but he could not seriously imagine leaving his village, his home for another country.

On the other hand, this place certainly wasn't any paradise! Now he was in real trouble – no job, no prospects – who was going to help him now? God? He had stopped going to church a long time ago, so God probably wasn't listening anymore.

Jozef got up from the stove and lit another cigarette. His eye fell on two small pictures by his wife's bed. One was a recent picture of Helena – she was a beautiful young woman now. She was actually one source of pride and comfort to him. The other photograph was of a little girl with big eyes like the stars and a shy smile tugging at her face. The old familiar pain gripped his heart and despair pulled him back down to his seat.

"*Nech sa paci*[17] – come and eat!" his wife announced as she ladled the soup into bowls.

He stared at her for a couple of minutes and then wearily moved over to the table. He crossed himself and began slurping his soup. Ondrej came noisily home from school and flopped down in his place at the table.

"Wash your hands," Zuzana warned him shaking a spoon at him. The young boy reluctantly went to the washbowl, poured fresh water in and washed his grimy hands. Then he crossed himself quickly muttering a hurried prayer.

Zuzana put a big bowl of homemade noodles on the table. Immediately, Ondrej leaned over to spoon them in his soup. Jozef growled at him, and Ondrej sat back in his chair as if he had been struck. Jozef reached over, took the noodles, and helped himself. Then he pushed the bowl towards Ondrej. Zuzana looked at her young son and rolled her eyes. They ate in silence.

When they finished, Jozef got up from the table and went outside to chop wood.

"Why does he act like that?" Ondrej asked his mother as soon as his father had left. "Why does he always have to go first?"

"Ondrejko, I have told you many times. He starved as a child! He never had enough to eat growing up," Zuzana replied.

"No food? Were they so poor?" Ondrej persisted. "Couldn't they catch fish in the river or kill a rabbit?"

---

17 Please help yourself

"You don't understand! You had to get permission from the count to hunt or fish – you could get in a lot of trouble if they caught you," Zuzana said sharply to her son.

After a short pause, she continued, "You know, when I met your father, I thought he was, well, really somebody," she chuckled. "You wouldn't believe how dapper he looked! I met him at a wedding. He and his brothers were playing in the band, and I hate to say it, but he was actually very charming – back then."

Ondrej snorted in unbelief as he took a sip of his soup. Zuzana grew silent thinking about the past. Then she said, "Do you know that he even managed to borrow a car from, God knows who, and drove it to my village to visit me? Can you imagine? That was in 1925!" Zuzana paused. "My parents thought he must be a great catch, but after we got married, I had to move here and live with his family." She lapsed into silence again. Ondrej continued to slurp his soup but waited patiently for her to continue.

"Let me tell you, that was a shock! People used to call them gypsies around here! They all ate and slept in one big room. When you walked in the hallway, you had to step around the goats who lived there! We were only separated by a little wall! There were no windows and we only had dirt floors. Such a dark, smoky place! When there was enough food, your Aunt Margita would set a big bowl of it on the table, and we all ate out of that one bowl!"

She shuddered at the recollection. To think about it was more than she could bear. "The point is that when he was a little boy, his mother died," she continued after collecting her thoughts, "and his brothers would push him away from that bowl of food. By the time he got to the bowl with his little spoon, it was all gone. Everyone for himself. If it wasn't for your Aunt Margita, your Apa probably would have starved to death."

Ondrej sat very still staring at his soup. "So, *that's* why he has to go first," mused the young boy wrinkling his forehead.

"*Presny tak!*[18]" Zuzana nodded as she cleared the table. She looked at the empty chair by the stove. "Poor fellow," she added quietly under her breath.

---

18 Exactly!

A New Arrival

It was quite hot and sticky that Sunday morning in late July. Zuzana opened her eyes and blinked at the sunrays coming through the east window. She flipped back the lightweight blanket and heaved her heavy body up. The springs on her bed creaked under the weight. She was a small woman and struggled with her protruding stomach, so to get out of the sagging mattress on the wrought iron bed took real effort. She slipped on her *papuchky*[19] and then knelt on the wooden floor. After she finished her prayers, she briskly began to dress herself. She then combed her fine blonde hair, streaked with gray, and pulled it tightly back in a bun.

Jozef was already outside in his usual spot by the stove in the summer kitchen and nodded as she shuffled by him. She put on her scarf, picked up her prayer book, and went to open the gate. Taking one fleeting look at the misty blue sky, she started on her way to church. She always went to church at eight thirty on Sunday mornings so that she could come back and prepare lunch for the others. The men in the family went to the later Mass.

The church began to fill up and Zuzana found her place among the other women. She sat down on the hard wooden bench and felt a slight twinge of pain in her lower back. The scarf clad *babkas* started singing in their high-pitched nasal voices, the altar boys ceremoniously filed in, and the priest began the Mass in his low sonorous voice. The men sat up in the chorus and observed what was happening below. A few minutes later, Zuzana stood as the gospel was being read. The smell of incense made her feel nauseated as the priest swung the censer at the Holy Book. Another sharp pain jabbed her; this one was much stronger. Zuzana clutched the front of the wooden pew until the gospel was finished. Beads of sweat rolled down her forehead, but she forced herself to endure the rest of the service. Her neighbors on the pew looked at her with concern and took her

---

19 House shoes

arm as they pushed their way out of the church. Just as she reached the door, a severe contraction struck her. She fell to her knees on the stone floor, and her friends called out frantically to the men to come help them. Milan Skalicky had just pulled his wagon up in front of the church to fetch his wife and son. He jumped out quickly and rushed over to help. He half carried her, half dragged her to the wagon, and without breaking stride lifted her up on the seat. They drove hurriedly down the street to her little house. Every bump and jolt in the wagon was agony for Zuzana as she clutched the sideboards. As they pulled up in front of the little house, Ondrej rushed out of the house.

"Mama, Mama! Are you all right?" he asked looking anxiously at his mother's pale face.

"Fetch the midwife! It's time! Please hurry," she said grimacing. Ondrej hesitated for a moment and then dashed towards the midwife's house. She lived on the other side of the village.

Jozef came out of the little house, and she almost fell from the wagon into his arms.

"You always have to go to church no matter what, don't you?" he scolded her as he helped her in the house.

"Looks like you are going to be a father again, Jozef," Milan said cheerfully nodding at him. Jozef didn't bother to look at him and shrugged. Milan waited politely until they went into the house and then slapped his horses with the reins.

"Do you want me to stay?" Jozef asked uncharacteristically. He was not used to showing too much consideration or affection to his wife.

"Just go on – *daj mi pokoj!*[20]" she said grimacing. A flash of concern crossed his face, but he turned and ran out into the garden.

Zuzana felt another contraction and tried to breathe normally. She stood up and began to pace the kitchen floor. *I am too old for this*, dear Lord, *I am too old for this,* she repeated silently. *Dear Jesus, Mary and Joseph, please help me,* she prayed silently looking at the picture of the holy family on the wall. Mary smiled back at her encouragingly.

She paced the floor and the pains were coming faster. She tried to peel some potatoes and warm up the soup from yesterday, but the contractions gripped her small-framed body. Ondrej rushed in the room with the old midwife. He took one look at his mother's pale face and cried, "Mamička!"

---

20 Leave me alone! Or literally, "Give me peace!"

"Ne boj sa, synchek moj!" she said trying to smile and stroking his curly hair. "Run along to church now or you will be late! Soon you will have a little sister!"

Ondrej's eyes began to well up with tears, and his face reflected the confusion he felt, but he obeyed his mother, running out the door. The old midwife looked knowingly at her, and Zuzana nodded back at her. She heard her eldest son coming in from the garden. Martin entered the room, and she grabbed his hand as another contraction gripped her.

"Mama, don't you think you had better lie down?" he asked her gently. He walked her to the bed in the kitchen and pulled back the feather comforter. He knelt by her and took off her slippers as she sat on the bed. "Don't worry about lunch. Helena is coming."

She shut her eyes and leaned back on the feather pillows.

"Jesus, Mary, and Joseph! Jesus, Mary, and Joseph," she whispered as another contraction tightened her stomach. Martin stroked her hair.

"Don't worry, Maminka, don't worry," he said soothingly.

"Just go to church, Martin, *moj*. Please go and pray for me," she said shutting her eyes. He nodded and then left.

The labor was not easy and dragged on the rest of the afternoon. Helena arrived and quickly took charge. Jozef sat outside on a little wooden stool smoking one cigarette after the other. He stared at the ground and studied the grass. Martin kept himself busy checking on the geese at the river, watering the pigs, and pulling a few weeds in the well-kept garden. Forgetting for a moment what was happening in the house, Ondrej sat in the corner of the small courtyard designing a big house in the sand with a stick. A little gray bird perched nearby observing his handiwork.

It was five o'clock and the air began to finally cool off. Helena emerged from the house to bring her father a bottle of beer. Suddenly, a baby's cry pierced the air. Helena gasped, almost dropping the bottle, and ran quickly back to the house. The men of the family stared at the house and waited in anticipation. After what seemed like an eternity, Helena stuck her head out the door and announced triumphantly, "It's a boy!"

Jozef sat back down, nodded his head, and lit another cigarette. Martin clapped his father on the back and jumped on the bicycle to tell his Aunt Margita the news. Ondrej ran around to the kitchen window and peeked in. He saw his mother's head leaning back on the pillows. Her face looked pale and exhausted, but she was smiling. She was holding some kind of bundle in her arms.

Ondrej ran back to the front door and quietly let himself in. He knocked on the kitchen door and peered around the corner. His mother noticed him and beckoned to him with a weak smile. The old midwife hastily picked up the bloody linens and stuffed them in a bag while Helena took the wash pan out to empty it. Ondrej swallowed hard. There was a strange smell in the kitchen.

"Come meet your little brother," Zuzana said. "His name is Pavol."

Ondrej looked at the small infant in his mother's arm. He saw a little red face peering up at him.

"His eyes are open! Look, he's smiling at me!" Ondrej exclaimed excitedly.

"I'm not sure he can see you yet, but, yes, he seems very alert," his mother said softly. She looked down at the infant who was nuzzling her breast. "*Palko, Palko*. I thought you were a little girl, but no matter. You will be a priest one day – a true man of God!"

"Why is he going to be a priest?" Ondrej asked puzzled.

"He is a gift from God in my old age," his mother replied wearily.

"Let your mother rest, boy," the midwife said to Ondrej shooing him out of the room. Ondrej felt relieved that his mother seemed out of danger and skipped down the front steps.

As Zuzana and her new baby fell into a deep sleep, the midwife slipped quietly out the door. Helena met her in the courtyard and paid her in crowns. The old woman clasped the money in her hand, kissed it, and bowed. Helena quietly opened the door and peeked in on her mother one more time before leaving to go home. The clock ticked quietly on the wall in the kitchen.

Suddenly at seven in the evening, Jozef stomped noisily in the kitchen and woke Zuzana up with a start. He rattled the drawers and slammed the cupboard doors as he searched for a cup. Miraculously, the baby kept sleeping.

"Time to feed the pigs," he said gruffly staring at her in the bed.

She looked at him in disbelief.

"Can't *you* do it this evening?"

"I am too busy. Get up, woman! You are not the first woman to have a baby in this world!"

Anger rose up in her but then quickly subsided. She was too tired to argue with him. Where was Martin or Ondrej? She stood up shakily clutching the bed. Blood oozed down her legs. Her husband went white at the sight, turned quickly around, and went to his bedroom. He slammed the door. She knew if she did not feed those pigs, they would go hungry that night. Then they would all starve. *Stubborn old man!* She looked at the baby who stirred nervously in his *slamicka.* [21]

"I know, I know. I chose him to be your father, but what can I do about it now?"

Sighing, she wrapped an old coat around her, slipped on her work boots and shakily went out to slop the pigs.

---

21 A type of blanket that was wrapped tightly around the baby to keep his/her back straight

Survival of the Fittest

"Why is that baby constantly screaming? This isn't normal!" Martin asked his mother as he came home from work. Zuzana looked worn out as she brushed a strand of hair out of her eyes.

"I don't know, I don't know!" she said with exasperation. "I nursed him, he slept, but I think he is still hungry. I am afraid my milk is drying up! I tried feeding him a little broth, but he just spat it out! His little tummy feels so hard!"

Martin picked up the baby and began gently bouncing him in his hands. "Shhhh, shhhhh," he said soothingly to the little infant. The baby became quiet and stared with big blue eyes at his eldest brother. Soon those eyes began to lull and he dozed off. Martin gently laid him in his perambulator.

"You have such a way with him," Zuzana whispered.

"Where's Apa?" Martin asked in hushed tones.

Zuzana shrugged and whispered, "I suppose he is playing cards again. He asked me for more crowns, but I refused to give him any."

Martin went to the *speise*[22] and pulled out a large loaf of dark, chewy bread. He deftly sliced himself a thick piece and pulled a hunk of bacon off the hook. Cutting himself a slab off the bacon, he popped off the beer cap and poured the amber colored beer into a glass. The foam spilled over.

"Mama, I think you should visit the doctor tomorrow," Martin said with his mouth full and gesturing with his knife. "She is coming to our clinic – you can ask her if everything is all right with our little one."

Zuzana stared thoughtfully into space. "Yes, you are probably right," she nodded. "I will take him tomorrow."

The next day, Zuzana dressed Pavol in his white knitted one-piece suit and sweater. Then she bound him skillfully in his *slamicka*. She put the pacifier in his mouth, which he began to vigorously suck. His intense blue

---

22 Walk in pantry

eyes looked trustingly at her. He was not growing and his little cheeks were waning. She placed him in his pram and eased it out the door and down the steps. He always became peaceful in the fresh air. As they walked outside, fall leaves danced in the street.

"*Pani Tesarova?*" the nurse read her name off the list. Zuzana picked up her baby and walked with the nurse inside.

The nurse quickly weighed him, measured his length, and handed him back to his mother. Pavol's eyes were big, and he whimpered a little. Soon the doctor walked in. She was a large Russian woman in a white jacket; she looked gruff, but her eyes were kind. She gently listened to the baby's heart, checked his eyes, ears, and throat. Pavol began to cry.

"*Pani Tesarova*, this baby is malnourished."

Zuzana looked shocked! She knew he was a little thin, but she thought he just took after her side of the family.

"How old are you?"

"Forty-six."

"Did you start your menstruation yet?"

"No, but I am nursing."

"Let me see your breasts."

Zuzana quickly unbuttoned her blouse and opened her camisole.

The doctor checked her carefully and squeezed the nipples.

"Your milk has dried up."

Zuzana's heart began to beat faster. She knew he had been sucking harder than usual, but she thought perhaps he was just trying to build up the milk supply. The doctor sat down and wrote out a prescription.

"Take this to the pharmacy. She will give you a supply of rice every week. You are to boil it with two cups of extra water. After you cook the rice, pour the water into one cup of boiled milk, let it cool to room temperature, and feed it to him with this bottle. He won't like it at first, but he will get used to it. I wish we had formula for you, but unfortunately, it's out of stock and who knows when the next supply will come."

Zuzana nodded respectfully and quickly left the doctor's office to visit the pharmacist next door to the clinic. She was grateful for the prescription as it was impossible to buy rice in the grocery store. Rushing home, she prepared the milk according the doctor's instructions, and carefully administered it to the three-month-old. Palko scrunched up his face when he tasted the first drops, but then tentatively began sucking. As the warm liquid flowed down his throat, his eyes brightened, and he began to suck in earnest. For the first time in several days, Zuzana felt his little body relax. She breathed a sigh of relief. She began to gently rock him while singing one of her favorite lullabies in Hungarian.

A Wedding

"Mama, I need to talk to you," Helena said one afternoon after Easter. Zuzana was drinking coffee in the kitchen, relishing a rare moment of peace. No one was home, and little Pavol was asleep in his pram.

Zuzana looked at her daughter with interest. Helena seemed to be glowing. Her usual serious face was animated, and her eyes were sparkling.

"Let me guess – you met a man!" Zuzana said. "What's his name?"

Helena blushed as she sat down.

"Jan. Jan Horvath," she said shyly.

"Well? So what's the problem? You are almost twenty-five years old – it is about time!"

"There is no problem! At least, I don't think there is any problem…" Her voice trailed off uneasily.

Zuzana stared at her daughter.

"Well, he is a widower!" Helena burst out suddenly.

"A widower!"

"Yes, his wife died a couple of years ago from tuberculosis – she was only twenty-three."

"I am very sorry to hear that, but why must you get involved? Can't you find a nice single man who isn't, well, second-hand?"

"Mama! Really! He isn't a piece of furniture or some old clothes!" Helena said exasperatedly.

"How old is he?"

"I think he must be about twenty-eight, but he looks older because he is bald."

"Bald! You want to marry a bald man? Is he fat, too?"

"No! Well, not really. He is a little shorter than me," Helena conceded but then said smilingly, "But Mama! You know that none of that really matters! He is a good Catholic!"

Zuzana stopped shaking her head and mused over her daughter's news. "I don't know why you didn't like Milan Skalicky! He was always chasing you, and you would not even give him the time of day! He has such a nice singing voice!"

"Milan Skalicky is a *sedlak*[23]! I am not going to be some peasant farmer's wife!" Helena said firmly. "I want to live in town and work in an office – not in the fields! I deserve better than that!"

"So, you think this short fat bald man is serious about you?" Zuzana said studying her daughter's face.

"Well," Helena began again hesitantly, "he has asked me to marry him and I – I have said yes."

Silence prevailed. Then Zuzana stood up suddenly, almost knocking her coffee cup over.

"Have you lost your mind?" she demanded. "How long have you known him?"

"Well, he has been working at our company for a few months, but we have only been seriously seeing each other the past two weeks. He told me that I am the one he wants to marry, but he does not have much time for a long engagement."

Zuzana began to pace the floor. "And why not? What's the rush?"

"Because, Mama, there is one more thing," Helena added cautiously.

Zuzana stopped in her tracks eyeing her daughter warily. She placed her hands on her hips.

"He has a four-year-old daughter – her name is Jana," Helena blurted out. She held up her arms in front of her face; she knew an explosion was coming.

Zuzana threw up her hands and looked up towards heaven in frustration. Hungarian words came spewing out of her mouth like a volcanic eruption. Zuzana always spoke in Hungarian when she was frustrated and didn't want her children to understand. Helena winced but sat bravely in her chair as her mother shouted and whacked her daughter on the back with the dishtowel.

After a few minutes, trying to gain some control, Zuzana grabbed her daughter by the shoulders and said breathlessly, "Now I know you are mad! You want to be a mother to somebody else's child? Do you know what that means? Do you think it will be easy?"

"Mama, he is a good man – you'll see! He wants to come to meet you and Apa this Sunday after church," Helena pleaded earnestly.

---

23 Peasant/farmer

Little Pavol began to cry. Zuzana took one more irritated look at her daughter and turned to pick up the baby. Helena took this opportunity to make her escape from the room, breathing a little sigh of relief. Zuzana continued muttering under her breath as she prepared the baby's bottle.

Sunday arrived and Zuzana grudgingly prepared a simple lunch consisting of a delicate chicken soup, homemade noodles, fried chicken, potato salad, pickles, and apricots she had put up in jars the previous summer. She put on her best blue Sunday dress with white polka dots. Going down to the cellar, Jozef fetched a bottle of wine he had saved from last year's vintage. Helena appeared at the gate with a short, broad-shouldered young man. He was indeed bald, but his features were friendly and handsome as he smiled and kissed Zuzana's hand. She liked him immediately in spite of her resolve to remain aloof. A bashful little girl with long brown braids and dark eyes stood next to her father clutching his hand. Zuzana's heart went out to her. She bent down, took the little girl's hand, and squeezed it. The little girl's sad eyes brightened, and she smiled rather wistfully.

The afternoon went better than expected and even Jozef took a liking to this young suitor who animatedly discussed politics and current events with him. Zuzana had to admit that he wasn't too bald or short in spite of her doubts. Then Helena's fiancé even took off his nice suit jacket and energetically repaired the water pump which had not been working for days. That did it. He had met Zuzana's approval.

The next month was busy as Helena prepared for her wedding. She managed to find some white satin on the black market and began designing her dress. There was not much time or money, but they arranged things with the priest and the local pub where they would celebrate the wedding dinner. They would keep it small as Helena hated fanfare and refused to go a penny over their budget. Zuzana was worried about a suit for Ondrej who had outgrown his church clothes, but Martin took him to town and bought him a nice blue jacket and pants for the wedding. Little Pavol was oblivious to all the commotion around him and sat contentedly in his pram sucking his *doodlik*[24] while Helena and Zuzana prepared the flowers and food.

Finally, the wedding day arrived, and Helena donned her simple white wedding dress. It was three-quarter length with a bit of lace and seed pearls that Zuzana had sewn around the border. She had been saving them for years wondering if they might come in handy one day. They all

_____

24 Pacifier

38

walked to the church. It was the end of May and roses were blooming on either side of the main street in the village. As they made their way down the street, friends and neighbors waved from their gardens. Jan and his little daughter Janka were waiting in front of the church. She was dressed in a pretty blue dress with white ribbons in her hair, and the expression in her dark brown eyes was hopeful. She shyly handed Helena a bouquet of roses and carnations. Jan looked very handsome in his black suit and tie, but the other men in the party looked as if they wished they were somewhere else. Martin's pants were two inches too short, and Ondrej could not stop pulling at his collar and tie. Zuzana grabbed her younger son's arm, and the party went inside the church.

After the wedding ceremony and dinner, Jozef Tesar and his wife Zuzana sat together gazing at their oldest daughter with her new family at the head of the table. Helena was quietly laughing, and her new husband Jan was smiling broadly.

"She looks beautiful, doesn't she?" Zuzana whispered aloud to no one in particular.

"Yes, she does. She reminds me of you when I first met you at that wedding," Jozef said absentmindedly as he ate another piece of schnitzel.

Zuzana gasped and stared at him in surprise. This was the closest thing to a compliment she had received in a long time. She was not able to eat one more bite of food from astonishment.

Religious Education

Things were tricky now as far as religion was concerned in the new communist state of Czechoslovakia. On April 13, 1951, the government had simultaneously closed all of the monasteries and cloisters throughout the land.[25] Monks, nuns, priests, bishops, and seminarians were sent to concentration camps as well as prisons and persuaded to leave their orders. Many of them returned home and were forced to look for work in factories or co-ops. Some continued practicing their faith in secret, and many left the country. Parish priests were strongly advised to compromise with the government and submit their sermons for approval. On the outside, it certainly appeared that freedom of religion existed in their country, but only those on the inside knew the price to be paid. Priests and bishops who refused to cooperate with the new government were jailed, interrogated, and often beaten. Some disappeared or were sent to small, remote villages where they "could do no harm." Professional people such as doctors, lawyers, professors and teachers were discouraged from going to church and often traveled to other towns to marry in the church or baptize their children. If they were recognized, their jobs could be in jeopardy. Sometimes their children were refused admission to colleges and vocational schools. The government was systematically attempting to dismember and eradicate the thousand-year-old church structure in Czechoslovakia. However, it was not that simple.

Zuzana accompanied Ondrej to school the first day in the fall of 1952. There had been an announcement over the loudspeaker that parents who wanted their children to attend religious classes must register at the school building. They had never had to worry about it before as religious education had always been a normal part of their children's education. They learned mathematics, literature, composition, science, handwork,

---

25 See Cardinal Korec's book, *Night of the Barbarians*

and Catholic catechism. If children lived in a Lutheran village, they were taught Luther's catechism.

"I hope your father keeps an eye on Pavol," Zuzana said worriedly looking back at the house as they walked out the gate together.

"Mama, look! Look at the line!" Ondrej pointed as they turned the corner. Parents were lined up at the main door and their number stretched like a snake down the road.

"Jesus, Mary, and Joseph! What is going on?" she wondered aloud quickening her pace.

Zuzana stopped at the end of the line. Shielding her eyes from the sun, she scanned the faces. She recognized many people from church and saw a few of her neighbors there.

"How long do you think we have to wait?" she asked one lady who was standing with her daughter.

"It's that Sykora! He is sitting there in that office telling every parent that they may be ruining their child's future if they sign them up for religious instruction!" the woman said angrily.

"What? What is he talking about?" Zuzana asked in astonishment.

"Who knows? It's hard to know what's happening anymore!" the lady replied.

Zuzana remained silent as she stood there besides Ondrej. The bell rang and the children ran to class. The parents continued standing quietly in line. After an hour, some people began to leave. The sky looked gray and heavy.

"I have to work in the fields! I can't wait here all day!" one woman complained.

"Look, he is coming out!" another man said and pointed at the main door of the school.

Ludo Sykora, the mayor, came to the door swaggering like a lord. He looked pompously at the crowd and declared, "Everybody go home! Registration is closed for today!"

People began to murmur angrily but hushed as he waved his arms and said in a condescending manner, "You can come back tomorrow – don't worry! I'll be here."

The next day, people once again lined up in front of the door, but Mayor Sykora did not show up. His secretary came hurriedly to the door and posted an announcement that he had to go to town for an important meeting. The peasants grumbled but went home. The next day, he did not show up yet again. The villagers waited for a while and the complaining became louder. Finally, on Thursday, he showed up, but he only allowed five people in the school office and then locked the door. Once again, the others were turned away. The air was becoming thick with tension.

Later that afternoon, there was an announcement over the loudspeakers in the village. Loudspeakers were on every street corner throughout the village and had replaced the old fashioned town crier who used to beat on his drum and announce the latest news. Peasants in the field stopped their harvesting and listened intently. The workers at the brick factory ceased their labors and went near the windows to take note. Old men in the streets and *babkas* at home in their gardens froze and strained their ears to hear the announcer's shrill words.

"Due to a lack of interest, the religious classes at the Čerešňa School have been cancelled! No more registration will take place! I repeat, due to a lack of interest and small numbers, the religious instruction will not be held this year!"

People turned and looked at each other. The village was deadly silent. Even the chickens, pigs, horses, and cows were hushed. All at once, the men and women in the fields began grabbing their tools and heading back towards the village. Workers in the brick factory filled their pockets and bags with bricks. People filled the streets and angrily marched towards the local government office.

Ludo Sykora was enjoying his afternoon coffee in his office as his secretary handed him a piece of cream filled pastry. He leaned back contentedly in his chair.

"I knew they wouldn't care! All they care about is their full stomachs! It's like Comrade Lenin said! He would not have closed the churches if he saw that it mattered to anyone!" he said slicking his greasy hair back.

He was just about to bite into his pastry when suddenly a brick flew through the window, shattering it and crashed onto the floor. Sykora's secretary ran out of the office screaming, "*Pomoc!*[26]" slamming the door behind her. Sykora dove under his desk. More bricks flew through the window and heavy footsteps could be heard on the stairs. Broken glass was all over the floor. Soon there was heavy banging on the door and shouting, "Sykora, you worm! Open the door!"

Sykora trembled under the desk not sure what to do. "Get the police! Get Kolar!" he screamed in vain at his absentee secretary. Bricks and rocks continued to fly through the window. Finally, realizing there was no escape, he emerged cautiously from under the desk as the banging became more intense. He dodged two more flying bricks and gingerly stepped

---

26 Help!

over the glass to reach for the door handle. At that very moment, the door burst open and people flooded through the entryway knocking him over.

He scrambled to his feet and backed up yelling, "Now, comrades, just quiet down! What is all of this commotion about?"

With each spoken word the infuriated crowd's shouting became louder and louder. Peasants stood there brandishing their hoes, spades, and scythes threateningly. Mayor Ludovit Sykora could see people in the streets holding bricks and stones in their waving hands. He sat down meekly in his chair and buried his face.

Monday morning the sun was shining brightly. Zuzana Tesarova proudly accompanied her son Ondrej to the schoolyard. She only waited a few minutes in line, registered her son for his religious education class, and happily went home after bidding him good-bye. Her heart had not felt so light in quite some time.

Worries

It was already evening as Ondrej brought their flock of geese home. The long-necked birds chattered noisily as they waited for him to open the wooden gate. He whistled, and they followed him into the courtyard. They were fat and sleek after picking through the leftover corn and grain in the fields. Settling down in front of the door, the snowy white birds tucked their heads under their wings.

"That's exactly what I'm going to do, too," Ondrej said stroking their long necks. He went inside. His mother had cooked *kasha*[27] for supper, and he hungrily ate the hot barley cereal with fried onions and bacon. She tied a dishcloth around Pavol's neck, plopped him on her lap and spooned it up into his waiting mouth.

"You're force feeding him just like you do the geese," Ondrej remarked. His little brother grinned at him. His cheeks were rosier now, and his blue eyes were bright.

"Mama, I am going to bed," yawned Ondrej sleepily.

"Did you finish all of your school work?" Zuzana asked as she fed Pavol another spoonful of kasha.

"Yes, Mamička," Ondrej said. He kissed her goodnight, and she made the sign of the cross on his forehead. He disappeared into the next room, and soon she heard him snoring.

The days were getting shorter, and darkness settled over their village like a heavy blanket. Zuzana continued to feed Pavol but did not pay much attention when the barley dribbled on the faded dishtowel. She was worried about their living quarters. They only had two rooms plus the pantry. Martin had moved his cot into the pantry after Pavol was born. It was quite cold in there, but he slept under a big feather comforter. Ondrej slept in the other room with his father, and she slept in the kitchen near the stove. Pavol still spent most of his time in his pram, but he would soon

---

27 Porridge

44

grow out of it. However, it wasn't entirely the space that was worrying her. It was their new landlords. A few months ago, new people from East Slovakia had bought the little complex of houses on the corner where they lived.

The rental house where the Tesar family had lived for the past few years was right on the intersection of the main road and a street leading down to the river. It was a small house but very cozy; Zuzana was content living there. The church was nearby, Ondrej's elementary school was across the street, and she could watch the village activities from her window. It made her feel secure to hear the wagons and tractors go by as well as the chattering of the villagers passing her little house. The villagers were friendly and stuck together through thick or thin. Even though she was technically an outsider from another village, she had lived there long enough that the people of Čerešňa had accepted her as one of their own – Zuzana was well-respected. They often stopped by to chat when they saw her in the yard tending her geese or sweeping the street in front of her gate. However, since the war, new people had come on the scene and were buying property in their little village.

This was the case with their new landlords, the Horniks. They were from the mountains in the east and had moved into the bigger house next door. Both houses shared the little courtyard and the clothesline outside. At first, they seemed to be quite amiable, but Zuzana could not understand why Mrs. Hornikova seemed to be studying her all the time. It made her feel a bit uncomfortable.

One day Zuzana was alone at home when there was a knock on the door. She opened the door and was surprised to see Mrs. Hornikova standing at the door. She was a large, stocky looking woman with dark, piercing eyes.

"*Dobry Den!*" she said hesitantly. "I was wondering if you had an egg I could borrow. I was making noodles and accidentally dropped the last one I had."

"Of course," Zuzana said good-naturedly. "Come in, please, and have a seat. I have several in my pantry." She wiped her hands on her apron and disappeared behind the door. Mrs. Hornikova sat down and looked around the tiny room.

"*Nech sa paci,*" Zuzana said smiling as she handed her a little basket full of eggs.

"Oh, I don't need so many," stammered her neighbor as she took the basket.

"Don't worry," Zuzana said. "My hens are laying well this time of year. We have plenty. Just keep them. Would you like a cup of coffee or tea?"

Her landlord nodded and sat down. They chatted a while and then Mrs. Hornikova left. Zuzana continued her chores and taking care of little Pavol. That afternoon, she felt very tired and decided to stretch out on the hard bench in the kitchen. It was not her practice to take a nap in the afternoon; she considered that to be almost a sin, but today she could not resist. Pavol was sound asleep in his pram, and Martin was working in the garden. As she dozed off, she heard the door quietly open. Thinking it was her husband, she continued resting and paid no attention to the approaching footsteps. The footsteps stopped. Suddenly, someone began rubbing her back. Opening her eyes and peering over her shoulder, she was shocked to see Mrs. Hornikova.

"Now, don't move," Mrs. Hornikova said in soothing tones. "I could see this morning that you are overworked taking care of your little one and this house. Just relax."

Stunned and not sure what she should do, she obeyed. Mrs. Hornikova continued massaging and moving her hands in circular patterns. Zuzana could feel heat radiating from her hands.

"I used to do this for the patients when I worked in the hospital," she said breathing heavily. "Now, don't stiffen up."

Zuzana bit her lip feeling awkward when suddenly she felt one hand on her breast and the other on her pelvic area.

"My, you are a fine built woman," the woman whispered. Zuzana leaped up from the bench and moved quickly away. She stared at Mrs. Hornikova with wide eyes.

"I-I... must check on Palo!" she said and flew out of the room. Zuzana went in her husband's room where Pavol was sleeping peacefully in his pram. She turned the key and locked the door. Burying her face in her hands, she began to cry. She could hear quick footsteps leaving the house.

After waiting for several minutes, she listened at the door. Hearing only the clock ticking on the shelf, she carefully unlocked the door and stepped out. Mercifully, the room was empty.

It was impossible to avoid their landlord and neighbors after this, but she tried. She did not breathe a word to anyone what had happened; however, she felt those black, piercing eyes staring at her when she went out to hang the laundry or feed the chickens. A couple of weeks later, Zuzana saw Mr. Hornik standing outside her house in the street. His wife joined him, and they seemed to be in deep discussion. When they noticed

Zuzana at the window, they moved quickly away. Their previously friendly behavior towards her and the rest of the family had cooled considerably. Mr. Hornik complained that Ondrej was making too much noise in the streets when he played ball with his friends. Neither one of them greeted her when they happened to meet.

Then yesterday, the postman delivered a letter to their house. It was from their landlords and simply stated that the monthly rent would be raised. If payment was not promptly made the first of each month, an eviction notice would be served. Shocked, Zuzana handed the letter to her husband. Jozef's face became livid with anger. He stomped out of the house and went immediately to the local government to file a complaint. Sykora calmly told him he was in no position to ask for help or file any legal complaints as Jozef was unemployed and not actively seeking a job in their new socialist system. Deflated, Jozef retreated to the pub. At least there he could commiserate with other villagers who were trying to solve their problems with a shot of slivowitz.

Then Martin stepped in and accompanied his mother to town to speak with a lawyer. Helena had arranged the meeting since the lawyer was married to her colleague and friend. The lawyer was also a party member but a strong advocate for the poorer families in their region. She listened to their case, took notes, and promised to look into it.

Zuzana sighed that night as she rocked Pavol to sleep. The moon had risen in the sky and was shining brightly. She stared absentmindedly at her reflection in the glass pane. Unexpectedly, a movement outside her window caught her eye. Someone had walked by the window! She stood up and peered through the glass with a cupped hand. She could see a shadowy figure standing by the tree in their little courtyard. Her heart beat faster.

Zuzana stood still as she watched the figure climb up into the tree; she could not tear her eyes away from the scene. Suddenly, electrical sparks flew in the sky. The light in the kitchen went out. She recognized their landlord's son-in-law as he slid back down the tree and disappeared over the fence. Tears of frustration welled up in her eyes.

"Why, God? Why is this happening to us? What have we done?" she asked helplessly looking up at the starry sky. The full moon shone through her window. She put her sleeping child in her bed and then groped her way to the pantry to look for a kerosene lamp. Čerešňa had recently gone electric, but Zuzana had kept all of the old lamps to use in case they needed them.

"I guess this constitutes an emergency," she muttered. Grasping the lamp, she pulled matches out of her apron pocket and lit the oil. A soft light flooded the room. She sat there for a moment and then pulled out her rosary beads.

"*Zdravas' Mária, milosti plná, Pán s tebou...*"

A loud knocking interrupted her prayers. She could hear the geese honking loudly at this unwelcome interruption of their sleep. She jumped up to the door and cautiously opened it. Two drunken villagers were standing there, swaying on the front porch. They were supporting her unconscious husband between them. She stepped back in horror as they dragged Jozef over the threshold. His face was pale and covered with blood. Zuzana let out a scream at the sight. The two men clumsily tried to hush her, but she could not control herself.

"Don't worry – he was just in a little skirmish down at the pub!" the taller one said thickly, dropping him heavily on the floor. Both men retreated hastily out of the kitchen.

"Wait! Don't leave me! Help me! Somebody help me! Oh, God, is he dead?" wailed Zuzana as she looked at her motionless man. "He's not breathing!"

Jozef moaned softly and turned his head.

"Jozef! Jozef! Do you hear me? What happened to you?"

Zuzana suddenly felt a light tapping on her left shoulder.

"Mama," a little voice said.

Zuzana turned around in surprise and saw her eighteen month old son Pavol standing there in his nightgown. He held a dishtowel in his chubby little hand and tried to hand it to her as he balanced himself. His face was full of concern and worry. Zuzana gasped and grabbed her little son. She stroked his cheeks and said, "Don't worry, *synchek moj*; Apa will be all right. Don't worry, little one."

She set him gently back in his pram marveling that he was able to climb out of it by himself. She quickly gritted her teeth, wiped the tears that were spilling on her cheeks, and poured water from the pitcher into the pan on the stove. Jozef stirred on the floor and sat up on his elbows. He touched his head and winced.

"What happened?" he said weakly. The smell of alcohol and tobacco permeated the room.

"Who knows? That is what I would like to know!" Zuzana said exasperatedly. She grabbed the soap and set the pan of warm water on the floor next to her dazed husband. She gently began to clean his cuts. Pavol sat quietly in his pram watching his mother with wide-open eyes. Her husband continued lying on the floor in a semi-stupor and flinched only slightly as she bathed his wounds. She found a roll of gauze in her work drawer, cut it, and taped it across the biggest gash on his forehead.

"I must have fallen down," he moaned as he staggered to his feet. He made his way to the next room. She could hear the springs squeaking as he fell into bed. Zuzana grabbed her wire brush and furiously scrubbed the bloodstains on the floor.

That night she tried to compose herself by finishing her rosary, but it was too difficult to concentrate – different thoughts kept rushing about in her head. A light breeze fluttered through the window, and she could hear the last train from Nitra blowing its whistle. Martin would be home soon. Ten minutes went by and she heard his footsteps crunching in the snow, his key fumbling at the door. Zuzana listened anxiously as her son tried to switch on the light. Picking up the kerosene lamp, she met him at the kitchen door.

"*Pochvalit Ježiš Kristus!*[28] What's the matter with the electricity? Is the power out?" Martin whispered as he came in the kitchen.

Zuzana sat him down and related all of the evening's events. She could see the muscles tensing in his jaw as he silently listened. When she had finished, he stood up and went out the door again. Peering out of the window, Zuzana saw him pacing back and forth in the yard. The geese woke up and sulkily scolded him for disturbing their rest. He came back in the house after a while and went straight to the pantry. No one slept very well that night including the geese.

The next morning, she woke up feeling tired even though the sun was beaming cheerfully through her window. The events of the night before came vividly back to her mind. After she prayed and dressed herself, she walked over to the bucket in the kitchen and went outside to pump the water she would need for the day's cooking and washing. She gasped as she turned the corner around the house. The pump was gone! Zuzana stared at the empty hole where the pump had stood and then threw down her bucket in frustration.

"What's the matter with you?" her husband asked as he stood on the front porch gingerly touching his aching head.

Wordlessly, Zuzana pointed at the spot where the pump used to be.

"Damn it, woman, what did you do with the pump?" Jozef asked angrily.

---

28 May Jesus Christ be praised!

"What did I do with the pump? Are you blind? If you had been home last night behaving yourself, maybe this would not have happened!" Zuzana yelled in vexation shaking her fist at her husband.

Quarreling ensued after this remark, which caused the chickens to start clucking and the geese to start honking. Wakened by all of the noise, Martin came outside buttoning his shirt. He took one look at the missing pump and immediately went into the garden muttering all the while under his breath. He had been forming a plan all night, and now he was ready to put it into action. Stationing himself behind the tree near the door of the Horniks' house, he waited. After a long twenty minutes, he saw his neighbors' door slowly open. The son-in-law poked his head out and looked cautiously around. Satisfied that the coast was clear, the stocky young man headed towards the main street. Martin followed him at a safe distance and watched him enter the grocery store on the corner. He soon came out of the shop with a beer in hand and talking cockily with another villager. As he walked backwards down the street still talking to his friend, Martin stepped out from behind the corner of the shop and roughly grabbed him by the collar dragging him down the street in the direction of the river. Taken by surprise, Hornik's son-in-law stumbled along behind him. He began to tremble when Martin released him on the bridge. They stood there for a few minutes not saying a word. Finally, Martin broke the silence.

"Why did you do it? You cut our power lines! And what about our water pump?" Martin demanded, staring accusingly at the young man. The morning air was frosty and his words hung like smoke between them.

"W-w-what d-d-do you mean? I-I-I don't know what you're t-t-talking about!" he stuttered.

Martin shoved him towards the rail and grabbed him by the shirt. "If you ever do anything to hurt my family again, you will live to regret it!"

He glared at him again and began to walk away. Suddenly the young man shouted at him, "Beggars! A family of beggars and gypsies, you son-of-a-bitch!"

Martin stopped. He turned slowly around and stared menacingly at him. Before the young man could get away, Martin grabbed him and threw him over the bridge's railing. He landed in the frigid water with a huge splash and shot out of the water gasping and sputtering. Martin spat in the river and stared at the floundering man below. Then he stomped off in anger.

"Where did you go?" Zuzana demanded as Martin burst into the kitchen. Martin didn't bother to answer her but stood by the window quietly waiting and watching. He began chuckling when he saw Hornik's son-in-law walk into the courtyard. He was shivering from cold and water dripped from his clothes but started with alarm when he saw that Martin was staring at him through the window. He scurried like a rat inside his house.

"Mama, we are going back to see that lawyer! Now!"

They spent all morning in Topolcany waiting for an appointment. Pavol kept trying to wander off down the hall, and Zuzana had a difficult time keeping him entertained. The waiting room was crowded. Finally, their turn came. Martin explained to the woman behind the desk what had happened in the last twenty-four hours.

"So, you threw him in the river, did you?" the lawyer asked with a grave expression on her face. Her mouth began twitching and her secretary turned to hide a smile.

Martin did not answer and just looked down at his hands. Zuzana stared at him with an open mouth.

"Well, I will draw up an official complaint. They cannot drive you out of your home or raise your rent without sufficient reason. However, if I were you, I would start looking for another place to live. It is never pleasant to live such an environment."

"The problem, *Pani Advokata*[29], is that my husband is not working. We have no place to go!"

"That is a very serious problem and could land your husband in jail. You know that it is against the law not to work in our new socialist government," the lawyer said sternly. "Tell him he better find something, anything, so that he can collect his retirement. Now, here is a letter – take it to your local government. Let me know if you have any further problems."

Martin thanked the lawyer and shook her hands. They rode home silently on the train.

"You know, Apa still has that field in Hrusovany. They took his other fields in Čerešňa away to build the new nursery school."

"Yes, that's true, but we don't have the money to build right now. Where would we get all of the material?" Zuzana asked nervously biting her lip.

"Well, we have some time. We need to think about it."

Zuzana nodded and they rode home in silence.

---

29 Mrs. Lawyer

Where's Ondrejko?

The sun came up early. Four-year-old Pavol jumped out of his bed, slipped on his shirt, and pulled on his knee pants. With his suspenders flying behind him, he ran to his father's room. Jozef was putting on his socks. He grunted good morning at Pavol.

"Apa, where's Ondrejko?" the little four-year-old asked his father, looking at his brother's empty bed.

His father shrugged and beckoned his little son to come closer. "Come here and let me button your pants."

"No!" Pavol said emphatically turning and running out the front door. He slipped on his shoes but did not bother to lace them. His older brother Martin had taught him how to tie his shoes, but he was too busy to be bothered. Holding his pants up in one hand and his hanging suspenders in the other, Pavol ran out the gate. He looked up and down the street and then made a beeline to the church. The morning Mass was almost finished when he pushed open the heavy door and slipped in. He spotted his mother's familiar polka dotted scarf and ran to the pew where she was sitting. Pushing past the other women, he struggled to get by their stiff petticoats in order to reach his mother. Zuzana feigned displeasure when she saw him, but even she could not hold back her smile as she saw him struggling to push past the other *babkas*. Finally, he stood triumphantly in front of her and held up his suspenders. The other women chuckled in the pew. She quietly fastened his suspenders, buttoned his pants, and sat him on her lap. The altar boys winked and pointed, but quickly stopped when they saw the priest glaring at them.

After the Mass, Zuzana bent over to tie her son's shoes. "Now why are you running around so early in the morning half-dressed? Couldn't your father help you?"

"I wanted you to help me," he said resolutely. He slipped his little hand in hers, and they walked home.

Plopping him on a chair, Zuzana tied the blue and white dishtowel around his neck and fixed his breakfast.

"Why do people have to eat?" he asked as he licked the apricot jam off of his bread and butter.

"Well, you have to eat in order to live," his mother replied as she kneaded the bread dough.

"What happens if you die?" he continued with his mouth full.

"If you believe in God and go to church like a good boy, you will go to heaven," she said slapping the dough soundly.

"Where is heaven?" he asked.

Zuzana turned around in exasperation and stared at her little son. "My goodness, you are full of questions this morning! Leave me alone now, or I will never get this bread ready to take to the baker!"

Pavol ate the rest of his breakfast in silence, but his mind was whirling. Soon his mother finished working the dough and deftly shaped it into two large loaves on a huge tin sheet. Taking a few crowns out of her pocket, she went out the door with her loaves. Jozef remained by the stove smoking.

Pavol started to follow her down the street but saw his brother Ondrej in the schoolyard. With a yell of delight, he pulled away from his mother and ran to the fence around the schoolyard. Zuzana was so preoccupied with getting her bread to the baker on time that she did not even notice his escape. Pavol stood at the fence waving at his older brother and trying to get his attention. Ondrej pretended not to see him and quickly walked back in the school building with the other boys. Undeterred, Pavol squeezed through the fence. However, he suddenly did not feel very brave, and he looked cautiously around. This was unsafe territory, and he knew that his nemesis could not be far away. Then he spotted him! A big red rooster came strutting around the corner of the school. It stopped and cocked its head when it saw the little child standing there. Pavol held his breath, not sure which way to run. The rooster began to flap his wings and started strutting towards him with his head outstretched. The small boy did not waste any time and headed towards the school door as fast as his chubby little legs could carry him. He tried to open the door, but he could not quite reach the handle. Becoming desperate, he hurled himself against it trying to push it open, but the door would not budge. The rooster was getting closer, and Pavol ran quickly around the building. After the second time around, he heard a voice call to him.

"Here! Over here!"

He looked up and saw a girl with brown curly hair beckoning to him from the window.

"Who is it?" Two other girls with long braids pushed past the other to peer down at him.

"Oh, it's *Palko*[30]! Isn't he sweet? Look at those dimples! Come here!"

Pavol ran to the window, held up his arms, and the girls hauled him into the classroom just as the rooster came tearing around the corner. Pavol looked down at the angry cock and sighed in relief.

"Where's Ondrejko?" he asked looking around the classroom.

"Oh, don't worry about him! Stay here with us!" They began to exclaim how tiny he was and how blue his eyes were. Then they began to play patty cake with him and hug him. Enjoying the attention, he forgot about Ondrej for a while until the teacher walked in the room. She looked with surprise at Pavol and shook her head smiling.

"*Palko moj*, you are the youngest pupil we have ever had in this school! Are you ready to learn how to read and write?"

Pavol nodded his head solemnly. The teacher laughed and said, "*Dobre!*[31] Then I will look forward to having you in my class one day!"

Pavol slid out of his seat, waved at everyone in the class, and left. He walked nonchalantly down the hall, opening every door and peering inside to see if Ondrej were there. The children roared with laughter every time his little head appeared. Finally, he opened one door and saw his brother sitting near the window with his classmate.

"Ondrejko!" Pavol cried happily.

Ondrej's face flushed with embarrassment when he heard his little brother's exuberant greeting. The teacher, a large, portly man, stared as Pavol ran to his elder brother.

"Ondrej! I have told you that your little brother cannot come here and interrupt our class! Take him home now!" the teacher said sternly.

Ondrej nodded unhappily and grabbed Pavol roughly, tucking him under his arm. He quickly disappeared out the door. Pavol looked up at the windows as they strode across the schoolyard and saw the girls looking at him from window. Pavol grinned at them and waved. They blew him kisses. Ondrej kicked the rooster out of the way as he opened the school gate.

"Where are we going?" Pavol asked hanging on for dear life as Ondrej began running with him towards the house.

---

30 Sweet nickname for Pavol – similar to "Petey"

31 Good!

"Home! Stop following me all the time! You are too little to go to school!" Ondrej opened the gate and pushed him inside.

"Now stay here!" His fourteen-year old brother marched off back to school.

Pavol watched until he disappeared around the corner and then trudged sadly in the house. His mother looked at him as he walked in the kitchen with his head down.

"So there you are! I thought you were going to the baker's with me!" she said as she prepared lunch. She smashed the garlic cloves with a closed fist.

"I went to see Ondrej, but he didn't want to see me," Pavol said sadly.

"Well, he is in school right now. He has to study and learn things. When you get big, you will go to school, too."

"Tomorrow?"

"No, not tomorrow, but soon. When you are this many years old." His mother held up six fingers.

"That's not for a long time!" Pavol protested.

His mother chuckled and said, "Oh, *Synchek moj*, time goes much faster than you think." She smashed a few more cloves in the bowl and sprinkled dark red paprika on top of them.

School let out at one, and Ondrej came noisily in the kitchen. He had grown a great deal in the last few years and looked very handsome with his dark wavy hair, blue eyes, and athletic build. He was the best football player in the village and could even do gymnastics. Last month, he impressed all of his classmates by doing a handstand on top of the school chimney.

"Ondrejko!" Pavol said with delight as his brother sat down. Ondrej looked at him and grinned slightly.

"Go and wash your hands, both of you!" their mother ordered.

Pavol watched Ondrej carefully as he poured the cold water from the pitcher into the pan and washed his hands with the creamy colored soap in the jar. Ondrej handed Pavol the soap and his little brother followed suit. Then they sat down at the table, and Pavol copied everything his older brother did. If Ondrej put his elbow on the table, Pavol put his elbow on the table. If Ondrej slurped his soup, Pavol slurped his soup. If he reached for a slice of bread, Pavol reached for a slice of bread. When he sneezed, Pavol sneezed.

"Hey, stop that!" Ondrej said with vexation when he noticed what his little brother was doing. Pavol just smiled happily finishing his lunch.

After lunch, Zuzana announced that Ondrej would have to take Pavol with him to watch the geese. She interrupted his protesting with a wave of her hand saying, "I have washing to do today, so, you will have to take care of your brother!"

Ondrej sighed, grabbed a cheese *kolache*[32], and walked out the door. Pavol grabbed his jacket singing out, "Ondrejko! Wait for me! Wait!"

Ondrej trudged quickly to the river whistling. Pavol struggled to catch up with him. When they got to the river, Ondrej spotted their flock of geese floating lazily on the water. There were several flocks of geese dotting the river never mingling with the geese from another flock. If one goose accidentally bumped into a strange flock of geese, all the birds would reprimand it loudly and chase it away. In the evening, each flock would go home: one flock of geese would turn left down the street and the other flock would turn right, waddling and honking like workers coming home from their shift at the factory. The Tesar geese looked up when they heard Ondrej whistling and began to climb up on the riverbank towards him. He broke off a thin branch from a nearby tree and herded the geese across the bridge.

They wandered past the fields until they came to a soft green meadow. Ondrej carefully guided them to the meadow making soft clucking noises in his throat; the geese began to furiously pluck at the green grass that grew there. Ondrej plopped down in the soft carpet with his hands behind his head. He looked up at the blue sky with big fluffy clouds. Pavol leaned back on his elbows and looked up at the sky, too.

"*Pozrie!*[33]" Ondrej pointed at one mass of clouds. "That looks like our priest when he is yelling at the altar boys."

Pavol giggled and nodded thinking about their overweight priest and his puffy red face. It wasn't too hard to make him lose his temper.

"That one looks like a chicken," Pavol said pointing at another clump of clouds.

"I think it looks more like you!" Ondrej said and began tickling him. Pavol squealed with laughter as they rolled in the grass.

"Ondrej! Hey, Ondrej!" Several village boys stood on the road. "Come and play football with us!"

"Can't! I have to watch the geese!" Ondrej called back.

"Oh, come on! We'll just play over in the field over there. Your little brother can keep an eye on them!" the boys pleaded.

---

32 Sweet yeast dough pastry

33 Look!

Easily persuaded, Ondrej bent down and said to Pavol, "Look, I'll be right over there! You can see me! Watch the geese and I'll be right back."

Before Pavol could answer, Ondrej ran off and joined his friends. Pavol watched as they became smaller and smaller dots on the horizon. Squatting in the grass, loneliness crept over him. He watched the geese as they busily ate. He tried looking at the clouds again, but he could no longer make out any funny shapes or animals. Sighing, he got up and began singing his favorite song that his mother taught him.

"*Prsi, Prsi, len sa leje…*" The geese began spreading out further and further, so Pavol began running around trying to gather them together. One large white gander opened his massive wings and began chasing him. Frantic, Pavol ran down the road as fast as he could until he tripped and sprawled face first in the dirt.

"Ha, ha, ha!" laughed a young voice. Pavol looked up and saw two girls in front of him. One of them was leading a young milk cow on a rope. The blonde haired girl looked to be about seven years old and her older sister with long braids must have been about ten. The blonde was laughing and the older one grinned mockingly at him. Standing up, he brushed the dirt off of his knees and the younger girl pushed him back down on the ground. His suspender popped and the button rolled away in the grass.

"What's the matter, baby? Still don't know how to walk? I'll bet you can't even keep your pants up!" she said teasingly.

"I think he's just scared of that big old gander over there," the older one said pushing his head down as she went by. She flicked her braids and laughed. Stunned, Pavol sat in the middle of the dirt road. He had never been treated like that. He could still hear them laughing as they walked down the road. Tears welled up in his eyes.

Ondrej came back from playing football and started to scold Pavol for not staying with the geese, but then he noticed his ripped suspenders and dirty tear-stained face. Without another word, he gathered the geese together, and the two brothers headed home with the flock in front of them. Pavol slipped his hand into Ondrej's free hand, carefully keeping his distance from the big gander. As they reached the river, Ondrej stooped down by the bank and washed his brother's hands and face. The geese slipped with delight into the water.

"Hey, what happened to him?"

Ondrej and Pavol looked up and saw Martin standing on the opposite side of the bank with a large bucket. He was hauling water as they still did not have a pump to replace the old one, and of course, the Hornik family had repeatedly denied that they had ever taken it. So everyone took turns hauling water from the river.

"I'm not sure. I just left him for a few minutes. When I came back, the geese were everywhere, and he looked like this," Ondrej replied shrugging.

Martin walked across the bridge, scooped Pavol up in his arms and strode back to get the bucket. Ondrej followed behind kicking a stone.

"So, tell me what happened to you?" Martin whispered in Pavol's ear.

Pavol pushed aside his brother's sandy hair from his ear and whispered loudly back, "Two girls pushed me down and laughed at me. They said I was just a baby."

"Girls? You let two girls push you?" Martin started chuckling.

"They were bigger than me!" Pavol protested.

"Everybody is bigger than you!" His brother stopped laughing and became very serious. "You know when I was small like you, I just took a little whip and POP – I let them have it. I never had any more problems."

Pavol was silent and thought about this all the way home. That night as he slept, he dreamt all night about big ganders and blonde haired girls with braids chasing him all over the village.

The next day after school, Ondrej and Pavol took the geese again to the fields. Once again, Ondrej's comrades came and left Pavol in charge of the geese. Pavol looked around and saw a thin branch hanging down from a poplar tree. He broke it off and flicked it in the air. When the big gander came threateningly towards him, he switched its wing and the surprised bird quickly backed off. Feeling quite proud that he had mastered the situation, he began strutting back and forth like a captain in the army.

"Eins, zwei, drei! Eins, zwei, drei!" He had heard soldiers in a movie counting like that. Suddenly, he heard voices.

"Look! There he is again! The little *krpec*[34]!"

"*Krpec! Krpec!*"

Pavol whirled around and saw the two braided girls walking their cow down the road again.

"I'm not a dwarf!" he yelled flicking his whip. The girls came closer and put their hands on their hips.

"You are, too, a dwarf! You'll never get big!"

"Will too!" Pavol shouted.

---

34 Dwarf

The girls began to dance around him singing, "*Krpec, krpec*, Palo is a little *krpec!*"

The older girl grabbed him by the collar and they began shoving him back and forth between them like a rag doll.

"Stop it! Leave me alone!" Pavol cried but the more he cried, the harder they pushed him until he fell on the ground again. Grabbing his little whip, he lashed the younger girl around the leg. Both girls stopped in astonishment and gazed at him with their mouths open. Then the older girl jerked the whip out of his hand and furiously began whipping his bare legs.

"Ow! Stop! Owwww!" Pavol cried trying to run away, but the girl seemed to have lost control as she kicked at him and popped the whip. Her sister cried out for her to stop. Pavol buried his face in his hands and tried to scrunch up in a ball in order to avoid the stinging of the lash.

"Hallo! What's going on? Leave him alone!" Ondrej came running up breathlessly. The two girls looked up in surprise. The elder dropped the whip and both girls dashed away leaving behind their grazing cow.

Pavol did not move. He slowly raised his head and moaned. Looking up at his brother he asked woefully, "Ondrejko?"

A pang of guilt went through Ondrej's heart. Quickly putting him on his back, Ondrej gathered the geese, and they hurriedly made their way home. As they pushed through their gate, Ondrej was panting. Zuzana looked out the window and rushed out the door.

"What happened? Oh, my God!"

Without asking any more questions, she heated water on the stove, filled up the big wash bucket with warm, soapy water and bathed him. She gasped as she noticed the bruises and whip marks. What disturbed her more was the sad, broken expression that had replaced his usual sunny countenance. Ondrej reluctantly related what had occurred and in turn received a sound scolding along with a slap on the back of his head. Ondrej hung his head and went in the other room.

"And where did he get the idea to take a switch and hit those girls?" she asked her eldest son suspiciously. Martin went quickly out the door to tend the animals.

The next morning, Zuzana waited outside the church door as Mrs. Strba came out.

"Mrs. Strba, may I speak to you a moment?" she asked tersely.

Mrs. Strba was not a friendly woman. Her husband had become a party member and did not attend church anymore; it had been rumored that he beat her when he drank. She looked down as Zuzana approached her.

"Your daughters yesterday— Well, my youngest son was tending the geese, you see…" Zuzana began quietly.

The woman's head snapped up and her eyes glittered. "He deserved it! My girls said he started it!" She walked quickly away muttering, barely looking at anyone. Zuzana stood there for a moment and then turned to go home. Pavol was sitting on a stool, swinging his legs and smiling as she walked in the door.

"*Pochvalit Jesis Kristus*," she said as she took off her sweater and put her purse in the cupboard.

"*Na veki*[35]," sang out Pavol.

Zuzana bent down in front of him and looked in his smoky blue eyes.

"Palko, I am sorry about what happened yesterday," she began. His smiled faded and he looked down at his shoes.

"You can come with me and Apa to the fields today if you want," she suggested softly stroking his cheek.

Pavol paused for a moment. He remembered when he was a baby sitting in the long grass and straining to see his parents small figures on the horizon as they worked in the fields. He could remember how forlorn he felt.

He looked up with a little defiance in his face. "No, I am going with Ondrejko," he said.

Zuzana hesitated and asked, "Are you sure?"

He nodded slowly at first, but then more vigorously. Sighing, she turned quickly around to prepare breakfast.

That afternoon, Ondrej and Pavol were sprawled in the grass as the geese busily pulled at the blades. Ondrej was reading his history lesson out loud, and Pavol listened attentively as a ladybug crawled up and down his hand.

"Ondrejko, come and play!" Several boys whistled and beckoned for him to come over.

Ondrej rolled over and hesitated, but then he said, "Let's play right here on the road."

The village boys looked at each other, shrugged, and nodded. Ondrej hoisted Pavol up on his shoulders. He began running up and down the dirt road kicking the ball. He skillfully weaved in and out of the boys who unsuccessfully tried to steal the ball away. Laughing, Pavol's head bobbed

---

35 May the name of Jesus Christ be praised forever

up and down as he rode his curly headed steed. Off in the distance, the Strba girls watched the game as their milk cow grazed. Finally, Ondrej scored a goal and ran off in the meadow whooping and jumping with Pavol still on his shoulders. Little Pavol brandished his fists in the air for victory.

"We make a good team, don't we?" Ondrej said winking as he set Pavol down. Pavol nodded joyfully as the sun began to set in the western sky.

Memories of Jozef and Zuzana's Courtship

The village of Čerešňa was almost seven hundred years old. In spite of wars and invasions, life remained fairly ordered. It was one of many little settlements situated on the Nitra River with the Tribec Mountains in the east. There were ruins of an old castle on the base of the hills, remnants of a feudalistic society. During the Austro-Hungarian Empire, there was a succession of wealthy Hungarian counts who ruled the land in this area. The peasants did the backbreaking work in their lord's fields, and they also served as butlers or maids in their households. As a result, there were more than a few bastard children running through the village who could truthfully claim aristocratic blood. Jozef's older sister Margita had a child by the former count near the village of Oponice. Of course, the count never acknowledged his handsome son, and the child grew up fatherless. However, Jozef's sister was quite proud that her son was from nobility and spoiled her little Vincent. The fact that he had difficulties holding down a job and preferred drinking in the pub was quite beside the point.

Besides working the fields and serving their master's household, the peasants had to get permission from the lord for hunting, trading, and even marrying. After World War I and World War II, major changes had occurred in the government and ruling families' lives, but village life seemed to carry on much the same way it always had.

When young people began to look around for a suitable life partner, it was customary that the young men would cross the mountains and look for their brides in other villages in order to "freshen" the gene pool. However, in some remote mountain villages, where this was not possible, all of the inhabitants looked strangely alike and were of a rather peculiar nature. Maybe it was this instinct that led Jozef Tesar to wander to another village in search of his bride.

The Tesar family was one of the founding families in Čerešňa and had weathered invasions from the Tatars, Turks, Hungarians, Nazis, and later

62

the Soviets. Sometimes they joked that it was time to start learning Chinese because that was probably where the next invasion would come from. They had originally been rich peasants, but multiple heirs had split and divided their property causing them to sink into poverty. Yet, they remained close and worked together.

Jozef and his many brothers played passionately in a band together, and it was rumored in the village that they had gypsy blood due to their musicality and dark hair, but the most striking characteristic was their intense blue eyes.

One summer evening when Jozef was in his early twenties, he and his brothers played at a wedding reception in the nearby village of Dolina. As Jozef played his *cimbalo*[36], he noticed a petite, energetic young woman with blonde hair and fiery blue eyes. She obviously loved dancing the *chardash*[37] and put all her heart in to it. He could not take his eyes off of her as she danced energetically and gracefully with her partner across the wooden floor. During the break, he came down from the stage to try and talk to her, but his tongue seemed to cleave to the roof of his mouth. However, summoning up his courage, he asked her to dance one *chardash* with him. She smilingly accepted this stranger's invitation although he detected a little reluctance on her part. As they danced, he found out her name and the street where she lived. He came home that night thinking only of her and for several nights afterwards, he could not sleep.

Towards the end of the next week, he managed to borrow the mayor's car (who was conveniently away at the time) and drove to Dolina to visit her. He had never driven before, and it took him a while to learn how to steer in the proper direction and shift the gears. She was surprised and her family impressed when he pulled up in front of the gate. They even politely pretended not to notice when he bumped into their hitching post. He invited her for a drive in the mountains and since her mother didn't insist on chaperoning them, they took off with a jolt. She sat stiffly clutching the seat as Jozef weaved back and forth over the narrow dirt roads. He managed to park the car, albeit rather jerkily, near a green meadow and they sat down in the soft grass.

As they chatted comfortably together, Jozef was surprised how well she could express herself. This one was different than any other girl he had ever known. Zuzana was intelligent as well as beautiful, and he could

36 A type of xylophone
37 A special Hungarian dance

not help but admire her. He tried to steal one kiss but she turned away. However, she smiled shyly and did not seem displeased.

Encouraged, he continued to visit her and soon they had meetings in the fields, in the barns, and under the stars. He wrote poetry for her, which seemed to please her even more. Then Jozef's cousin decided to relate a story to him one day that shifted the current of their burgeoning love. They were riding together on the train to Topolcany when his cousin decided to bring up the subject.

"She had a boyfriend, you know," his cousin began.

"Who had a boyfriend?" Jozef asked.

"Your Zuzana! She liked a boy in Dolina, but the parents refused to let them marry! His father is the *Richter*[38] and they think their son is too good for her. They are forcing him to marry this other girl, but they say he still loves Zuzana."

"So? What is that to me? Now Zuzana is going with me," Jozef said impatiently.

"Well, listen to this." Jozef's cousin leaned over and whispered in his ear, "I heard that he came secretly to her home in the middle of the night, not too long ago, and asked her to run away with him to Argentina!"

"That can't be true!"

"It is, I swear! A friend of mine saw them together in her garden and overheard the whole conversation!"

Jozef's face flushed with anger and he stood up. "Stop! I don't want to hear anymore! Do you think I am interested in your gossip? *Daj mi pokoj*!"

Jozef made his way to a different part of the train as it swayed noisily along the tracks. He stared out the window at the passing fields and blur of tracks. He was sure that Zuzana cared about him, but sometimes he saw a faraway look in her eyes that troubled him. He felt insecure around her even though he never showed it.

Several days later, Jozef saw Zuzana at the butcher shop in town. He was not yet ready to talk to her and tried to duck out of the shop.

"Jozef! Wait a moment!" she cried as he pretended not to see her.

"Jozef, where have you been?" she said breathlessly running up to him. He felt helpless and turned his face away. He had desperately wanted to go and see her, but jealously was choking him. Her smile faded.

"Is something wrong?" she asked worriedly.

---

38 The count's main foreman or superintendant

He looked down at her and gazed in her eyes. His face softened and he relaxed. "No, I have just been very busy."

She smiled with relief, and they walked down the street together chatting. They lost track of the time and ended up in her village just as the sun was setting. As they approached her house, a young married couple passed them. The young man stared intently at Zuzana and then looked sharply at Jozef. Jozef glanced over at Zuzana and noticed that she was blushing furiously.

"Who is that?" Jozef asked trying to sound disinterested.

"That's my classmate Stefan and his new wife," Zuzana said also trying to sound casual.

Jozef walked her to her house, and they sat down together on the bench in the garden. Jozef held her hand and said nothing.

"Jozef, there is something I need to tell you," Zuzana stammered. The urgency in her voice made his heart beat faster.

"I'm going to have a baby," she said looking down at her hands and tears began to flow.

Jozef stared at her wordlessly. Zuzana looked up at him through her tears and tried to smile.

"I haven't told my mother yet, but if we were to get married, no one would have to know right now..." Her voice trailed off as she saw Jozef's face.

He threw her hand down, stood up, and turned around. Without saying a word, he left the garden. Zuzana sat on the bench frozen not daring to move. As she sat there, she began to tremble. She hugged herself rocking back and forth.

Nine months later, Jozef Tesar was working in the mayor's office. He was notarizing some documents when the mail carrier walked in. He handed Jozef a telegram and waited to be paid. Jozef pulled out a few crowns from his pocket, and the mail carrier nodded at him knowingly. Jozef stared at him a moment and then tore open the telegram. It read as follows:

YOU HAVE BEEN HEREBY SUMMONED TO APPEAR AT THE TOPOPLCANY CITY COURT ON SEPTEMBER 10TH AT 2:00. BRING YOUR BIRTH CERTIFICATE AND IDENTIFICATION PAPERS.

Jozef swallowed hard, crumpled up the telegram, and sat down at his desk. The clock struck twelve o'clock on the wall and the cuckoo began singing its song.

It was unusually warm that day as he entered the courthouse. Zuzana was sitting outside the judge's office holding a small bundle. She looked thinner than when he had last met her. Her rounded cheeks looked sunken in. Sitting next to Zuzana was her mother who glared at Jozef as he approached. He sat down on the opposite side of the hall and tried not to look at them, but their eyes met and he was struck by the hurt and resentment he saw there. A distinguished man with an air of importance called their names, and they approached the bench where the judge presided. The magistrate flipped through the pages in the file, looked sharply at Jozef, and said bluntly, "Are you the father of this child?"

Jozef took a deep breath and answered, "No, sir, I am not."

Zuzana turned deathly white and looked as if she were about to faint. Her mother grabbed the baby out of her daughter's arms as the man with the moustache helped the young mother to her seat.

"She claims that you are the only man that she has ever had"—the judge cleared his throat and looked down at the file— "relations with."

"I'm not so certain of that, your honor," Jozef said quietly.

Zuzana's head shot up; her face was filled with horror.

"How dare you!" she hissed. "Whose baby do you think this is?"

She started crying. Jozef's heart began beating faster. Her mother rushed over to him before anyone could stop him.

"Young man, do you realize what you have done to my daughter? You have ruined her reputation! My daughter does not lie! If she says you are the father, then you are the father, you no good lazy—" shouted her mother as the judge began banging on his desk for order.

"An investigation will be conducted. Witnesses will be called. Mr. Tesar, you will appear here in this office next week for an in-depth interview. You will have the opportunity at that time to express your, uh, doubts on the subject. Court adjourned."

Zuzana stood up sobbing and left the room without even looking back at Jozef. Her mother rushed over and snatched up the baby.

"Here! Don't you want to see your own daughter?" She held out the baby in front of her.

Jozef looked at the solemn little face, and an intense pair of blue eyes stared back at him. Something inside him crumpled. The baby's grandmother noticed the change in his expression and said triumphantly, "There! I told you she was your daughter, but you don't deserve her!" She marched out of the room with the baby in her arms.

The investigation took place, and it was determined by the court that Jozef was indeed the father, so he was to pay a monthly stipend for her support. He knew in his heart that the infant was his as soon as he saw her. He recognized the family resemblance, but he could not shake off the jealousy that there might have been someone else in Zuzana's life.

A few days later, he rode his bike to Dolina and parked it in front of her house. He knocked tentatively at the gate. No one seemed to be home, when suddenly he heard quick steps. The gate swung open and Zuzana stood there looking at him. Her eyes were flashing.

"What do you want?" she asked bitterly.

"I need to talk to you," he said tersely.

She paused and then stepped back to let him in the courtyard. No one was at home.

"Look, I realize that the baby is mine," he began.

"Na, finally!" she said shaking her head in disgust.

Jozef held up his hand to signal a truce. She became silent.

"I heard rumors that you had somebody else. Were those rumors true?"

Zuzana sighed and folded her hands. "Jozef, you are the only man that I have ever been with – like that." She bit her lip. "Yes, I liked a boy in our village, but all that finished long before I met you. Anyway, nothing ever happened between us. Now, he is married to someone else."

"So, you are not going to Argentina with him?"

"Where did you hear that?" she stammered.

"People talk," he shrugged and then looked at her sharply. "So are you going or not?"

Zuzana stood up and began pacing in the room. Then she whirled around and looked at Jozef with her hands on her hips. Her eyes were flashing again.

"He is a married man in the eyes of God and our Holy Church! I can't go with him! I would never do that to my parents or to myself! I have already sinned enough with you!" She broke down and began to weep.

Jozef moved over by her and took her hand. "Do you still love him?" he asked.

She did not answer immediately. He squeezed her hand and asked her more urgently, "Zuzana, do you still love him?"

"Yes!"

Jozef looked down at his feet and then stood up. His face was hard and his voice cold.

"I want to see my daughter," he said.

Zuzana stopped sobbing and stiffened. "What are you going to do?"

"Let me see my daughter!" he said raising his voice.

She ran inside and brought the baby out in to the courtyard. He held out his arms, and Zuzana hesitantly placed the baby in them. The baby looked gravely at him as he began to walk slowly around the courtyard. She watched them as Jozef began talking to the baby and gently rocking her. She paused, staring at them, and then went quietly in the house. Jozef began humming as he gently bounced his child in his arms.

Every week for the next few months, Jozef visited Zuzana and their little daughter. Her heart softened towards him as she saw him smiling and playing with Helena, but she could not forgive him for his denial in court. His cold attitude unnerved her. Jozef absolutely refused to talk of marriage or their relationship. He was civil to her, but nothing more. Inwardly, he was struggling as his passion became even more intense every time he saw her, but he tried to maintain a cool exterior. Zuzana, hurt by his rejection, tolerated his behavior for the sake of her daughter. She was relieved that he had at least accepted fatherhood and was contributing a little money to support her.

Neighbors no longer spoke to her in the village of Dolina. Even though her grandfather was a butler to the count and her family had always held a position of respect, Zuzana's illegitimate pregnancy had tainted their reputation. She often stayed at home in order to avoid meddling looks and remarks. She was not happy.

One day in early spring, she began coughing. At first, she thought it was just a cold, but the coughing became worse. Soon she could not sleep from the constant attacks. Jozef came and took baby Helena to his sister's house as Zuzana's condition became rapidly worse; her distraught mother had her hands full taking care of her. Jozef was also becoming uneasy. He had already lost his mother and another sibling to tuberculosis.

One fitful night of coughing caused Zuzana's mother to send for the doctor. The young woman lay pale and feverish on the pillow. The kindly old physician examined the handkerchief next to her pillow and sighed when he saw the red blood stains.

"I am sending her to the sanatorium in Lefantovce. She needs to stay there for at least six weeks."

"Doctor, tell me the truth! Is she going to die?" her mother asked anxiously.

The doctor looked at Zuzana's mother intently and shook his head. "We must never give up hope. She is a strong young woman. Only – she must exert herself a little more – she needs to fight." He patted Zuzana's thin hand and left the room.

Jozef came the next day to check on Zuzana. He knocked on the gate, but no one answered. He deftly swung himself over the wall and looked through the window where she had been convalescing. The bed was neatly made, and there was no sign of her. Suddenly, Zuzana's younger brother walked out the door. Surprised to see Jozef, he greeted him.

"Where is she?" Jozef asked anxiously.

"They took her to Lefantovce," her brother replied sadly.

"You mean...?"

"Jozef, don't worry—" He did not have time to finish his statement as Jozef was rushing out the gate. He took the difficult shortcut over the mountains to reach the Sanatorium as quickly as he could. Pesky gnats flew in his face as he ran through the forest paths and salty drops of sweat burned his eyes. He finally reached the village and asked for directions. After several minutes of hard running, he saw the white walls of the clinic behind the trees. Still panting, he approached the building. A woman in a starched white uniform sat at a desk filling out papers.

"I'm looking for a woman named Zuzana. Can you help me find her?" he asked breathlessly.

The nurse looked sharply at the wild looking young man, but simply asked, "Are you family?"

"I am her fiancé," he said without a moment's hesitation.

The nurse nodded and pointed to the deck outside. Several people were resting on lounge chairs. Bowing his head in thanks, he slowly walked outside. Carefully scanning the faces, he walked tentatively in front of the patients. Suddenly he stopped.

She had her eyes closed and he stood there looking down at her fragile face. She was so pale but beautiful in the morning light. Her eyes flickered open and she gazed at him as if she were in a trance. He knelt beside her bed and took her hand. He began to cry, "Oh, Zuzka, I am so sorry. Please, don't leave me – don't leave me!"

She stared at him in amazement and then a beautiful smile spread across her face. Heartened by her smile, he stopped weeping and clasped her small hand in his. Kissing it, he murmured, "Zuzana, can you accept a fool like me?"

She let out a small cry and began laughing and coughing.

"Yes, I will," she said weakly after the coughing subsided. He stroked her hair and then her hand. They lost track of time as the evening shadows approached.

The Beginnings of a Long Education

"Mama, I signed myself up for kindergarten this morning," Pavol announced at lunch.

"What?" His mother nearly choked on her soup.

"I went to school and signed myself up, but we have to pay two crowns," he continued.

Zuzana stared at her little five-year-old in amazement.

"You went all by yourself and registered for school? Don't you want to stay at home with me? You have time! Why are you rushing?" she asked tenderly.

"Mama! I want to learn things! I want to play with the other children!" Pavol replied exasperated. "School is a wonderful place!"

Zuzana gazed at her little son and then patted his face.

"*Dobre*. I'll go pay *Pani Ucitelka*[39] right now. You stay here and don't go anywhere!" Zuzana stood up taking two crowns from her wallet and ran quickly out the door. Pavol felt very happy. He had watched the other village children running to school for a long time. Now was his chance!

As the first day of school approached, he no longer dragged his feet when his mother woke him up to go to Mass in the mornings. Every day at five thirty, his mother would gently shake him and dress him in the dark kitchen. Some winter mornings it was so bitterly cold in the house, and it was difficult to leave the comfort of his warm bed.

One morning, his father, Jozef, unexpectedly opened his mouth and scolded Zuzana, "Let the boy be! He needs his sleep!"

"Jozef! Don't you understand? When this child was born, I dedicated him to God! I know what I am doing! He is going to be a priest one day!" Zuzana replied defiantly.

---

39 Miss Teacher

"I don't know if he will be a priest or not and neither do you!" Jozef said, shaking his finger at her. "Don't you see how pale he is? You are making him sick!"

Pavol listened to their bickering for a few minutes and then sighed. He slid out from under the warm feather bed, dressed himself and met his mother in the doorway.

"See? He wants to go!" Zuzana said triumphantly.

Jozef looked down at his little son with pity in his eyes but gestured with his hand in resignation. He turned away and never interfered again.

The first day of school finally arrived, so after they came back from church, his mother carefully washed his face and hands. She examined his nails, straightened his collar, and kissed him goodbye. As he walked across the street clutching his new notebook and pencil, his heartbeat quickened. He walked to the kindergarten class and the teacher showed him where his table was. His feet dangled from the seat. Looking next to him, he saw the little girl who shared his table. Maya! He felt so happy! He had been in love with Maya and her dark brown eyes ever since he first saw her sitting on the front row in church. She smiled shyly at him and giggled. He sighed happily. However, the large picture of a dark headed man with a big moustache on the wall made him feel a little uneasy – he looked strange and scary.

At school they read stories, sang songs, and played. He put all his energy into the activities, and the teachers soon noticed his precociousness. He could memorize and recite long poems with ease. Soon he was the star at school programs, and his little voice could be heard over the loudspeaker in the village. Zuzana felt very proud of him in spite of herself. She tried to check those feelings. This was all very good, but Pavol was going to be a priest – not an actor or an orator.

One day, the teacher announced that the kindergarten class would be putting on a special program for the upcoming May first holiday. One child would be selected to recite at the program. This program was very important because members of the city and local government would be there. Pavol felt excited and knew this honor should be his! He rushed home to his mother and told her the news. While his father puffed on his cigarettes by the stove, Pavol practiced his poem with his mother until he had it perfectly memorized. Zuzana hugged him when he recited the entire poem without one mistake. Even his father nodded his head approvingly.

Finally, the day arrived when the teacher announced who would open the program with his poem. Pavol leaned forward eagerly in his desk to hear the news.

"Vladimir Sykora will be our poet," the teacher announced with a hint of resignation in her voice. She looked sadly at Pavol.

Pavol sat stunned by the news. Vlado Sykora was the mayor's plump son who could barely speak without stuttering. For the rest of the morning, Pavol sat quietly at his table and did not join in the games. Not even Maya could cheer him up. He stared at the picture of the man with the bushy moustache. A sneaking suspicion came to his mind that the man on the wall was responsible for what had happened.

The day of the program arrived, and all of the children were assembled in the first row of the auditorium to watch the pageantry of another communist holiday. A big red star hung over their heads, and the children wore red scarves around their white collars as they marched up and down the aisles carrying pictures of Lenin and Marx. Vladimir Sykora was perched nervously on a chair next to his proud father and mother. Not paying much attention to the parade, Pavol stared remorsefully at his classmate who had taken his place. Vlado looked pale and sweaty as he tugged at the red scarf around his fat neck.

Mayor Sykora opened the ceremony with a short speech on stage and then proudly introduced his son. Little Vladimir was positively gray by this time and walked slowly to the podium. He opened his mouth. Nothing came out. He opened his mouth again but not a sound came out. Silence reigned in the hall. Suddenly, he turned desperately towards his parents and started gagging, throwing up all over the stage. The auditorium was still for several seconds, but then all pandemonium broke out. The villagers roared with laughter, and Vladimir began to sob. His father jumped on the stage and started scolding him harshly, cuffing him on the back of his head. His mother rushed over, grabbed him by the collar, and whisked him off the stage wiping his face and expensive new suit with his red scarf. Some of the other children started to heave in the front row from the stench. The kindergarten teacher furiously beckoned to Pavol to come on stage while someone fetched a mop. Pavol walked up on the stage carefully avoiding Vladimir's mess and holding his nose. His teacher nodded at him, and the laughing in the audience slowly subsided. He loved standing in front of an audience with all eyes looking at him expectantly; the lights became dim and the spotlight was on him. Effortlessly, he began to recite the poem that Vlado had intended to say. He spoke clearly without hesitation and put feeling into every line. The audience sat quietly mesmerized by his voice. When he finished, he bowed and everyone began clapping enthusiastically. As he walked back to his seat in the auditorium, the villagers patted him on the back and said, "Well done, Palko! Well done!"

The next day in school, Vladimir did not show up to class and the children were all talking about the previous day's events. Maya shyly gave Pavol a candy, and the teacher praised him, "Our poet laureate!"

After school, Pavol rushed home and proudly told his mother the news. She stared at him for a few minutes and then took him firmly by the shoulders.

"That's all fine – you did very well, but don't forget, you are going to be a priest one day!"

Pavol wrinkled his forehead and hung his head. He mumbled, "Mama, I don't want to be a priest. I... I don't really know what I want to be – maybe a singer." Then he looked up hopefully. "Or what about a policeman? They get to use guns! Or I could fly a plane and be an airplane pilot!"

Zuzana's jaw was clenched and her voice uncharacteristically cold as she said, "You are too young to know what you want. We will talk about it later." She marched out of the kitchen. Pavol looked over at his father, who was carefully inspecting his fingernails by the stove. He looked up at his son and winked. Plopping down in his chair, Pavol shrugged and began slurping his soup.

The River

Years went by and the youngest son of Jozef Tesar grew. He was a small-boned boy with intense blue eyes and a big smile who fiercely loved his parents and his siblings. Most of all, Pavol was attached to his village and all of its sparkling features. It was the closest thing to heaven that he knew. Every season had its distinct flavors and scents. In the fall, the leaves turned fiery gold and red, the grapes grew plump and sweet until they were finally ready to harvest and turned into wine. In addition, the villagers' cellars became full of fragrant scented apples. In the winter, the river froze for ice-skating and there was exuberant sledding on the hills with thermoses of hot chocolate and slivovitz to warm frosty fingers and toes. When spring finally arrived, the village bloomed and looked like a bride with pink cherry blossoms. Then summer would burst forth; it was perhaps Pavol's favorite season. School was out and every day after breakfast, he would slip out the door and join his friends at the Nitra River, which meandered lazily along the village and its fields. The cool and refreshing water sparkled so invitingly on those hot summer days. He and his friends would have races to determine the fastest swimmer or start jumping contests from the highest branches to discover the bravest village boy. Then they would rest and eat on the soft sand bars that projected into the river. Cherries, plums, and apricots grew everywhere at various times during the summer, and the boys ate until their stomachs ached. Sometimes they would build a little fire on the banks and roast slanina[40] 'til it was crisp and dripping; it went perfectly with the thick chewy hunks of bread they had brought along in their knapsacks. Life could not get any better.

Pavol's mother would often protest and forbid him to go the river, but after constant wheedling and begging, she would ultimately give in. While she knew only too well the dangers of the river, she did not have the heart

---

40 Bacon

to keep her children captive in their own home. Children needed discipline, but they still needed freedom to grow. The problem was that the adults were too busy working to supervise. The river had many facets – not only was it a place of fun and recreation as well as a necessary means to their daily life, it also had a darker sinister side. Many stories had circulated over the years throughout the village.

Some said a *vodnik* or a water troll lived in the depths of the water. Pavol had listened to tales about the *vodnik* since he was a little boy. There were tales of the water creature stealing a goose paddling on the surface or a sheep that happened to graze too close to the riverbanks. One story involved a friendly old villager named Petrik. He worked in the co-op, but one night, he came home visibly wet and shaken.

He had been out planting in the fields, and when he had finally finished, he discovered that he was all alone after dark. The river lay between the village and the fields. He began wearily walking home that moonless night and was silently cursing the distance to the bridge where he could cross over to go home. Eyeing the water, he decided to take a shortcut and swim across a narrow part of the river. As he descended down into the water and began to swim across the cool still waters, he suddenly felt something jump on him from behind and yank him backwards into the water! The startled man began to choke and struggle for air as something or someone pulled him under the turbulent water. Crying out to the Holy Family and fighting with all his might, he managed to free himself and scrambled quickly onto the banks of the water.

The villagers had listened gravely to this story and did not laugh or smirk as Petrik had the reputation of being a serious, honest man. Pavol tried not to take these stories about the vodnik too seriously when he was swimming and laughing with his friends, but sometimes when the shadows of the evening approached, those accounts would come to mind. He could not help scanning the water rather apprehensively.

In Čerešňa, the village boys prided themselves on being tough, and they were always competing to see who had the most courage. As the smallest and most agile, Pavol would climb to the highest tree and dive into the river below, but he was careful to make sure the water was deep enough and free of rocks or debris. Further down the river was a dam that the new local communist government had built. They began regulating the river to prevent annual flooding, but they had constructed dangerous concrete pillars and vacuums below the surface of the water. Some of the more rash boys would cross the dam and dare each other to jump between the "teeth" below where the water churned and bubbled. Many jumped successfully, but there were a few who never came up.

Čerešňa's villagers took these events in stride. This was just fate. If it was your destiny to drown in the river, what could anyone do about it? The children grew up free and wild, toughened by both hardships and tragedy.

One day in early August, Pavol came in the kitchen hungry and exhausted from swimming and playing with friends. He found his mother weeping in the corner clutching a photograph in her hand.

"Mama, what's the matter," he cried with concern. He ran to her and began to stroke her hair. She didn't look up and started rocking back and forth.

"My baby, my baby," she murmured.

Pavol began to feel alarmed as she seemed oblivious to his presence in the room.

"Mama? Mama!"

Zuzana didn't react and continued to weep. He ran out of the house and saw Jozef squatting in the courtyard smoking a cigarette. His father looked up at him sadly and beckoned for him to come over.

"Is she still crying?" Jozef asked as he threw down his cigarette into the dirt.

"Yes, but why? Why is she crying? She did not even know I was there!" Pavol exclaimed.

"She is crying for your poor sister Maria. This is the anniversary of her death. You know the story, don't you?" Jozef said in a flat voice, devoid of emotion.

"All I know is that she drowned in the river when she was five years old," Pavol said thinking about the little gravestone he had seen in the cemetery. It had a little angel carved into the stone.

Jozef sighed and folded his hands. He looked up, and Pavol could see his father's clear blue eyes uncharacteristically misting up. The little boy felt awkward; he had never seen his father like this before.

"I was working in the local government that day. Your mother had to go to the fields and help with the wheat harvest. She left Helena at home in charge with Martin to watch their younger sister. I was supposed to check on them, but I got involved in my work and forgot the time. It was Helena's twelfth birthday, and she was excited about a new dress your mother was making for her. She and Martin were playing with their friends in the garden, and Maria wandered down to the river with some other little girls. Apparently, they had seen some of them playing near the bridge, on the other side" —Jozef paused and winced—"and they thought they would try to cross the river.

"That damn river has so many holes. You think it's shallow and then it drops."

Pavol nodded. He had fallen into many of the holes but had always popped back up to the surface.

"Apparently, she and the other little girl waded in and fell into one of the holes. Her friend was bigger and managed to swim to the surface, but our little girl, s-she did not make it."

Pavol waited in silence as his father stared at the sky and slowly began wringing his hands.

After a few moments, he continued, "The other children screamed; Helena and Martin ran to see what was wrong. Martin jumped immediately into the river, but he could not find her. They came to my office wailing and screaming, not making any sense. When I finally got them to calm down, I understood, and ran without stopping to the river."

"Soon the entire village was there looking for her. Your poor mother fainted when she heard the news. Hours went by and then days! We simply could not find her!" Jozef paused again recalling that dreadful time.

"Finally, I went down the river towards Lefantovce and started dredging the water with a rake. I remembered during the war, the soldiers' bodies would often appear in that particular bend of the river. But, at the same time, I was dreading that I would be the one to find her – dear God, please help me!"

Jozef wiped his forehead nervously. "I have never been a good one to be around dea— uh, such things."

Pavol nodded sympathetically.

"Suddenly, I dropped my rake in the water and there was a tug. I knew it. It was her and sure enough, her body popped to the surface." His father buried his head in his hands. The tears began to flow freely. Pavol held his breath.

"It was horrible how she looked – her sweet little body was swollen and black. Oh, *Majka moja*[41]!"

Pavol sat in silence. The evening shadows grew longer and the wind began to blow. Rain clouds began to build, and Pavol felt the first drops on his cheeks. Thunder rumbled off in the distance. His father roused himself and shuffled off towards the summer kitchen, wiping his face with

---

41 My dear sweet Maria

the back of his hands. Pavol debated with himself if he should follow, but decided to go back inside where his mother still sat.

Helena came that evening and fixed a small supper of soup, bread, cheese, and salami for them. Then she sat by her mother who was quietly praying her rosary. When Pavol tried to wish Helena a happy birthday, she forced a smile, shook her head, and said, "Thank you, Palko, but I don't celebrate my birthday anymore. Not since—" She broke off abruptly and went quickly to the pantry.

Pavol ran outside and walked down to the bridge as the rain continued to fall lightly. He stood on the banks looking at the pebbles until he found a beautiful blue shiny stone, then he walked onto the bridge. He sat down, hanging his feet from the bridge, and observed the rings that formed in the water as the raindrops softly fell. Kissing the small stone, he tossed it lightly into the water and watched it sink. Then he went home.

Sand

It was finally happening. Zuzana's prayers were finally answered. The government had announced that low-income families would receive assistance to build new homes, so the Tesar family applied and was granted the appropriate funds. In the meantime, Zuzana had been scrimping and saving what little she could to put towards the house and now that spring had arrived, they could start laying the foundation. There were always problems getting the building materials, but through connections, paying under the counter, and being resourceful, nothing was impossible. The biggest obstacle facing them was the lack of sand. There was no way to mix concrete without sand!

It was late March, and Jozef squatted on the riverbanks of the Nitra. He was fishing and thinking about the new house. The water sparkled in the morning sun, but he didn't notice its brilliance as he was deep in thought. Where, oh where, was he going to get sand? He scratched his head and accidentally knocked his old cap off. As he picked it up, he brushed a few grains of sand off the bill. A few grains of sand! Jozef dropped his fishing pole and began digging where his hat had fallen. Sand! Beautiful white grainy sand! He grabbed his gear and hurried home.

Bursting into the kitchen he shouted at his wife, "Where are the boys?"

Zuzana, taken somewhat aback by this rush of energy, looked at her husband with open mouth.

"Come on, woman! Where are they?" he demanded impatiently.

"Ondrej and Martin are working in the garden, and I just sent Palko to the store to fetch some flour."

"Oh, no! Palko will be standing in line for an hour!"

"What can I do? We need flour! We're out of bread!"

"No matter – send him to the river when he comes home. I think I solved our sand problem!"

Jozef ran outside and whistled at his sons. As they came running up, their father shouted at them to bring the shovel and dustpan as well as the old wheelbarrow. Surprised to see their father so animated, they quickly obeyed and followed him to the river.

All afternoon, they mined the riverbanks for the white sand. As they dug, they discovered different qualities of sand – some of the grains were finer and had a whiter tinge while others were coarse and yellow. They dug and scooped, hauling several loads back and forth to their property where they planned to build. As they were digging, one man rode up on his bicycle and observed them for a while.

"Hey, how much would you sell that pile to me?" he asked pointing at the pile of sand they had near their little mine.

Jozef looked at him with a glint in his eye.

"Well, how much would you offer?"

"I'll give you twenty crowns for this much." The man measured out how much he wanted.

"Make it twenty-five and it is yours."

"Done. I'll need five times that amount. I'll bring my tractor if your boys will load it up for me."

Jozef nodded in satisfaction. Soon the word got around and more people began to come with their wheelbarrows, horse drawn wagons, and tractors. People came from several kilometers as the supply stores did not have any sand, and there were many new houses being built in the surrounding villages.

Later, more mines began to appear along the riverbanks, but no one worked as industriously as Jozef Tesar and his sons. As the sand mining business progressed, an unspoken law began to develop that no one disturbed another person's spot. Occasionally it happened that neighboring miners would combine their efforts if there were a particularly large demand that day. Men and boys would work side by side pleased that they were meeting the needs of their friends and neighbors. They would take breaks and share their *pivo* they had brought along to quench their thirst.

Zuzana was delighted to receive the extra income and gave her husband an approving smile each time he handed her the extra crowns to tuck away in her secret hiding spot. Jozef would then immediately go to bed after a quick supper as he was too weary to go to the pub and spend money on drink or cards. His wife was feeling very satisfied.

The sand business lasted a couple of summers as it was impossible to work on the riverbanks during the cold winter months. It was not long before they had enough sand and extra money to purchase the rest of the materials they needed for their house, and with Helena and Martin's added financial support, Zuzana's dream began to become a reality. Her daughter and son-in-law would come on weekends to help with the building. Of course this meant that their little daughter, Maria, would also come and play in the garden. She liked to hide in the corn and entertain herself by braiding the silken hair on each stalk. Jana, who was twelve years old now, helped with the cooking and fetched water for the workers. Zuzana liked walking around the grounds with her hands behind her back as the men dug, mixed cement, and laid bricks.

"Thank you, Lord," she whispered, "thank you!"

Soon, by the end of the second summer, their house was finished. Moving day finally arrived and, with great satisfaction, Zuzana handed the key to their little rent house back to Mrs. Hornikova. Their landlady still lived in the same house but was all alone as her husband had passed away the previous year from a sudden heart attack, and strangely enough the son-in-law had also died in a tragic car accident. Zuzana refused to rejoice over her neighbor's misfortunes and even felt sympathy for her, but it was a relief to leave – no looking back.

Milan Skalicky came one fall morning with his horses and wagon to load up their belongings. Eight-year-old Pavol felt a pain in his heart as he sat on top of the wagon next to his mother's wood burning stove. This had been his home! He was born in that house and had spent many happy hours there! This was where his mother taught him his ABCs and fed him her delicious cheese kolaches in their cozy kitchen. This was the street where he and the neighborhood children played street hockey or ball for hours. He swallowed hard and fought back his tears as they rode away in Mr. Skalicky's wagon. They were not going far, but their new house was right on the opposite side of their village, Čerešňa. It was going to be a whole new world. However, Pavol could not remain sad long as he observed how happy his mother and father seemed to be as they unloaded all of their worldly belongings into the new house. Helena and Jana joined Zuzana and immediately began sweeping, wiping, and arranging the kitchen, the most important room in the house. The men carried and unloaded the meagre furniture wherever the women directed, but they often took time to rest in the courtyard and drink a cool beer. The next day the priest came quietly to bless their house, and they celebrated outside with food and new wine from the vineyards where Martin was working. It was a joyful time.

As they settled in and grew accustomed to their new home and garden, Jozef and his three sons continued their business at the river. Pavol was his father's main assistant as Ondrej and Martin could only help on the weekends.

One morning, Pavol woke up and went with his father to the riverbanks to dig more sand. Fridays were usually busy, and many people would come in the afternoon. As they neared their mine, they noticed one mine that seemed unattended.

"Why don't you dig there, Synchek moj?" Jozef prodded Pavol towards the spot.

"Doesn't that belong to Kleister?" Pavol asked.

"He's a lazy bastard! He hasn't dug in that mine for weeks. Go ahead!" Jozef ordered.

Pavol obeyed and took his shovel and dustpan to the abandon mine along the river. He loved the smell of the fresh river sand and worked happily digging himself deeper and deeper down into the riverbank. After about an hour, he heard a noise above him.

"Hhrrmph!"

Pavol looked up and saw old man Kleister glaring down at him.

"What do you think you are doing? This spot belongs to me!"

Pavol scrambled out of the mine and stared at the unshaven man. Then he blurted out, "We thought you had stopped digging!"

"Clear off, boy! Your father thinks he is so smart – making himself a small fortune! We'll see about this!" He turned around and stomped away.

Pavol watched him until he disappeared and then ran quickly to his father. After explaining what had just happened, Jozef shrugged and replied, "Don't pay any attention to him. Now come on and help me with this."

A few days later, a letter came in the mail. Zuzana opened it up and sat down again.

"Jozef, look at this."

She handed him the letter. He put on his reading glasses and read it aloud:

"Dear Comrades:

It has come to our attention that illegal activity has been taking place on the banks of the Nitra River in Čerešňa, district Topoľčany. Capitalistic activity of any kind is forbidden and considered a serious crime. This property belongs to the state and therefore to the people;

anyone found mining sand will be fined 400 crowns. If it continues, perpetrators will be charged with criminal violation.

Signed by the Mayor of Čerešňa
Ludovit Sykora

Jozef cleared his throat nervously and put the letter down. He thought for a moment.

"Kleister! He reported us!"

"Why would he do that?"

"Because he is a jealous old fool. Ach, 400 crowns! I had better go and warn the others at the river."

And that was the end of the sand mining. There was still some illicit mining going on by the light of the moon as shortages still persisted, but the Tesar family business had to shut down much to Pavol's dismay. During the past two summers at the sand mine, there had been a sparkle in his father's blue eyes. He had even been standing up a little bit straighter and looking taller. Now he was slumping down again in his old spot by the stove. Jozef Tesar looked like an old man.

Another Wedding

It was the middle of June and unusually warm. The cherries were darkening on the trees along the road. They looked so plump and juicy that Pavol could not resist pulling a few off as he walked home from school. As he approached the gate, he saw his oldest brother's bicycle parked outside. He spat the pits out of his mouth and went inside. His mother and Martin were talking quietly in the corner of the kitchen. Martin had a resigned look on his face while his mother was gesturing with her wooden spoon and talking earnestly in his ear. They both jumped in surprise when they heard Pavol's book bag plop on the table.

"Oh, Palko! You are home?" his mother said hurriedly as she turned her back on Martin and resumed stirring the soup on the stove.

"It's one o'clock, Mama. I always come home at this time," Pavol replied looking at her curiously. "What's for lunch?"

"Noodles! But eat your soup first!" Zuzana smiled rather nervously first at Pavol and then at Martin.

"Do I have to?"

"Yes, of course. It's full of vegetables from the garden. Don't you want to grow up to be as big as your brother?"

Martin stood up from his chair, ruffled his younger brother's dark hair, and walked to the door. His mother looked up at him anxiously. He smiled, shrugged, and walked out of the door. Zuzana shook her head slightly.

"What were you and Martin talking about?" Pavol asked.

"Oh, nothing that concerns you!" Zuzana said breezily. "Now, when are you going to take those geese out?"

"Oh, Mama, I am almost 13 years old! Do I still have to take care of the geese?"

"Who else is going to do it? They need some fresh green grass, so I am depending upon you!"

"Why can't Ondrej do it?" Pavol said with some annoyance in his voice. "My teacher gave me a book about Captain Cooke. He sailed around the whole world – I want to start reading it!"

"You know that your brother has to study for his exams. He doesn't have time to help us now. Besides, you can still read your book a little and watch the geese."

Pavol ate his soup in silence. He had just seen his middle brother talking and laughing in front of the pub with a group of village girls. They were all teasing him and admiring his muscles as he flexed them.

"Hmmph! Ondrej is really studying hard," Pavol muttered as he blew a hot carrot off his spoon.

Zuzana did not seem to notice what her youngest son had just said. As she ladled the soup in her white ceramic bowl, her mind wandered to a scene in the kitchen that had occurred a few years ago. She and her husband Jozef were having a violent argument.

"You did what?" Jozef asked incredulously.

"I had to, Jozef! Otherwise they won't admit Ondrej into the university! I had to sign our fields over to the co-op!" she retorted.

"Our fields? You mean my fields! Why? Why did you do that? You had no right! Those were my father's fields and my grandfather's fields! They have been in the Tesar family for generations! You had no right!" Jozef slumped in the chair and put his head in his hands.

"The head of the co-op told me that Ondrej would not be admitted if we did not sign over those fields! They threatened me! You were not at home! What could I do?"

Jozef shook his head and pounded his fist on the table. Then he stood up and moved menacingly towards her. Her heart skipped a beat. After glaring at her in a strange, wild way, he grabbed her arm very tightly and yelled, "You did it without my permission! Without my permission!" He dropped her arm and looked at her helplessly, shaking his head. Then he whirled around and stomped clumsily out of the room. His card playing and drinking seemed to increase after that day.

Zuzana winced as she pulled her thoughts back to the present. What could she have done? *I really had no choice*, she told herself again. The government had threatened everyone that if they did not cooperate, their children would not be allowed to attend a university or trade school. She could not imagine her children not having the advantages of being well-educated. She wanted them to have more opportunities than she or Jozef had ever had. Helena had gone to secretarial school and was happily working as an office clerk at a local company in Topolcany. She was busy raising Jana and their new little daughter, Maria. But what about her own sons? Zuzana had always hoped that one of them would go to medical school and be a doctor, but she had given up on that idea. Martin was too busy working at the new agricultural complex with his cows and horses as well as being an active communist party member. From all appearances, he was advancing in his career, but he was attending church less and less. He thought it was hypocritical to profess Marxism and then sneak off to church in another village or town like many of the other party members did. He was too straightforward for that. Some of them would drive for miles to have their children baptized in a strange parish where nobody knew them or could report them to headquarters. For Martin it was an open and shut issue.

Then there was her Ondrejko. He was a handsome, amiable boy who was always surrounded by friends. Since he was very skillful at designing and building things, she was sure he would make a fine engineer. So, after she signed the fields over to the co-op, she made sure he would study engineering in Bratislava. He started out well, but his active social life took precedence, and he did not pass his classes at the end of the third year. He came home in disgrace. Zuzana could not even look at him for a week, which wounded him more deeply than a fierce scolding. However, a year later he began his coursework anew at the agricultural university in Nitra and threw himself into studies. He was doing well, but he still preferred the soccer field and parties over his textbooks and lectures.

As far as Pavol was concerned, there was no need for her to speculate. He was going to be a priest. It was fate. She had conceived him late in life like Sarah and Elizabeth in the Bible, so Zuzana had consecrated her youngest son to God. Every morning at five thirty, she woke him up to go to Mass where he would don the altar server's big white robes and assist the priest. However, their new priest shouted a great deal at the altar servers and boxed their ears when they did something wrong, especially her son. Their priest wasn't a bad person, but he had a short fuse and the slightest thing could set him off.

And she was worried – Pavol did not seem to have any great ambitions about being a priest. The priest they had before was a good and gentle man who was not afraid to speak openly against the government when he preached. He was the same priest who had baptized Pavol when he was only three weeks old. However, one evening big black cars pulled up in front of the rectory and their village priest was escorted away by men in dark coats and hats. Some said he was still in prison in the Czech lands. Others said he had already died. *That Mayor Sykora informed the authorities about him*, sniffed Zuzana.

"That godly man would have encouraged my Pavol to be a priest," she whispered aloud.

Pavol did not even want to discuss the matter and was either out playing with his friends or had his nose buried in another Karol Maj story. He was such a dreamer! The other morning he had woken up and told her that he had dreamed about being in New York City. He described in detail the skyscrapers and how crowded the streets were with people.

"Mama! It was so real! I am sure that I will be there one day!" he said with a faraway look in his eyes.

Zuzana was concerned about him. He was often sick with migraines, and he just didn't seem as strong as her other boys. He was intelligent enough to study medicine, but he could not stand the sight of blood! He almost fainted when she took him to the doctor last time. What kind of physician would that be? *No, he must become a priest. He doesn't have the nerves for anything else*, she thought. *But what if he does not want to be a priest?* Zuzana hesitated. *Well, then - he'll be on his own.*

"Oh, Lord, am I doing the right thing?" she said absentmindedly aloud.

"What did you say, Mama?" Pavol asked as he dug into the big pot of noodles. He topped them with his mother's homemade cottage cheese and sour cream – mmm, delicious!

"Nothing, *synchek moj*, nothing. Now, run along and feed those poor geese finally!"

Pavol finished his lunch and then dutifully gathered the geese in the courtyard, escorting them through the gate. He whistled and called as they followed him towards the bridge. As he walked past the local government, he saw some kind of commotion going on in front of the mayor's door. As Pavol came nearer with his flock of geese, he saw the mayor's secretary trying to push a large, stubborn goat out of the front door. Mayor Sykora was standing in front of the steps trying to pull the obstinate animal from behind and yelling at his secretary. The goat seemed to be more interested in the secretary's colorful dress and took a little nibble of her sleeve much to the secretary's dismay.

Pavol chuckled, "Belo's goat got loose again. I wonder why he always likes to call on the mayor? Maybe they have something in common to talk about."

He turned the street corner towards the bridge and saw his classmate Belo asleep under a tree. A tattered rope dangled in his hands.

Pavol put his fingers in his mouth and whistled shrilly. Then he cupped his hands around his mouth and yelled, "Hey, Belo! Your goat is paying the mayor another visit!"

"W-w-what?" Belo opened his sleepy eyes and looked at the loose rope in his hand. "Betka? *Pane moj!* Where are you?" He staggered to his feet and stumbled towards the mayor's office.

Pavol crossed the bridge with his flock of geese and headed towards the green meadows along the riverbanks. The geese waddled eagerly towards the lush grass. Pavol settled himself down under a tree and was soon lost in the South Pacific with Captain Cook and his crew.

"Palko, Palko! Come here!"

Pavol roused himself from his book and looked up. He saw his friends Jakub and Michal.

"Ahoj," he said shutting his books. "What are you doing?"

"The same thing you are," Jakub said pointing at his own flock of geese. "What are you reading?"

"Oh, it's about Captain Cook and his adventures at sea. What's that in your hands?"

Jakub smiled smugly at him and held out his hand. "It's a cigarette. I stole it from my brother. Do you wanna try it?"

Michal looked at it in awe and said, "If my mother sees me, I won't be able to sit down for a week."

"Don't worry," Jakub said confidently. "Nobody will see us out here. Look, I brought matches."

He struck the match, lit the cigarette and started puffing on it. Pavol and Michal looked at him admiringly. Then he held it out to them. "Here, try it!"

Michal shook his head, but Pavol could not resist taking the burning cigarette into his hand. He had often watched his father take deep drags off of his cigarettes and blow smoke rings in the air when he was deep in thought. Pavol took a tentative puff on the cigarette and immediately began to cough and sputter. Michal and Jakub laughed at him.

"Phewy! Forget this! Let's go kick the ball," Peter said throwing the cigarette away.

That night, Pavol lay in his bed half asleep dreaming about ships, Tahitian girls, burning cigarettes, and exotic islands. His dreams were interrupted by his oldest brother's heavy boots on the stairs.

Zuzana was sitting at the kitchen table reading her prayer book when Martin came through the door. His face was serious but he looked pleased. She looked up at him with expectation in her eyes.

"Well, congratulate me, Mama! I am going to be married!"

Zuzana's face broke into a smile but there was a flicker of worry in her eyes.

Pavol sat straight up in the bed and yelled, "Married! To whom?"

"Dalena Skalicky! That's who, little brother!"

Pavol lay back in the bed dazed. Dalena Skalicky! Why in the world was he going to marry her? She never even opened her mouth. How can you marry someone who never talks? Martin had brought her home one Sunday afternoon for coffee and cake, but she just sat like a stone on her chair and stared at the table for one hour. Finally, she jumped up and said rather abruptly, "I have to go home!" Then she dashed liked a scared rabbit out the door. Martin had been embarrassed and rushed out the door after her.

Pavol had to admit she *was* pretty, and she did have a very good reputation in the village like her father Bolek, but Pavol was not entirely convinced she was the right one for Martin. He clenched his fists under the bed cover.

Zuzana stood up and kissed her oldest son on both cheeks to congratulate him.

"You did the right thing, my son! My goodness, you have been seeing each other for five years! What would people think?" She walked slowly out of the room, nodding her head and repeating that last phrase as if to assure herself that this was the correct course of action.

The wedding took place later that summer. Dalena wore a modern wedding dress that flared at the skirt just below her knees. She blushed and smiled uncomfortably as the villagers came by one by one to congratulate her. Martin looked tall and slender in his dark suit. His hair was blond from working out in the sun all summer. His tanned face was peaceful and grave. Pavol could not understand why his own church pants from last year had become so short and his shoes seemed to be too small, but he forgot about them when he saw his friends playing in the churchyard. Helena's eight-year-old daughter Maria preened and curtsied showing off her new white taffeta dress while she held her sister Jana's hand. Ondrej stood with a crowd of friends around him, flashing his movie star smile at the girls who blushed and giggled. Their father only wanted to know when it would finally be over and time to eat.

The church was quite hot and the bridal pair, as well as the congregation, were sweating as they took their holy vows. Even the priest had to stop halfway through his sermon to wipe his brow during the ceremony. After the ceremony, everyone went to Bolek Skalicky's house for the wedding supper. No one mentioned the incident anymore when Sykora came to collect his farm goods and had thrown Bolek in jail for several weeks. Bolek and his wife worked for the co-op now and seemed resigned to their fate, but there was still a bitter look on his face when he looked out over the land that used to be his. Instead, they turned their focus on their only daughter Dalena and gave her everything she wanted.

Much to Jozef Tesar's delight, the table was loaded with sausages, sauerkraut, bread, beer, and wine. He was able to eat to his heart's content, but Zuzana's mouth felt dry and she could only pick at her cake. She tried to share in her son's joy, but this nagging feeling of apprehension would not go away. Martin was going to move out of their house and take up residence in the Skalicky home since Dalena refused to leave her parents' house and village. He had been offered an apartment through his company in Nitra and had been quite excited about moving to town, but his new wife had flatly refused to go.

"Will Martin still come to see us, Mama?" Pavol asked his mother wistfully as they walked home that evening from the Skalicky's house. The wind was blowing slightly and the red poppies in the fields were bowing in unison as they passed by.

"Of course he will! Nothing will change!" his mother said with determination in her voice. Pavol looked up at her, but noticed that she still had a troubled look in her eyes. He turned his eyes towards the ground and did not look up again until they came to their gate.

School and Friends

The seasons quickly passed and before anyone knew it, spring had once again appeared. Pavol was in middle school, and his days were full with church, friends, and school. All of nature was beckoning to him to come outside; life was exhilarating. The most exciting events were the impromptu games of football in the streets. The boys played so furiously that they didn't even take time to eat. Sometimes their mothers would come outside and give them thick slices of bread with delicious goose fat spread on top. They would balance the bread in one hand and run wildly chasing the ball and eating at the same time. They were free and unshackled.

One day after school, Pavol was on his way to the store for his mother. He carried the big flowered shopping bag full of empty beer bottles and milk bottles. Suddenly he heard someone trying to get his attention.

"Psst! Palo! Over here!"

He looked around but didn't see anyone.

"Over here!"

He saw his friend Jakub sticking his head around the corner of the brick factory and waving sharply for him to come over. Curious, he wandered over to the building. Jakub was his best friend and always full of ideas. Pavol came around the corner with Jakub pulling him quickly behind the bushes where Michal and two other boys were crouching.

"What are you doing?" Pavol asked surprisedly. "Are you hiding from someone?"

"Look! Lubinko figured out how to make cigarettes out of the dried potato tops! Here, try it!"

Pavol stared at the clumsily rolled up paper. Jakub lit one end of it and smoke curled up.

"I don't know…" Pavol's voice trailed off.

"Aw, come on! Just try it! It's not going to kill you! You already smoked one of my brother's cigarettes, remember?"

Pavol tentatively took the rolled up cigarette and took a puff. A strange taste filled his throat and nostrils. His eyes began to water.

"Bleh! That tastes terrible," Pavol said spitting on the ground.

"Go on! Try another!"

He took another puff and began to choke and cough. The other boys laughed at him, and Lubinko took the cigarette away from him.

"Look! You do it like this!" He demonstrated by taking a deep drag and blowing the smoke out of his nose.

"I have to go," Pavol said admiring Lubinko's finesse.

"Meet us here after school tomorrow!"

Pavol promised and hurried to the store.

The following days, the boys met regularly either at the river with their geese or behind the brick factory after school. They felt very grown up kicking the soccer ball with a cigarette hanging out of their mouths. The burning and coughing subsided, and they actually began to enjoy their homemade cigarettes or the ones they snitched from their fathers' packs. Sometimes, they hid down in the quarry while the workers were on lunch break and played cards, puffing and practicing their smoke rings.

One day Zuzana was walking home from church when one neighbor came rushing up behind her on a bicycle.

"Pani Tesarova! Pani Tesarova! Wait!"

"What is it, Pani Gajdosova?" Zuzana stopped and stared at her neighbor.

The other woman's face was flushed and bursting with untold information as she got off of her bike.

"Did you know," she huffed and puffed, "that, that, your son is smoking with his friends behind the brick factory? They almost burned the entire place down!"

"What?"

"It's true! I was walking past there yesterday, and I thought I smelled something strange. Then I could her them laughing! I looked around the corner and there those little *pangarts*[42] were playing cards and smoking! They are no more than twelve or thirteen and already smoking! Shame on them!"

Pani Gajdosova paused to catch her breath and then continued, "If I were you, I would give him a good switching!" She then nodded sharply at Zuzana and mounted her bicycle riding quickly away.

---

42 Bastards

Shocked, Zuzana walked slowly home pondering this news. As she pushed through the gate, she saw Jozef squatting in the corner of the yard rolling a cigarette.

"No wonder," she muttered to herself shaking her head.

That night Pavol came in from taking care of the geese. He looked hot and disheveled. There were dark circles under his eyes. Zuzana suspected he had been playing more football with his friends than looking out for the geese, but she did not say a word as he washed his hands and sat down to eat the evening bread.

She sat quietly, staring at him from the other end of the table. Pavol could feel her eyes burning into his soul, and he began to feel uncomfortable under her gaze.

"Is something wrong, Mama?" he asked squirming a little in his seat.

"Pani Gajdosova said she saw you inside the brick factory today smoking with your friends. She said that you almost burned the factory down!"

"We weren't in the brick factory! We were behind it!"

"Ahhh," she said showing a look of satisfaction that he had confessed.

Pavol felt his face grow hot as he realized he had fallen into a trap. Zuzana got up from the table, and Pavol was sure that she was looking for the braided leather whip she kept in the pantry for switching naughty boys. But instead, she looked up sadly at the crucifix on the wall. She stood there silently for several minutes without moving a muscle. Pavol began to get nervous as the clock ticked. Then he heard her sigh – a deep, heavy sigh. Without another word she left the room.

Pavol felt terrible. That sigh was worse than any beating she could have given him. He could not bear to disappoint his mother like this. He had seen that look of sadness when his brother Martin stopped attending church in their village. He had seen that same look when his father came home drunk and penniless. He had also seen that look when his brother Ondrej had failed school. That was it. No more smoking. Surprisingly enough, he actually felt a little relieved.

The next day in school, the teacher stood up to make a special announcement. He tried to look stern as he stared at Pavol and his friends.

"It has come to my attention that some of you are trying to end your lives a little early!"

The children looked at each other.

"Now you may think that smoking is the grown-up thing to do, but it is a stupid and dirty habit!"

"But Pan Ucitel, I saw you smoking at the bus stop the other day!" one of the girls said in the front row.

The teacher's face turned red as he said hurriedly, "Well, never mind that now. Now, Pavol Tesar, stand up!"

Pavol looked around at his friends Jakub and Michael. They shrugged and gestured for him to stand up, so he slowly rose from his chair. He looked down at his hands and was quiet.

The teacher walked over to him and asked loudly, "May I ask, why you were late to school again this morning? For the fourth time this month?"

Pavol's heart began to beat a little faster. He didn't know what to say and shuffled his feet nervously on the floor.

"I know, Pan Ucitel." Beata, a little girl with long brown braids, raised her hand eagerly.

The teacher nodded at Beata, so she said smugly, "Palo was late today because he was serving as an altar boy at Mass this morning."

The teacher's face became pale and his eyes bulged out in fury. He took a step nearer to Pavol and stood trembling in front of him.

"Is this true?" he demanded.

Pavol nodded uncertainly still looking down at his hands. Suddenly the teacher grabbed his hair and started yanking his head back and forth like a rag doll while he slapped it with his other free hand.

"Owww," Pavol wailed. "Stop, Pan Ucitel, stop!"

"I don't every want to hear that one of my students is late because he was attending church with *babkas*! Do you understand? Do you want to be a superstitious old lady, too? Do you understand me?"

"Ano, Pan Ucitel, ano," Pavol cried his face turning red as paprika. Pavol glanced over bitterly at Beata who was stifling a giggle.

The teacher released his hold and stepped back to his desk. Trying to gain his composure, he addressed the class. "What I really wanted to tell you all is that we have a special speaker today. You all know Pan Krachik. I want all of you to sit quietly and give him your full attention."

Mr. Krachik was sitting in the corner of the room, observing everyone in the classroom. He was a prominent communist member in the village, but Pavol had never heard anyone speaking very highly of him. He used to attend church but no longer showed up during Mass since he began working for the local government. Shooting Pavol a withering look, Mr. Krachik put some strange pictures of creatures who looked half man and half monkey on the chalkboard.

"These pictures, boys and girls, are your ancestors!" The children looked at each other again. The girls began to giggle and one of the boys gave a loud snort.

"Now, stop laughing. I am serious! If you study science, you will discover that all human beings descended from these ape-like creatures."

Then Mr. Krachik went into a long discussion that was over the children's heads about Darwin and the evolutionary theory.

Pavol stared curiously at the pictures and in spite of his recent punishment began to feel angry. He raised his hand.

"Yes?"

"If we are descended from monkeys, then why aren't we still swinging from trees?"

The class roared with laughter. Mr. Krachik frowned angrily at Pavol and took a threatening step towards him but then composed himself.

"Don't tell me that you believe all of those silly stories that your mother has told you about Adam and Eve! Our new socialist government is here to teach you the truth! You cannot believe those lies they tell you in church!"

"They're not lies!" Pavol protested. He felt that not only his head but his whole world was being shaken.

"Young man, there is no God! There is only science and evolution – that is how the world came to be! Those stories in the Bible are only myths and fairy tales. Religion is the opiate of the people!"

Jakub leaned over and whispered into Pavol's ear, "What does 'opiate' mean?"

Pavol shrugged and whispered back, "I think it means drug or some kind of opium – you know like they get from poppies!"

"Oh," Jakub said still looking dubiously at the strange pictures.

Mr. Krachik pointed his finger at Pavol and said, "Just study science, boy. Then you will find out all your answers! Science will solve all of the world's problems!"

Mr. Krachik continued to talk about Darwin's theories while the children sat quietly in their seats. Their teacher looked bored as he stared absentmindedly out of the window.

Finally, the mini-lecture finished, the teacher thanked Mr. Krachik for coming, and the children were dismissed.

Pavol felt depressed and kicked a rock into the street. Jakub followed him on his bike, but neither one of them said a word. Jakub tried to cheer him up, but Pavol brushed off his overtures. Giving him a hurt look, his friend rode slowly away swinging his bike from one side of the road to the other. Pavol did not even notice Jakub had left; his world had just been shattered. Was Mr. Krachik right? Were all of the stories in the Bible just that – simply fairy tales?

As he walked along the main street deep in thought, he suddenly heard the screeching of brakes, a woman's scream, and a thudding noise. He ran around the corner and saw Jakub's bike wheel spinning wildly on the ground. Pavol's heart was in his throat, and his feet felt glued to the ground. He stood frozen as he saw people rushing towards the crumpled figure lying on the side of the road. A *babka* stood wringing her hands and moaning as an elderly man gently bent down. Pavol forced himself to move and started running towards the bicycle. He pushed through the crowd and saw Jakub lying very pale and still in an awkward position with his leg bent backwards over the frame of the bike. Blood trickled from his mouth. Pavol began to shake and he could feel his head start to spin. He sat down and put his head between his legs.

"Go home, boy! Go home!"

Pavol was roughly pulled up and pushed away. He ran blindly home sobbing all the way.

He had always hated funerals and always looked for an excuse when the priest asked him to serve. Death made him angry and sometimes doubt the existence of a loving God.

Marching silently beside his mother, they followed the procession to the cemetery at the end of the village. He saw Jakub's mother weeping and leaning on her husband's arm. Vainly trying to blink back his tears, Pavol agonized over those last few minutes he had spent with his friend. *Why didn't I just stop and talk to him a little longer? He might still be alive! All that stupid talk about evolution and monkeys!*

That evening, Pavol sat at the table staring at the *halusky*[43] his mother had made earlier for lunch. Normally, it was his favorite dish, but he had no appetite.

"What's the matter with you? Are you sick? I hope all that silly smoking hasn't ruined your health!" his mother asked worriedly feeling his forehead. Pavol grimaced as he remembered his friend Jakub laughing and smoking behind the brick factory. Tears sprang to his eyes, and he ran outside.

The fruit trees were in full blossom and a warm, scented breeze floated through the evening air. He stared up at the dusky sky and looked

---

43 Pasta – something between a noodle and a dumpling; usually eaten with Bryndza, sheep cheese

around at the new life springing up around him. The stars were slowly appearing one by one.

Pavol had always implicitly believed that God had created the world and everything in it, but he wasn't exactly sure how. And what about his friend Jakub? Was he in heaven now? He studied the twinkling stars for a few minutes, and then he clenched his fists.

"I will study science and learn the truth!" he said resolutely. "They'll see. I'll prove to them that God does exist; it's not just a story! Jakub must be in heaven – he must!"

"Palko, come inside and finish eating! What are you doing out there? Do you want me to give your supper to the chickens?"

Taking one last look at the night sky, Pavol nodded resolutely and turned to go inside.

Changes in the Family

Martin was now married and living permanently with his new in-laws, but he still tried to visit his own family on Saturdays. He wanted to help his mother and his *apa* with some of the gardening and chores, but his new bride would show up and tap her foot until he returned home. Soon his visits became less frequent, and his financial help ceased altogether. As a communist party member, he also stopped attending church, so his family no longer had the pleasure of seeing his long lanky body leaning against the chapel wall and singing his favorite hymns.

It was not long before a little daughter named Barbora arrived, and two years later a son was born. Zuzana thought that they would name their new son after his father or grandfather, but Dalena shook her head vigorously and announced his name was Alexis. Martin was very proud of his two children and paraded them around the village on his shoulders. They received a great deal of attention, not only from their doting father but from their grandparents and great-grandparents as well. Dalena kept her job as a bookkeeper at the brick factory, so her mother and her elderly *babka* looked after the children while she was gone. She was a difficult woman to keep up with, that Dalena. She never walked but ran or rode her bicycle so furiously through the village that one would think she had a train to catch. She loved her children, but seemed eager to leave them with her mother and dash off to work.

Martin's hard work and activity in the party was going well; promotions kept coming. It wasn't long before he was appointed the director of the huge agricultural complex located in Nitra. He even had his own driver and car picking him up early each morning and then returning him late in the evening.

On the weekends, he began building a new house next to the old one that belonged to his father-in-law, Bolek. He solicited his father and brothers to help him with the construction as well as other villagers, and they obliged him by mixing cement, hauling wood, and hammering.

Perhaps he did not consciously mean to think this way, but there was an underlying attitude on Martin's side that his family owed him. After all, he had taken care of them while Jozef was out of work and too depressed to look for a job to care for his wife and younger sons. Those were desperate times and Martin was their rock.

Work on Martin's new house went on for months, even years, but once it was finished, he stopped calling on his way home from work. Feeling a sense of loss and hoping to chat with her eldest son, Zuzana started dropping by his new home after church on Sundays. Pavol often accompanied his mother as he also missed his eldest brother. Martin was more than just a brother to him; he was like a second father to Pavol.

His own father, Jozef, had never mistreated Pavol, but there was a certain amount of neglect and a sense of apathy. During his bouts of depression, Jozef was not able to shower much love or affection on his youngest son. It was his eldest brother Martin who used to swing Pavol up on his shoulders and bring him little presents from his various trips, but now there were only presents for his own two children. Any free time he had from his demanding job was spent with them.

"I already did my duty – no more," Zuzana once heard him say as he waved his hand to signify that his support was over.

However, Martin seemed pleased to see them whenever they stopped by, but he was not his usual self. They often sat in an uncomfortable silence until someone would try to say something about the weather, politics, or even the pigs or chickens. Pavol's eldest brother had built an invisible wall around him and after a while there was nothing more to say, so he would retreat to the living room to watch a football game on his new color TV. They could no longer even pray the rosary together as they used to when he lived at home.

Zuzana and Pavol would admire and sometimes longingly look at the beautiful Spanish oranges or yellow bananas Dalena had on display in her shiny, modern kitchen. She was always a good hostess and waited on them, sharing what they had, but it was impossible to buy such fruit in the normal stores – they could only buy those green oranges from Cuba and stand in line for hours if bananas were in stock. In contrast, the communist party leaders had their own shops and connections. They were the new elite in their socialist government, and now Martin was one of them.

After playing with little Barbora and Alexis, Zuzana and Pavol would usually go home.

Pavol entered the gymnasium in Topolcany and started taking the train every morning to town. He had taught himself Latin during the summer and had already been accepted into the advanced class. He enjoyed the history and science classes, muddled through his Slovak language classes, despised his Russian classes, and worked hard to learn German. What wearied and bored him the most were the daily classes in Marxism and Leninism. He could repeat verbatim the lines that "religion was the opiate of the people," and America was an imperialist nation full of pigs that exploited its workers and wanted to take over the world. Sometimes, when he came home from class, he would leave his books on the table and dash to the fields to escape the barrage of red stars and pictures of Lenin draped across the village streets and buildings. He would take a deep breath and feel his body relax from the tension and stress he had to experience each day.

They can't find me here, he thought. *No one knows where I am! Just let them come and try to watch me here.*

Music was another world where he could escape, so he continued his lessons at the conservatory switching from playing the trumpet to voice. His baritone voice was developing well, and he sang the psalm in church every day. The villagers enjoyed hearing his resonant voice ring out from the balcony above, and when he sang, he noticed their crotchety priest actually became a little less cranky.

Meanwhile, girls had become even a bigger attraction, but he actually felt shyer since the onset of puberty; he was not quite ready for a serious relationship yet. The thoughts of physical intimacy overpowered him and shook him to the core. Playing football or hockey helped calm his hormones down as well as diving into books about far-off lands; they were conducive in diverting his mind to other topics. However, he had a romantic soul, and the songs of Karel Gott, a popular new Czech singer from Prague, inspired him. He would absolutely forget everything else when he played those songs or French *chansons* on their old record player. Even his mother would get a nostalgic look in her eyes when the notes would drift into the kitchen from Pavol's room.

Another new development in their lives was that his middle brother Ondrej had a new steady girlfriend – Agata. She was a tall, pretty girl from the neighboring village. They were always together and Pavol quickly grew tired of discovering them making out behind the house. Agata would sometimes wait for Pavol whenever he left the house or church, grab him by the arm and demand to know, "Where's Ondrejko? What is he doing? Can you tell me where he is?"

Pavol would pull away, shrug angrily, and retort, "How should I know? Go look for him yourself!"

It was not new for girls to be chasing his handsome brother, but Agata had a jealous streak and was determined to keep him under her control. He was playing football less and less and spending more and more time with her. Zuzana would shake her head and worry about all of this "togetherness," so as a result it wasn't long before another wedding took place, and a new bride took up residence in their house.

The Tesar family had been living fairly contentedly in their newly-built house. Zuzana was so pleased to have her own home and garden, and she was especially satisfied to have a brand new water well with a hand pump. Everyone had more space in the new house and was assigned his or her own territory. Pavol was given the sitting room which converted into a bedroom at night. Helena and Jan had purchased new furniture for it, which received Zuzana's seal of approval. She loved new things and hated old junk.

She still insisted on sleeping in the kitchen, which was her domain and kingdom, but Pavol was a little embarrassed when his friends would come over and see his mother's big wrought iron bed next to the kitchen table and stove. Jozef had a small bedroom next to the kitchen. His window faced the mountains and the apple trees that Martin had planted in the garden. His eldest son had also given them his old portable black and white TV to put on the stand in the corner of the small bedroom.

It became a tradition to gather there on Saturday nights when the one TV channel out of Bratislava would broadcast movies from the West, usually French or Italian detective stories. Zuzana would become easily engrossed in those stories. She would sit on the edge of her chair fascinated by how evil these criminals could be and delighted when justice was served. Ondrej and Agata moved into the back bedroom next to Pavol's room. They spent a great deal of time there, and no one had any desire to see or disturb them.

Pavol was not happy with the arrival of his new sister-in-law or the near proximity of their bedroom. Stuffing his pillow into his ears at night, he would toss and turn until he finally fell asleep. In the morning, his quiet existence with his parents was disturbed by Agata's booming voice and her take-control attitude in the kitchen. Sunday lunch was especially difficult as she and Jozef would argue over who would get their favorite piece of chicken. Pavol did not even know his father liked that part of the chicken so well, but suspected he reached for it just to provoke his new daughter-in-law. However, Agata was a good-hearted girl and was not afraid of hard work; she was just a strong-willed peasant used to having her own way.

One good point was that she liked cooking, which delighted her mother-in-law. Zuzana was tired of the daily culinary duties and ready to turn it over to her younger, stronger daughter-in-law.

"My mother always makes the *halushky* with milk!" Agata stated flatly one Friday morning as the two women worked side by side in the kitchen.

"Really? Isn't that a little *tazky*[44]?" Zuzana asked mildly.

"Of course not! It is the only way to make them!" Agata replied briskly. "See? Mix the milk, beat the egg, and add the flour. There! Now all we need is boiling water, so let's turn up this heat a little bit."

Zuzana did not say a word but thought to herself that these were going to be the heaviest *halusky* she had ever eaten.

"Ondrejko! Where are you?" Agata yelled through the door as she vigorously mixed the dough for the *halushky*.

"What's the matter? Why are you screaming at me, woman?" Ondrej yawned as he came in from their room barely dressed in his boxer shorts.

"Ondrej! Go and put your clothes on!" Zuzana scolded him.

Ondrej just smiled lazily and winked at Agata. She grinned back at him and said, "I need your help with these *halushky*! Dice them into the water while I prepare the soup."

"I am supposed to meet—" Ondrej began to say when Agata interrupted him, "Meet your silly friends to play football? I don't think so! You will stay home and help me!"

Zuzana stared at her daughter-in-law with open mouth. Even Pavol and his father stopped chewing their food to look up from their breakfast. Ondrej blushed, mumbled something, and went back to his room to get dressed. Agata continued beating the dough oblivious to the censure around her. Pavol shook his head and made a mental note that when he got married, his wife would never dictate to him when he could or could not play football.

One morning, Agata was unusually quiet and looking rather pale at the breakfast table. Zuzana pushed a cup of coffee at her.

"What's wrong with you this morning?"

"I don't know. I just feel strange. I am not hungry."

Jozef and Zuzana looked at each other.

---

44 Heavy

Pavol drank his cocoa and asked her wiping his mouth, "Are you sick?"

Zuzana snorted and stood up to clear the dishes patting Agata on the arm. "She's not sick, *synchek moj!*"

Agata suddenly gagged, running quickly outside where they could hear her retching in the garden.

Pavol shrugged saying, "She sure sounds sick to me," and then took another bite of his jam and bread.

Spring had finally arrived and the family got the garden ready. Agata was able to help them dig and plant in spite of her morning sickness. They planted potatoes, beans, onions, carrots, parsnips, as well as corn and pumpkins. The black soil was rich and promised them a good harvest. Martin had given them several different kinds of fruit trees from the Agrokomplex: apricot, plum, apple, cherry, and peach. He also came to help his father plant grape vines along the fence. The garden soon became their own little Eden, and it was easy to shut out the rest of the world when they worked and rested there.

Fall arrived, and Ondrej helped his brother Martin to harvest the grapes in his garden and they made several bottles of wine. It was a crisp white wine causing their father to smack his lips in satisfaction when he tasted it. Wine helped the winter go by a little more pleasantly, and it was used to celebrate when a new addition joined their family.

In February, Ondrej and Agata had a beautiful baby girl with big blue eyes and golden hair. Agata had been sure it was going to be a boy and was determined to name him after his father, but when the baby turned out to be a girl, she decided to call her Gabriela.

Zuzana felt that there was nothing more that she could wish for: their own home, a healthy and happy family, a new granddaughter, plenty of fresh water to use for drinking and washing as well as a decent supply of food in the pantry.

"We are truly blessed," she said contentedly looking around the kitchen. Ondrej was cooing lovingly to his new baby daughter while Agata knitted a new little blue sweater. Pavol was lost in a book, and Jozef dozed by the warm stove.

She bowed her head and murmured thanks.

The University

"Mama, I am leaving now," Pavol called to his mother in the garden.

It was Sunday afternoon and his mother was standing under the apple tree with her hands behind her back. Her little granddaughter Gabriela was toddling around the garden examining the fallen apples on the ground. It was late August, and the air was just beginning to cool off. The grapes were hanging in big bunches on the fence, and the plums were turning a dark blue color. Zuzana turned reluctantly around and saw her youngest son standing at the picket fence with his backpack and his suitcases in his hand. She felt a tremor go through her body, but she swallowed hard, and tried to smile as she walked towards her son.

"Do you have everything?" she asked.

Pavol tried to smile back and said, "I think so."

"Wait a moment! I packed some food for you," Zuzana remembered suddenly.

"Oh, it's all right, Mama, you don't have to do that," Pavol said raising his hand.

"No, no, you must take it. Just a moment." She ran in the house to the pantry where she had a bag prepared with schnitzels, cheese kolaches, and fruit. She stuck a bottle of mineral water in the side.

"Mama, I have to go! The train will be here soon!" Pavol called to her anxiously. Zuzana came quickly out the door and handed him the bag.

"I look like St. Nicholas – is it almost Christmas?" Pavol joked.

"Here, take this, too," Zuzana said pressing a prayer card in his hand. Pavol looked at the prayer card of Jesus praying in the Garden of Gethsemane before His passion. He took a deep breath and kissed his mother goodbye. She hugged him fiercely and then slowly released him.

"Call Janka if you need anything!" she hollered as he disappeared through their iron gate.

Pavol rushed down the street past the brick factory with his bags bumping him on his legs and back. He could hear the train's whistle as it approached the Čerešňa station. The train screeched to a halt and he quickly scrambled on, finding a seat near the window. Settling back in his chair, he could feel his heart pounding. He was excited to start his university study, but he was nervous about living in the big city. He peered out the dirty window at the gardens, trees, fields, and mountains whizzing by, and a wave of sadness swept over his entire being as the distance between him and his sweet little village grew greater and greater.

After a couple of hours, the train began to slow down as it approached the capital city. There was a smell of chemicals in the air, and the buildings looked gray. In contrast to the rectangular socialist buildings, Pavol saw the Bratislava Castle up on the hill overlooking the Danube River – a reminder of past worlds.

The train pulled into the station, and Pavol took his place in line to get off the train. People jostled him and shoved past to get to the door. As he finally got off, he looked around and saw crowds of unsmiling people rushing through the station. A gypsy woman sat on a bench holding a baby. She had colorful ribbons in her hair, but her face looked hard and unhappy. Two other children in dirty torn clothes were running in circles around her. She held out a bony hand towards him, and Pavol found a few coins in his pocket to give her. She smiled up at him, revealing an array of missing teeth. Pavol noticed a bruise on the side of her face. Swallowing nervously, he quickly grabbed his bags and headed up the stairs.

"Pavol! Pavol!"

Pavol looked up the stairs and saw Jana standing at the top of the stairs. She was no longer the shy little girl with long braids who had stood so shyly next to her father. She was a beautiful young woman with big brown eyes and delicate skin. Many people said she looked just like the Hollywood movie star Audrey Hepburn. She was waving at him and holding the arm of her new husband Albert. Pavol felt happy to see a familiar face and hurried up the steps.

"Well, now, you made it!" she cried happily. Albert shook his hand and smiled warmly.

"I didn't know you were coming to meet me," Pavol began.

"Papa called me and told me you were moving into your dormitory this afternoon. Albert and I thought you might need some help! Afterwards, you can come to our flat for supper."

They took the streetcar outside of the train station and headed towards the student housing.

"How is your new job working out at the newspaper?" Pavol asked her.

"Oh, it's wonderful! I get to travel to Prague sometimes and meet with many important people. It's very exciting! And Albert is dubbing the text for a new Italian movie that just came out!"

Pavol looked at Jana's husband Albert who nodded in affirmation. Jana's husband had studied in Bologna and could speak Italian fluently. He was a pleasant, distinguished man of noble lineage, but he had a rather nervous twitch in his face. He often shooed them along when they were dawdling too long in front of a store window. Pavol looked out the window and was amazed at all the people crowded on the sidewalks, the high-rise buildings, cars, and shops. This was definitely not his little village with one small grocery store!

They arrived at the dormitory, and Jana asked the elderly watchman where they should register. He pointed to a glass window where a strict looking woman with bright red hair sat.

"Stay here, Palo, I'll take care of this for you!" Jana walked over to the glass window. The redheaded woman looked up from her papers. Jana began talking and the woman started looking over a long list. Soon, she was shaking her head, and Jana began talking louder with a note of agitation in her voice. Pavol and Albert looked at each other anxiously and waited for her to come back. Finally, the woman emphatically shook her head and slammed the glass window. Jana walked quickly over to them.

"Well, they don't have your name on the list, and all of the rooms are booked up," she said sadly.

"But I signed up for a dorm room! I made all of the arrangements! I paid the deposit!"

"She said that we can come back tomorrow when the housing director is here," Jana said grabbing his arm. "Don't worry! You can stay with us tonight!"

"But classes begin tomorrow!" Pavol said worriedly.

"Don't worry!"

Pavol sat in silence as they rode the streetcar towards Jana and Albert's's neighborhood. The streetlights were beginning to come on as the sun disappeared slowly on the horizon. Their apartments were part of a huge complex of unattractive concrete "vertical shoeboxes" that the communist government had built. They were proudly proclaimed as "modern" and "progressive." Pavol found them quite depressing. They rode the dirty elevator up to the third floor and Egon opened the door to their flat. A nice, clean smell greeted them, and Pavol felt more cheerful as he took off his shoes in the tiny foyer.

"Go and wash your hands. I'll get us something to eat," Jana said pushing him towards the tiny washroom. Pavol squeezed between the washing machine and the sink. He looked at himself in the mirror. He was a young man now with intense blue eyes, dark hair, and an intelligent expression on his face. His skin was smooth with no signs of any whiskers. He felt a little insecure as he was on the shorter side and thin.

He carefully dried his hands and went into the living room. As he walked through the door, he gasped. Elegant antique furniture from the Austro-Hungarian period was crammed into the tiny space, and a gold brocaded mirror adorned the plastered wall. Albert's's family paintings also hung there, and Pavol felt as if he had entered a small, cramped palace. Jana took note of his surprise and remarked smilingly, "That's Albert's's Hungarian grandmother. She was a countess!"

Then she brought out slices of bread, salami, and cheese for them to eat along with cakes she had bought at one of the local bakeries. Pavol fetched his mother's food and set it on the table. Jana poured wine for them to drink and after toasting, they sat down to eat and discuss politics.

Albert was quite bitter about the communist government, as his lawyer father had lost all of his property and holdings in the early 1950s. His mother had come from an aristocratic family, and she too had been reduced to poverty. He had managed to salvage some of the family's furniture, paintings, and gold, but unfortunately robbers were also aware of his family's treasure and had already robbed him twice. However, Albert tried to stay optimistic and threw himself into his business. Pavol was never quite sure what kind of work he was involved in; it was simply better not to ask.

"Mmmm, *Babka* makes the best kolaches!" Jana said with her mouth full of the sweet pastry.

Albert and Pavol heartily agreed, and the evening finished on a pleasant note.

The next day, Jana and Pavol took the streetcar downtown.

"Palo, I have to go to work and I know you have your first class now, so I will meet you here at noon. We will try to solve this problem with your dorm room. 'Til then! Ciao!" Jana hurried down the street and disappeared around the corner. Pavol looked around him and headed down the street to the Geography building.

A pretty young girl at a desk directed him to his classroom, and Pavol joined the class already in progress. The professor glared at him over his glasses but nodded in the direction of an empty seat. Soon Pavol lost himself in the professor's lecture about regional geography and took several pages of notes. After the class, one of the students sitting next to him said to him in a friendly tone, "So, is this your first year?"

Pavol smiled and nodded. "I just got here yesterday."

"Where are you living?" the young man asked.

"Well, actually, nowhere right now. I was supposed to live in the dormitory on Laska Street, but I'm not on the list. I'm trying to find something else."

"I live at home in Trnava with my parents, so I don't have to worry about that. It's a problem to find inexpensive housing in this city. What's your name?"

Pavol introduced himself and found out his companion's name was Viliam Lauko. After class, they talked together in the hallway and then parted with a friendly handshake. Pavol felt a little more at ease in his new surroundings.

The rest of the day was spent wrangling with offices, paperwork, and bureaucracy, but finally they were successful and Pavol had a room in the dorm. Albert brought his bags, Jana held the door, and together they took the elevator up to the third floor. Pavol checked the number on his key and looked for his door, but when he finally found it and tried the key, he discovered that the lock was bolted. He knocked loudly and a voice within yelled, "Go away!"

Jana and Albert glanced at each other. Pavol knocked again. A flood of cursing ensued, and Pavol backed up a few steps. The door flew open, and a tall naked man stood there in full view. Jana turned her head quickly away as Albert and Pavol gasped. The man gulped to see the three of them standing in the hallway and darted quickly inside to fetch a towel. Pavol felt his face grow hot; he felt like running away, too.

The young man's unshaven face appeared again at the door, and he asked roughly, "What do you want?"

Pavol answered gruffly back, "I live here. Would you mind letting us in?"

The man looked surprised and said apologetically, "I'm sorry – I did not think they were going to assign anyone here. Please come in!"

Jana nodded for Pavol to go in and said weakly, "I'll stay here. You go on in."

Pavol walked in and saw a young woman in one of the beds. Her face was full of astonishment as she clutched a blanket to her bare breasts.

"This is my wife Tanya. My name is Vlado. Welcome to Bratislava." He reached out shaking Pavol's hand as he hurriedly pulled on his pants. He tossed his wife's dress to her.

"Your wife?" Pavol said stunned.

"Yes, she comes to visit me now and then. I hope you don't mind."

"No, no, of course not," Pavol said a bit confused and feeling rather foolish. "I'll just put my bags here and I will come back later."

His new roommate nodded in relief, and Pavol soon slipped out the door.

Jana and Albert looked at him anxiously. "Is everything in order?"

"Oh, yes, perfect order," Pavol said a little sarcastically and then began to laugh. "Let's get out of here. I think I need a drink. A big one!"

On the Other Side of the Ocean

While Pavol was getting settled into his new dorm room in Bratislava, a ten-year old girl was furiously riding her bike down a wide street through a residential neighborhood in West Texas. Her tangled curly hair blew in the wind as she glanced back to see if her dog Buster was following. The two of them arrived home hot and panting. She threw her bike down on the crispy brown lawn and took Buster in her arms. He was a Jack Russell terrier and had been her closest friend since she was two. She opened the gate on the cinderblock fence and put him down in the backyard. He tried to escape, but she stopped him with her foot before he made it through.

"Oh, no you don't! You want to go and visit your girlfriend down the street again, don't you? Well, I don't want Mrs. Shepherd calling me again! Last time I could hardly get you away from her little, precious, pure-bred beagle!"

Buster licked her hand and panted good-naturedly. The little girl laughed and petted him before she quickly shut the gate. Walking around to the front door, she tried to go in, but it was locked. She knocked, and she could hear her grandfather's shuffling footsteps as he approached the door. An elderly man peeked at her through the window. She waved, and the door quickly opened.

"Hi, Grandpa, how's it going?" she said breezily walking in the hallway. The air conditioning felt cool on her sweaty face.

"Hi, hi, yourself," he said jokingly turning slowly around to make his long journey back to his captain's chair under the window. He sat down heavily in the captain's chair and picked up the *Time Magazine* he had been reading.

She headed towards the kitchen and poured herself a glass of ice water and grabbed some cookies out of the big ceramic jar that looked like a big red and yellow apple. Then she grabbed the phone and called her mother at work.

"Mama? I'm home!"

"How was school?"

"Fine. Just the same boring stuff. Buster came to my classroom again today."

"Oh, no! Did he jump the fence again?"

"I don't know – probably. He walked right in the classroom and sat down beside me. The teacher didn't even notice him until an hour later when some kid told her."

"What did she do?"

"She put him in the janitor's closet and made him stay there the rest of the day. I picked him up when school was out."

"That dog is going to be the smartest dog in town if he keeps going to school like that," her mother chuckled.

"Mrs. Mayberry said she is going to call the dog pound if it happens again," her daughter replied in between bites of her cookie.

"Oh, well, Mrs. Mayberry can just—" Her mother abruptly changed her tone asking, "Did you clean your room yet or make your bed?"

"Mom, I gotta go! I'll talk to you later!"

"Katie! Wait a minute!"

Click! Katie hung up the phone and wandered into the living room.

She turned on the TV and started watching an old version of *Leave It to Beaver*. Her Grandpa moved his chair where he could see the TV set. He liked to watch the reruns with her. She sat there for a while but soon became bored as it was one she had already seen five times before. Finishing off another cookie, she walked in the living room where the piano stood. She played Beethoven's *Fuer Elise* for a while and flipped through her music books; Cleo, her Siamese cat, gracefully entered the room and positioned herself behind Katie to enjoy the short concert.

Finally, after stalling for thirty more minutes, Katie stood up and went to her room. It was definitely messy. The bed was unmade, her pajamas still lay on the floor where she had thrown them in the morning, and all of her dresser drawers were open.

"Kelly Martin's family has a maid – she never has to clean her room," she muttered. Reluctantly, she started picking up her clothes, sighing heavily as she bent over. Then, she saw one of her library books on the desk and picked it up. Fairy tales were her favorite. She stretched out on her bed and quickly became engrossed in some far away land where beautiful princesses and castles were the rule. Cleo jumped on the bed and settled herself down near the small of Katie's back. Katie could feel the warmth of her body and her steady purring in the background.

The front door slammed. Startled, Katie jumped up from her bed and ran down the hall. It was her mother. She was a tall, beautiful woman dressed in high heels and a dark blue suit. Her short wiry hair was dark but sprinkled with shiny gray hair that glistened in the light. Katie flung her arms around her mother, breathing deeply in. Her mother always smelled of Chanel No. 5. Pushing Katie gently away, she headed quickly down the hall to change into something more comfortable.

"It is so hot outside! I can't wait to get out of this girdle! Oh, Katie, I told you to clean your room," she said disgustedly as she poked her head in the room.

"I'm working on it!"

Katie's mother shook her head and just pointed at the mess. "Keep that cat off your bed! You know you have allergies!"

That night, the family sat around the table together. There were five of them: Grandpa, John, and Paula, and their two daughters, Katie and Margaret. Katie's eldest brother Rick was away at college, and Margaret was a senior in high school, who liked to go out and drive around Midland with her friends. However, there were days when she locked herself in her room sketching and painting late into the night. Her room also looked like a tornado had hit it, but her mother defended her and simply stated, "She's an artist. It's her creative right."

Katie's grandpa was usually silent while the rest of the family chatted about work, school, and the news. He liked her mother's cooking and did not want to waste time talking when it was time to eat. Katie watched him noisily slurp his soup, so she did the same. He ate his salad with his fingers, and Katie followed suit. Her mother glared at both of them and then said pointedly, "Would you mind using a fork, young lady?"

It was the weekend, and Margaret was going to the movies with her friends. Katie peeked in her room. She could see posters of the Beatles staring back at her. George Harrison was her favorite, but her older sister raved about John Lennon and Paul McCartney. Katie watched for a few moments as her sister carefully put on thick black eyeliner.

"What do you want, punk?" her sister said out of the corner of her mouth.

"Can I go with you and Pam tonight?"

"Are you kidding? I wouldn't be caught dead taking you!"

"But Mom and Dad have bridge club over at the Manuliks' house and I don't want to stay home alone!"

"Grandpa's here!"

"I know, but he goes to sleep so early."

"Look, you know what happened last time!"

"I promise I won't tell Mom and Dad anything!"

"Yeah, right! I got a ticket for speeding, and who told them before I even got in the door?"

Katie hung her head and dug her big toe in the green shag carpet.

"But—"

"Just forget it!"

"Fine! Who wants to go with you anyway?" Katie stomped off to her room.

That night after she had her bath, she filled a bowl full of M&Ms and knocked on her Grandpa's door.

He was sitting in his chair with his feet up on his hassock. His little black and white TV was glowing in the dark room.

"Grandpa, can I come in?"

He beckoned for her to enter.

"What are you watching?"

"I don't even know. Watch what you want."

Katie turned the channel until she found re-runs of the Andy Griffith Show. She settled down on the floor and held up the bowl to her Grandpa. He grabbed a fistful of the candy. Katie was always amazed at how big his hands were. He had worked in a machinist shop almost all his life in Chicago.

"Katka, where are your parents tonight?"

"They're playing bridge over at Laura and Al's."

He nodded and munched on the M&Ms.

"Grandpa?"

"What?"

"Why did you come to this country?"

Her grandfather groaned. Katie had heard his story before, but she never tired of hearing about her grandfather's earlier life. It seemed so different than the one she knew.

"I think this is the fiftieth time I have told you this," he said good-naturedly. "All right. Here we go. I didn't want to serve in the Austro-Hungarian army – they were inhumane! One time, I saw them in the street army whipping a man with a heavy chain. I told myself that was never going to happen to me. Besides, I needed work, and I could not find a job."

"I thought you were from Czecho-, Czechosl-, oh, you know what I mean."

"Well, it was different back then. It was called Austria-Hungary."

"Are you Hungarian?"

"That's what it said in my identity papers, but we were actually Slovak. Slovakia belonged to Hungary at that time."

"Do you speak Hungarian and Slovak?"

The elderly man nodded, looking at her amusedly.

"Wow, two languages." Katie was silent for a few minutes as she thought about that.

"When did you come to this country?" she asked starting a new line of questioning.

"Well, I was about 18 years old, I think. It was around 1900. It's so long ago that I can't really remember anymore," he answered rubbing his forehead.

Katie tried to imagine her Grandpa at 18. He was in his eighties now and reminded her a little of Fred Mertz on *I love Lucy* with his shirt buttoned all the way to the top and his pants buckled high above his protruding stomach. He wasn't really fat, but he was a short, strong stocky man with thick glasses and thinning hair on top. He stood up and pulled out a picture from his closet and handed it to her. She saw a handsome young man with thick wavy brown hair and a big handlebar moustache. His white, starched collar came up high on his neck, and he looked a little cocky standing there with his hands on his hips.

"Who's that?" she asked giggling.

"That's me!"

"You're kidding! That's you?"

"Yes! This photograph was taken right after I arrived in Pennsylvania."

"Why did you go to Pennsylvania?"

"My mother had a cousin who lived there, so when I got off the boat in New York, I made my way there."

"Did you speak English?"

"Nope!"

"Did you go to school to learn?"

"I was too old for school, and I had to find a job. I finally found one digging ditches."

"So, how did you learn to speak English?"

"I taught myself to read with a newspaper and a German dictionary. The other workers helped me, too."

"You can speak German, too?"

"Everyone in my country speaks at least three languages. I spoke Slovak at home, Hungarian in the school, and we learned German along the way. Vienna, Austria was very close to my home."

"Speak something in German!"

"*Du redest zuviel, mein Liebchen*!" he smiled.

"What did you say? What did you say?" she asked fascinated that there were other languages in the world besides English.

"You talk too much, my dear."

"Grandpa!"

Miffed, Katie turned around and watched Barney and Andy on television.

After a few minutes, she asked him quietly, "Did you ever see your mother and father again?"

Her grandpa was quiet for a moment and sighed, "No, I did not."

"Why?"

Growing exasperated, he replied roughly, "You just couldn't hop on an airplane back then. The boat ride was too long and expensive! Then the war came, then the Depression, and then another war."

Katie was silent as she watched the rest of the show. When it was finished, she saw that her Grandfather had nodded off, so she tiptoed out of the room and went to her room.

She was lonely. She missed her brother Ricky; he only came home in the summer. When he was around, he would often take her for rides on his motorcycle. They would go to the A&W to get root beers in big, frothy mugs. However, work and friends kept him occupied, and he didn't really have much time for a little sister either. Her sister Margaret, needing her own space, got tired of her tagging around and was tired of being the built-in babysitter at home.

Katie's parents loved her, but they were usually drained when they got home from a long day at their respective offices. Most evenings, her father retreated behind the newspaper with his beer until supper was ready, or he worked outside in the garden to get a little fresh air and exercise. He had made many attempts to turn the dry, sandy ground into black, fertile soil, but it wasn't easy in the scorching West Texas heat.

One Saturday afternoon, Katie followed him into his garden.

"What are you going to plant there?"

"Well, I want to put in some onions, tomatoes over there, and I'm also going to try and grow a few green peppers," he said enthusiastically.

Katie made a face.

"Now, don't look like that! You can't beat fresh grown tomatoes!"

"Why do you like to garden so much? Mama doesn't like it."

"When I grew up in Chicago, the Slovak, Czech, and Polish families had the nicest gardens in the entire city. I guess it's in my blood."

"Did your family have a garden?"

"No, but my dad had one before I was born when your Aunt Mick was little. But after my mother died, he sold the house."

"What did she die of?"

"Stomach cancer."

"And where did she come from?"

Katie, you know that story!"

"Daddy, just tell me again!" Katie said trying to catch a horned toad.

Her father stopped his digging and stood up to wipe his forehead with his handkerchief.

"She was from a small town in Czechoslovakia called Modra. It was about 20 miles from where Grandpa lived, but they didn't meet each other until they both immigrated to the United States. I think they met in the Slovak church in Chicago."

"What did she look like?" Katie asked stroking the horned toad's spiky head.

"I don't remember her. I was just a baby when she passed away. Your grandpa said she had dark, curly hair like you!"

"Can we go there?"

"Go where?"

"To Cheko-cheko-slobonia?"

"Czechoslovakia," he said chuckling. "It's pretty far away, Katie. Besides, it's behind the Iron Curtain now and they won't let you in."

"What the heck is an iron curtain?" Katie asked, trying to visualize drapes made of iron.

"That's just an expression. Those are all the countries where the communists have taken over. The Soviets are in charge now."

"Soviets? What are they? And what's a communist?"

Her father smiled at her and said, "Go and get me a beer."

Katie grudgingly stood up and went to the kitchen.

"Mama, there's nothing to do!" she complained as her mother handed her a can of Schlitz beer from the fridge.

"Why don't you go outside and play?"

"There's no one to play with since Bee Bee moved away, and the girls down the street are so boring with their stupid Barbies."

Katie thought about her former neighbor Bee Bee that she used to play with. He had turned his storage shed into a laboratory and was always

116

creating something. They fried bacon once over his Bunsen burner, and he even showed her how to make stink bombs and firecrackers.

"When I was your age, we entertained ourselves! Where are those paper dolls I brought you last week? Now go and take this to your father." Her mother pushed her out the backdoor.

Katie rolled her eyes and snorted. Who wants to play with paper dolls? Her mother told her that it was one of her favorite things to do when she was a little girl. Parents. They could be so weird sometimes. She ran to the garden to give her father his drink.

Draining the can in one gulp, he handed it back to her after crushing it.

"Throw it in the big garbage can in the garage. I'm collecting aluminum cans there." He turned his back on her and began breaking up the hard clods of dirt.

As she walked to the garage, Buster came running eagerly up to her with an old tennis ball in his mouth. He dropped it in front of her and waited expectantly for her to throw it.

"Okay, you win," she said petting him as he wriggled in anticipation.

After a few rounds of ball, she went into the house and headed towards her room at the end of the hallway. She pulled one of the Oz books from her tall stack of library books and started reading. She had read the same story many times before, but it didn't matter; it was an escape with Dorothy and Toto into an exciting, magical land with odd creatures – one that she wouldn't emerge from until supper.

Heaven and Back

"How did it go?" the geography student in the hall asked Pavol anxiously.

"He gave me a 1," Pavol replied. "It wasn't so bad."

"That's easy for you to say! You always get good grades!"

Pavol shrugged and walked down the stairs relieved that his oral exam was over. It was November and he hadn't been home since he moved into his dorm. As he entered the front door, he heard someone calling his name.

"Pavol!"

Pavol looked around and saw a young man walking quickly towards him.

"*Ahoj, Ferko! Ako sa maš?*"[45]

"*Dobre, dobre!*[46] I wanted to ask you if you had any plans this weekend."

Ferdinand was a mathematician that Pavol had met in church a few weeks ago. They had to be careful as there were informants everywhere, and it wasn't always clear who was a true believer or simply a mole sent by the government.

"Well, I am planning to go home and visit my parents over the break. I haven't seen them in two months!"

"Let's go outside," Ferdinand said taking him by the shoulder.

The two young men walked casually out of the building. The days were already getting shorter and it was getting dusky at three thirty.

Ferko pulled him closer and said quietly, "I am going on a secret retreat in the mountains in Central Slovakia. A priest will be there that I would like you to meet."

Pavol's attention was immediately caught. Secret religious meetings and retreats were strictly forbidden by the communist government.

---

45 Hi, Ferko, how are you?

46 Fine, fine!

"Who is this priest?"

"His name is Jan Korec. He's actually a bishop and was secretly ordained by the Vatican in the early fifties, but ever since that time he has been working in factories and doing manual labor. The government won't allow him to be a bishop, much less a priest! He was in jail in Vaduce for several years. He is a fascinating man – I know you will think so, too."

Pavol's interest mounted with every word. He paused.

"I don't know, Ferko. I haven't been home for quite a while. Let me think about it."

"Well, if you decide to go, meet me at the train station tonight at seven. We want to get there after dark so no one will notice us walking towards the parish."

Pavol nodded and shook his hand. Riding up in the creaking elevator, he stepped out in the foyer. Some of the boys were playing a game of football in the hall, and he dodged out of the way to get to his room. Knocking before he entered the room, just in case Vlado's wife was visiting again, he walked cautiously through the door. The room was empty. Sighing with relief, he grabbed the sack of *piškoty*[47] off the desk and shoved a few of the sweet biscuits in his mouth. He was hungry and hadn't had time to eat. Usually he ate his breakfast and lunch in the student cafeteria, but today he had been too busy studying for his tests. Plopping down on his bed, he could not help but listen to the boys outside in the hall. The dorm was a lively place and it was hard adjusting to the late night hours and the parties that seemed to be going on twenty-four hours. He had asked some of them to hold it down, but they just laughed mockingly in his face. He even went so far as to make an official complaint, but the ladies in the office just shrugged.

One particular night, he had been working very diligently on a project for his biology class. His roommate Vlado was snoring in his bed, and he couldn't take the shrieking and yelling from the party upstairs anymore. His nerves were shot. It had been going on for hours and seemed to be getting worse, so he banged on the ceiling with the broom. The students upstairs banged back in reply and continued their whooping and hollering.

"That does it!" He grabbed his jacket and ran out of his room. The night watchman was dozing on his chair. Pavol walked quietly past him and went out the front door. Looking up at the fourth floor, he could see the drunken students through the window, their noise and music echoing over the entire street. He leaned over, picked up a brick from a pile of

---

47 Vanilla wafers

rubble, aimed carefully, and threw it towards the window. Crash! The glass shattered and a stunned silence reigned. Pavol ducked behind a tree and held his breath. One large young man came out on the balcony and yelled, "Who did that? Who's out there?"

After standing nervously there for a few seconds, the young man went back inside through the broken window. The party soon broke up and the lights went out. Staying carefully in the shadows, Pavol slipped back in the dorm with a group of boys who were just returning from a football game. He finished his project and went to bed. That was two weeks ago.

Munching on the stale wafers, he reflected how relatively quiet it had been in the dorm since that time. He stood up and began packing his things. It was time to go home; his mother had written him one of her rare letters, asking him when they might expect him.

That evening, Pavol boarded the streetcar with his backpack. He did not bring too many things along – just his jacket, toothbrush, wallet, and an extra pair of socks. He sat quietly in meditation as the streetcar rumbled along the track, swaying like a rope around the corners. The streetcar stopped and a disheveled man boarded the tram and plopped down heavily in front of Pavol. He stank of urine and alcohol. Pavol turned his face away repulsed by the smell.

As they neared the train station, Pavol noticed a beautiful shapely woman walking by the station. He forgot everything as he stood up and stepped out of the train mesmerized, in spite of himself. She turned and smiled slyly at him. Suddenly, the tram door slammed behind him and Pavol realized he had left his backpack on the tram. He turned around to bang on the door, but the tram driver was already leaving. The drunk who had been sitting in front of him smiled a toothless smile as he waved Pavol's wallet at him through the window. Pavol's heart sank and he looked around helplessly.

"Now what am I going to do? I don't have any money to buy a ticket. I'm not going anywhere now! God forgive me for not paying attention!" He shook his head angry at himself and went inside the train station. Ferko was standing in front of the departures/arrivals sign; he waved for him to come over.

"*Ahoj*! I'm glad you made it!"

"Well, to tell you the truth, I was planning to go to my village, but I just lost my wallet. I don't have any money!"

Ferdinand got a funny smile on his face and said quietly, "Maybe it's a sign that you are supposed to go with us! I don't have enough cash to loan you, but I think you should just go—"

"B-b-but, I don't have a ticket!"

Ferdinand didn't say another word but just started pushing him in the direction of the train. Pavol's heart started racing and he sat down nervously in the train compartment. The trained creaked and swayed as it pulled out of the train station picking up speed. Pavol peeked down the hall waiting for the conductor to come at any moment and throw him off of the train, but the corridor was empty.

The two young men started talking quietly, and Pavol soon found out that Ferdinand was involved in more than just underground Christian activities. He was involved in covert political activities as well.

"Here, look at this." Ferdinand shoved a newspaper in his hands.

Pavol looked at it and gasped, "Where did you get this?"

Ferdinand looked sharply around and then quietly replied, "I printed it."

Pavol stared at the newspaper. It was the first one he had ever held in his hands that published anti-communist sentiment and news. He and his family had listened for years to *Radio Free Europe* and the *Voice of America*, but he had never seen a newspaper other than the standard *Pravda* or others published under communist control.

"Hide it and take it with you," Ferdinand said tensely. He sat back and stared at the window. Pavol tucked the paper into a pocket inside his coat and looked at Ferdinand.

"How long have you been involved with…?"

"A long time. It isn't easy, but we are making headway. Things will change. You'll see."

Pavol was quietly musing over this information as the train rocked back and forth. Soon Pavol nodded off and fell asleep.

"Palo! Wake up! We're here!" Ferdinand was shaking his shoulder. Pavol stood up, yawned, and stretched.

"Let's go! They are expecting us!"

The two students stepped off the train. There was a small station there, but the windows were dark and empty. Everyone had gone home. There was a light frost on the ground, and Pavol gulped the fresh mountain air. He pulled his jacket closer around him.

"*Zima*[4]!" he said straining to see through the darkness. "Where are we going?"

"Come on," Ferdinand said picking up his bag. "You'll see."

The two young men walked for what seemed like several kilometers when finally they saw the lights of a small village twinkling in the distance. After several minutes, they arrived and walked quietly through the dark streets. One drunken man stared at them stupidly as they passed him. Soon they came to a house that looked quiet. The shades were pulled, and no light could be seen. There were no cars around or bicycles. Ferdinand walked through the wrought iron gate with Pavol following. Knocking lightly on the door, Ferdinand and Pavol waited nervously. Soon, the door opened slightly and a young girl's voice said, "Ferko? Is that you?"

"*Ano*[5]!" The door swung open and they were quickly ushered into a small foyer.

"This is my friend I told you about – Pavol. Pavol, this is Milka."

A round-faced girl in her twenties looked at Pavol and nodded at him. Pavol nodded silently back. They walked through a long, dark hallway until they came to a large door. Pavol could see a glimmer of light proceeding from under the door. Not a sound could be heard. The young girl knocked twice and the door swung open. Pavol blinked his eyes. Light filled the hall, and he was astounded to see sixty people, maybe more, squeezed in what looked like a large living room. Young people ranging in age from sixteen to thirty sat on the floor, chairs, tables, and two couches. An intelligent looking man with glasses who appeared to be in his early fifties was standing at the front of the room. He smiled and greeted them.

"Welcome! Welcome! Please come in! We just started!"

Pavol and Ferdinand walked in the room. Milka quickly closed the door. Two teenage boys scooted over on the couch and invited them to sit down.

"Again, welcome to all of you! Let us begin with prayer." The man in front of the room crossed himself and bowed his head. Everyone in the room followed suit.

"Heavenly Father, we know that the only true freedom exists in you. Neither bars nor prison cells can imprison our souls. Please bless these young people who are gathered here to learn more about your ways – please send us your Holy Spirit. Our Father, who art in heaven…"

Pavol sat entranced as he listened to the man. This was the secret bishop Ferdinand had been telling him about. He looked like an ordinary person dressed in ordinary street clothes, but there was something different about him. His face looked tired and a little worn, yet there was a twinkle in his eyes. The next two days passed quickly as they studied the Bible, prayed, hiked in the mountains, and meditated. Saturday afternoon, they sat in a circle around a big campfire. Bishop Korec led them in prayer and song; Pavol borrowed one of the boy's guitars and accompanied them. He felt very satisfied and somehow free from the feeling that he was locked in a cage. He had been spiritually hungry for more, but the churches were limited due to governmental control.

Pavol had so many questions about faith, but he could never get any straight answers from those government-appointed priests. This man seemed so different – an intellectual person who had been forced to leave the Jesuit seminary where he had been studying as a young man. Most priests had soft white hands as they never did any manual labor, but this man's hands were calloused and worn from working in factories as well as warehouses. Here was a man who had been arrested, interrogated, and jailed for his faith, yet he seemed to have so much peace and confidence. Pavol wished his faith were stronger. Going to daily Mass and praying with his mother had definitely influenced him, but doubts crept in and he worried, what if it was all just a big lie, like his teachers said? He took confession with the Bishop Korec and expressed all of his uncertainties.

The bishop listened respectfully to him until he finished and nodded. Then he laid his hand on his arm and told him, "Pavol, don't worry. Science and religion do not have to be enemies. I have studied for many years, and you will find that they are not in contradiction to each other. On the contrary, both are means of seeking the truth and introducing us to new ideas. God and faith cannot be put in a box; we shall know the truth and it shall set us free."

They talked a little longer and the bishop invited him to come to meetings that he held in his small apartment in Bratislava. Pavol thanked him happily and left.

Sunday morning the retreat finished with a Mass. One of the students in the group heard of Pavol's predicament with his wallet and offered him a ride to Topolcany where his sister Helena lived. Pavol accepted gratefully. As they rode back towards West Slovakia, Pavol's mind was whirling with all that he had seen and heard. He felt like he had moved on to a new plane of awareness, and he wanted more. Suddenly, he realized they were coming closer to his village.

"Can you let me out here?" he asked. "I don't live very far away from here."

The blue Skoda slowed down and Pavol hopped out. Waving, the driver drove off. Pavol walked slowly home. His mother saw him approaching from the window and began smiling broadly. Zuzana met him at the door. "I thought you would be here Friday! I was so worried that something had happened! You should have called your sister. Where have you been?"

"To a little piece of heaven and back," he said picking his petite mother up with a hug.

Italy

Katie held her breath as the huge jumbo jet left the ground. The New York skyscrapers became smaller and smaller.

"Daddy, it's simply unreal! It looks like some kind of toy land!" she exclaimed.

Her father John was sitting next to her and squeezed her hand. The fifteen-year-old closed her eyes until the plane leveled off, but cautiously opened them again after a few minutes. She looked around to study her surroundings. Rome, Italy was their destination and the farthest point Katie had ever traveled. Her father John, a geologist, was being sent to watch a well in the Adriatic Sea, and as the company thought it might be for at least a year, she and her mother Paula were allowed to accompany him. He had been traveling to Europe more frequently the last few years and meeting with other oil companies to discuss joint ventures in the North Sea and Adriatic Sea.

Every time he returned home, he brought Katie souvenirs from his trips to Paris, London, Aberdeen, Dublin, and Rome. She was fascinated by the pictures and proudly displayed her growing collection of dolls in her bedroom. She loved looking at the colorful folk costumes and different styles. Now it was her turn to go exploring, but she felt nervous.

The first class seats were large and comfortable in the jumbo jet, which was in stark contrast to the airplane they had taken from Dallas to New York. On that first leg of their journey, Katie had gotten so airsick from the smell of martinis and tobacco smoke that she thought she was going to have to say goodbye to her parents and end it all. However, she was still alive, albeit very pale, when they arrived at the JFK airport, so Paula immediately sent John to look for some motion sickness pills. They waited for over an hour for his return and became very uneasy during his absence. Both of them had heard stories about the horrific crimes in New York, and it didn't help matters much when a scruffy looking man began telling them stories about a burglary in one of the airport shops. He made sure to mention that the owner had been shot to death in the process.

The clock ticked on and Paula's shoe began impatiently tapping the floor. They both sighed in relief when John strode in the lobby with a brown paper sack in his hands. Katie popped the pills and they quickly ran to board their plane. They settled down in their seats, and her mother began to quietly pray. After several minutes of unexpected waiting, the captain came on the intercom and made an announcement. His tone was a little embarrassed. "Uh, folks, we just discovered some mechanical problems. Bear with us as our mechanics work on it. It shouldn't be too long."

Paula looked over at her daughter and nodded knowingly. Katie smiled to herself and thought, *I'm glad Mama is praying. I should probably say a prayer, too.*

Thirty minutes passed. One hour passed. Two hours passed and the passengers were getting restless. After what seemed like an eternity, the captain finally announced that they would soon be on their way. Everyone clapped and the engines roared. The take-off was quite thrilling, and Katie felt like she was embarking on the biggest adventure of her life.

After several minutes, the airplane levelled off and she could barely perceive that they were moving. Unbuckling her seat belt, she decided to look around. She stood up and slipped past her parents into the aisle. Her mother looked pretty in a dark slack suit with her Navajo turquoise jewelry. No one would suspect that Paula was just a country girl from a small farming community in the Midwest, and her father John looked smart in his leisure suit. He was cleaning his glasses while listening to his effervescent wife chat. A dark-skinned, well-dressed man in the next seat glanced up at her and winked. Katie swallowed and walked down the aisle. She had never seen such a variety of people! There was a cowboy decked out in his best wranglers and Stetson hat reading the newspaper. Another woman with bleached blonde hair and big diamond earrings sat sipping her wine and reading a magazine called *Town and Country.* Another Italian looking man and woman in dark glasses sat closely together talking and smoking. The stewardesses smiled at her and asked her if she needed anything. She smiled shakily back and shook her head. She peeked in the bathrooms and looked around the curtains in the other section of the plane. She saw businessmen, students, tired mothers, and squirming children hanging on the crowded seats. The stewardess headed towards her with a big cart, so she moved back in the direction of her seat.

When she returned, John said, "Let's go upstairs and have our dinner! They have a little restaurant area up there."

"They have a restaurant on the plane?" Katie asked wonderingly.

"Yep! Let's go!"

They made their way up a narrow spiral staircase and a waiter greeted them at the top of the landing. After studying the menu, Katie decided to eat shrimp scampi while her mother ordered lobster. After explaining that he wanted his steak well-done, John looked at his youngest daughter and wife with a twinkle in his eyes. "Now, this is the life, isn't it?"

They readily agreed. Soon, the man who had winked at her appeared at the top of the stairs. He asked if he could join them, and John nodded, politely offering him a chair. Soon they were in a deep conversation about business, politics, and famous people. Katie soon learned that their table companion was from Mexico and was in the business of exporting Gulf Coast shrimp. He had traveled all over the world and nonchalantly told them how the Shah of Iran was one of his closest friends. Katie was fascinated as he talked about exotic travels and celebrities.

After lunch they returned to their seats and decided to watch a movie, *The Man Who Would Be King*. After watching Sean Connery and Michael Caine's adventures, Katie shut her eyes and tried to nap.

There had been a lot of changes the last few years. She was no longer a plump curly haired girl with scraped knees. She had grown tall and lanky with long thick frizzy hair cascading down her back; she definitely preferred wearing jeans to dresses. She wasn't quite at ease yet with her blossoming body, so she was a little shy in mixed company.

Grandpa had passed away the previous year, and the captain chair now sat empty under the window. She missed his presence, and felt guilty that she had spent so little time with him the last several months. She had bought a horse with her birthday money she had saved, so every weekend and evening after school was spent horseback riding with her friends. She had felt happier and freer than she ever had before but knew she was neglecting her grandfather. He seemed resigned to being alone and retreated to his room at the back of the house – just silently fading away.

There were other changes in the family. Her sister Margaret had moved out when she turned nineteen. Now her new abode was a lime green school bus painted with psychedelic flowers. She and her friends were traveling up and down the California coast and across the Southwest region spreading peace and love. Last summer, Katie and her parents had headed towards the Rocky Mountains in Colorado on a fishing trip, and they stopped over in Santa Fe, New Mexico. There they met up with

Margaret along with some of her friends. She showed up at the restaurant wearing only a scratchy green army blanket, looking thin, even a little gaunt. She had pasted little colorful rhinestones all over her face, and the expression in her eyes had a far-away look.

Mesmerized and a little disturbed, Katie stared at her sister realizing she really didn't know who this person was. They gave each other a hug, and Katie almost gagged from the strong body odor.

"Don't you take a bath anymore?" she whispered to her sister remembering the days when Margaret spent hours in the bathroom washing her hair and putting on makeup.

Margaret laughed and said, "No, not very often! All that bathing isn't natural – besides, we need to conserve Mother Earth's resources!"

John had bought lunch at the café for his oldest daughter and her friends. He sat silently across from them as he watched them hungrily wolf down their food. After lunch, they said goodbye without any emotional scenes, but Katie noticed her mother wore dark glasses the rest of the trip. Once Katie was sure she saw a tear trickle down her cheek, but her mother quickly brushed it away. John didn't say a word, but the muscles in his jaw were tense.

Her brother Rick had graduated from college a couple of years ago. The whole family had gone to his graduation, and even Grandpa had sat proudly in the university chapel as his grandson marched down the aisle in his cap and gown. The procession of graduating students walked slowly passed them and the elderly Slovak man reached out to squeeze his grandson's arm. Rick smiled slightly, looking pleased, and marched forward to get his diploma.

Her brother had earned a degree in economics and went on to the U.T. law school where he had a promising future (according to his professors). However, that all came to a screeching halt when his live-in girlfriend left him for someone else. So, even though he was on the dean's list and in his last semester, he dropped out and camped on a mesa in the desert for several weeks. However, after dodging *javelinas*[48] and rattlesnakes, he had enough and returned home sporting a beard and long hair past his shoulders. He soon found a job at a few construction sites in town and started working with a hammer. His parents were not pleased, but relieved that he was working and supporting himself.

Holidays were not very pleasant any more as family get-togethers ended in shouting matches between her more liberal siblings and her

---

48 Wild pigs

conservative parents. There seemed to be a cultural gap one hundred miles wide, and Katie didn't know which side she should stand on. When they argued, she would just sigh and wonder what it would be like to live in a family that seemed to enjoy time together. Running to her room was her escape and there she prayed; she desperately needed someone to listen. She needed a change!

Then one evening, her father came home with a big smile on his face and said, "Guess what! We are going to Italy this spring!"

Paula's dark eyes became wide as she gasped, "Oh, Johnny! Are you serious?"

"Well, Forest Oil wants to send me over to supervise a well in the Adriatic Sea. They told me that it may take some time, so I can take you both with me!"

"Even me?" Katie asked excitedly.

"Even you!" John said hugging his daughter.

The seatbelt light came on and Katie's thoughts jolted back to the present. A stewardess passed by and asked, "Hot towel?"

Katie gratefully took the fragrant, steaming towel and pressed it on her face. Her stomach began to flip flop again as the Captain announced they would soon be landing at the International Airport in Rome. She looked out the window and was surprised to see how flat it was except for tall juniper trees in the distance. It almost reminded her of home, but much greener.

Soon, they were in the airport gathering their bags. Feeling groggy and a little wobbly from the long flight, they looked for a taxi. A driver in a small cab drove up, and John began loading the bags in the trunk.

"Do you think all of our suitcases will fit in there?" Katie whispered to her mother worriedly.

"It's certainly smaller than our cars back home," Paula smiled wearily.

Katie and Paula squeezed in the back seat and tucked the remaining bags around their legs. The taxi driver shook his head and muttered something about crazy Americans. Her father showed him the address of the hotel, and the taxi took off with a jolt. Katie and her mother stiffened as the taxi weaved in and out of traffic at a very high speed. Even her father did not look too relaxed in the front seat, and Katie noticed he seemed to be pushing an imaginary brake in the floorboard while he clenched the sides of his seat. After a hair-raising ride, the taxi pulled up in front of the Grand Hotel, and they quickly hopped out.

John mopped his brow with a handkerchief and said, "Whew! Am I glad to be on solid ground again!"

They laughed a little nervously as he went in to find a porter. In a few minutes, he came back alone looking annoyed.

"Well, apparently the bellhops are all on strike today, so there is no one to carry our bags. Stay here while I take them in to the lobby."

Katie and her mother stood awkwardly by their huge pile of bags as people walked quickly around them on the sidewalks. There were such different smells, sounds, and sights. Katie began to feel ill again when suddenly her father appeared with a short little man in a suit.

"Okay! This is Giovanni. He is going to show us to our room." Giovanni nodded smilingly and ushered them down a long hall.

"I'm sorry that you had to carry your own bags. We are going to give you an extra special room for the inconvenience," Giovanni said in a thick accent as he unlocked the double doors.

Katie gasped as they walked into the living room. She had never seen such beautiful furnishings and elegance in all her life. A large crystal chandelier hung from the ceiling; tall windows were framed by sweeping blue drapes. The brocaded wallpaper and the crown molding brought the sense of another era to mind.

"This is one of our finest suites!" Giovanni said proudly looking around. "Gromeko, the Soviet Ambassador, stayed here only last week!"

Katie's parents looked at each other. Katie had never heard of Gromeko before, but she couldn't help but being impressed. Giovanni showed them the attaching bedrooms and bathrooms.

"You mean, I get my own room?" she asked wonderingly. She had always shared a room with her parents when they went on trips together. *Boy, this beats the Holiday Inn, hands down*, she thought as they followed Giovanni through the suite. Feeling extremely sleepy, Katie flopped down on the bed.

"Hey! It's okay if you take a nap, but I'm going to wake you up in about an hour as you need to get used to the new time. That's the only way to get over jet lag!" her father warned.

Katie nodded drowsily and closed her eyes. What seemed like only a few minutes turned into several hours. The room was dark and she could hear the muffled sound of traffic from the streets below, but something was rumbling like thunder in the next room! *Maybe it's a storm*, she thought. Tiptoeing through the suite, the rumbling became increasingly louder and suddenly she realized it was her parents snoring in their bedroom. Stifling a laugh, she checked the clock and was shocked to see it was six p.m. It was only ten thirty in the morning when they had laid down to take a "short" nap!

"Daddy! Mama! Wake up!"

Her father and mother looked at her dazedly. "What time is it?"

"Later than you think! I'm hungry! Can we get a hamburger or something?"

Soon, they were out on the streets walking up and down looking for a restaurant. Katie's mother had insisted she put a dress on and her best white patent leather shoes.

"You have to dress up when you go out! People will be looking at you!"

Well, the Roman citizens were certainly looking at them, snickering and whispering "Americanos" as they passed by. Their search for a restaurant or café ended in failure.

"What's the deal?" Katie asked her father hungrily.

"I don't know. Maybe Italians don't eat supper here," her father replied irritably. "I'm going to ask this guy if he speaks English."

He went in the café while Katie and her mother waited outside. Katie looked down at her shoes and her flower print dress. She felt like she stuck out like a sore thumb among the sophisticated and chicly dressed Roman women. Paula didn't look too comfortable either.

"Well, they open at nine p.m.," John said dryly.

"Nine p.m.!" Katie and Paula exclaimed together.

"Yup! Italians eat very late. Sometimes it's ten or eleven. We'll just have to buy something in the shops and take it back to our room."

They stopped in a store and bought a loaf of bread, ham, and cheese. Katie was relieved to see they were selling bottles of Coca Cola – something familiar! They went back to their hotel, and Giovanni waved at them from behind the hotel desk.

"We have wonderful sightseeing tours of the city, if your wife and daughter are interested!" said Giovanni holding out an accordion brochure with colorful pictures.

The next couple of weeks were spent seeing the sights in the city and the countryside. Museums, ruins, cathedrals, carriage rides, boat rides, and hikes revealed Italy's romantic and historical beauty. They visited the touristy but beautiful Isle of Capri and its blue grotto. They admired the breathtaking beauty of the Amalfi drive with its citrus groves and villas perched above the blue Mediterranean Sea. The bus driver pointed out Sophia Loren's house overlooking the Mediterranean Sea. Florence's art filled them with awe, and Venice was like a fairy tale as they drifted through the canals on a gondola. It was exciting to see what was around every corner. Arias floated out of the windows and the laundry hanging on the balconies seemed to wave in time to the music.

However, the climax of the tours and Katie's childhood dream came true was when they visited the ancient city of Pompeii. She had read about it as a little girl in her third grade class and had always been interested to see the inhabitants of an ancient city that had been covered and preserved by volcanic ash. It was incredible to imagine a thriving city some two thousand years ago.

She and her parents toured, ate, drank, talked with new acquaintances from all over the world; but most of all, they relaxed. Katie had never seen her parents in such a good mood.

One afternoon, Paula was feeling a little sick with a stomach bug, so Katie and John decided to set off on their own and find the city zoo. As they walked through a park, she noticed a young guy with long curly hair bouncing on top of a girl sprawled in the overgrown grass.

Katie suddenly felt one of her father's hand being clapped tightly over her eyes and his other hand pulling her in another direction. She struggled a little, but she couldn't budge from his grip.

"What's going on, Daddy? What are you doing?" she cried as she stumbled beside him on the path.

"Just never mind! Never mind!" he said tensely as he dragged her along towards the zoo's entrance. After making sure the coast was clear, he released her at the gate.

The rest of the day was spent pleasantly enough viewing the animals, but the previous scene from the park kept flashing in her mind, and she was puzzled at her father's reaction. That evening back in the hotel, it finally dawned on her what was going on back there. She gasped as they were sitting and eating their dinner in the restaurant downstairs.

"What on earth is the matter with you?" her mother asked in surprise.

"Oh, nothing, Mama, uh, I just remembered I, uh, forgot to pack my, um – sunglasses!"

The next day, they sat outside in an outdoor cafe eating Italian *gelato*[49] and watching the people go by. John looked up from his ice cream and announced that they would be leaving for Pescara by the end of the week.

"So, what are you going to do there exactly?" Katie asked.

"Well, I'll drive every day to Ortona – it's a small town close to Pescara. Our offices will be there. Then I'll fly out to the rig on a

---

49 Ice cream

helicopter and check the samples," he said pleased at the thought of not being stuck at a desk in a stuffy office.

"What are Mom and I going to do while you are gone? You'll have the car!" Katie asked as she took a bite of her spaghetti ice cream.

"Katie, this is not Texas. Everything is in walking distance, and if it isn't, you can take the bus! Besides, Pescara is a resort town on the Italian Riviera! I think you will find plenty of things to do."

Katie and her mother smiled at each other, exclaiming in unison, "Shopping!"

John rolled his eyes and groaned.

They packed their bags, loaded their green Fiat, and headed east across the peninsula. Katie's mother began praying again before they started driving as the traffic was fast and heavy in Rome. No one seemed to pay attention to lights, stop signs or traffic signals, yet the drivers could stop on a dime if someone stepped out in front of them. As they drove through the center of the city, they were shocked to see a pregnant woman and a young man pushing their car through the heaviest traffic. Not long after that, they saw a horse and wagon meandering its way through the streets with cars zooming by on all sides. However, once they got out into the countryside, they breathed a sigh of relief and enjoyed exploring the countryside. Noon arrived and John drove them on a side road back into the hills. "There's an old monastery back here – Gino told me about it at work. Let's see if we can find it."

Katie had liked meeting Gino and his wife Ada. They worked in the headquarters office in Rome and were kind enough to take John, Paula, and Katie out one day to see the sights around Rome. They drove up towards the Mediterranean coast and stopped at the top of a hill for refreshments.

"Now, what would you like to drink, *Signorina*?" Gino asked her smiling.

"What is that red stuff everyone is drinking?" Katie asked pointing at a couple standing near the lookout point.

"Katie! Don't point! It's not polite!" her mother admonished.

Gino looked in the direction she indicated and said, "Ah, that's *campari*! It's a liqueur, but they also make a soda pop. Excellent idea – you and your parents should try it. *Cameriere!*"

The waiter brought the colorful drink with orange wedges on the glasses.

Katie eagerly took a big sip and then sputtered, "Wow, it's really bitter!"

Gino laughed and said, "Oh, you'll learn to love it just like I learned to drink your root beer! You know I was a prisoner of war in an American camp! They found out I spoke English and I got a good job translating for all of the officers. Look, here's my picture from back then!"

Gino pulled out his wallet and showed them a crinkled black and white photo on an old ID.

John gasped and said, "You look just like—"

"I know! I know! Humphrey Bogart! I think that's why all of the American soldiers liked me so well!" Gino smiled with satisfaction that they had recognized his double. "Come on, now, let's go to our village. They make the best pasta you have ever eaten!"

The rest of the day was spent pleasantly touring the seaside and eating clam linguini in Gino's hometown. It was a lovely day.

"Hey, there's the monastery!" John pointed up at the hill at some old ruins. They pulled over and noticed people slowly coming out of their houses and staring at them.

"I don't think they see a lot of tourists here, do you?" whispered Katie to her mother. Paula shook her head smiling as she pulled out the basket of food they had brought along. They hiked towards the monastery, stopping now and then to admire the beautiful view of terraced hills and green meadows.

Munching, Katie remarked, "You know, I'm getting used to this bread. It's really chewy – not like our American bread. It's pretty good!"

"You're not kidding, kiddo!" her father replied as he poured his wine into a paper cup. "This stuff is the real thing. Our white bread just sticks to the roof of your mouth and clogs up the pipes…"

Katie giggled and lay down in the soft, green grass.

They drove into Pescara late that afternoon, and with the help of Gino's instructions, Paula navigated them through the town to the Sea Lion Hotel.

"Okay, the directions say that you cross this railroad track and go around the curve," Paula said studying her notes.

As they approached the railroad track, the bar came down and the cars in front of them stopped.

"Uh-oh… damn. Looks like a train's coming," sighed John exasperatedly.

Katie craned her neck out the window but couldn't see an approaching train. People started getting out of their car, lighting cigarettes, and talking to each other. Some of them seemed to be sharing a bottle of wine.

"Why am I getting the feeling that we are going to be here for a while?" Paula asked nervously.

Suddenly, all of the people jumped back in their cars and quickly rolled up the windows. Katie peered over her father's shoulders to see if the train was on its way, but the tracks were empty. Then she saw them – a large group of women, children, and men approaching the vehicles. They were dressed in colorful clothes, and the girls had ribbons in their hair. Gypsies! Soon they came to their car and spoke to John through his opened window.

"Sorry, I don't speak Italian!" he said as the woman stared at him. She thrust her hand in the car and showed him some beads.

"Cinquanta Lira! Cinquanta Lira![50] "she cried pushing him with her hand.

"Hey, back off, lady," John said growing angry.

"Just give her the money, Johnny. It's not that much!"

Grudgingly, he pulled out the money and handed it to her. She smiled a toothless smile and pointed at the beads. *"Buono Fortuna! Buono Fortuna*[4]!"

As John rolled up the window, the train went rumbling by. "Thank God!" he said shaking his head and starting the engine.

In a short time, they drove up to the Sea Lion Hotel and parked the car.

"Look!" Paula gasped pointing at the pool and the beach. "It's just like the dream I had a few weeks ago. See, I told you the Lord was taking us somewhere special!"

The porter came out and loaded up their suitcases and directed them towards the elevator. A tall, slender man with dark glasses greeted them in the hallway and introduced himself as "Vic," the manager of the hotel.

"If there is anything you need while you are staying with us, please let us know. That's the restaurant over there where you will have all your meals. We have an agreement with your company."

Katie peered into the dining area and saw a beautiful expansive area with big windows overlooking the beach. A huge table in the middle of the room was covered with a large assortment of fruit and cheeses.

"Hmmm," she said approvingly.

Vic took them up the elevator to their rooms and said apologetically, "I'm sorry that we could not get adjoining rooms, but your daughter's

---

[50] Fifty Lira!

room will be right above yours. I hope that is all right with you. I assure you that it is very safe here."

He unlocked the door and ushered them in. The room was airy with large windows and a beautiful view of the Adriatic Sea. Blue and white wallpaper adorned the walls; it was a pleasant, clean room with modern furniture. Katie's parents looked pleased, and the tension lines in their faces began to relax.

"Look, we have balconies," Katie exclaimed. Vic opened the doors to the balcony and they stepped out. A balmy sea breeze stroked their faces, and Katie took a deep breath.

"Oh, man," was all she could say.

That night she ate the best minestrone soup she had every eaten. It was packed with vegetables, and the waiter grated fresh Parmesan cheese on top. She knew right then and there that she was going to like this place.

Back in Texas, the Mexican girls had *quinceanera* parties when they were fifteen, and some of her friends had sweet sixteen parties. Pescara was to be Katie's coming out party. The attention she received there was something she had never experienced before. The so-called jocks and socialites in high school had never paid much attention to her, and she didn't even try to talk to the so-called "popular girls." One of them told her once that "she was just too serious" and that she should lighten up and wear more make-up.

Now in Italy, it was a whole new world. Suddenly handsome Italian boys her age were giving her admiring glances and nodding at her. Romeo, the waiter assigned to their table, prepared exotic flaming desserts out of fruit and ice cream placing them triumphantly in front of her with a flamboyant flourish, impatiently waiting for her approval. Luigi, the bar boy with dark curly hair and a big nose, tried to practice his English with her and prepared her beautiful tropical fruit juice drinks. He introduced her and her parents to their first cappuccinos, much to her mother's delight.

Along with the hotel staff members, there were French divers from the oil rig; they would try to impress her by doing fancy flips off the board and the side of the pool. The icing on the cake though was Mimo, the handsome lifeguard, who would nonchalantly do some bodybuilding poses in his black speedo whenever she was sunning by the pool. She had to admit that his physique looked pretty good. All of the attention, not to mention her parents' knowing looks, embarrassed her greatly, but she was flattered. Her confidence definitely took a turn in the right direction.

The next few weeks were spent enjoying the beach and pool as well as interesting boutiques, salons and museums. Paula, who never met a stranger, was soon trying to communicate in broken Italian with people she met on the street. They seemed to appreciate her efforts and laughed as she tried to converse.

One June morning, they had been in town shopping for shoes as Paula had heard from one of the other wives that Italian leather shoes were the best quality. However, it wasn't so easy as mother and daughter wore an American size ten and most Italian women shoes were just not that big. When the shoes associate bent down to measure their feet, he looked up with exasperation, slapped his forehead, and cried, "*Grosso! Grosso!*[51]" So, they ended up buying sandals. Katie tried to tell herself it didn't matter too much if her toes hung out just a little over the edge.

"Oh, my darlin', oh, my darlin', oh, my darlin' Clementine… she wore boxes without topses…" Katie sang quietly as she and Paula hurried out of the boutique. Her mother giggled and pushed her out the door.

Coming home exhausted and hot, they decided to head towards the beach. The healthy Mediterranean diet had helped Katie to shed a few pounds, so she was eager to try out a new red Hawaiian print bikini she had bought back in Texas. She had never been brave enough to wear it before but felt sufficiently "skinny" to put it on. Her mother settled down on a lounge chair and started a conversation with the woman next to her. Katie spread out a towel on the soft sand and lay down to sun. After several minutes, the heat got to her and she decided to cool off. Her mother was deep in conversation by this time and didn't notice as her youngest daughter waded out into the sea. The sand and water felt delicious.

A group of tall, good-looking boys stopped their volleyball game and watched her as she swam further out towards the buoys and rocks. One of them left the group and began to follow her. She had never been out that far, but she was a fair swimmer and felt confident. Suddenly, she heard a voice with a strong Slavic accent behind her.

"Do you always swim to here?"

Katie whirled around in the water and saw a young man swimming too closely behind her. Feeling uncomfortable and surprised, she backstroked a little and said, "No, not usually."

"Maybe you just wanted the two of us to be alone!" he smiled unpleasantly swimming closer.

---

51 Huge! Huge!

"Hey, I don't even know you!" Katie said with growing alarm.

"Oh, you American girls like to play games, don't you? Just relax," he said.

Katie turned and tried to swim back to shore, but he grabbed her around the waist. She could feel his hands sliding down towards her bottom piece trying to pull them off. She managed to flip over on her back and started kicking the guy in the chest. He just smiled but was a little surprised when she started screaming. He let go and held his hands up in the air saying, "Okay! Okay!"

Swimming as fast as she could, she pulled herself out of the water and dropped onto the towel next to her mother. Her mother didn't even notice her panting there as she continued chatting pleasantly with the other woman, who was smiling vaguely at them both.

"Did you have a nice swim, sweetie?" her mother asked in between sentences.

Katie just buried her face in her towel and lay still. Unbeknown to her, Luigi and Romeo were watching from the balcony of the restaurant.

That night she told her parents what had happened, and her father jumped up to talk to the manager. He came back to their room and sat down looking a little embarrassed.

"Well, I spoke to Vic, and he told me that they belong to a Yugoslavian water polo team that is competing here in Pescara. He said the boys didn't mean any harm," he said looking a little uncomfortable. "He didn't really do anything to you, did he?"

Katie just stared at her father and then said, "You know, I am really tired. I think I'll go to bed. Goodnight!" She kissed her parents and slipped out the door to go to her room. As she turned the key to her room, she decided to make a quick trip to the restaurant and get a glass of milk.

Luigi and Romeo met her at the door with smiles.

"*Buona Sera, Senorigna*[52]*!*"

"*Buona Sera*! Uh, can I get a glass of *Latte, per favore*?" she asked trying to remember the Italian word for milk.

They looked at each other with a confused expression.

"You know, *Latte* – milk!"

"Ahhh, milch! Si, si!"

Good grief, my pronunciation must be terrible, Katie thought to herself as Romeo fetched a glass and poured the creamy beverage into it. He offered to seat her, but she smilingly shook her head and thanked him.

---

52 Good evening, Miss!

As she turned to leave, Katie noticed the water polo team sitting at the bar. They began nudging each other and pointing at her. One of them stood up and bowed mockingly at her. Recognizing him, her face went crimson. Turning abruptly to flee the room, she managed to get through the swinging door without spilling her milk.

Puzzled by her hasty departure, Romeo, the headwaiter, glanced over at the group. Luigi was behind the bar shaking drinks when Romeo caught his eye. He nodded in the direction of the tall water polo player. Luigi winked and nonchalantly moved over to the other side where the unsuspecting boy was laughing loudly with his companions. Suddenly the lid flew off the shaker and splashed the water polo player directly in the face with his mouth wide open.

"Idiot!" the tall Yugoslavian man sputtered jumping up from the stool and grabbing Luigi by the collar.

"*Mi Scusi, scusi*[53]," Luigi said apologetically offering him a bar towel as he hung helplessly in the air.

At that moment, Mimo strolled in the room, took stock of the situation, and gave the water polo player a threatening look while clenching his fists. The young man stared at the lifeguard, snorted, and then let go of Luigi with a flourish.

Romeo was having difficulty controlling his laughter on the other side of the room as a shaky Luigi gave him the thumbs up. Vic, the manager, walked in and looked questioningly at all of them. Everyone got busily back to work, and the water polo team dispersed.

"Good work," Romeo whispered to Luigi while they cleaned the bar.

Luigi smiled and winked, "Just doing my job."

---

53 Excuse me!

Trnava

"Daddy, what's the matter?" Katie asked at dinner one evening. John had been unusually silent most of the evening. Paula glanced at him sympathetically.

"Well, they decided to can the well," he said abruptly without looking up from his antipasto.

"Can the well?"

"The French company decided to pull out, and since they have the major share in the operation, there isn't much we can do but go home."

Go home! Katie was shocked by the words. How could they go home now? She was supposed to attend the International School in Rome that fall while her parents continued to live in Pescara for the next two years.

As she was mulling the news over in her head, her father interrupted her thoughts by saying, "I'm disappointed, too, Katie. I was sure that we would strike oil if we just kept going, but what can I do? A lot of money down the drain for nothing. Well, I have an idea," he leaned back in his chair. "What would you think about driving to Czechoslovakia before we leave? I have some vacation time left, and to tell you the truth, I am curious to see our relatives there."

"Oh, Johnny, I think that's a wonderful idea! You can finally meet some of your family!" Paula answered excitedly. "But can we get in the country? I mean, isn't it difficult to travel there?"

"I called the embassy in Rome and they told me we just have to come in and fill out the visa applications before we leave. You are forced to exchange a certain amount of money every day, but I think we can handle that. What do you say, kiddo?"

Katie shrugged still feeling numb about the end of their Italian adventure. When she had first arrived in Italy she felt homesick for her friends, her horse, and everything that was familiar back home, but the past two months had changed her outlook and this place had become a significant component of her life now.

"I guess so. When do we leave?" she asked quietly.

"Well, we'll pack things up over the next couple of days and then we will drive to Rome to arrange our visas. I already sent a telegram to Aunt Josefina that we will get there the end of this week."

Katie thought again about her grandfather and wished he could have accompanied them on this trip. Two years before he passed away, he had received a letter from his cousin Joe Petrovic in Chicago. In the letter, Joe had written how he had traveled to Czechoslovakia to visit relatives. While he was there, he noticed an elderly lady in the Lutheran church and discovered she was Katie's great-aunt. Joe had approached her along with her children, got her address and forwarded it on to Katie's grandfather. Grandpa was stunned when he read this news as he had not been in touch with any of his family members since the Depression; there had been absolutely no contact. The next afternoon was spent writing a letter to his baby sister Josefina, but it was a struggle for the elderly man as he hadn't spoken or written in Slovak for many years. John sent the letter off, and they all waited in suspense for an answer. Finally, the mailman delivered a letter with strange looking stamps on it. Grandpa got out his magnifying glass and carefully read the letter. It was written by Josefina's daughter who introduced herself as Marta. She started the letter out by telling him the difficulties they had in reading his letter as no one could read the old script that people used to use in Grandpa's day, and Aunt Josefina couldn't see well enough to help them. However, they found someone who could decipher the old style of writing, and that person had conveyed the contents of the letter to them. They were very happy to hear that their Uncle Stefan was still alive and well in America. The letter went on to elaborate about Aunt Josefina and her family. Katie had watched her grandfather's lips move as he silently read the letter. He looked up with a broad smile across his face.

"So, it's true. My youngest sister is still alive! She has two children, five grandchildren, and six great-grandchildren!" he said in amazement to the rest of the family. "It's my fault that we didn't keep in touch…"

After this first communication was made, letters from Czechoslovakia came frequently, and Katie's grandfather awaited each one of them with eager anticipation. He learned information about his late parents, his brothers and sisters, and all of the younger family members he had never met. Katie had always been curious about her father's side of the family, and now they were going to actually meet them!

The next two days were a blur at the Sea Lion Hotel. Katie and her parents were busy packing and shopping for last minute gifts to take home as well as to their newfound relatives in Czechoslovakia. After tearful goodbyes to all the staff at the hotel and one last flaming dessert passionately created by Romeo, they were on their way back to Rome.

"I heard the young people in Eastern Europe really like jeans, especially Levis," Paula said as she checked her purse for her passport.

"Well, you certainly bought enough of them," John said wryly. "You could probably open your own shop there."

"I don't think the communist government would appreciate that somehow," she retorted.

They finally arrived at their hotel and checked in for the night. The next day, they walked to the Czechoslovakian embassy and spent most of the morning filling out their application forms. While they were there, an elderly Catholic nun engaged them in conversation and helped them with the hefty amounts of paperwork. She gave them her blessing and kissed them goodbye when they left. They made it as far as the Austrian border that night and decided to stop over in a *Gasthaus*[54] in a little mining town. The next morning after dining on coffee, fresh hard Kaiser rolls, butter, and jelly, they continued their journey towards Vienna.

Vienna was a bustling city but seemed a little more organized than Rome. Drivers followed the rules! As they approached a bridge, John said excitedly, "It's the Danube! We are going to cross the Danube River!" and he began whistling Strauss's *Blue Danube Waltz*.

Katie peered out the car window as they crossed the canal. "Daddy, it's not all that blue…"

That night they found accommodations in a beautiful Gothic looking hotel near the Ringstrasse in Vienna. Paula had gotten the address from an Austrian doctor and her family who were vacationing in Pescara. The next day they strolled through the *Altstadt*[55], tasted their first delicious piece of *Sachertorte*[56], and enjoyed the Strauss waltzes floating through the parks. Katie noticed several American students who were eating apple strudel and drinking coffee at the outdoor cafes. She felt a chill go up her spine when she thought about how exciting it must be to study in a European city like Vienna. They spent the next couple of days visiting *Schoenbrunn*[57], the art museum, and the stables where the world famous

---

54 Inn

55 "Old City" – the city center

56 A special chocolate cake created at the Sacher Hotel

57 The summer palace of Maria Theresa – Empress of the former Austro-Hungarian Empire

Lippizaner horses were housed. Europe seemed to be full of treasures that were just waiting to be discovered!

The next morning, John roused his family and they set off for the Austrian/Czechoslovakian border.

"So, where are we going exactly after we cross the border?" Katie asked as she looked at the map.

"Do you see a city named Bratislava?"

"Yes," she replied squinting at the map.

"Well, that's the capital city of the Slovak part. Prague is the capital of the entire country, but the country has three different regions: Bohemia, Moravia, and Slovakia."

"What's the capital of the Moravian part?"

"I think it's called Brno," he said concentrating on passing a flashy red Mercedes.

As the neared the border, fewer and fewer people were visible in the villages they drove through. In fact, the streets looked rather empty and a little desolate.

"Where is everybody?" Paula asked in astonishment.

"I guess they don't like living so close to the Iron Curtain," John shrugged in reply.

He slowed the car down as they approached a line of cars in front of the Austrian border. They moved slowly forward until it was their turn to show their passports. The Austrian border guard glanced quickly at their passports and waved them on. They looked forward and saw another border station, but this one was manned with soldiers in olive green uniforms and red stars. These particular border guards carried guns strapped across their backs with huge German Shepherds straining at their leashes. John swallowed hard and drove slowly forward.

"Papiere!" a burly looking guard with an unsmiling face held out his hand.

John handed him their passports with their visas. The guard examined each one and peered in the car to see if the photographs matched the inhabitants of the green Fiat. Then he looked at the last one and began to shake his head. He pointed at the section that concerned their car and started muttering something in Czech. Then he took the paper and tore it up into little pieces. Katie and her parents stared at him with open mouths. He began yelling at John who sat in the car looking totally bewildered. A sympathetic tourist who was waiting in line behind them came up and offered to help translate. After several minutes of shouting, the gentleman explained to John that something was wrong with the vehicle number, and that he would have to pull over and reapply in the station. John silently obeyed and walked behind the unpleasant guard into the station office where a large greasy looking man in uniform sat stamping papers. Katie and her mother sat stiffly in the car, watching the other border guards as they checked cars, suitcases, and trunks. She looked across the countryside and tried to see the end of the barbed wire fences and watch towers that crisscrossed the land.

It looks like a prison camp, she mused shuddering. Looking up at the sky, she saw a flock of birds flying across the border. *At least they don't need passports*, she thought slightly comforted by the sight.

"What are you thinking about?" her mother asked tensely.

"Nothing. I was just thinking."

"Well, don't think too loudly... I'm not sure if that's allowed here! What on earth is taking your father so long?"

John came back to the car looking a little pale but relieved.

"Okay, all we have to do now is exchange the money," he said mopping his brow with a handkerchief. He pulled the car forward and stopped in front of the exchange window.

"How many days?" a woman soldier with bright red hair asked sharply.

"Four days," John replied pointing at the visa dates.

"How many people?" she asked again, ignoring the visas.

"Three," my father replied.

"It is sixteen dollars per person per day, so that will be 192 dollars," she answered briskly.

John counted out the bills, and she handed him Czechoslovak crowns in exchange. He got back in the car, and they continued driving past barbed wire fences, guards, and more dogs. Finally, they emerged from the crossing and entered the city. Smog hung in the air and she could sense a strong chemical odor in the air. Off in the distance, she could see a large gray castle, perched on the top of a hill, overlooking the Danube River. Grimy looking buses with people packed in like sardines passed them. The expressionless look on people's faces resembled something out of a science fiction movie. Streetcars rumbled past and ladies pushing large prams walked through the streets stopping to look at the store windows with their sparse displays. Stone-faced people turned and stared at the strange foreign car driving through the streets. It looked strangely out of place next to all of the East German *Trabants*[58] and Czechoslovakian *Skodas*[59].

"What a gray place!" Katie exclaimed.

Her parents nodded their heads in agreement while navigating their way through the city. There weren't many cars, but there were people of all ages walking and riding their bicycles. Somehow, their clothes and styles looked a little different. Red stars and pictures of the "Fathers of the Revolution" were omnipresent.

"You know, this kind of reminds me of Chicago back in the 1930s somehow," John remarked looking around as he drove. "Except for him," he added thumbing at a particular striking pose of Lenin.

"There's supposed to be a sign saying 'Trnava' somewhere, but I haven't seen it yet," grumbled Paula.

Finally, after driving around for almost an hour and too intimidated to ask for directions, they came to an intersection where they spied a small sign with the word "Trnava" written on it. An arrow was pointing right.

"Aha!" Katie's father said smiling with relief. They took the right exit and drove out of the city.

The landscape looked immediately brighter once they left the polluted city, and they began to feel a little more cheerful. The terrain was rolling and the corn looked healthy growing in the fields. Poppies dotted the green grass and brightened up the scenery.

"There aren't many billboards or advertisements, are there?" Katie remarked as they sped along the two-lane road. "Hey, there's one!" She pointed at a sign that had the numbers of a radio station on it. In the upper right hand corner was a red hammer and a sickle.

"Oh, Toto, we are a long way from Kansas," John remarked wryly.

After driving for an hour, they came to the city limits of Trnava. Tall, boxy looking apartments lined the outskirts of the city, but onion dome churches could be seen in the center.

"Now where?" Paula asked looking at her husband who was supposed to have all of the answers.

"Good question," he said scratching his head. A man on a bicycle pulled up beside them curiously staring at the Fiat and the people within.

"Excuse me, do you know where this address is?" John showed him the paper where he had scribbled it down.

---

58 A very small, boxy East German car

59 A small car made in Czechoslovakia

The man pulled out his reading glasses, stared at the paper and then waved for them to follow him. He started riding furiously on his bicycle, and John slowly followed him up and down the city blocks. Finally, they pulled up in front of a pleasant looking two-story house that was surrounded by a beautiful garden and a wrought iron fence. The man on the bicycle rang the bell, and a short heavy woman with brown curly hair appeared at the door. When she saw Katie and her parents standing awkwardly in front of the gate, she ran down the garden path with open arms to let them in. The man on the bicycle tipped his hat to them, and John quickly pressed a few American dollars in his hands. His face brightened up immediately, and he jumped on his bike whistling as he rode away.

"*Vitaj, Vitaj*[60]!" the woman smiled as she fumbled with a huge key in the lock. The door swung open and the corpulent woman grabbed them and swallowed them up with big, sweaty hugs.

"*Pod, pod! Kommen Sie, Kommen Sie! Ich bin Marta*[61]!" she said excitedly pointing to herself and waving them towards the house.

At the door entrance, a white haired man, who vaguely resembled Danny Kaye, came running out nodding and grinning broadly. Katie could see a gold tooth glinting in the sun. He bowed before them, shook John's hands, and kissed Paula's and Katie's hands. As they entered the house, he brought them three pairs of old house shoes that looked like the dog had been chewing on them.

Taking the hint, they slipped off their shoes, placing them in the rack near the door, and put on the oversized house slippers. Shuffling through the hall, the woman ushered them into a parlor where a long table was set with open-faced sandwiches, pickles, hard boiled eggs, cakes, pretzels, wine, and soda.

"*Setzen Sie, bitte! Setzen Sie*[62]!" their hostess ordered in broken German shoving chairs behind them.

The American family gratefully sat down and looked with admiration at the beautifully set table and room. The walls were white plaster, stenciled with beautiful ornamental patterns. Asparagus ferns and ivy hung from the ceiling, and a huge china closet filled with crystal filled one side of the room. The wooden floors were covered with Oriental rugs. Even the food on the table displayed an air of old world elegance. They

---

60 Welcome! Welcome!

61 Come! Come! I am Marta!

62 Sit, please! Sit!

admired the artistically created sandwiches of salami, ham, and grated white cheese; homemade pickles and red peppers were decoratively placed with slices of egg as the finishing touch.

"*Was trinken Sie*[63]?" the white haired man asked.

Before they could answer, he filled their glasses with white wine and brought out little schnaps glasses filled with an amber colored liquor.

"*Slivowitz*[64]!" he said triumphantly setting the glasses in front of them.

He held up a glass and said something in Slovak as a toast. They all raised their glasses and as Katie sipped the drink, she started to choke as the burning liquid went down her esophagus.

Soon, an elderly lady walked shyly in the room. Katie gasped when she saw her. She looked like a female version of her grandfather! A plump little woman with hair pulled tightly back in a bun came forward, wiping her puffy hands on her apron. The expression on her face was kind and gentle as she kissed Paula and Katie on each cheek.

"*Janko*[65]?" she asked hesitantly turning to look at John. With tears in his eyes, he stood up and embraced his aunt. They stood there a few minutes while Aunt Josefina squeezed his hand and looked up at him admiringly. She stroked his tanned, leather face and sat down gingerly on the edge of the chair. Soon, more family members entered the room and John was suddenly surrounded by relatives. They could not speak each other's language, but the laughter and hearty handshakes made up for their lack of communication.

"Hello! Hello! I hear there are some Americans here!"

John, Paula, and Katie whirled around to see an elderly lady with snow-white hair and sparkling blue eyes smiling at them.

"Hi, there! I'm Lottie Holčik! From New York! I've come to translate for you!"

"From New York? Oh, are we glad to see you," John said jumping up and shaking her hand enthusiastically.

Soon they were all gathered around the table with Mrs. Holčik busily translating questions and answers from every member of the group. During the course of the conversation, they found out that she was the widow of a Slovak Lutheran pastor, whom she had met in New York when he was studying at the seminary; they married and then her husband brought her back to Slovakia in 1933.

---

63 What will you drink?

64 Hard alcohol made from plums or other fresh fruits

65 Johnny?

"Just in time for fun and games with Nazi Germany! It was a time of insanity, let me tell you!" she said, her sharp blue eyes flashing.

She went on to talk about the war with Marta and Karol adding their stories about German and Russian soldier occupation in Trnava.

"Did you ever go back home?"

"No, my dear, after the war I had so much work to do raising my three daughters. My husband was ill, and I had to help him, too. He passed away several years ago, you know."

"Why don't you go now?"

"My youngest daughter and grandchildren need me here! How are those children going to learn about the Bible if I don't teach them? My older daughters live in the States now, and they send me what I need."

"What do they send? Can't you buy everything here?" Katie asked naively.

Mrs. Holcik translated this last question to Marta, and they both burst into laughter. She started talking quickly while Mrs. Holcik translated.

"Before the war and communism, the Czechoslovakian economy was doing very well. We had a fairly high standard of living. But we regressed over the last several years, and it is difficult to buy what you need here. Even basic things can be a problem! During the winter is the worst time as it is almost impossible to buy fresh fruits and vegetables. That's why everyone here tries to garden and raise their own produce. Marta and Karol always give me what I need in that area," she said smiling and patting Marta on the arm. "However, we do have special stores here that only accept Western currency. They are called Tuzek shops. You can buy all sorts of things from the West there, but as I mentioned before, my daughters in the States send me little care packages from time to time. They are always full of coffee, chocolate, and my favorite – Jello pudding!"

Paula made a mental note to start buying extra coffee and packets of Jello pudding at the grocery store when she got back home.

"And you see? I can be of help to you, too," Mrs. Holcik said smiling triumphantly.

Evening came and Karol, Marta's husband, turned on the lights while carefully pulling the curtains across the open windows. He put his fingers to his lips and gestured with his head towards the window.

"He is worried that nosy neighbors might be peeking at us," Mrs. Holčik remarked as the Americans looked at him curiously. "There are always informants in every neighborhood, and it's better to avoid trouble, you know."

148

"Are, uh, Marta and Karol communist party members?" John asked hesitantly watching the curtains blow in the summer breeze.

Mrs. Holcik smiled broadly and translated the question. This provoked another loud uproar of laughter. Karol jumped up from the table making mock military salutes and goose-stepping across the room.

"Karol is a retired railroad worker whose name is on the party list, but everyone here knows that he has no respect for them. In fact, when he goes to the city offices to take care of any business, they greet him by saying, 'Oh, here comes that Lutheran Communist again...' They leave him alone as he is basically retired and just works part-time as a janitor in the girls' dormitory at the university. Marta here works as a cook in the high school. She likes to eat as you can tell," Mrs. Holčik nodded at Marta.

Marta responded by smiling a big toothless smile and brushing back the sweaty curls hanging around her plump round face. She disappeared through the kitchen, returning with a big tureen full of steaming soup.

"Uh-oh, here comes more food," Paula said. "I thought the sandwiches and cake were supper!"

"Oh, no!" Mrs. Holčik chuckled. "That was only a small appetizer – just wait 'til you see what Marta has whipped up for you!"

Soon, schnitzels, fried potatoes, and salads fresh from the garden followed. The rest of the evening was spent talking, laughing, eating, and drinking until they all thought they were going to burst. Their cheeks became flushed from the excitement as well as the new wine. Katie began to feel very tired.

"*Schlafen? Gehen Sie schlafen?*"[66] Marta asked holding her hands up to her cheek and shutting her eyes.

John, Paula, and Katie nodded wearily, so she led them to their bedrooms. She and Karol gave up their bedroom on the ground floor to John and Paula. When they tried to protest, Marta just laughed and shook her head pushing them towards the room. There was a large painting of Jesus praying in the Garden of Gethsemane over the bed.

Katie was taken upstairs to their sons' old bedroom. It reminded her of something from the TV show *My Three Sons* with school pictures, sports posters, wooden tennis racquets and boyish paraphernalia around the room. She spied one of the boys' confirmation pictures on the wall. The pastor looked very strict and unpleasant. Katie wondered if it might be Mrs. Holcik's husband.

---

66 Sleep? Go to sleep?

Marta opened the door to the balcony and said, *"Es ist heiss! Brauchen Frische Luft!"*[67]

She pulled back a big down comforter on the bed and plumped the goose feather pillows up for her. Giving Katie an affectionate squeeze, she closed the door. Katie could hear the stairs creaking under her cousin's heavy weight. She slowly undressed in the moonlight streaming through the window. She felt a little nervous in this new environment so far away from home. She had certainly never been in a communist country before, but it was definitely different than what she had imagined. Slipping under the comforter, she soon fell asleep.

Bong! Bong! Katie jumped up with a start as the clock in her room struck twelve o'clock. She peered around the dark room and suddenly felt very ill to her stomach. Jumping up from the bed, she ran to the door and tried to open it. It was locked! After a few futile attempts to open it, she ran to the balcony and eyeballed the drop to the ground. *Too far! What am I going to do?* she thought worriedly. *Oh, dear Lord, please open this door!* She pulled on the knob again and the door suddenly popped open. Scrambling down the stairs, she barely made it to the bathroom. The outhouse smell of the toilet overpowered her as she threw up repeatedly in the toilet. Too much rich food and alcohol had put her body on red alert. After several minutes, she exhaustedly pulled the chain to flush the toilet. Turning on the light, she peered at herself in the small mirror over the sink. A scared, pale face looked back at her. She shook her head before bathing her face and rinsing her mouth with fresh cool water. Feeling somewhat better, she turned to open the door, but it was locked, too! *What is going on in this place?* Katie thought wildly. *Are they trying to imprison me?*

Suddenly, the door flew open and a worried Aunt Josefina stood there in her nightgown holding a light, *"Jako? Jako?"*[68] Katie smiled weakly at her great-aunt and slipped past her to go up the stairs, quickly retreating to her bed.

Early the next morning, bright sunlight bathed her face. Opening her eyes, Katie could hear water splashing outside. Yawning, she pulled back the covers and slipped on her worn house slippers. Looking at her watch, she was shocked to see it was only 4:30 a.m.

"It's so bright outside," she said aloud in amazement.

---

67 It is hot! Need fresh air!
68 What? What?

Walking rather unsteadily out on the balcony, she saw Marta's husband Karol standing in the garden pumping water and vigorously washing his face and upper body. He looked up at her and grinned. She smiled dazedly back at him and looked around the garden. Pink, yellow, red, and white roses lined the street in front of the house. People were already walking to work or riding their bicycles. Morning glories draped themselves around the gate and cherries hung in abundance on the tree near the balcony. The fragrant scent of fruits and flowers wafted up to her nose, and she took a deep breath. She tried to go back to sleep and managed to doze another hour, but feeling somewhat refreshed, she dressed herself and walked down the stairs. Aunt Josefina and Marta were busy in the kitchen cooking breakfast and making coffee.

Aunt Josefina whispered as she went by, *"Dobre Rano! Lepšie?"*[69] and rubbed her tummy sympathetically.

Katie ruefully nodded, not sure what she said but guessed from her expression and gestures that she was asking if she felt better. She moved quietly out the door and into the garden. Karol came around the corner, wiping himself with a towel.

"Dobre rano! Dobre Rano!" he said smiling at her as he buttoned his shirt.

He beckoned to her, and she followed him behind the house. As she walked around the corner of the stucco house, she stared in amazement. She had never seen a garden like that before in her life. Her father could only dream of having a plot like that! A greenhouse stood in the corner, and she could see tomato and pepper plants growing in abundance. Fragrant flowers bloomed along the borders while fruit trees dotted the garden that stretched at least a half an acre behind the house. Lush rows of beans, potatoes, lettuce, carrots, and parsnips were planted neatly in between the walkways. Karol led her over to a far corner of the garden where there was a chicken coop and a pigpen. He went quickly inside to collect a few eggs. Coming back out, he handed her the few he had gathered in his big hands, and she carefully placed them in her t-shirt. Behind the chicken coop were two baby pigs snorting and chasing each other in the pen.

"Slanina[70]!" Karol said laughingly as he pointed at the pigs.

Katie smiled back not sure what he had said, but didn't want to appear rude. Carefully, balancing the eggs in her shirt, she followed him back to

---

69 Good morning! Better?

70 Bacon

the house. She took the eggs into the kitchen where Marta and her mother were busy cooking. Marta took the eggs from her and lovingly patted her on the cheek before shooing her out of the kitchen.

Then she walked across the foyer into the room where they had sat the night before and sat down on the settee. She began looking at the pictures of all their newfound relatives. Marta and Karol had three sons: Karol Jr., Viliam, and Ondrej. Karol Jr. and Viliam were already married and living in their own apartments or houses, but Ondrej the youngest still lived at home. He was a round-faced teenager who looked like he enjoyed his mother's cooking a little too much. He was obviously her favorite out of the three as he obeyed her every order and helped her serve. He sometimes sat a little too closely to Katie, in her opinion, but she gradually understood that people in other countries have different ideas of space. His brothers Karol Jr. and Viliam were also present with their wives. The oldest son was very handsome and athletic. He wasn't too friendly at first and eyed them suspiciously, but soon warmed up to them and began asking them questions about America. The second son was a scholar and studied geography at the university. He could speak a little English with them, but got flustered and blushed when the words came out wrong. Aunt Josefina also had another son named Viliam, Marta's brother, and he was married with two children: Viliam and Marta. Katie had never met so many Viliams, Karols, and Martas in all her life. The house had been very crowded last night with all of the newfound family members, but the atmosphere was warm and jovial as they tried to speak with each other. Sometimes they all started laughing until the tears flowed. Suddenly, the door buzzer rang loudly, giving Katie a start. Looking through the window, she saw Karol walking quickly to the gate to let Mrs. Holčik in.

"Well, good morning! You're up early! Did you sleep well?" she asked Katie as she walked into the parlor.

Relieved to hear her own language again, she eagerly replied, "Good morning! Yes, I slept well except for one little incident. I'm afraid I ate too much last night and was a little sick in the night."

Mrs. Holčik laughed good-naturedly and said, "That's easy to do! Slovaks will stuff you full of food and drink when you come to visit. They have a proverb that you should treat every visitor as if it were God Himself visiting! But be careful – Marta's cooking is delicious, but it's very rich!"

Katie moved over on the settee, and Mrs. Holcik sat down next to her still chatting good-naturedly about Slovak and American cuisine. Aunt

Josefina soon joined them and tentatively asked her new American niece a few questions about her older brother Stefan. Did she know him well? What was he like? Katie eagerly began telling her stories about her grandfather.

Aunt Josefina listened attentively as Mrs. Holcik faithfully translated. She nodded now and then looking pleased. Soon John and Paula joined them and they gathered around the table as Marta brought in steaming cups of Turkish coffee, boiled eggs, salami, long white rolls, butter, thick apricot jam, cheese, and red pepper slices.

"This sure beats cornflakes, doesn't it," John said looking happily at the breakfast table. Sitting down, he began stirring his coffee but was a little disconcerted to see thick grounds at the bottom of the cup. His attentive wife noticed and quickly took his cup into the kitchen to run it through her tea strainer.

"I guess I could have strained them through my teeth," he whispered to Paula as she returned the cup. She elbowed him to be quiet.

As they ate, Mrs. Holcik began asking John questions about his Slovak mother.

"Johnny, Marta tells me that your mother was from *Modra*, right?" she asked spooning jam onto her roll.

"Yes, she immigrated to America when she was only sixteen, but died of cancer when I was just a baby. I don't remember her, but my older sister was six years old at the time; she remembers her a little," he replied thoughtfully. "When my mother passed away, my father took us to a Lutheran orphanage run by German ladies – my dad was working long shifts and didn't have anyone to help him," John said reflectively. "They said my sister cried for two weeks hoping that he would come and take her home. That did not happen; however, he was there every Sunday afternoon to visit us."

"That's very sad that you grew up without a mother! Where is your sister now?" Mrs. Holcik asked.

"Mick died last year – two weeks before my father did," John replied sadly.

"Oh, I am so sorry!" Mrs. Holcik exclaimed. She turned to the others and quickly translated as they listened patiently. When she finished, they shook their heads in sympathy and patted John on the arm.

"I wish I knew more about my mother, but all I have is this picture that my father left me before he died." John stood up and went quickly to the bedroom where his suitcase was.

He came back with an old photograph. On the front was a young woman with dark curly hair, big dark eyes, and a full oval face. She was elegantly dressed in a high-necked lace blouse and a belted black skirt. Their Slovak relatives passed the picture to each other nodding and saying, *"Pekna! Pekna žena!"*[71] Marta suddenly became very excited and with her mouth full of salami and bread, she began talking to Mrs. Holcik.

"She says that she can take you to your mother's hometown and perhaps you can find some of your relatives there," Mrs. Holčik translated. "What do you think?"

"That would be great," John nodded enthusiastically. "When can we go?"

"No time like the present, I always say," Mrs. Holcik said briskly.

So after breakfast and washing up, Marta put on her best dress and squeezed into the front seat of their Fiat. Mrs. Holčik, Katie, and Paula managed to fit in the backseat and quickly rolled down the windows. Katie was always surprised how many people you could fit into these small cars.

Marta directed John with her broken German, and Mrs. Holčik helped them when the communication lines broke down. Katie soon learned that her grandmother's town was famous for its ceramics, and that the word "Modra" was the name for the color blue. The woods became thicker as they came closer to the town, and they could see clearings on the side of the hills with expansive vineyards.

Pulling up to the town square near the church, they parked under a big chestnut tree. Marta struggled to get out of the car, but managed to do so as gracefully as possible. She asked John for the picture and walked towards an elderly man sitting on a park bench. She greeted him and he nodded in return. Then she began to explain to him that this was her cousin from America, and that he was searching for his relatives in Slovakia. He listened to her in silence as she rambled on, and then she showed him the picture of John's mother. Pulling a pair of reading glasses out of his pocket, he peered at the photograph. Then the elderly man sat up with a start staring intensely at the photograph. No one spoke.

Trembling, he looked up at Marta and said, *"To je moja najštarša sestra!"* Marta and Mrs. Holčik gasped. Katie and her parents looked at them expectantly and asked in unison, "What did he say?"

---

71 Pretty! Pretty woman!

Mrs. Holčik turned and looked very solemnly at John saying, "The Lord must be directing your paths, Johnny. He said that the woman in this picture is his older sister."

You could have heard a pin drop. Katie and her parents gazed at the elderly gentleman as he began sobbing. He stood up shakily on his cane and beckoned them to follow him.

The rest of the afternoon was spent getting to know Uncle Michael. He showed them a few old photographs when he was a boy, posing with his sister when she was a young girl. When Katie saw those pictures, she recognized him from photos she had seen in an old family album her grandfather had brought with him to Midland. There were also pictures when he was a handsome young man posing with his older brother – both looking cocky and dapper in new suits. Another picture revealed a more serious and bitter side as the two unshaven brothers posed in their World War One military uniforms.

After looking at the old photographs, they met his son and daughter-in-law who quickly told them that there were other cousins in the neighborhood. They brought out pitchers of homemade wine and gave them a tour of their vineyards in the back of the house.

John looked happy as he sat next to his uncle. Michael told them he was quite young when his sister left for America, and that he had cried nonstop for days after she left. He couldn't understand why she had to go, but learned when he was older that they were in the midst of a famine, and she went away to help out the family. Working as a maid for one rich family, she would send money home as often as she could. Katie sat quietly wondering how she would feel if she would have to leave her family and friends to go to an unknown far-away land and work for strangers. A chill went down her spine.

Then Uncle Michael's daughter-in-law brought out beautiful handcrafted plates and bowls that she insisted on wrapping up and sending home with them. Paula looked with delight at the presents, and John tried to give them some money. They vigorously shook their heads and refused, but then he said, "Please, for my mother." Mrs. Holčik translated, and Uncle Michael reluctantly took the bills he pressed in his hands. They exchanged addresses, shook hands, kissed and walked back to their car. Everyone was quiet as they drove back to Trnava.

The next couple of days were spent touring Trnava and places Katie's Grandpa had grown up. They learned that his father was a miller and one of the richest men in a nearby village. However, he had a reputation among his children and grandchildren to be a rather cruel and abusive man. All five children with the exception of Josefina had immigrated either to Austria or America. Katie recalled how her grandpa had always talked about how sweet his mother Elizabeth was, but rarely mentioned his father in their conversations.

The town of Trnava was beautiful with Byzantine spires of churches and cathedrals. Mrs. Holcik told them that it was called "Little Rome" and was famous before the war for its Jesuit seminaries and schools. The old city was surrounded by an ancient wall and on the gate of the wall was the head of Jesus. However, the little river that flowed around the wall was yellow and foamy. There was a strong chemical smell surrounding the older part of the city, and it was obvious that laws protecting the environment either did not exist or were not being enforced. However, they tried to ignore those unpleasant aspects of the tour and happily continued sightseeing and shopping in the state souvenir shops.

"You know, Johnny, Marta tells me that your father was working as an apprentice to a tailor right here in this street," Mrs. Holcik said as they walked down an older section of the city. "He was making fur coats and hats, but when he finished his apprenticeship, he couldn't find any work. She says that he applied for a job at the sugar factory and was waiting for weeks to hear from them. Finally, he gave up, and since there was a strong possibility that he might be drafted into the Austro-Hungarian army, he just left for America." She paused for a moment wetting her lips. "The day after he left, a letter came from the sugar factory offering him a job. Marta said her grandmother broke down crying when she read that letter, but it was too late – he was already on his way to Hamburg to board the ship for New York."

John was very quiet the rest of the day as he reflected on the many turns life can take. What if he had never been born? Or what if he had been born in Czechoslovakia instead of the United States? If he had grown up in Trnava, he would not have most likely had all of the educational opportunities and freedom he had in America, but he would have been surrounded by grandparents, aunts, uncles, and cousins who cared about his welfare. He would not have grown up in an orphanage and always wondering what it was like to have a real family. He sighed.

On the last day of their visit, John made his relatives a promise to visit them again in one or two years, and that he would bring his older children to meet them. Aunt Josefina cried and worried that it was their last meeting together. Marta and Karol ladened them down with gifts of crystal glassware and embroidered tablecloths. While Paula struggled to pack everything into their suitcases, John quietly put some money in an envelope and placed it behind the vase on the table. Their goodbyes were sad and heartfelt. Katie could not believe how close they had all become in such a short time. She felt like she had known them all her life.

As they drove slowly away, waving goodbye, John remarked with his voice full of emotion, "You know, besides you two along with Rick and Margaret, these people are the only family members I have left in this world."

"God is looking out for you, Johnny. I think He always has," Paula said squeezing his arm.

He nodded wordlessly in agreement and shifted the gears.

The Dating Game

"Palo, I really think it's time you made a decision!" Vaclav said sternly.

Pavol looked up from his tea with surprise. Vaclav was peering at him over his glasses as he took a bite of his cake and then waved his fork at Pavol. "You are twenty-seven years old; it's time to get married or become a... a priest!"

Vaclav was himself a young Catholic priest, only a few years older than Pavol, but he had decided to take on the big brother role. They had become friends in Trnava along with two other young priests in the seminary. Pavol had just finished his second degree in geography and was employed as an assistant professor at the Trnava Pedagogical College as well as the University in Bratislava. He was also busily working on his *Candidatus*[72] degree, and even though he was very busy, life was good – he was free and single! They were sitting in a *Lahodky*[73] as Vaclav lectured Pavol.

Pavol rolled his eyes at this last statement and took another bite of his pudding. "Look, Vaclav, you are beginning to sound like my mother! She has been telling me I was going to be a priest since I was born. 'It's my destiny!'"

"Well? Have you seriously considered it? You attend Mass every day, you are heavily involved with the underground church, and you like spending time with us." He paused and quietly added, "Don't you think it's time you made up your mind?"

Pavol was silent for a moment and then slowly replied, "I'm just not ready yet to make a decision either way." He then added smiling, "I'm afraid the opposite sex is too attractive."

"So? What's the problem then?"

---

72 Equivalent to Ph.D.

73 Milk bar where they serve pudding, ice cream, cakes and coffee

"Well, I dated in Bratislava, but it was nothing serious, but I don't really trust these girls here," Pavol said wiping his mouth. "You know, this retired man I know works part-time as a janitor in our dormitory – he is the father of one of my colleagues, Viliam Lauko." Pavol leaned in closer to Vaclav. "He told me that he has seen a queue of our female students in front of the doctor's office. They get pregnant, they get rid of the child, and then they go back to school pretending like nothing ever happened. I'm not saying it is all their fault, but it's disappointing," he sighed sitting back in his chair. "I don't know what I'm really looking for exactly, but I would just like to find a girl who… who is, uh…"

"Who is what?"

"Who thought I was worth waiting for! That's all!"

Vaclav shrugged, "Well, what about the girls in your village? Surely, you can find a nice girl there. You need to take the first step! She is not going to just fall in your lap."

Pavol grinned and looked at his friend. "I didn't know you were such an expert in these things! I'll think about it. I promise. Now, I have to go and catch the train to Bratislava – we are having a departmental meeting this afternoon. I'll come by to see you tomorrow."

The train pulled into Bratislava around two-thirty and he made his way to the geography department. As he walked down the hall, he spied two of his colleagues sitting in one of the offices.

"Ahoj! What's new?" Pavol stuck his head in the door greeting the two young men. The customary wine bottle and glasses sat in the middle of the table. They invited him to sit down with them and have a drink. One of them had a worried look on his face.

"What's the matter, Viliam?" Pavol asked as he plopped down on a chair, shaking his head when they offered him wine. Red wine triggered migraines.

"Well, I'll tell you. I have American relatives coming next month to visit our fair socialist republic, and my dear parents have asked me to escort them to the Tatra Mountains for two weeks. Can you imagine? I am trying to finish my dissertation, I have a wife with two small children, and I have to try and communicate with people in English or German for two entire weeks and keep them entertained! That means Helenka will be at home alone with our two boys. She is going to go crazy!"

Pavol's interest mounted as he listened to his friend talk. He felt a strange stirring inside to meet these Americans. A scheme to offer himself as an assistant tour guide started to form in his mind. But what would

Viliam think? He might think he was being too pushy. Besides, he couldn't even speak English, and his German was a little rusty.

"How many are coming?" he asked curiously.

"It's my mother's first cousin, his wife, and I think his daughter will be with them."

"How old is the daughter?"

"She's eighteen. I met her a couple of years ago. She seems very sweet, and they are nice people, but this is such a stressful time for me right now. My parents just don't understand how much work I have to do!"

Puzzled by this strong urge to offer his services, Pavol began inwardly arguing with himself. Why should he even care about these strangers from abroad? They're not his relatives! *You should go with him!* He forced himself to remain silent as Viliam continued to bemoan his fate.

Pavol glanced at his watch. "Well, *chlapsi,* it's time for our departmental meeting. We had better go. By the way, Vilo, I saw your father at breakfast this morning..."

For the next couple of weeks, Vaclav's words kept coming to mind. He had noticed the last couple of years that he was beginning to get strange looks from his parish priest and other people in the village. Most of his former classmates and colleagues were already married with small children, but he instinctively felt that he still had time. Even his first girlfriend from kindergarten, Maja, was married now and the mother of two little girls.

One Saturday afternoon when he was playing football with some of the younger boys from his village, one of his childhood friends stopped by on his way to the train. He was carrying two heavy suitcases and followed by his wife and sons.

"Palko, Palko, how long are you going to keep playing these games?" Milan said trying to look old and wise in his overcoat and hat, but came across as more tired and irritated. "When are you finally going to grow up?"

His two little children tugged at his hands and his wife impatiently tapped her foot. "Milan, we are going to miss the train!"

"I don't know!" Pavol yelled as he went running by chasing the ball. "I'm not in any hurry!"

His friend shook his head but could not help glancing back at Pavol as he triumphantly scored a goal. A flash of envy crossed the young man's face as he dutifully headed towards the train station with his wife and children in tow.

The following Sunday, Pavol was playing the organ in the village church. As he sang the psalm and pressed the yellowed keys, he was distracted by the girls sitting in the balcony. Usually only the men sat next to the organ, but a girl's choir had been formed and young, giggly girls had invaded the men's space. His eyes rested on one of the young ladies who seemed to be the leader of the group. She wasn't the prettiest girl he had ever seen but seemed to have a self-assurance about her that impressed him and was very attractive at the same time. He knew her family and was well aware that they were respected in the village. Everyone seemed to like Kristina. Vaclav's words were ringing in his head, so he decided to try and talk to her after the Mass. She seemed pleased when he approached her and gave him enough encouragement to ask her for a walk that afternoon.

After the litany prayers finished at three o'clock, Pavol and Kristina strolled across the bridge and along the river. He talked about music and books he had read; she listened respectfully. She seemed to have a natural intelligence, even though she was not a highly educated girl. She worked as an assistant bookkeeper with his sister-in-law at the brick factory. They spent a pleasant afternoon talking together, her smiles and attention giving him sufficient confidence to invite her to the movies that evening.

Over the next couple of weeks, he began coming home more frequently just to see and talk to her at church, prayer meetings, in the store, or at the culture house. He observed her closely during these encounters and was impressed with her pleasant demeanor; she seemed like a responsible hard-working girl. He noticed the other village boys seemed to admire her as well. She gave him a black and white photograph of herself, and he took it home hiding it in one of his Karl Maj books. At night, he would take it out and look at it before he went to bed.

"I think she is a good girl," he remarked one afternoon in his older brother's house as they sat drinking tea. His sister-in-law, Dalena, confirmed his thoughts and spoke highly of her as she served them apple strudel sprinkled with poppy seed.

"Who are you talking about?" Zuzana asked sharply coming into the kitchen.

"Kristina Palovic. You know which one she is! She works with me at the brick factory," Dalena said hurriedly running to fetch sugar from the pantry.

"Oh, the one with the big nose? Well, they all have big noses in that family. Palo, I have told you before! You should stay away from those people!" his mother said impatiently stirring her coffee.

161

"I like her nose! But why should I stay away, Mama? She goes to Mass every day! Everyone thinks highly of them," Pavol protested as he took a big bite of Dalena's strudel.

"Just because people go to church every day doesn't mean they are saints! Some of the villagers used to work for them. The Palovic people are... well, they are mean people! I knew her grandfather and his father. They'll smile sweetly at you as they pay only half the wage they promised!"

"Mama, you're being ridiculous! Everyone in the village respects them."

"Because they are rich and used to own a lot of property. Now they are the big bosses at the co-op," Zuzana said loudly waving her spoon at him. "Mark my words! Don't say I didn't tell you so. I've lived in this village a long time, and I know the people who live here. All that family thinks about is money. They are *lacomy*[74]! Her *babka*[75] used to pay their workers in milk and she was very careful not to give them one extra drop! They're rich peasants all right, but how did they get that way? By using people!" She paused for breath and then said quietly, "Besides, you have no business thinking about girls!"

Pavol's head snapped up at this last remark. His mother was now busy arguing with Dalena as she protested her mother-in-law's portrayal of the Palovic family. Zuzana didn't notice the grim expression on her son's face. He was starting to feel something for Kristina Palovic, more than he had felt for any other girl before. He shook his head and left the room. He was not going to listen to his mother's negative comments anymore.

"What do you think about Kristina Palovic, Janko?" Pavol asked his friend Jan Skrtel one Saturday evening as they watched American boxing on television. Jan was several years older than Pavol and a worker in the brick factory, but they had become friends through the new fellowship group that a young priest had formed in their village. The group would meet in various houses and learn more about their faith and a personal relationship with the Lord. Jan, who was previously known in the village as a thief and someone who dabbled in witchcraft, had undergone a true conversion experience; he was now actively involved with the fellowship group.

Jan leaned back on the settee and thought for a moment. "I think she would be a good choice. She works hard, goes to church every day, and I

---

74 Stingy
75 Grandmother

think you could come to a good understanding with her. I don't know though – I don't exactly trust her family even though they have a very good reputation, but I think she is a good girl…" His voice trailed off with a little uncertainty as the boxing on TV got more interesting. "You know, there's a dance going on tonight in the culture house – why don't you go and see if she's there? I'll walk over there with you when this is finished!"

Pavol thought for a minute and shrugged, "Why not?"

They watched the match on TV a little while longer and then got up to go. As they pulled on their jackets, Jan's wife looked at them questioningly. Her husband nodded knowingly at her and said, "I'll be back soon," as they walked out the door.

There was no moon out that night, and a smoky haze and the smell of burning coal hung in the air. Pavol could hear the music from a distance. As they approached the culture house, Pavol could see the light streaming from the windows and young people dancing. A few tough looking guys were hanging outside smoking and drinking. Pavol nodded at them as he and Jan went inside. He looked around the room searching for her face, but couldn't see her. Then he spied her laughing with two girls near the stage. He took a deep breath and walked over.

"*Nazdar!*" he said smiling at her.

"*Servus!*" she said shyly but a little flirtatiously. Her friends turned to hide their smiles.

"Shall we?" he asked holding out his hand.

She nodded and stood up. A traditional polka was playing and couples were flying around the room. She was light and kept good time to the music. Pavol felt a new energy coursing through his veins and they danced the next two dances plus one "modern" pop dance. When they finished, the bandleader beckoned for her to come on the stage and sing. Trying to catch her breath, she thanked Pavol and gave him a quick peck on the cheek. Feeling enormously pleased, he watched her sing and dance on the stage before going outside to cool off. Jan was leaning against the back wall smoking and observing the couples.

"Well, you two looked pretty good together out there!" Jan remarked as he puffed on his cigarette. His dark eyes glittered in the lamplight.

Pavol brushed a lock of hair out of his blue eyes and grinned. "Who knows, Jan, maybe she's the one…"

Jan threw his cigarette down on the ground and stamped on it. "I'm going home now. I'll see you tomorrow."

The rest of the evening, Pavol danced with various girls from his village, but he noticed Kristina smiling at him from across the room.

When the party was over, he walked over to her and asked if he could walk her home. She nodded and they went out in the dark street.

"Goodbye, Terka! Goodbye, Jozko!" she said smiling as she walked down the street with Pavol. As they walked further along, she took his arm and squeezed it slightly. His heart raced a little.

"Do you mind if we walk down this street before we go home? I am so hot from being in that stuffy room," she said as they walked along.

"Of course," Pavol said.

She smiled gratefully at him and he stood a little taller. There was no moon out that night and it was unusually dark, but a few stars peeked out from behind the clouds.

"See that old house over there? It belongs to my father. Do you want to see it? No one is living there now."

Pavol shrugged as she pushed open the gate. She opened the door and stepped inside the darkness.

"Kristina? It's too dark in here – we don't have a light," he said stepping hesitantly in the dark hallway. Suddenly he felt her lips pressed against his and her hands on his shoulders. Surprised, he hesitated but then firmly returned the kiss.

"I think we had better go," she whispered in his ear. Pavol was breathing heavily but nodded reluctantly as she pulled him out into the cool air. Pavol wiped his forehead and tried to compose himself.

"You don't have to walk me home from here," she said giggling. "I'll see you later!" With that she darted away down the street.

Pavol stared as she disappeared into the darkness. His heart was racing wildly and his blood was pumping. Taking a few deep breaths, he sprinted home. He felt like he could have run all the way to Nitra that night! The next morning at breakfast, his mother was looking at him as he delved into the breakfast she had prepared.

"You came home quite late last night," she remarked.

"Jan and I went to the party at the culture house. I stayed there 'til it finished – you know how long they go on!"

"Yes, I do," she said still staring at him. "Aren't you going back to Trnava this afternoon?"

"Yes, but I'll be back on Thursday. We are giving oral exams and then it's the summer break."

"Hmmm," she said turning away from the table. His father poked the fire with a stick.

Back in Trnava, Pavol tried to focus on his students and prepare exam questions, but his mind kept going back to Kristina and their evening together. He pulled out her picture and put it on his mirror. It was difficult to concentrate. He could hardly wait for the week to be over! Finally, he finished up the last oral exam, filed his report, and ran to the bus station. When he arrived home late that afternoon, he met Kristina's cousin waiting at the bus stop.

"Richo! *Ako sa maš?*"

"Dobre!" Richo smiled broadly, shaking Pavol's hand. "Where are you going?"

"Home! Where are you going?" Pavol replied.

"There's a dance in Hrusovany tonight. Lubinko and I are going to sell wine, so I am going over there to set it up. Are you coming? Kristina is going to be there," he said winking at Pavol.

A little surprised, Pavol smiled hesitantly and shrugged as they walked home together. Later that night, he washed himself by candlelight in the kitchen. Glancing at the mirror, he flexed his biceps. His muscles were looking more defined since he had started working out in the gym at school. He had a smaller body frame and knew he would never be like his hero Arnold Schwarzenegger, but he wanted to at least put on a little more weight. His mother sat at the table chatting about the latest news in the village. He slipped on his shirt and sprayed a little breath freshener in his mouth.

"Since when do you like going to all of these village parties?" Zuzana asked her youngest son suspiciously.

"You know I have always liked music and dancing! Just like you! Plus, I used to play in that band until you made me stop!"

"What kind of life is that going from place to place and staying up all hours of the night? With your migraines, you would have been dead in a year! Besides, you were too young for that sort of thing!"

"Apa and his brothers played in a band, didn't they?" he asked combing his hair carefully.

"Yes, they did…" her voice trailed off.

"I'll see you tomorrow. Don't wait up for me," he said kissing his mother on her soft white hair. She sighed as the door slammed.

Pavol arrived at the party and saw that it was in full swing. He talked to a few old friends and then went over to the table to buy a paper cup of wine. Richo served him and pointed to a corner of the room. Pavol looked in that direction and saw Kristina sitting and watching the dance. She seemed to be watching someone intently. Pavol swaggered over to her and sat down. He greeted her, but she didn't answer. Surprised, he asked her if she wanted to dance. Looking right and then left, she said yes but rather reluctantly. As they danced, he noticed she was pulling slightly from him. After they finished dancing, she ran to talk to some friends. Going back to Richo, he looked at him questioningly. Kristina's cousin just shrugged and whispered loudly, "*Ženy!*[76] Who can understand them?"

The rest of the evening, Pavol had the distinct impression that she was trying to avoid him. She danced and flirted with other boys, but when he called her to come over and sit by him at the table, she pretended not to hear and sat down by some other fellow. Hurt, he left the dance early.

"So how was the party?" his mother asked as she looked at him through her big magnifying reading glasses.

"Okay, I guess," Pavol answered without any enthusiasm.

"Was your Kristina there?"

"Yes," Pavol said quietly, but his mother saw the flash of pain in his eyes.

"*Syncek moj*, I told you to be careful! Didn't I tell you?"

Feeling depressed, he could not answer her and went to his room. He tried to read a little Jules Verne but just couldn't focus on the story. The rest of the day, he helped his mother wash the floors and beat the rugs outside. *Why was she acting like that? Wasn't she his girl?* He beat the rugs a little harder.

The next day after church, her behavior was different. She gave him sweet smiles and chatted happily with him. But after a few minutes, she ignored him again and flirted with some of the other boys in church. Richo came over and they stood together under the shade tree near the priest's house.

"I think she really likes you," Richo whispered to him confidentially. "She's just playing games to make you jealous."

"Well, it's working," Pavol said angrily as he watched her laughing with another boy. "Who is going to escort her to Milka's wedding this week? Milka invited me, but I didn't hear who was escorting the bridesmaids."

Richo looked a little uncomfortable and said, "Well, I think they paired her with Lubo."

Pavol stared at him. Lubo Bolchazy! Lubo was his classmate and the one boy who had attended Mass with him every day. He was a nice guy, but why him?

"Does he like her as well?" Pavol asked tensely.

---

76 Women!

"All the guys like her. She's a good catch and her family is pretty well off."

At that moment, one of the boys laughingly kissed Kristina. She playfully slapped his face. That did it. Pavol abruptly left his friend and walked over to Kristina.

"Can I talk to you for a moment?" he asked tensely. Something in his flashing eyes made the smile on her face disappear. She nodded hesitantly as Pavol grabbed her hand. As they walked down the street together towards her house, Pavol confronted her. "What's going on with you?"

Tossing her head and pulling her hand out of his grasp, she looked at him nonchalantly and said, "What are you talking about?"

"I mean, why did you ignore me at the party last night, and why are you going to the wedding with Lubo Bolchazy?"

"I don't know what you are talking about. And I can go to the wedding with anyone I like! You don't own me!" She stared at him as if he were from the moon.

"Fine. Go with him. See if I care." He turned abruptly to leave but suddenly spun around. "You know, Kristina, you are not who I thought you were – I thought you were a good and decent girl, but I see that I was wrong. You just like pulling boys along on a string! I am not going to be part of it!"

Kristina's face turned bright red and she angrily retorted, "I am good! You are the one who is crazy! Just leave me alone!" With that parting statement, she ran into the house.

Pavol stood at her gate for a moment and then walked quickly home without greeting anyone he met. He spent the rest of the day in his room and refused to come out even when his mother called him to lunch. His mind was in turmoil and total frustration. Grabbing his book, her picture fell out. Picking it up carefully, he stared at it. Her smile that he had admired so often seemed to be mocking him. Ripping the photo in half, he let it flutter to the floor.

"That's it! I've had enough!" he muttered aloud and ran out of the house.

Zuzana was washing dishes in the kitchen when she heard the door slam.

"Palko? Are you there?" No answer.

She pushed open the glass door to his room and walked in. Papers and books were strewn all over the table and his church clothes hung haphazardly on the back of the chair. As she began tidying up the mess, she noticed something else lying on the floor. Bending down, she picked up the two torn pieces of a photograph. She looked at them thoughtfully and then tossed them in a drawer.

"*Synchek moj!*[77] You just never listen," she murmured softly. "I may be old, but I know what I am talking about." Quietly shutting the door, she went back to work.

---

77 My dear son

The Scholarship

"When are they finally going to make the announcement?" Katie asked impatiently. She and two of her college friends sat nervously in the auditorium.

"I don't know. I wish they would hurry up," Ann Dee replied tapping her fingers on the armchair.

"You know they only give five scholarships out," James leaned over and whispered. "There are at least fifty people here hoping to get one of them."

"I'll bet you and Ann Dee get one," Katie said. "You guys are way ahead of me. I just finished my undergraduate degree this summer!"

"Shhh! He's coming to the podium!"

A tall portly man in a blue suit and red tie came to the microphone.

"As you know, we will be awarding five study abroad scholarships this morning to candidates that we believe will represent our country and its values as an ambassador for Rotary International. We have been interviewing highly qualified candidates all morning and have been impressed at the caliber of students who have applied. Scholarship applicants have listed five schools that they would be interested in attending the year after next. Today, the five scholarship recipients will find out where they will be studying in 1982-1983. You will be receiving the necessary information and instructions after the assembly. When you hear your name called out, please remain in the auditorium until our program concludes. Thank you for your interest in Rotary International, and we wish you all the best."

Katie, James, and Ann Dee sat holding hands as he began to read the names.

"First, Debra Smith... Congratulations! Debra will be studying in Paris, France!"

"Second, Ann Dee Johnson! Ann Dee is studying German and will travel to Bremerhafen, West Germany!"

Ann Dee squealed and jumped in her seat hugging James and Katie.

"John Amos has been chosen to study abroad in Buenos Aires, Argentina!"

Katie held her breath.

"Katherine Boszko will be studying in Heidelberg, West Germany!" Katie gasped and clasped her hands over her mouth.

"The last name to be called"—the man paused while James anxiously leaned forward—"is Madeline Carlyle who will be traveling all the way to Osaka, Japan!" James slumped down in his chair disappointed.

Katie and Ann Dee sat quietly not sure what to say to their friend. After a few minutes, Ann Dee broke the silence. "James, maybe your Fulbright will come through! Didn't you just apply for one?"

James brightened up a little and nodded. The auditorium emptied out and the scholarship recipients moved closer to the stage. They received their packets of information, a handshake of congratulations, and headed out towards the door.

"Shall we celebrate? Do you want to go to lunch?" Ann Dee asked as they walked through the student center.

"No, sorry. I've got to go home and get ready for class tomorrow. I'll see you later," Katie said.

She walked out of the Spanish style building and looked up at the blue sky. White, puffy clouds floated idyllically by. She raised her hands upward and smiled. As she walked across campus, the news began to sink in: she was going back to Europe! For a whole year! Since her first trip to Italy, she had been back twice – once with her family in 1978 and later with a student group from her university. Europe seemed to be pulling her with an irresistible force.

Since graduating with her high school class, she wasn't really sure what she wanted to study at the university. She had tried music studies for a while, but realized along the way that it was not what she really wanted to do.

"You know, Caroline, I just don't have any goals. I might drop out of school. What do you think?" she asked her roommate in despair one afternoon.

"No! No! Don't do that! Talk to the counselor and see what else you can major in," her roommate exclaimed. "Get your degree in something, but for heaven's sakes, don't drop out!"

Katie took her advice and made an appointment with the guidance counselor at Texas Tech.

"Well, let's see… So you don't want to study music anymore?" The blonde haired lady gave her a curious look.

"No, ma'am."

"You have enough hours in music theory, history, and performance for a minor – we just need to find a major. Hmmmm, let me see…"

The counselor studied her transcripts and started counting hours.

"Well, I see you have had quite a bit of German and have made all A's. If you really focus on that area, you could finish your degree in about three semesters!"

"Really?"

"What made you study so much German?"

"My relatives in Czechoslovakia speak a little German, and I wanted to be able to communicate with them. We visited last summer, and I could already converse with them," Katie said starting to feel excited.

"Oh, that's wonderful. Take a look at this. Here is a degree plan that you can work on for your bachelor's degree. Take it to the German department and talk to Dr. McClain. She can advise you further and approve the plan. Bring me her signature."

Katie thanked her and hurried over to the foreign languages department. Soon, it was all settled and she had a new major – German. She felt like she was finally on the right track. Music would always have a special place in her heart – nothing gave her more pleasure than composing her own little songs on the piano and guitar – but she knew there was another path she needed to explore; it was calling her. Foreign languages could open all kinds of doors to new adventures; how could you ever really get to know a country and its people if you did not speak their language?

For the next few semesters, Katie worked hard to catch up with the students in her class. Soon, she was at the top of her class and at the end of the year, she received many awards at the German Student Awards Banquet.

One day, her professor, Herr Alexander, brought her an application for the Rotary International Scholarship.

"All you are lacking with your language skills, Fraulein Boszko, is a chance to study abroad. This will help your comprehension and speaking abilities. I think this would be a good opportunity for you and more intense than our six week trip abroad," he advised her in his thick Viennese accent. "Dr. Goebel will write you a recommendation, and I will, of course, write you one as well. Let's try!"

Katie took the application and studied it for a few days. Finally, she got the courage to sit down and fill it out.

In the required essay, she talked about the need for American students to learn a foreign language and how important it is not to be isolated from other cultures. She was also convinced that it was imperative for children to learn a second language as soon as possible. Programs could be implemented into the elementary schools and young children could be bilingual. Herr Alexander had taught her how to teach young children with pictures, songs, and games, and she heartily agreed with him that other languages should be an integral part of a child's education. She also went on to mention how study abroad promotes understanding between countries and creates good relationships.

"Okay, Lord, it's in your hands," she said as she sealed the envelope.

Now, several months had gone by. In the meantime, she had gone on a short study abroad trip to Vienna with seven other students from the German department. Dr. Goebel, one of her professors, led the group, and they had a marvelous time studying at one of the Viennese academies, attending plays, touring the area, and practicing their German. One afternoon as she and her group munched on a delicious piece of Sachertorte at an outdoor café, Katie smiled recalling her first visit to Vienna five years ago. *Another dream come true,* she thought happily.

She earned her undergraduate degree at the end of that summer and immediately started her graduate studies in German. However, graduate school was much more difficult than her previous studies, and it was a struggle to keep up with the more experienced students in her class. They were fluent and used very sophisticated vocabulary. She had to fight overwhelming feelings of helplessness.

One day, she felt so frustrated and lost in her "Middle High German" class that she began to cry in the chairman's office. He patiently held out a box of tissue and listened to her complaints between sobs.

"Katie, you can do this. I know it's hard and you were thrown into a group that already has a couple of semesters under their belt. But just hang in there; it will get better," he said briskly.

Dr. Goebel was originally from northern Germany but had spent most of his growing-up years in the United States. Some of the students thought he was rather abrupt and brusque, but Katie knew him to be a very kind and caring man. She nodded between sobs and gathered up her books.

With a lot of prayer and determination, she managed to get through the next two semesters as well as teach her beginning undergraduate German classes. That had been the real surprise. She was shocked at how much she actually enjoyed teaching. The students responded enthusiastically to her lessons in class, and her other German professor, Herr Alexander, boosted her self-esteem.

"Some people are born to be teachers, Fraulein Boszko, and you are definitely one of them!"

Summer came and Katie packed her things to go home to Midland. She had a big trip in front of her. She felt a little nervous about being so far away from home for a whole year, but excitement took over her fears.

One evening, her best friend Phyllis came over and they sat at the kitchen table looking at old pictures from high school.

"Do you want a Diet Dr. Pepper?" Katie asked as she opened the refrigerator.

"Yeah, sure. Do you remember our choir trip to Kansas City?" Phyllis asked as she pointed to a picture.

"How could I forget? That's when I decided I was in love with Dan," Katie laughed pointing at a blonde, curly haired boy standing next to them on the bus.

"I liked him, too, but decided to let you have him, since you gave up John for me," Phyllis teased.

"Hey, what are friends for!" Katie said smiling sweetly and fluttering her eyelashes.

"He was a big guy in the band. Hey, I heard that trumpet players make excellent kissers. Is it true?"

"How should I know?" Katie looked at her slyly and then burst out laughing.

She and Phyllis had been friends since they were eleven years old and had gone through a lot together. Phyllis was the one person Katie felt she could trust.

"Are you excited about your trip this year? Oh my gosh, I would be so scared!" Phyllis said as she continued to flip the pages of the photo album.

Katie took a deep breath and said, "You know, every time I think about it, my stomach does flip flops. But yes, I am thrilled. I need to do this."

Phyllis nodded and then asked, "What about that guy in Lubbock? Jack? Are you and he still dating?"

Katie's smile faded a little and she shook her head. "No, that's over, thank God. Hey, why don't we go out in your Carmen Ghia and cruise around town like we used to? Does it still backfire every five minutes?"

"Of course! How else would my parents know what time I get home each night?" Phyllis said her eyes twinkling. "Daddy refuses to fix it!"

After a fun summer evening of driving around town, Katie plopped down on the floor of her room and picked up the photo album. One of the pictures that floated out was of Jack; they were posed together in the mountains near her sister's home. Her sister Margaret had married a man who reminded her of Willie Nelson, and they lived a very rustic life on a mesa in northern New Mexico.

Katie had spent a great deal of time last summer in those mountains as she had gone on a six-week archaeology dig to earn her last six hours of science credits.

"I need what?" Katie had almost yelled at the blonde-haired counselor who was looking very perturbed.

"You need six more hours to graduate! I don't know how we missed it, but that's what it is!"

"What the heck am I going to do? I'm supposed to start graduate school this fall!" Katie slumped down in the chair.

The graduate counselor began hastily flipping through the course catalogue. "Now just a moment, don't panic. Look! Here's an archaeology field trip that will give you the exact hours you need! Shall I register you?"

And that's how Katie found herself living in an army tent under the baking hot sun of New Mexico. Her dusty days were filled with sore muscles from the intense hiking and digging, but on the weekends she would drive up to Taos and visit her sister. There wasn't much luxury there. They didn't even have any running water or electricity, but they had a snug little outhouse with a great view of the Sangre de Cristo Mountains. And, what's more, you could wave at the occasional cars passing by on the road since there was no door to the outhouse. She and her sister spent several desert evenings sitting by the campfire and gazing up at the myriad of dazzling stars in the sky.

One weekend, her friend Jack drove all the way from Lubbock on his Harley Davidson to visit her there that summer. She couldn't help but like Jack with his dry sense of humor and cynical commentaries, but she could not ignore the fact that alarm bells went off inside when he moved in too close. They had met in a summer German class, and Jack had persistently asked her out on a daily basis until she finally said yes. He was a tall well-built man with sandy colored hair and a moustache. She had to admit it was fun riding on the back of his Harley; it felt so free as they toured down the highway through the cotton fields.

One afternoon, before she left on the study abroad program to Vienna, she was outside in the backyard petting her old dog Buster when she heard her sister calling, "Katie! Telephone!"

Katie opened the screened door, careful not to let Buster in, and picked up the receiver. "Hello?"

"Hey, it's me – Jack."

Katie could barely conceal her surprise. She hadn't talked to him since the semester had finished.

"I just called and wanted to tell you to watch out for those guys in Austria. I've heard about them... They're all losers, you know," he chuckled in his deep husky voice.

Katie laughed. "What's the matter, Jack? You worried I won't come back?"

"That's exactly what I am worried about! Just remember I'm waiting here for you!"

They talked a little longer and Katie's sister, who was visiting, looked at her curiously when she hung up the phone.

"Well? So who is he?"

"He's a guy I've gone out with a few times – nothing serious," Katie said trying to sound casual.

"Yeah? He has a great voice," Margaret nodded, smiling at her knowingly.

Katie just shrugged, but had to admit she was surprised he had called. Jack was the first American guy who seemed to put his cards on the table and tell her how much he liked her. Most guys she knew usually kept you guessing. Jack was the first one who made her feel special.

Well, she didn't meet "Mr. Right" while she was in Vienna or in New Mexico on the field trip, so they continued to see each other when she came back. But the relationship started to become strained. Different philosophies and attitudes began to surface.

"Katie, you know what the Bible says!" her mother confronted her one morning.

Katie rolled her eyes and moaned, "Oh, Mom, come on. It's not like that."

"It says that you cannot be unequally yoked! I know you like him; I like him, too! You both looked like you were made for each other when I saw you dancing together at the party, but I just don't think he's the one for you!"

Katie sighed. They had had this conversation before, and deep down, she knew her mother was right, but it was hard to let go. Whenever she tried to talk about her faith in God, Jack would change the subject. In addition, he had a few bad habits that she didn't want any part of. He had made promises to give them up, but then she would catch him sneaking behind her back. And then there was the matter of sex.

"Look, we love each other, right?" he said puffing on his cigarette as he pulled over.

"Yeah, I think so," Katie smiled, "but I'm still not hopping in the sack with you!"

"Why not?"

"Jack, I told you: I'm only giving it up to my husband. And you, darlin', well you're not my husband yet!"

"Hey, if I had the money and a job, I would propose right away!"

"Uh-huh, sure you would."

"I would, so what are you worried about?"

"I'm not worried! You are the one who's getting a little pushy here!"

"It's just I haven't, uh… practiced celibacy this long in quite a while."

"Poor baby."

Jack smoothed his moustache and looked slyly at her. "Well, maybe you wouldn't like sex anyway. Maybeee you're just too cold," he suggested waiting to see her reaction.

Katie glared at him and said, "You know what, Jack? When I get married, and I'm on my honeymoon, I'll send you a postcard that says, 'Dear Jack, It was great! Love, Katie'."

Jack smiled wryly and repeated, "It was great… Do you really think you are going to find someone who has waited – someone like you?"

Katie stopped smiling and looked at him intently. "Yes, I think it's possible."

John mounted onto his motorcycle and pulled on his gloves. Shaking his head, he looked at her with mock pity and said, "Sucker!"

Katie just shrugged as he drove off. As the semester went on, they saw less and less of each other. Sometimes she saw him laughing and flirting with some of the other girls in their class. She tried to focus on her studies and teaching, but she missed him. On the last day of class, she saw him outside the foreign language building smoking. He reminded her of James Dean in his jeans and leather jacket.

"Hey, Jack, I haven't seen you for a while!" she said coming up behind him.

Startled, he turned around and backed up a little. Surprised by his reaction, she tried to keep her composure, but she could not help noticing that he was still staring at her in shock.

Hurt, she turned to go, but suddenly coming to, he grabbed her by the hand and said, "Katie, wait... please. There's something I have got to tell you. Let's sit down."

They walked over to the concrete bench.

"You know, I have been thinking a lot about you this past semester. You might not believe this, but I almost drove down over Thanksgiving to ask you something." His voice trailed off a little.

"Ask me what?" Katie looked at him questioningly.

"Well, uh, to marry me."

Katie's mouth fell open.

Avoiding her eyes, he continued, "During the break, I got my bike ready and was all set to come down to Midland when, get this, I'm on my bike and was about to take off when I felt a – uh... a..."

He stopped unable to go on. His face was white as a sheet. Katie stared at him. Jack looked around to see if anyone was listening.

He leaned forward and hissed, "I felt a hand on my shoulder, stopping me! A real hand! Someone's hand was on my shoulder! Katie, there was no one in that garage! And that's not all! Then I heard a voice!"

"You heard a voice?" Katie asked incredulously.

"I swear to God, I heard a voice!" He sat there staring off into space.

"So," Katie prompted, "what did this 'voice' say?"

"It said, 'She's not for you.' I turned around, but there was nobody there. Look, you know I'm not making this up. You know I don't believe in that kind of stuff, but it's all true!"

Neither one of them said anything for a few minutes.

Katie broke the silence and mustered a smile. "Okay. Well, I guess that's what we both needed to hear." She stood up and picked up her books. "I'll see you around."

He pulled her gently back down on the bench and then said quietly, "Look, I would never want to admit this to anyone, but I know I am not good enough for you. I just want you to know, you are the best girl I have ever met." With one last earnest look and a kiss on the cheek, he quickly left.

She never saw Jack again. She felt sad but at the same time a distinct feeling of relief waved over her. She had been tempted to give in to his demands when they were dating, but she realized now it would not have worked out. Even her father told her once, "Katie, you know I like Jack, but he's, well, he's the kind of guy that I'm afraid will hurt you one day."

"I guess he was right," she said softly as she tossed Jack's picture back in the drawer. She looked out her window at the stars. *What next?*

Quiet for a few minutes, she began thinking about her upcoming year in Heidelberg. She opened the closet and started pulling clothes out to pack.

Trials

"Pan Professor! Dr. Toth is looking for you! Please, come with me!"

Lucia, the departmental secretary, was chasing Pavol down the hall. He turned around in surprise.

"Lucia, I can't! I am on my way to Trnava! I have a meeting later this morning!"

Lucia stopped and leaned against the wall panting, "He said it was urgent."

Pavol hesitated and then nodded reluctantly. Dr. Toth was the head of the department and his advisor. They used to be on good terms, but lately the older professor seemed displeased about something.

Pavol knocked tentatively on the door.

"*Pod Daly*[78]!"

Pavol walked in the office and stood hesitantly at the door.

"Come in! Come in! Shut the door and sit down!"

Obeying, Pavol sat on the edge of the wooden chair. Dr. Toth looked up at him and stared for a few minutes. Clearing his throat, he said brusquely, "I know about you, Tesar! You think you are fooling all of us, but we know about people like you!"

Pavol swallowed nervously and said nothing.

"Do you know that you are being watched? Observed? And I have reports here how you hop from church to church in this city, and even how you visit that so-called Catholic bishop in his apartment. Do you think they are so blind? The secret police has been conducting an investigation! They informed me that they even checked with the party officials in your village, but lucky for you, they gave you a good report."

Pavol felt some relief as he heard that last statement. He knew the communist officials in his village; they were people he had grown up with

---

78 Come in

and knew well. They didn't always agree with each other, but they would not betray their own villagers to outsiders.

Dr. Toth stood up and started pacing back and forth in his office. Stopping in front of Pavol, he attempted to muster a kindly voice.

"Look, Pavol, you can't seriously believe in religion and faith," he said putting his hand on his shoulder. "I used to be like you and even considered studying at the seminary. But I realized those people are just hypocrites – it's all a lie! Don't jeopardize your career over this!"

Pavol didn't look up at him. It was true that he had doubts about his faith and wondered sometimes if the communists were right, but something deep inside him screamed, 'No!' He just could not give it up. He looked up, his eyes flashing.

"So, what do you recommend?" he asked testing his boss to see what he would say.

Dr. Toth looked pleased and sat down behind his desk. Leaning forward on his elbows, he said, "I want you to start attending night school. I know you are busy doing research on your dissertation and teaching in Trnava, but this is critical. You haven't joined the party, and I am not telling you that you must, but you need to show your, well, your solidarity with the party and your willingness to learn more about Marx and Lenin's teachings on religion."

Pavol groaned inwardly but remained silent. Since he was a small child, Marx and Lenin had been pounded into his brain in the classroom. Every state holiday, they were forced to march through the streets and carry signs with pictures of Marx, Engels, and Lenin. The last few years, he had simply refused to go and waited until the parades were over. He had also been forced to sign a contract that he would teach in the spirit of Marx and Lenin, but he told himself that it meant nothing. Dr. Toth waited impatiently for his answer.

"Well?"

"All right. I agree. When does it start?"

Toth rubbed his hands in satisfaction and said, "Good, good! The first class is tomorrow evening. I'll tell Lucia to register you. Now run along. Don't you have a meeting to go to?"

Pavol nodded, flying out the door, barely catching the bus to Trnava. Sitting next to the window, he stared outside at the passing fields. He loved his country, the nature and culture, but the strain of keeping up appearances was beginning to wear him down. He was thirty years old, and he had already been teaching for a few years. He believed he had a calling to teach, and whenever he could, he quietly encouraged his students to explore their faith and ask questions about God.

However, he had been aware for quite some time that the secret police had been watching him. It was a feeling that had become part of his daily life. He had gotten in the habit of looking over his shoulder before he entered a church, and he often sensed he was being followed when he walked through the streets.

One night, in the dormitory, he had been awoken by a sharp knock on the door. It was the secret police. They began asking him questions under the pretense that something had been stolen on his floor, and they were trying to investigate. Pavol answered their questions and endured their intense piercing looks as they looked around his room while checking his identification papers. After a half an hour, they left. Feeling shaken, he could not sleep the rest of the night. The jolt of the bus pulling into the station shook him from his reverie. He ran to his office.

The next morning while sitting at breakfast with two of his students, Karol Lauko, the janitor, came up to the table and greeted him. Pavol shook his hands warmly. He had always liked Karol and appreciated his friendship.

"Pan Professor, I need your help," Karol said respectfully as he sat down on the edge of the chair.

"What is it, Pan Lauko?" Pavol asked munching on a *roshky*[79].

"Two of my wife's relatives from America are visiting us for a few days. Mrs. Holcik, the organist at our church, usually translates for us when they are here, but she has gone to visit her daughter in Nitra. Do you think you could help us while they are here? My son Viliam is also very busy in Bratislava and won't be home."

Pavol thought for a moment. He had started taking English classes in Bratislava the year before as well as a few lessons with Mrs. Holcik, who was a Slovak-American, but he didn't feel very confident about his English skills. Then suddenly he recalled how Viliam had been talking about these same American relatives a few years ago and how he had wanted to volunteer his services but felt too shy.

And now? Why not? Visitors from the West were a rare occurrence, and he had to admit he was curious.

"Well, I have to go back to Bratislava this afternoon, but I will be free on Wednesday if that would help you," Pavol replied.

Karol nodded looking pleased and ran back to his work.

---

79 A long hard roll

That evening in Trnava, Pavol strolled into the building where his Marxism/Leninism class was to be held. After walking up the dirty stairs, he located the room number and walked inside. He was surprised to see only a few students there. A woman and a man were seated at the desk. Pavol signed his name, took a seat and the lecture began. He had heard it all before and his mind drifted as the two instructors took turns discussing various topics. Suddenly he realized that the woman instructor was standing directly in front of him with her arms crossed in an authoritative manner.

"And what about you, Pan Professor? Do you believe in God?"

Pavol was startled by this unexpected question. He had never been so blatantly confronted with such a question and had always been able to sidestep the issue in the past. His mind began racing as he searched for a good answer. He knew if he said, 'Yes, I believe in God,' that it would all be over; he would lose his job and that would be the end of his career. However, if he lied and said, 'No, I don't believe in God,' he would be denying his own faith and conscience; he simply could not live with that.

"I believe... that..." he hesitated but then forged ahead, "this is a question that every person must, uh, independently decide for himself. In fact, there needs to be more freedom about this issue in our country!"

Silence reigned in the room. He could feel her eyes boring holes into his head. The woman turned sharply away and walked quickly back to her desk. She looked at the other instructor who in turn wrote something in a black notebook. She looked sharply at Pavol one more time, but continued teaching the class. Pavol traveled to Bratislava after it was finished and stayed that night with Jana and Albert in their flat.

"You said what?" Jana asked looking at him incredulously.

"I simply told them that it should be up to each person to decide if they believe or not. I didn't really tell them what I believe. I think it will be okay."

"Pavol, have you gone mad? They're going to fire you!"

"What did you expect me to say? To deny my beliefs?"

"No, of course not, but you know what you believe in your heart. It's none of their business. They don't have to know the truth."

Pavol slumped down in a chair and looked up in despair.

"Janka, I can't keep living like this. I can't keep up one face for work and another for my private life. This is killing me."

"You know, Pavol, I heard it's no different in the West. It's just a different kind of game we have to play here." She went quickly in the kitchen to prepare supper.

The next morning, Pavol headed to the geography department. As he passed Lucia's desk, she looked up at him sadly.

"He wants to see you," she said pointing her head at Toth's office. Pavol's heart began pounding as he walked towards the door. Before he could turn the handle, Toth opened the door and glared at him. He pointed at the chair in front of his desk. Wordlessly, Pavol went in and sat down. The door slammed shut.

Lucia poured herself a cup of coffee and sat down near the door. There was silence for a few minutes and then Toth barked loudly, "Tesar! What have you done?" Lucia almost spilled her coffee.

"Just go back and tell them that you were drunk! That's it! Just tell them you didn't mean it! Don't you understand what this means? You are out! Finished!"

Pavol sat silently for a moment and then mumbled, "I can't do that."

"Why the hell not?"

"That's the reason why! I don't want to go to hell!" he blurted out suddenly.

Toth's face turned red and he began to stomp his foot on the floor.

"That's it. It's over! I can't help you anymore. It's nothing personal; it's just business! Do you understand? I can't help you anymore! Now, get out of my sight!" He turned around and sat on the edge of his desk mopping his brow with a handkerchief.

Pavol walked slowly out of the building feeling dazed. The sky was dark and stormy. Rain began to pour, so he jumped quickly on a passing streetcar and rode around the city for hours just staring at the raindrops coursing down the smudged window. Suddenly the streetcar stopped, and the conductor stepped out for a break.

Pavol looked around and realized he was in Devin, a small town outside of Bratislava near the Austrian border. The rain had slowed to a drizzle, and the clouds were breaking up. He got out and began walking toward the river. He had been there many times before and knew the way well. As he climbed a hill where the ruins of an old fortress stood, he began taking deep breaths of air. Standing at the top of the hill, he looked out over the Danube basin where he could see Austria on the other side of the river. Barbed wire fences, dogs, guards and even boats patrolled the area. Pavol sat down in the long grass and stared. What was it like on the other side? How did it feel to be able to come and go whenever you pleased? What was it like to worship in freedom? Something brushed against his hand. Looking down, he noticed a beautiful butterfly perched on his knee.

"Now, where did you come from?"

The butterfly seemed to be waiting, its brilliant yellow wings slowly waving back and forth as it remained poised upon his pant leg.

"Can you fly to the other side, and let someone know I am here?" Pavol whispered hopefully.

A breeze began to blow and lifted the butterfly in the air. Pavol stood up and watched it flutter into the sky. Then, it took a westward turn and began flying across the Danube. With open mouth, Pavol watched it reach the other side and disappear into the meadows.

The sky began to take on a gold-reddish glow as the sun set in the West. Pavol felt strangely comforted. He brushed the wet grass off the seat of his pants and headed back to town.

***

Wednesday morning, Pavol traveled by bus to Trnava. As he strolled into the departmental office, the secretary handed him a letter. It was his letter of termination. They allowed him to continue for one more year, but then he was finished. Crumpling up the letter, he threw it in the basket.

"Is everything all right, Pan Professor?" the secretary asked in surprise.

"No, everything is not all right," he said grimly walking out the door.

It was a hot, muggy day and beads of sweat rolled down his forehead. He went to the nearest church and pushed the doors open. Cool, damp air touched his face. He went inside and knelt in front of the altar. The church was empty except for one *babka* who was lighting a candle under the Blessed Virgin's picture.

"It's not personal, he said! Just business! What kind of business is this? Dear God, why? Why does this have to happen to me?" he whispered tensely. "What am I going to do?" He continued praying intensely for several minutes. Afterwards, feeling exhausted, he sat back in the pew and stared up at the crucifix.

The next morning as he stepped out of his dorm room, Karol Lauko stopped him and asked, "You haven't forgotten about today, have you, Pan Professor?"

Pavol stared at him a moment and then realized what Karol was talking about. "No, no, of course not, Pan Lauko! What time shall I come?"

"Could you meet us at the museum at ten? My wife's relatives will be there. There are only two of them: Paula and Katerina. Janko didn't come this time."

Pavol nodded, "I'll be there, Karol. *Ne bojte sa*[80]!"

As he walked out of his room and headed towards the cafeteria, he felt a little lightheaded. The news from the day before had upset him and he had not been able to eat. He picked up a mug of cocoa and a roll. Sitting down, he became lost in his thoughts and was oblivious to anyone in the room.

Suddenly, he looked up at the clock and saw that it was almost ten! He wiped his mouth and quickly left the dining hall. It would take him about ten minutes to walk to the museum in the old part of the city.

Hurrying down the street, his heart began beating faster, but it wasn't just from the exercise. He could not explain it, but he felt that something momentous, something life-changing was about to happen. Strong waves of emotion began to wash over him, bewildering feelings. As he passed the soccer stadium, he slowed his pace down and began having an internal argument with himself.

He sensed that if he continued on his way, the direction of his life would shift. However, he also felt that he still had a choice and could turn back. His life would continue like it always had.

He paced back and forth in front of the stadium not sure what to do. He stopped abruptly. He had made his decision. Taking a deep breath, he resolutely headed towards the museum. No looking back.

---

80 Don't worry

Meeting New Friends

A pleasant summer breeze was blowing in front of the Trnava Museum as Katie sat perched on the brick wall. A large shade tree provided some relief from the sun. Her mother was standing on the sidewalk once again trying to explain something to Karol Lauko who smiled and nodded; however, it was obvious to Katie from the blank look on his face that he didn't understand a word in spite of her mother's frantic gesturing.

Marta had told her at breakfast that they had arranged for someone to come and help translate at the museum, so they were waiting in front of the historic building. Meanwhile, Katie's mind wandered back to the events of the last few days and how things had been working out so far.

Paula had accompanied her daughter to Germany to help her get settled for her "year abroad" on her Rotary Scholarship. It was a good excuse for a trip to Europe, and Katie was grateful to have her along for moral support. They had arrived on a rainy Sunday afternoon in late August and managed to find a hotel room in a small town outside of Heidelberg.

One of her colleagues, a former U.S. soldier, had given her the name of an American woman who might be able to help her find a room in that area. The German universities had dormitories, but space was limited, and most students had to find their own accommodations. Heidelberg was the headquarters for NATO, so Katie decided it might be better to live where there were fewer Americans; otherwise, she would be tempted to speak only English instead of practicing her German. As they settled into their hotel room and unpacked, Katie stared out the window at the Neckar River where long, flat barges transported various goods. Cold, gloomy weather created a depressing atmosphere. She wondered why on earth did everyone think that studying in Europe was so glamorous. The sky was a heavy gray, and people were not very friendly. However, there was no time to sit around and mope, so she went down the stairs and outside to the public phone booth on the corner. After carefully dialing the number on the sheet of paper, she waited nervously.

"Schalich hier!"

"Uh, hello, this is Katie Boszko. Hazel Johnson, your former student, gave me your phone number."

"Oh, hello, Katie! Yes, Hazel wrote me and said you were coming! Welcome to Germany!"

"Thank you!" Katie murmured, relieved to hear a friendly voice.

"Where are you staying?"

"My mother is here with me. We're in Neckargemünd at a hotel – *Zum Ritter*."

"Ah, yes, I know that place. Hazel said you needed to find more permanent accommodation for the school year, right?"

"Yes, that's right, and I am really not sure how to go about it."

"Look, there's a friend of ours that we play tennis with. He is renovating a room that he lets. Let me call him and see if we can work something out!"

"Oh, I really appreciate that!"

"In the meantime, why don't you and your mother join us for lunch today? Nothing fancy, of course, but it will give us a chance to meet!"

"We'd love to!"

"Fine. I'll send my husband Gunther around twelve o'clock to pick you up. He speaks English, but you speak German, of course?"

"Well, that's why I am here – to try and improve my speaking skills!"

"Good! We live up on the Dilsberg which is very near to Neckargemünd; look out your window and you can see it! Bye now!"

Katie hung up feeling a bit more optimistic. She looked in the direction of the river and saw the sun peeking out over the clouds. There it was – the Dilsberg! She could see an ancient edifice that looked like a fortress up on top of a distant hill.

Her mother, who loved meeting new people, heard the news with delight. They quickly dressed themselves and waited. Soon Katie opened the door to a tall, intellectual looking gentleman. After introductions, he ushered them to his Volvo and they were driving up a winding two-lane road with wild apple trees on either side. When they reached the top of the hill, they could see a large iron gate and an old stone wall surrounding a medieval village. Shops, bakeries, and outdoor cafes were busy with local inhabitants and tourists walking along the small, cobblestone streets. Katie and her mother were thoroughly enchanted.

Gunther pulled up in the driveway of a new two-story house built in the typical German white stucco style complete with flower boxes. A tall, athletic woman came out to meet them and introduced herself as Arlene. She immediately took them inside and out on the balcony where she had white asparagus, ham, salad, and fresh *broetchen*[81] waiting on the table. Pink, yellow, and lavender wildflowers adorned the vase in the middle of the setting.

"Please, please sit down! We are not very formal here!" Gunther said pleasantly.

During the course of the conversation, Katie and Paula discovered that Arlene's husband was actually born in Czechoslovakia, a "Sudetan Deutsch."

"Czechs forced the German inhabitants out of their country after the war, so my mother and I settled near here. I studied at the university and now I teach *Germanistik*[82]. So, if you need any help while you are here, please let me know!"

"Yes, please feel free to contact me, too, Katie," Arlene added as she handed her a piece of apple cake. "I know how it feels to be a 'foreign student.' I was one myself."

"Really?"

Arlene got up and showed her a picture of a young round-faced girl with bright eyes and brown hair.

"That's me when I first came to Heidelberg to study twenty years ago! I met Gunther and never went home to Boston."

Katie studied the picture and then handed it back to her smiling. "You remind me a little of someone I know."

Arlene winked at her and nodded cheerfully. After lunch, they strolled down to the town square where there was a small jazz festival going on. The sun peeked out from behind the clouds and the music was relaxing. Katie's mood definitely felt lighter.

By the end of the afternoon, Arlene had contacted her friend Herr Wagner and set up an appointment to view his rental room at ten the next morning.

"I'll take you there and introduce you to him. He is divorced and has a young boy who plays tennis with my son. He's very nice, so don't worry!"

---

81 German hard rolls – Kaiser rolls
82 German language and literature

Katie and Paula thanked Arlene profusely who brushed it off with a smile. That night, as they walked back up the stairs to their hotel room, Paula suddenly muttered, "Great – he's divorced! I hope he is not looking for a sweet young American girl!"

"What? Oh, Mom! Don't be ridiculous!"

The next morning, Arlene picked them up at the hotel and drove them a few blocks up through the *Altstadt*[83] of Neckargemuend.

"Here we are! I'll ring the bell."

The three women waited outside on the sidewalk. The streets were narrow, and people pushed past them on their way to the butcher shop next door. Katie could hear quick footsteps approaching the door. The heavy door creaked open and a handsome, tanned man dressed in tennis clothes greeted Arlene. She introduced Katie and her mother, and then led them through the arched hallway where metal mailboxes hung on the wall.

"The room is at the very top of the stairs. This is an old house, so I am afraid I don't have an elevator. I hope you don't mind walking up a couple of flights," he said with a slight German accent.

Katie could see her mother's face grimace a little as she had knee problems, but she quickly hid her dismay and bravely started walking up. They arrived at the top with Paula huffing and puffing. Herr Wagner opened the door to the room and Katie stepped inside. Her first impression charmed her. There was a small entryway that led to two rooms. The first room was a small makeshift kitchen. It had a built-in counter with a sink, a hot plate and a small refrigerator. The adjoining room was a little larger with a slanted roof. The walls were paneled in knotty pine, and there was a twin bed that doubled as a couch during the day. A large heater stood in the corner of the room. She was pleased with the coziness of the room. She peeked through the lace curtains at the people and street below.

"Oh, it's perfect!" she said turning around and clapping her hands.

"You don't think it's too small?" Arlene asked looking around a little anxiously.

"No, not at all – it's just right!" Katie exclaimed.

Arlene and Herr Wagner looked satisfied, and he promised to hold the room for her.

"I still have to put a few finishing touches on the ceiling and walls, but it should be ready by the middle of September. What is your full name, please?"

"Katherine Marie Boszko."

---

83 The Old City

"That sounds like a good Catholic name!" he said as he wrote it down in a little black notebook.

"Well, actually, I grew up in the Lutheran church," Katie replied.

"Oh, we have a Lutheran church just down the street. I was baptized there! Anyway, call me when you get back in September and we will arrange for you to move in," he said politely shaking their hands.

Herr Wagner's schedule fit exactly into Katie's plans since she and her mother were going to visit Czechoslovakia for several days as well as do a little sightseeing through Southern Germany and Austria. There was plenty of time before the semester began in October.

After Arlene dropped them off at their hotel, Paula looked at her daughter and hugged her.

"Isn't God good? We were praying he would prepare a place for you, and He did!"

Her daughter nodded happily and began to feel better. She tried not to worry about the future, but it was intimidating trying to communicate in another language and getting accustomed to a different culture.

The next day was very busy registering at the university and meeting her Rotary Advisor, Herr Dr. Mittler, who was the director of the library. He was also an acquaintance of the Schalichs and proved to be a very pleasant, friendly man who put her quickly at ease. She was a little nervous about speaking German with him and the other office clerks, but she was treated with patience and kindness. Katie found out where her classes would meet as well as the location of the *Mensa,* a student cafeteria in the middle of town where she could eat a hot meal for a very inexpensive price. Dr. Mittler also told her how she could use her student ID to get in for free to museums, theater performances, and concerts. Katie was surprised that the university buildings were scattered across the city of Heidelberg and did not have a centralized campus like the American universities.

"Ruprecht-Karl is one of the oldest universities in Europe! We have a reputation here to uphold. We take good care of our students!" he said reassuringly. Katie thanked him profusely and promised to contact him as soon as she returned from Czechoslovakia.

That night, she and her mother discussed their plans.

"I think we should rent a car and drive to Marta and Karol's. I checked with Daddy, and he thought it would be better than taking the train. We have too much luggage! Besides, we will be freer to explore. However, I want you to drive; you're younger and have better reflexes than I do."

"But Mama, I don't know how to drive standard shift! I've only driven automatic!"

"Don't worry! It's easy! I'll show you how…"

The next day, after much jerking and stalling, they made their way on the *Autobahn*[84] towards Austria. Katie couldn't suppress a smile as she saw how her mother pretended not to be nervous.

"What? Why are you grinning at me?" Paula asked with surprise.

"At least my driving is keeping you close to the Lord. You were practically on your knees when I merged onto the Autobahn in Wurzburg!"

Her mother laughed and muttered, "Well, you did give me a few more gray hairs…"

As they cruised along the German countryside, Paula suddenly spoke up. "You know, Katie, I had the most vivid dream last night."

Katie was used to listening to her mother's dreams and didn't treat them lightly. She turned the radio down.

"I dreamed I met a young man when we went to Czechoslovakia. He had long dark hair that curled at the ends and the most intense blue eyes. I was talking to him about the Lord and America. I think he is someone special that we are supposed to meet."

"Hmmm," her daughter replied thoughtfully as she admired the beautiful Alpine scenery.

By now, this was Katie's fourth visit to Czechoslovakia, and she knew the routine. They got their visas in Vienna, drove to the border, opened their suitcases for inspection, answered a few questions, exchanged their dollars for crowns, and drove on through the barbed wire and dogs towards Trnava. Visiting Karol and Marta was like coming home, and as usual, they were treated like royalty. She and her mother tried to help wash dishes, but Marta usually shooed them out of the kitchen.

However, there was something missing this visit. Aunt Josefina's chair stood empty at the end of the table. She had passed away shortly after their last visit. Marta shed tears every time she mentioned her mother, and Katie could see how they all missed their sweet *babka*.

While Marta did the dishes, she asked Paula to sing 'Alleluja' and she wept as she tried to harmonize with her. *"Das war das lieblingslied meiner Mutter*[85]," Marta sniffed as they finished singing.

---

84 German highway

85 That was my mother's favorite song

The next day, they saw Mrs. Holcik and hugged her warmly as she bustled into the hallway, taking her coat off with a flourish.

"Thank you, thank you my dears for the jello and coffee! And I love those Mounds candy bars! Coconut is my favorite! Now, tell me how is Johnny and your son Richard?" Her animated blue eyes sparkled.

Marta and Karol joined them at the table for coffee and cake while they talked.

"You know, I am leaving for Nitra tonight to visit my daughter. She just had another grandbaby and needs a little help with the children, but don't worry! Karol has found someone to help translate for you! He is a young professor at the college here. I think he is a friend of Viliam, too. They study together at the University in Bratislava."

"Does he speak English well?" Paula asked.

"Well, he speaks some, but he also speaks German, so he and Katie can figure it out, I think!" she said with a twinkle in her eye.

Marta began speaking in Slovak with Karol interjecting and laughing. Katie and Paula waited for Mrs. Holcik to translate.

"Marta says that this professor is single. They tried to fix him up with a girl here in town, but when he came to the house and saw her, he said, 'Ahoj, Sonya! How are you?' Turns out they were already acquainted from school in Bratislava. He's a very nice young man. Karol likes him immensely."

Katie listened attentively and felt a little jab of jealousy when she heard how they were trying to play matchmaker for this young professor.

"You don't even know him," she muttered to herself puzzled as the others continued talking. She went upstairs to unpack and soon forgot about the conversation, but was reminded the next day as she and her mother waited in front of the museum.

"Dobry Den, Pan Professor!" Karol turned abruptly around and started waving.

Katie looked up from her reverie and saw a young man coming down the street. She eased off the wall and moved closer to her mother. She watched with interest as he walked, half-strutting towards them. He had rather long dark, wavy hair and was dressed in a flannel shirt with black corduroy overalls. He smiled hesitantly as he approached and stopped to greet Karol who shook his hand vigorously.

"Pavol! Thank you for coming!"

As Karol introduced them, the young man shook Katie's hand and gazed for a moment into her eyes. She was struck by their intense blue color, but didn't have time to reflect on them as a sudden gust of wind blew up her skirt. Embarrassed, she quickly tried to hold her cotton print skirt down. Glancing over at the stranger, she saw him looking politely away, but the twinkle in his eye did not escape her. Katie turned around in embarrassment. He walked ahead of them towards the museum and her mother suddenly whispered in her ear, "That's him! That's the one I dreamed about!"

Katie looked at her mother with wide-eyes but didn't have time to reply as Pavol was holding the door open for them.

They spent a pleasant morning in the museum looking at old Slovak costumes, artifacts, and folk art. As they moved from room to room, Paula asked Pavol several questions and tried to talk to him, but he had to stop and ask her to speak a little more slowly so that he could understand. He spoke with a heavy accent, but he managed to express himself well as he answered their questions and talked about Slovak history. When he didn't know a word in English, he would look questioningly at Katie and say the word in German. She would then supply him with the English translation, so in this fashion, they got on quite well.

After a while Paula became interested in a display of ceramics, and Katie wandered into a room that was full of elegant clocks, some gilded in gold. She looked around in wonder at all the different sizes and designs. As she turned around to find the others, she was startled to see Pavol standing right behind her. He was looking at her intently and moved closer to her face. Katie started to step back but caught herself, remembering the cultural differences on space.

"Do you like clocks?" he asked finally, not knowing what else to say.

"Well, yes – I do like clocks!"

"Really?" he asked looking a little surprised.

"These are beautiful! I have never seen so many different kinds," Katie exclaimed, amused at his question. The clocks ticked noisily in the background.

Paula joined them at that point and they continued the tour. In one of the next rooms, there was a beautiful piano. Pavol asked her if she played and would she like to try this one.

"Is it all right?" she asked looking around.

Pavol shrugged nonchalantly and nodded.

Katie sat down at the piano, but couldn't recall any of the classical tunes she used to play, so she played a simple melody that she had composed herself. When she finished, she looked up and Pavol clapped approvingly. A little lady from the museum rushed over and started scolding Pavol; Katie guessed that she wasn't supposed to touch the piano, but Pavol just winked and smiled at Katie. *Hmmm, a rule-breaker*, thought Katie. *That's definitely not for me!*

Afterwards, they went outside where Karol Lauko was patiently waiting. Paula was already busy carrying out her mission work with Pavol and talking about the Lord. He listened intently trying to comprehend her rapid speech and idiomatic expressions.

Karol went up to him and said in Slovak, "Pan Professor, why don't you join us for supper this evening? I think my relatives would enjoy talking with you!"

Pavol accepted gratefully, and after shaking their hands goodbye, he said, "Mr. Lauko has invited me to visit you this evening, so I will see you again – very soon." With those parting words, he quickly disappeared around the corner.

"Isn't this amazing? I wonder what it's all about!" Paula took her daughter's arm as they began walking down the street.

Katie was silent, but wondered as well what God had in mind. That night, around six o'clock, the bell rang at the Lauko's house and Karol hurried out to answer it. He returned with the young professor. He had changed his clothes and had on a nice white, buttoned shirt and pair of black pants. Katie noticed his long, wavy hair seemed a little more carefully combed. He slipped his shoes off in the hall and put on the traditional *papuchky* that Karol offered him. She hid a smile as she looked at his shoes in the corner. They were red and pointy with very high heels. As Pavol approached her to shake her hand, she noticed that he was a little shorter. He seemed to realize it as well, but they soon forgot about height differences after they started talking and were seated around the dining room table. As usual, Marta outdid herself by cooking a wonderful supper; as usual, the food and wine flowed. Katie noticed Pavol did not drink much wine, mumbling something in Slovak about his stomach when Karol tried to pour him another glass.

Pavol had many questions for them about the United States, freedom of religion, and politics. He mentioned how difficult it was in his home country, and how hard it was to get news from the West. After supper, Marta urged Paula and Katie to sing. Paula loved singing gospel songs and her youngest daughter often joined her by singing harmony. Paula immediately began with one of her favorites. "Something beautiful, something good, all my confusion, He understood. All I had to offer Him was brokenness and strife, but he made something beautiful of my life…"

Katie joined in and the others listened attentively. When they finished, Pavol's eyes seemed to be misting up as he applauded. Then he cleared his throat and said rather reluctantly, "Well, it is getting late and I should be going home. When are you leaving for West Germany?" he said addressing the question to Katie.

Paula spoke up before Katie could answer. "We leave on Monday, Pavol. Will we see you again?"

"I hope so! I must go to my village to visit my parents tomorrow, but I will come back before you leave. It was very nice meeting you!" he said earnestly, shaking their hands. Then he thanked Marta and Karol in Slovak, and with one final wave, he left the house.

That night as Katie lay in her bed, she thought about that young man. He was handsome with very fine features – no doubt about that. He reminded her of the famous Russian ballet dancer Baryshnikov whom she had developed a big crush on after seeing him in the *Nutcracker*. However, Pavol was thin and had a worried expression on his face. He didn't look like he took very good care of himself. *Maybe his life is really difficult here,* she mused. Her mind wandered back to the pointy red shoes, but then she chided herself for noticing such details. Men in this part of the world didn't seem so concerned about looking tough or macho like the guys back home. He did have interesting eyes though... She drifted off to sleep.

The next day, Marta put on her best dress and shoes to take Paula and Katie to some of the tourist areas nearby. It wasn't easy for her to walk due to her excessive weight, but she managed. On Saturday, they visited the spa town of Piestany and tasted the sulphur water at the mineral baths. The water was poured into exquisitely designed cups that had a graceful spigot for drinking.

"Smells like rotten eggs," Katie said whispering to her mother.

"I guess it must be good for you then!" Paula said bravely as she took a sip. However, the look on her face said everything, and they both burst out laughing.

"*Trink! Trink! Das ist gesund!*"[86] Marta said urging them. They waited until she turned around and quickly poured their water out.

After leaving the spa, Marta sat down heavily on a park bench and indicated that she wanted to rest. Katie and Paula wandered down the street and peered in the shop windows. After a few minutes, Katie became aware that someone seemed to be following them through the streets.

---

86 Drink! Drink! That is healthy for you!

While they looked at Russian and Czech *Prim* watches as well as garnet jewelry in the window, a curly headed man with a dark mustache stood right by her elbow. He came so close that she could smell the garlic on his breath. Moving aside, she disappeared in the store. Later, she saw him again in a music shop when her mother was looking at a mandolin. Thinking it was just a coincidence, she didn't pay any attention to him.

After shopping for a couple of hours, she and Paula went back to where Marta was resting. They decided to go to a *Cukrovinky*[87]. There was a display of all kinds of cakes that were cut in long rectangular pieces: chocolate with layers of nuts and cream, punch cake with delicate pink icing, and chestnut cake with nougat. Katie was trying to make up her mind when she noticed the same curly headed man sitting down at a table next to theirs. He ordered a mineral water to drink and pretended to read his newspaper.

The salesgirl behind the counter looked questioningly at her, and Katie pointed at one of the chestnut cakes. As she brought her plate back to the table and sat down, Marta asked to see the items they had bought, so they began pulling them out of their bags. The man appeared to be listening to their conversation and was apparently curious about their new purchases. Even Marta and Paula began noticing his interest in them. Marta raised her eyebrows and slightly jerked her head in the direction of the door. Taking the hint, Paula and Katie gathered up their parcels and headed towards the exit.

As the ladies walked out of the café, the man immediately folded up his newspaper and paid his bill. He took note which way they turned as they walked out the door. Stepping outside in the street, he looked around. They were gone! He ran to the right and then back to the left, but they had disappeared. While he was standing on the corner scratching his head, a large bus rumbled by. Looking up, he saw them behind the bus windows. Marta was perspiring; she wasn't used to running like that. Katie waved at him as they drove past. He stared at the bus as it disappeared down the dusty road and then lit a short stubby cigarette. With a wave of resignation and disgust, he headed back to the police station.

On the bus route back to Trnava, they stopped in a town called Topolcany. Katie stepped off the bus to stretch and gazed at the hazy, blue mountains off on the horizon. The air had a clean, fresh scent and the

---

87 Sweets shop

streets and homes looked neat and well-kept. Marta leaned out the window and said, *"Das ist Pavol's Heimat! Sein Dorf ist nicht weit!"*[88]

Katie felt a strange stirring inside her stomach, and she looked more closely at the people passing by hoping she might catch a glimpse of Pavol's face in the crowd. With one last fleeting look around, she bordered the bus, and they headed back to Trnava.

Monday morning arrived, and Katie took her suitcases outside to load in the car. Marta and Karol were busy running back and forth from the kitchen to the dining room, bringing out fresh rolls, salami, cheese, and butter to the table. As she loaded her bags in the trunk, a wave of sadness hit her that she could not explain. She did not want to leave! The thought of being on her own with no family or friends around for support was beginning to overwhelm her. Her mother would be flying back to America soon, and then she would be really alone.

"Stop it!" she told herself angrily as a tear welled up in her eye. "You're acting like a baby!"

"Did you say something?" a voice asked from behind the wrought iron gate.

Katie whirled around and saw Pavol smiling at her through the bars.

"Oh, hello! Just a moment, let me go and get the key!" She quickly brushed the tear from her cheek and ran back up the stairs to the house, grabbing the big key off the nail. Feeling excited, she forced herself to walk more slowly, trying to appear cool and dignified. However, as she struggled to unlock the rusty gate, Pavol reached through the bars and quietly took the keys out of her hand.

"Perhaps you do not have keys like this in America," he said looking at her as he unlocked the massive gate.

"Well, they are a little different," she said, feeling a little confused. "Come on in, we are about to eat breakfast."

"I do not want to disturb you!"

"You are not disturbing us! Please come in!"

While they were eating breakfast, Viliam Lauko arrived with his brother Karol. Viliam seemed pleased to see his colleague Pavol and shook his hand warmly. He introduced him to his brother and then asked Katie and Paula how they liked Piestany as well as the other towns they had toured the past few days. While they were talking, Marta brought in a beautifully embroidered tablecloth and laid it on Katie's lap. She said something in Slovak to Pavol, which he translated for her.

---

88 This is Pavol's home! His village is not far!

"She wants you to have this and put it in your room in Germany so that you will feel more at home. She said to tell you that this is also your home, and you should come whenever you can. She is counting on Christmas!"

Katie looked up at Marta and couldn't hold back the tears any longer. A little sob escaped her mouth, and Marta gave her a long hug, stroking her curly hair saying, "*Moja mila! Nie plač! My sme Rodina!*"

"She said, don't cry, *Katka*. We are your family," Pavol translated gently.

After breakfast, everyone accompanied them outside and began their goodbyes. As Katie hugged and kissed her cousins goodbye, Pavol suddenly stepped in and pulled her close, kissing her soundly on each cheek.

"I will write you," he said softly in her ear. Surprised, she pulled back blushing a little. Viliam looked amused while his older brother Karol Jr. stared curiously at them both.

"*Dovidenia! Dovidenia!*" Marta said waving her handkerchief. Her husband opened the gate, and they carefully pulled out into the street. Katie could see them all in the rearview mirror still waving as she and her mother drove down the road.

"You know, that Pavol isn't bad looking," her mother remarked after a few minutes.

Katie was silent for a few moments and then suddenly blurted out, "Well, he better not be getting any ideas about me!"

Her mother looked at her with surprise and then muttered, "Hmmm, the fish is fighting the hook, I see."

"What?"

"Nothing, nothing. Just keep your eyes on the road!"

Heidelberg

It was October, and the hills were glowing with red and gold colors. Katie stared at their reflection in the Neckar River as the bus followed its winding road. She was starting to feel more comfortable in her new environment. Classes had started, and they were exactly what she needed to help her improve her German. At the beginning of the semester, the institute had given her a test to assess her language ability. She had passed the reading and writing sections but failed in the listening and oral parts. She wasn't used to poor results and felt rather humiliated, but they had placed her in the appropriate classes, so she began working hard to improve her language skills. In the morning she attended her reading and writing class, and afternoons concentrated on listening and speaking. The teachers in the *Sprachinstitütt* were from different German speaking communities: Austria, West Germany, East Germany, Poland, and Hungary. The Hungarian teacher noticed the spelling of her last name and smiled at her approvingly.

Her classmates, on the other hand, were from all over the world: Asia, North America, Europe, and Latin America. The cultural difference among the students was striking. There was the group of French students who had difficulties pronouncing the "H" sound; they looked fashionably pale smoking their long cigarettes outside the building during the breaks. American students clad in jeans and t-shirts greeted her and chatted in English when she passed them in the hall. She always said hi but didn't stop to talk. Instead, she sat down on the first day of school next to a shy looking girl with big dark eyes and dark skin. She was from Sri Lanka and her name was Samantha. They each tried to communicate a little in German and when it didn't come out just right, they both burst out laughing and all shyness disappeared. Georgina, from Mexico City, soon joined their group and the three of them began hanging out together after class to wander through the *Altstadt*, and munch on fresh chewy pretzels from the bakery, or drink tea at the outdoor cafes. Loneliness faded away, and it was good to find friends who were in the same boat.

She still saw Arlene and Gunther occasionally, but one German couple she had met through the Rotary Club took an avid interest in her. Their family name was Brandl, and they took it upon themselves to be her surrogate family while she lived in Neckargemuend. Every day she went to their home for lunch, so she received a great deal of conversational practice as well as instruction in whole foods and healthy living. Ursel, her adopted mother, ground her own grains every night with a hand-turned mill, soaked them in milk or water, and served them up for breakfast with yogurt or quark. She also used them to bake rich, chewy breads. Katie, an eager student of the culinary arts, paid close attention.

In addition to cooking and baking with the whole grains, she and Ursel would go for long walks through the beautiful woods near the Neckar River where they discussed every topic imaginable. Ursel would gently correct Katie's mistakes in German and patiently listen to the talkative American as she tried to express herself. The German woman seemed to enjoy listening to Katie's opinions and often laughed as they walked in the shady, cool woods.

The forest reminded Katie of the fairy tales she had read as a child. Little red and white mushrooms peeked out at the base of the trees and dark green moss carpeted the ground. She would not have been surprised if a little gnome or dwarf were to suddenly pop out from behind one of those colorful mushrooms.

One day when she came back home after class, she opened her mailbox and found a postcard. The picture had a Slovakian woman in folk costumes along with a scenic view of the mountains. Running up the stairs to her room, she dropped her things on the bed and sat down to read the card.

Dear Katie,
I am in Lehota picking up potatoes with my students. We call it Brigade. How do you like Germany?
Many greetings from Slovakia.
Pavol

Katie smiled, studying the postcard, and then pulled out some paper and a pen.

Dear Pavol,

Thank you for the beautiful postcard. What exactly is 'Brigade'? I am fine and living in Neckargemund. It is a very pretty little town on the Neckar River. I take the bus everyday into Heidelberg where I go to class. Heidelberg has a castle on the hill and there are many paths in the woods and hills where I can go walking. The people here have been very kind to me, and I eat my meals with one family almost every day. I think my German is getting better!

Take care,

Katie

Now where should I send it? He didn't give me an address, she thought as she studied the card. Pulling out her address book, she found Karol and Marta's address and wrote it on the envelope. Maybe Karol could give it to him at the dormitory, she mused.

That Sunday, she decided to go to church down the street. As she walked down the hill on the cobblestone street, she sighed. Sundays were very quiet in Germany – the shops were closed, and no one was out.

She missed the bustle of the workweek and felt a pang of homesickness. As she approached the Lutheran Church doors, she looked around. *Where is everybody,* she wondered. She tried to open the door, but it was locked. She checked the times of the services and then her watch. Puzzled, she leaned against the brick wall. Two elderly ladies came around the corner and slowly approached the door. They said something to her in a German dialect. She didn't understand and paused trying to figure out what they had said. They repeated their question, and Katie shyly answered in German, *"Entschuldigung, Ich bin Amerikanerin, und ich habe Sie nicht verstanden."*[89]

The two ladies looked at her in surprise and one of them repeated her question in *Hochdeutsch.* *"Gibt es Gottesdienst heute?"*[90]

"I am not sure," Katie replied in German. She looked at her watch and then gasped. "Oh, I forgot to change my watch. The time has changed!" She tried to explain to the German ladies about the time change and they began laughing. When they realized they had missed the church service, they began walking back up the street.

They asked Katie what in the world she was doing in their little town, and she explained that she was a student and renting a room from Herr

---

89 Excuse me. I am an American and didn't understand you.
90 High German; Is there a church service today?

Wagner. This seemed to please them, and they issued her an invitation to come visit them for tea that afternoon. Ready for some company, Katie readily agreed and got directions to their house. As she let herself into Herr Wagner's hallway, she noticed a letter in her mailbox.

"I guess I forgot to check the mail yesterday," she said in surprise as she opened the box. Thinking her parents had written, she stuck the letter in her purse and climbed the stairs.

"Okay, let's set these clocks," she said as she came in the room. After adjusting her watch and alarm clock, she poured herself a glass of juice and pulled out a slice of Ursel's dark whole grain bread.

"Mmmm, this bread is the best! I am going to be as fat as a pig when I go home," she said to no one in particular as she took a bite.

Pulling out the letter from her bag, she settled into the chair by the stove. She looked at the envelope and was surprised to see Slovak stamps. Her heart began to beat a little faster. Yes, it was true. Pavol had written.

Dear Katie,

I was very happy to get your letter. Karol brought it to me this morning at breakfast. I am very glad you are settled and enjoying your life in Germany. My classes are keeping me busy...

Katie continued reading as Pavol described his daily schedule. She sensed a little wistfulness in his writing. At the end of his letter he wrote, *"I am wishing you all the best. Please write me at this address. I hope we will meet again soon. May God walk over you! Pavol"*

Katie giggled as she read that last statement, but then she stopped and sighed. It would be nice to see him again. She folded the letter carefully and put it back in the envelope. Wiping the jam off her mouth, she stood up to prepare for her visit that afternoon.

***

"Now, this is my husband you see – he was an officer during World War II – and this is my brother who was killed when they bombed Berlin."

Katie was sitting in the elderly ladies' home looking at old photographs. At the appointed time, she had walked up the hill with a box of chocolates under her arm. She knew it was customary to bring flowers or candy when you visited, so she was glad she had an extra box in her cupboard since all the shops were closed. The two ladies she had met in the church greeted her at the door, introduced themselves formally as the Frau Muellers and whisked her into the cottage style house. It sat on top of a hill and was surrounded by a beautiful green garden. Flowers grew everywhere. The house was dark inside, but as her eyes adjusted to the dim light, she saw beautiful polished wood floors and elegant furniture. She soon learned that her new friends were sisters and lived together in this house with two more of their siblings.

"This house belonged to our parents and we have lived here all our lives. Herr Wagner's parents used to have a bakery, and we went there every day to buy our bread and rolls..." The eldest Frau Mueller chatted happily.

Katie listened politely and ate the apple cake they offered her, but her mind was on the letter she had received that day. After an hour, she stood up to leave and the ladies urged her to come again to see them. Patting her on the shoulder, they gave her some cake to take home.

October turned into November, and the days grew very short. Katie was surprised that it was getting dusky at four in the afternoon. Meanwhile, letters flew between Germany and Slovakia. In each new letter, Pavol became more expressive about his life, politics, and views of the world. In one of the letters, he wrote, "A friend told me that I should be careful what I write to you because all our mail is censored by the government. So, let me take this opportunity to greet the officer reading our mail! I hope you are enjoying reading about our personal business!" Katie smiled at Pavol's boldness, but sometimes she felt worried about him.

One day a letter came inviting her and her friends to visit over Christmas.

I know that Marta Laukova is expecting you at Christmas, and after the holiday, I would like to take you and your American friends to the mountains where we can ski or hike in the snow. Can you come?

Katie immediately called Ann Dee in Bremen.

"Hey, Ann Dee, how are you doing?"

"I'm okay. It's raining again and I'm feeling a little down, but that's the story of my life. So what's happening?"

"Listen, what are you doing over the Christmas holiday? Do you have plans?"

"Well, James and I were talking about traveling together, but nothing set in stone. What's up?"

Katie told her about Pavol's letter, and Ann Dee perked up with interest over the phone.

"That sounds really great! I would love to see Czechoslovakia – how cool would that be! Let me talk to James. He just got settled into his apartment in Kassel and doesn't have a phone yet, but I am going to see him this weekend. I'll call you Sunday night, okay?"

Katie hung up. As she got ready for bed, she opened her Bible and read a random verse from Isaiah. "Eye has not seen, nor ear heard, the things that God has prepared for them who love Him…"

Christmas

It was December and there was a light snow on the ground. After class, Katie and Samantha walked towards the Christmas market in Heidelberg. The smell of *Glühwein*[91] filled the air, and the streets were filled with decorated lighted booths. Vendors were busy selling delicious *Lebkuchen*[92] and wooden Christmas ornaments. Children squealed in delight as they clamored on the small choo-choo train that drove through the streets.

"Mmmm, this tastes so good," Katie said as she sipped the mulled wine. Samantha nodded and looked in wonder at the Christmas tree in front of the church.

"We don't really celebrate Christmas in Sri Lanka. I mean we do buy some presents for each other, but I don't really know what it is all about," she said.

They stopped at a booth where a gentleman was selling nativity scenes. Hand-carved wooden figurines were on display. He smiled at the girls and proudly showed them his handiwork. Katie pointed at the little infant in the manger.

"That's the baby Jesus, Samantha. We believe He is God's son, and that God sent Him to this world to save us."

"Save us from what?"

"Well, our sins." Katie stumbled over the word in German and looked helplessly at Samantha who had a puzzled expression on her face. "You know, sins are the bad things we do. If we believe in Jesus and tell him we are sorry, we are free again. He brings peace to our hearts."

Samantha suddenly smiled and nodded, "Oh, I think I understand. Then He is a very special child."

---

91 Hot red wine that has been spiced with cinnamon, cardamom, and nutmeg
92 Gingerbread cookies

"Yes, He is," Katie whispered. The little baby Jesus smiled at her. German Christmas carols floated down the street as the girls hurried to the town square to hear the choir sing.

"You know, I pray, too. I like to go to the temple in my country and pray; sometimes, I sit in the tree in our garden and talk to God." Samantha looked at her shyly as they stood listening to the choir.

"I knew we were soulmates!" Katie said throwing her arm around Samantha's shoulder.

"Adestes Fideles..." the choir sang joyfully.

"What are you going to do over the Christmas break, Katie?" Samantha asked with concern as they walked home. "You can come and stay with me and my cousins if you are here during the break."

"Thanks, Sam, but I am going to visit my relatives in Czechoslovakia. I'll be all right," Katie said.

"Are you going to visit someone else, too?" Samantha asked slyly.

"Hey!" Katie said pushing her playfully and bursting out laughing. "Well, maybe!"

That night she threw her backpack on the bed. Her heater was glowing, keeping her little room nice and toasty. Checking the list she had made, she assembled her clothes and items she wanted to pack for her trip to Czechoslovakia. She felt a thrill of excitement as she carefully packed her presents for everyone. She had bought several pairs of jeans for her many cousins, and an extra pair for Pavol. *I wonder if he has ever had a pair of jeans*, she mused. "But he'll look good in these Levis," she said aloud nodding her head with satisfaction, rolling the jeans into her backpack.

***

"Ann Dee! James! I'm over here!" Katie said waving to her friends as they got off the train in the Kölner train station. Ann Dee and James grinned and waved back when they saw her.

"Can you believe we are really here?" Ann Dee said giving her a hug. "The last time we saw each other was in Texas! Now we are in Europe together!"

"I know! It's amazing! Listen, we need to hurry and get over to the consulate as soon as possible. Sometimes it takes forever to get visas. Did you bring some passport photos?"

The rest of the morning was spent in the Czechoslovak embassy arranging their papers, but there was still a little time to sightsee in

Cologne that afternoon. That evening they headed back to the *Hauptbahnhof*[93] to wait for the *Franz Josef Express* train to Vienna. The train station was full of people traveling for the Christmas holidays. Everyone seemed to be in a good mood and chatted cheerfully in spite of the nippy air outside on the platform.

"How far is it to the border from Vienna?" James asked rubbing his gloved hands together. He had grown a beard while he was in Kassel, and his nose was red.

"It's not very far," Katie replied. "It only takes about an hour once we board the bus. The problem is on the border. It depends on how many people are there and how carefully they check everyone. That can go on quite a while."

James and Ann Dee looked at their friend with new respect. She had always seemed so quiet and reserved in class, but they were seeing a new side to her.

"How many times have you been there?" Ann Dee asked curiously.

Katie started counting her fingers trying to remember.

"Hmmm, I think this will be my fifth trip to see my relatives. I can't wait for you to meet everyone."

Ann Dee and James glanced at each other a little apprehensively.

"What's it like behind the Iron Curtain?" James asked.

Katie stared at them for a minute and then smiled. "It's like stepping back in time. You'll see."

The train came screeching up and they grabbed their suitcases and backpacks. In addition to the jeans, Katie's bags were loaded with coffee, chocolate and other things her relatives could not buy in the stores.

"Oh, man, these bags are so heavy," she groaned as she swung them up on the train.

Equally loaded, Ann Dee and James pushed ahead through the corridor.

"Here's our sleeping compartment," James said looking up at the number. The conductor handed them each a bundle containing sheets, blankets, and a pillow.

"I'm so glad we booked this for the night. I have got to stretch out to sleep," Ann Dee said.

"Not me," said James. "I can sleep anywhere."

"I'll bet you have!" Ann Dee said rolling her eyes at Katie.

---

93 Main train station

There were no signs of the bunk beds as they settled in the compartment with three other travelers. They spent the evening talking and reading their books while everyone shared snacks they had brought along. Around ten, one of the German women said, "*Gehen wir schlafen, nicht?*"[94]

Everyone agreed and began pulling out the bunk beds from the side of the walls. Soon there were three bunk beds on each side of the compartment.

"This is really cool," Ann Dee said admiringly as she claimed the bottom bunk.

"I get the top one," Katie sang out scrambling up the ladder and pulling out the neatly folded blanket. It wasn't long before they were snuggled under the covers and the swaying of the train lulled them to sleep. The young Americans were so tired they didn't even hear the train whistle blow as it pulled into various stations during the night.

"Passport! May I see your passport, please!"

Katie jumped up bumping her head on the ceiling. The lights had been turned on. Looking down and blinking in the bright lights, she saw a short man in a dark uniform peering up at her. She sleepily fumbled for her purse to look for her passport. After checking everyone's papers, the custom's officer touched his hat, turned off the lights, and left the compartment. Katie fell back asleep.

The train rumbled down the track as the sun began to peek over the snow-covered hills. Katie sleepily opened her eyes and stared at the ceiling. "Where am I?" she wondered as she sat up. The heating was on, and the train compartment was warm and cozy. Katie looked down from her bunk and saw her friends Ann Dee and James still sound asleep. Two other travelers in the compartment were also still dozing, but one of the young men was putting on his boots.

"*Guten Morgen! Guck mal,*" he said nodding at the window. "*Schnee! Ist das nicht wundervoll?*"[95]

Katie turned and blinked at the scene. Soft white snow covered the rolling Austrian landscape dotted with woods and meadows.

"Ohhh," she gasped. It looked like a Christmas card. They stared in silence for a few minutes, and then the young man stood up and went out to get his morning coffee. As the sliding door shut, Ann Dee yawned and asked, "Where are we?"

---

94 Shall we go to sleep?

95 Good morning! Just look! Snow! Isn't it wonderful?

"I'm not sure, but we must be getting closer to Vienna," Katie said feeling a thrill of delight.

Ann Dee poked James who smiled when he looked out the window.

"Wow! Have you ever seen so much snow?" he said rubbing his eyes.

"Not in Texas," Ann Dee said.

At precisely 6:05 the train pulled into the Westbahnhof in Vienna.

As the three American students stood on the icy platform shivering, Ann Dee and James looked at Katie expectantly.

"Well, the bus leaves for Bratislava at eight o'clock. Let's take the streetcar over there and get our tickets. Then we can eat some breakfast. Okay?" Katie was not used to ordering her friends around, but this was new territory for them.

They shrugged and pulled on their backpacks.

"Can I get coffee anywhere in this place?" Ann Dee said looking around as they walked through the train station. They saw workers already sitting around tables drinking beer with little glasses of schnaps.

"*Trink doch ein Bier!*"[96] James said teasingly. "That schnaps will get your blood circulating!"

"No, thanks," Ann Dee snapped feeling a little crabby so early in the morning.

"Look, there's a booth where they are selling coffee, rolls and hot chocolate. That should hold us until we can find something better," Katie said pointing.

"Now that's more like it!" Ann Dee said with satisfaction.

Vienna looked beautiful in its Christmas garb and snow. As they rode around the Ringstrasse on the streetcar, they could see the gothic towers of the Votiv Kirche behind the park trees.

"I love Vienna," Ann Dee whispered as they looked out the window. James and Katie nodded.

The bus was already there and people were lined up to get on. The three friends quickly bought their tickets and got in line.

"Well, there goes our big American breakfast," James said glumly.

"We just drank hot chocolate," Katie said trying to peek over the heads of the people in front of her. "If we lose our place in line, we might not get to sit down."

Soon they were tightly boarded on the bus. People pushed by loaded with shopping bags and suitcases. People were talking but they didn't hear much German. It was a mixture of Czech, Slovak, and Hungarian. James

---

96 Just drink a beer!

and Ann Dee looked amused as a lady with bright red hair asked them a question in Slovak. Ann Dee asked her, "Sprechen Sie Deutsch?" The lady just smiled and shook her head. Then she offered them some type of pastries. James nodded eagerly and turned to Katie. "How do you say 'thank you'?"

Katie smiled and said, "Dakujem."

James repeated the Slovak word carefully, and the woman smiled delightedly nodding, "Prosim!"

"Does that mean, 'you're welcome'?" Ann Dee whispered.

"Yup."

Ann Dee and James practiced those two words all the way to the border. As the bus slowed down and approached the Austrian border, everyone became quiet. The Austrian guards came quickly through and checked their passports. Then they waved the bus on through. Then they drove towards the Czechoslovakian border; guards in green woolen coats and German shepherds waited for them under the big red star. Ann Dee and James tried not to look anxious.

"Don't worry," Katie said pulling out her passport, "we'll be all right. You guys aren't trying to smuggle any drugs or guns, are you?"

Ann Dee and James just stared at her.

"I'm kidding, I'm kidding!" Katie said laughing at their expressions.

The bus driver stopped the bus and quickly got off to open the luggage compartment below. Two tall soldiers in fur hats boarded the bus. Their faces were unfriendly as they gazed at the passengers.

"Papiere! Ausweis!"

Everyone scrambled to pull out their papers and held them out towards the guards. They slowly walked down the narrow aisle looking carefully at each passport and then coolly staring at its owner in order to verify the passport's validity. Katie sighed in relief after they handed her back her passport.

"As if anyone would want to sneak in their country!" Ann Dee whispered in Katie's ear.

The guard looked sharply at Ann Dee, and she became silent. Then they stopped in front of James. After examining his papers, they started talking to each other. Motioning for him to follow, he had to get off the bus. They pointed at the luggage compartment, and he quickly grasped what they wanted. Looking a little nervous, he pulled the suitcase out and put it on the wooden table next to the bus. The guards nodded brusquely at him, so he quickly opened it. Soon all of James unmentionables, books, shoes, and clothes were all over the wooden table. They nodded at him and waved their hands for him to pack it up. Looking up at Ann Dee and Katie, he shrugged helplessly. After a few minutes, he managed to cram everything back into his bag and reboarded the bus.

"Cute Santa Claus boxers," Ann Dee whispered to him teasingly.

He punched her lightly in the arm. Other passengers were pulled off the bus and had to open their bags. After about an hour, the guards finally waved them through the border. Ann Dee and James stared as they passed more dogs and guards with automatic weapons. Then the bus entered "No Man's Land." Endless rows of barbed wire fences crisscrossed the countryside. No one said a word as they passed through this area, but there was an audible sigh of relief and a few nervous giggles as they entered the city of Bratislava. The streets and buildings looked dirty and gray, but Katie didn't care. She felt like she was almost home.

Her cousin Viliam met them at the bus station and after quick introductions helped them find the bus to Trnava. The bus was already crowded with people, but the door opened and they managed to wedge themselves and their bags in the standing room area.

"Whew, they don't use much deodorant here, do they?" Ann Dee said in dismay as her face was pushed into one woman's armpit.

"You should come in the summertime! This is nothing!" Katie replied trying not to knock over an elderly lady next to her.

After about an hour, Katie felt like she was going to faint if they didn't get some fresh air, but finally they arrived in Trnava. The town was quiet and the streets looked clean covered in fresh fallen snow. They walked silently down the dimly lit street as Vili led them towards his parent's home.

Karol and Marta greeted them joyfully and ushered them into the hallway taking their heavy coats and boots. Karol presented them with fancy new house shoes.

"Wow, you guys must really rate," Katie remarked carefully examining the oversized slippers. "The dog hasn't even chewed on these yet."

Ann Dee and James grinned as they shuffled into the parlor behind Marta. Soon they were dining on soup, sandwiches, chicken, and pickled salads. Marta had outdone herself again. Karol kept their glasses full of his homemade wine, and soon everyone was laughing and trying to communicate. After supper, Marta took them up to their rooms. She and Ann Dee shared a room and James was across the hall.

As they slipped into bed under the big feather comforters, Ann Dee smiled and squeezed Katie's hand. "Thank you for bringing us here. I think this is going to be fun!"

Katie smiled back, and soon both girls were fast asleep.

The next morning as they sat down to breakfast, the bell rang. Karol ran to the gate and came back with Pavol at his side. Katie's heart jumped when she saw him; his eyes sparkled as they shook hands. She introduced him to James and Ann Dee.

"Well, I am your tour guide today! I show you and your friends around the Stadt— uh, I mean town. What you think?"

They spent the rest of the day following Pavol through the old part of the city where they visited cathedrals and churches.

"This is John the Baptist Church," Pavol said as he ushered them inside. An exquisite painted altar made of wood adorned the entire wall.

"You know, Trnava used to be called 'Little Roma' because of the many cathedrals, churches, and seminaries we have here," Pavol said as they gazed up at the altar in admiration. "However, that all changed after the war."

He looked around a little nervously to see if anyone was listening. "The communists closed all of the seminaries here and are trying to turn these buildings into museums; they won't even allow us to celebrate Mass in this church anymore. It's very sad," he said bitterly.

Katie slipped her hand into the crook of Pavol's arm as they left the church. He stood a little straighter and smiled, obviously pleased.

"Let's go shopping," Ann Dee said. "Do they have any souvenir shops around here?"

"Just follow me," Pavol said as he headed down the street.

***

That evening after one of Marta's hearty suppers, Pavol stood slowly up to leave. Shaking hands with each one of them, he then said, "Well, I want to wish you a very happy Christmas!"

"Aren't you going to spend the holiday with us?" Katie asked trying to hide her disappointment. Looking pleasantly surprised by her question, he stared at her for a moment and then shook his head.

"No, I must spend Christmas Eve with my parents, but I will come on the second Christmas day to take you to my friend's home in Orava. It's near the Polish border and in the mountains. I think you will like it there."

Katie walked with him out to the gate. He seemed to be in a good mood and the usual melancholy expression on his face had been replaced with a peaceful, more optimistic look. He bent down to kiss her hand and then he was gone.

The next evening, the family gathered at Marta and Karol's home to celebrate Christmas Eve. Viliam, Ondrej, and Ondrej's little son took the three Americans to the Lutheran church for the Christmas Eve service. Mrs. Holcik waved at them from the organ where she was playing *Joy to the World*.

"She's playing that for us," Katie whispered to her American friends. They sat down quietly in the narrow, hard pews and looked around. There were no Christmas decorations adorning the church and the walls were bare. Most of the pews were empty and the only people in the church must have all been over seventy years old. Viliam and Ondrej looked a little uncomfortable, and little Ondrej pressed his body next to his father's. The pastor, a stern looking man, stood up to the pulpit and began to preach. He delivered the entire sermon with his eyes closed. Katie wondered if he might not get dizzy and fall down from his lofty position. They were all relieved when it was over, and they were able to get outside and breathe the fresh air.

"Kommen Sie! Kommen Sie!" Marta said waiting at the door as they carefully picked their way along the frozen sidewalk.

James, Ann Dee, and Katie gasped as they stepped into the parlor. A beautiful fir tree stood in the corner adorned with lighted candles and a smiling angel on top. Wrapped candies and cookies were the ornaments along with a few old-fashioned glass balls. Garlands of pine branches and pinecones adorned the walls while two tall red candles glowed on the beautifully decorated table. Marta had pulled out her finest dishes and crystal. She had outdone herself.

"Oh, it's so lovely!"

"Wow, look at this food!"

"Have you ever seen such a beautiful tree?"

Marta looked satisfied with the expressions on their faces, and soon they were happily eating the Christmas feast she had prepared. After the meal, Marta disappeared for a few minutes, and then came in the room with a magnificent looking chocolate torte; sparklers were on top of it spurting out their glowing embers. Marta's son lit more sparklers on the tree, and his little boy Ondrej ran around the table waving his handheld firework. Everyone applauded as Marta acknowledged their praise. Then she opened a special box and pulled out some long thin wafers. They were stamped with a beautiful Christmas designs of bells, ribbons, and pine branches.

"*Oplatky!*" she announced. Pulling out the paper-thin cookies, she poured a little honey on the plate, sliced a piece of garlic next to it, and handed it around.

James looked surprised and said, "Are we supposed to eat it?"

Katie shrugged and said, "It's a tradition on Christmas Eve! Try it – it's very good!"

Ann Dee nibbled at one corner of the delicately sweet wafer and said, "Mmmm, it's good! But I don't know about eating garlic with it!"

The rest of the evening was spent opening presents and savoring the luscious chocolate torte. The Americans enjoyed their host's response to their "presents from the West" and James and Ann Dee oohed and ahhed over the embroidered handwork and ceramics they received. Little Ondrej and his father put on the cowboy hats and toy gun sets from Texas demonstrating their rendition of a gunfight in front of the Christmas tree. After the shoot-out, little Ondrej was left standing – much to his delight.

Then it was time for music. First the Slovaks sang some of their traditional carols, and then the Americans sang theirs. The evening was full of music, laughter, good food, and presents.

"Katie, I will never forget this Christmas," Ann Dee said as they began clearing the table.

"Me neither," James agreed.

Early Sunday afternoon, Pavol arrived to take them to his village. He came in a small red Renault driven by his brother-in-law. Both men were dressed in pinstriped suits, and Katie could not help but think that they both looked like characters from the *Godfather*. Pavol's brother-in-law Jan, a short, stocky man, smiled and shook her hand warmly. They piled their backpacks in the trunk, and then said their thanks and goodbyes to the Lauko family. It was dark by the time they arrived in Pavol's village. They pulled up in front of a house, and Pavol's brother-in-law quickly and efficiently unloaded their things and carried them to the gate. Pavol rang the bell.

"You will be staying with my friend Janko tonight. We have a special event planned for you! Tomorrow we will take the train to Orava, but just rest and enjoy your visit here. Ah, here he is," Pavol said as his friend unlocked the gate.

"*Ahoj, Palko! Pekny Vitam!*" Pavol's village friends seemed delighted to meet real Americans, and treated their guests with great respect. As usual, they were first ushered to a large table where their hosts loaded their plates up with food.

***

"Wow, you don't starve here, do you?" James said admiring the big schnitzel on his plate.

"No, I don't think you have to worry about that," Katie said.

"We are having a little 'cabaret' in our cultural center tonight. I will be performing there with my friends, so I hope you will enjoy it," Pavol said as they finished eating. "Shall we go?"

As they walked out into the dark street, a tiny figure dressed in black was just passing by.

"Mama!" Pavol cried out. "Katie, James, Ann Dee – I want you to meet my mother."

Peering through the darkness, Katie held out her hand and felt someone give her a hearty handshake. She could barely see the little woman's face, but saw the flash of a big smile. As they walked together to the culture house, Pavol ran ahead to buy their tickets. He brushed aside their overtures to pay, handed them the tickets, and ushered them to their seats.

The auditorium was filled with people and curious eyes followed them as they sat down. Pavol's mother sat a row in front of them with her friends. She turned and looked at them as they settled down into their seats. Catching Katie's eye, her face spread again into that beautiful smile. Katie was struck by the way her tired, wrinkled face became so illuminated. Soon the lights dimmed, the curtains opened, and the performance began. They didn't understand much of the dialogue, but the skits and dancing were very entertaining. The audience roared in laughter as mock soldiers strutted across the stage barking and shouting orders at one another.

"They're really good," Ann Dee whispered after the village girls danced on stage in their embroidered folk costumes.

The last act came, and Pavol appeared with his guitar and stool. He was wearing what looked like cargo pants and a denim shirt. He sat down, adjusted his microphone, and introduced his song by John Lennon. Speaking in his own language, he waved his hand in their direction; Katie understood that he was dedicating the song to his American visitors. She felt her face grow hot as he began to sing:

"Woman I can hardly express

My mixed emotions at my thoughtlessness
After all I'm forever in your debt
And woman I will try to express
My inner feelings and thankfulness
For showing me the meaning of success
Ooh well well
Doo doo doo doo doo
Ooh well well
Doo doo doo doo doo..."

His voice was resonant and clear; Katie was surprised at how well he sang. She smiled a little as he rolled the Rs on some of his words, but decided that his version was just as good as John Lennon's – maybe even better! At the end of his performance, the audience cheered and applauded. As they filed out into the foyer, people passed them, smiled and shook their hands. Ann Dee and James looked a little overwhelmed by their welcoming, but tried to respond warmly. Pavol soon appeared.

"We are having a dancing party downstairs. I hope you will all join us. We have been performing this cabaret at several different villages, so we want to celebrate our closing night."

He took them down the stairs to a large open room. A band was assembled on a stage on one side of the room; the musicians were busy tuning up their instruments. Katie noticed that several of the cabaret performers were also playing instruments in the band. Soon the music began to play, and the Americans found themselves being whisked on the dance floor.

"I don't know how to polka!" Ann Dee whispered tersely as she was pulled to the dance floor.

"Just bounce to the music on each foot," James advised.

Katie danced with one young man after the other. She flashed her brightest smile and concentrated all her energy into the dancing, but after a while, she glanced over at the table and noticed Pavol sitting there looking rather pale and tired. She thanked her partner when the music ended and walked back to their table.

"Whew! I am out of breath," she said sitting down.

Pavol forced a smile and said, "Are you having fun?"

"Oh, this is great! Thank you for bringing us here! Everyone has been so nice to us."

Pavol smiled again this time with more warmth and handed her a paper cup full of homemade wine.

"You and your friends are very popular here. Our villagers haven't met many Americans, so you are a new, how do you say… uh, sensation!"

Katie noticed a girl sitting at the other end of the table staring curiously at her.

"Who is that?" Katie asked.

Pavol looked in the direction Katie nodded, and turned back.

"That's Anna," he said a little wearily. "I used to date her sister, and later, I dated her."

"Wow, you dated her sister?"

"It's not a smart thing to do. I would not advise it to anyone," he said rubbing his forehead.

"She looks like she is still interested," Katie said.

"She is just curious about you. All the boys like her; she has many to choose from," he said quickly. Then standing up rather abruptly, he bowed and offered her his hand. "Would you give me the honor?"

Katie took a sip of her drink and then stood up kicking off her high heels.

"Now, we are the same height!"

Pavol smiled appreciatively, and they whirled away. He was a good dancer, and Katie admired his sudden burst of energy. She felt like she was flying. *I never knew so many guys who liked to dance,* she thought to herself. The rest of the evening passed quickly.

Later that evening, Pavol walked them back to Janko's house and bid them goodnight.

"I will come for breakfast at six thirty. I am sorry we must get up so early, but the train leaves at seven forty-five. We will be traveling most of the day to reach Orava."

The next morning, Katie and Ann Dee came down the stairs. Janko's dark haired wife, Betka, met them at the door with a smile. "Dobre rano!"

Katie had heard that expression enough at Marta's to know it was 'good morning' in Slovak.

"Dobre rano!" she answered back. Betka looked delighted and beckoned for them to come in the parlor where she had the table set with rolls, pastries, and coffee.

"Oh, man, this looks so good," Ann Dee murmured. "I am going to gain so much weight over here!"

"I don't think so with all the walking we are doing! You'll burn it up."

James soon came in, and it wasn't long before Pavol joined them. After finishing their delicious breakfast, they bid their hosts goodbye, and Katie and Ann Dee pressed money into their hands. They protested a little,

217

but the Western currency was not unwelcome. The small party walked through the streets to the little village train station. Soon a big, green train rumbled on the tracks. They found seats and settled into a quarter where the seats faced each other with a table in between.

"Hey, we can play cards," James said pulling a pack out of his pocket. Soon they had a card game going and the hours quickly passed. After finishing, they sat back to rest. Katie and Ann Dee pulled magazines out of their bags and began to read about the latest European fashion. James took out a book in German by Heinrich Böll and began to read. Looking over Katie's shoulder, Pavol looked at the models in her Vogue magazine.

"Those girls are too, how do you say… they don't have enough meat on their bones!" Pavol exclaimed.

"You think these models are too skinny?" Katie asked in surprise.

"Look at them! They have legs like a chicken!"

"Oh, bless you, bless you!" Katie said squeezing his arm.

"What did I say?" Pavol said smiling in surprise.

"Everyone in my country is always trying to lose weight and look like these models," Katie explained. "The boys don't like us if we are too fat."

"They must be crazy," Pavol said staring thoughtfully at the pictures. "Who wants a girl who looks like a boy? They have no, no, no…" Struggling to find the right word, he used his hands to show the curves of a woman.

Suddenly, one elderly gentleman in their train compartment began to cough. He paused for a moment as if trying to control himself but then he burst out with a loud guffaw hacking and wheezing incessantly for the next several minutes. Pavol looked at his companions and decided to have some fun. Clasping his chest, he started to cough as well. Ann Dee and Katie looked at him aghast. James caught on to the joke and started his own fit of coughing. Soon both of the young men were choking, gasping, and hacking in their seats.

"Stop it, you two!" Ann Dee warned the boys as they began rolling in their seats laughing and coughing. The elderly gentleman behind them glared between outbursts of coughing. Katie slumped down in her seat and pulled her magazine closer to her face. Noticing her expression, the two young men slowly stopped the tirade. James winked at Pavol and nonchalantly went back to reading his book.

"Is anyone hungry?" Pavol said deciding it was time to change the mood of the moment. He pulled out a cloth bag. "Betka packed schnitzels, bread, and kolaches for us."

Soon the coughing episode was forgotten as they began eating their lunch. That afternoon, the train stopped and Pavol said, "Well, this is our stop – this is Orava! Let's go!"

Katie looked out the window. Tall majestic mountains towered over the forest of pine trees. A tall, stocky young man wearing a ski cap was waiting outside on the platform of the small train station. He smiled when he saw Pavol getting off the train.

"Stano! Ako sa mas?" Pavol said smiling broadly and shaking his friend's hand.

"Dobre! Dobre!" Stano answered. The tall young man turned and looked at the Americans.

"My name is Stanislav, but please call me Stan. My English is very bad, but I will try my best!"

Ann Dee and James assured him that his English was great. Stan grabbed their bags with his big muscular arms and said, "I don't have car, so we walk, but it's not far."

Katie looked around as Stan led them through his village called Tvrdosin. He laughed at their futile attempts to pronounce it correctly. The sidewalks were covered with fresh fallen snow, and Stan broke a path through the snowdrifts. Regal mountains looked benevolently down at them. Katie inhaled the clean crisp air fragrant with pine needles and the slight smell of wood smoke.

"You ski?" Stan asked looking at Ann Dee and James.

"Actually, no, I have never been skiing, have you?" Ann Dee looked at Katie and James.

Katie and James shrugged, shaking their heads.

"Not too much of that in Texas," Katie said apologetically.

"It's okay," Stan said. "We will plan schedule for next couple days. There is castle I would like you to see and old wooden village that shows how people live here long time ago. I think we will have much to do."

The next couple of days were spent touring the area and hiking in the mountains. They had fierce snowball fights and the girls were initiated into the culture by getting their faces washed in the snow. One afternoon they visited an ancient medieval castle on the side of a steep mountain. Instruments of torture were still on display in the dungeon, so Ann Dee pulled out her camera as Pavol hung his head in the stockade, James was chained to the wall, and Katie grimaced on the stretching machine. "Great shot!" she said holding a thumbs-up.

They moved ahead down the dark passage way. Katie stopped trying to adjust her eyes to the dim light.

"This place is pretty eerie," she whispered to no one in particular.

Suddenly she felt a kiss pressed upon her lips. Surprised, she didn't have time to react as the perpetrator moved quickly away. It happened again as they explored the beautiful model Slovak village that was set deep in the snowy woods. As they walked outside, Pavol suddenly pulled her behind a large fir tree in the center of the square, and secretly stole another kiss. Taken aback, she didn't protest, but she tried not to react too much. She felt her face growing hot. Looking around, she checked to see if her companions had noticed, but Stan was showing them the log homes and the little rooms. She moved closer to the group and tried to focus on the exhibit, trying not to think too much about what had just happened. Old black and white pictures displayed peasant women cooking over the open fire in the kitchen as well as men herding their sheep in the meadows. The snugness and coziness of their living quarters were similar to Stan's home.

Each day at noon, his mother prepared a hearty lunch for them consisting of steaming hot soups, chewy breads, and homemade sausage. Stan's parents quietly served the noisy Americans and took their meals in another room. Evenings were spent sitting around the kitchen table near the wood-burning stove. The young people talked about politics, the outside world, music, films, and their different experiences.

"Who's your favorite author?"

"I like Heinrich Böll, but James is into Günther Grass right now…"

The Americans' respect grew as they listened to the two young men's struggles to live under an oppressive government.

"We are in a prison camp here," Pavol said chewing on a piece of dark sourdough bread. "Vienna is only a short distance away from Bratislava, but I cannot even cross the border to go to the libraries to do research. It isn't normal."

Stan was quieter, but his face became tense as he told them how he was watched when he attended daily Mass.

"They told my parents that my scholarship would be taken away if I didn't stop attending church. So, I just started going to different churches in other towns. It cost me some money and time, but at least I was free to practice my faith."

Ann Dee, James, and Katie listened quietly thinking about the incredible differences between their lives and the lives of their new friends.

"Sometimes, I go into the fields and crouch down on the ground in the cornfields. Then, I look up to the sky and say, 'Ha! You cannot control me

220

now! You can't see me here with your red stars!'" Pavol's eyes were flashing defiantly. Stan nodded at him with a face full of empathy.

One evening, as they sat playing cards, Pavol walked in the kitchen brushing off the snow.

"I met an old friend and classmate today at the store. We studied together in Bratislava. He has invited me for supper at the ski lodge. Would any of you like to go with me?"

Ann Dee and James declined, using the snowstorm as an excuse to stay home, but Katie was silent. Pavol then looked at her tentatively, and she made her decision. She smiled up at him and said, "Yes, I'll go with you."

Stan glanced up from his cards and said, "Good. I stay here with guests." He then shot Katie a meaningful look.

"Let me just get my coat," Katie said blushing as she ran across the hall to the bedroom.

They walked silently through the quiet darkening streets towards the ski area. Katie's hands were cold, so she kept them in her pockets. Pavol had a big furry bear coat on, but he didn't have gloves or boots, so he periodically bent down to rub his hands in the snow.

"It's good for your blood circulation!" he said briskly rubbing his hands together.

"You are nuts!" Katie said.

"Nuts?"

"Crazy!"

"Yes, I am a little bit crazy! It's true!" he said starting to run towards a patch of ice on the streets.

"Whoo hoo!" he yelled skidding across the long sheet of ice.

"Come on, Katie, just try it!"

She could just make out the outline of his big furry coat and skinny legs in the distance. His stocking cap was bobbing on his head as he danced in the snow.

"I'll fall on my butt!" Katie protested.

"What is a butt?"

"Oh, never mind."

"I'll help you!" Pavol slid back across the ice and grabbed her arm. "Okay, start running!"

The two started floundering through the snow and then hit the ice. Katie felt herself falling backwards, but Pavol kept a tight grip on her arm. They slid across the ice and both tumbled down in the snow bank laughing.

"How did you like it?"

"G-g-great! I'm not used to this back home, so this is something new for me!"

"So in Texas, you just ride horses across the hot desert?" Pavol asked smiling as he helped her up.

"Well, sometimes, but Texas isn't just a big desert, you know, and believe it or not, not everyone is a cowboy there," Katie said brushing the snow off her coat. Her cheeks were flushed and her eyes sparkled.

"I used to read books by a German writer called Karl May. He wrote about the Llano Estacado and the Indians there, but I don't think he ever travelled there. He just wrote about it from some travel brochures he had while he sat in jail. I loved those books!" Pavol said. He couldn't help but admire the glow in her face.

"I go to school in the Llano Estacado – Texas Tech University in Lubbock! That's amazing you have heard of it!"

They continued talking as they approached the lit buildings of the resort. People dressed in colorful woolen jackets and sweaters strolled down the paths carrying skis. Pavol and Katie had to duck in order to avoid being sideswiped with their equipment.

He took her hand and led her to the restaurant area. It was a cozy eating area with knotty pine walls, hand carved tables, and red embroidered tablecloths. A short, balding young man stood up at one of the tables.

"Jaro! Tu sme!" Pavol said shaking his friend's hand. "This is my friend from America, Katie! Katie, this is Jaro!"

"Excuse me, I don't speak English well," stammered the young man blushing. "Ah, Sprechen Sie Deutsch?"

"Ja, ich spreche ein bisschen Deutsch – kein problem!" Katie said smiling in such a disarming way that it put the young Slovak man at ease.

Pavol took Katie's coat and she sat down. She looked quite pretty in her cream colored cable knit sweater. Her dark chestnut curls framed her face and her cheeks were flushed from their walk in the snow. Jaro looked at her with admiration and nodded at Pavol with newfound respect.

The rest of the evening was spent in pleasant conversation. Sometimes the two young men talked together in Slovak, and Katie listened silently to their dialogue, trying to pick out words she could understand. It was a pretty language, she decided. Sometimes, they would remember themselves, and the conversation became a mixture of English and German. Pavol looked respectfully at her as she conversed with his friend.

He thought to himself, *she is educated and has traveled. Certainly different from the girls in my village…*

After supper and bidding Jaro farewell, Katie and Pavol walked back through the woods to Stan's house. The moon was full and shining brightly, so the forest seemed to be glowing. Snow sparkled like sugar in the soft light. *It's like a wonderland*, she thought. Pavol took her hand and squeezed it tightly as if guessing her thoughts. They walked along quietly a few minutes when Pavol suddenly turned and looked at her squarely in the face. His young, handsome face looked hopeful and earnest as he began speaking.

"You know, Katie, I don't speak your language well, but I need to tell you something. I don't like to play games, and well, I don't think we have time for that."

Katie held her breath as she listened.

"You know that God and the church are first in my life. Everything else comes second, but when I met you for first time in Trnava, I thought maybe, perhaps, God is sending you – to me. I don't know if it is possible, but if he were to give you to me, that would be the greatest gift I have ever received."

Katie caught her breath. She had never met someone like this who wasn't afraid to lay his cards out on the table and open up his heart in such a straightforward manner. He looked at her a little anxiously as the snow fell on his face and eyelashes.

"I don't know what to say, but I feel the same way," she said shyly. His face took on a look of delight as he pulled her closer to him.

There was no more need for words. He kissed her lightly on the lips as he held her face in his hands. The moonlight danced as Katie felt herself engulfed in the big bear coat.

The rest of the evening seemed like a dream as they made their way back to Stan's house. As they walked into the kitchen, the card game was still going full speed, so no one even noticed them. Pavol pulled her back out into the hallway.

"Goodnight, Katka. I will see you in the morning." Kissing her once more, he started up the stairs whistling. Katie's head was whirling as she lay down upon her bed.

***

"Mom? It's me, Katie. I'm back in Germany." The twenty-three year old was in a phone booth at the post office in Heidelberg.

223

"Katie! Is that you? Oh, I'm so glad you got back safely. How was your Christmas?"

"I'm writing you a long letter with all the details, but let me tell you it was just great – really, really great."

"Yes? Tell me about it!"

"Well, first I met Ann Dee and James in Cologne – you know, we had to get our visas there…"

After several minutes of replying with an occasional 'uh-huh,' Paula Boszko hung up the phone and looked at her husband. He was sitting on the couch and reading his newspaper. He put it down and looked at her expectantly.

"Well, how's our girl?"

"Well, our girl is back home in Germany and she sounds pretty happy."

"What's she so happy about?"

"I think she's in love."

"In love! With whom?"

"A boy we met at the museum. Well, he's not a boy really, he's at least thirty years old…"

"Thirty years old! Are you serious?"

Paula just shrugged with a smile and went into the kitchen. John sat on the couch for a moment without moving. Then he groaned and went to get another beer out of the fridge.

Pavol burst into the kitchen startling his mother who was cooking soup on the stove. He pulled her into an impromptu dance around the kitchen.

"Prosim Ta'! Leave me be – daj mi pokoj!" She protested as he picked her up and gave her a big hug. She stepped back and adjusted her apron.

"What are you so happy about? Did you have such a good time on that trip of yours?"

Pavol sat down at the table and took a bite of a roshky. He just grinned. Zuzana stared at him for a few minutes then started with a sudden realization.

"It's that American girl! The tall one with the curly hair, isn't it?"

Pavol's eyes sparkled as he continued to chew. Zuzana sighed, turning back to her cooking.

New Adventures

It was difficult concentrating on her studies. After a semester of intensive German language classes, Katie had passed the German language test with flying colors and was now eligible to take regular classes at the university.

"You know, Katie, the beauty of the German system is that you can go to any class you want. If you want to go and observe a surgery in the department of medicine, you can do it. In fact, I would highly recommend you visiting as many different classes as possible," Dr. Mittler advised her as she sat in his office.

"I'll try. I am a little nervous about it all," Katie replied as she filled out the paperwork for the coming semester.

"You don't even have to attend class regularly like you do in America. You just need to pass the exams – that's all," he said checking her forms. "Anyway, you are not seeking a degree." He leaned forward and whispered, "I would advise you to travel. You are young! Enjoy yourself!"

Katie smiled and handed him the papers. The next few weeks were busy with new classes and professors. In her free time, she wrote letters to Pavol and her parents as well as visiting her friends the Brandls. In February, there was a long semester break, so she decided to meet her friend Ann Dee in Berlin and do some sightseeing. Then they planned to travel to Great Britain for the rest of the month.

"I've got it all planned," Ann Dee announced. Katie had traveled up to Bremen on the train and was sitting on Ann Dee's bed drinking hot tea.

"See this book?" She showed Katie a big paperback manual. "This has all the information we need – hostels, trains, buses, restaurants, tours – everything! I can't wait!"

"Yeah, it'll be great," Katie said trying to sound enthusiastic.

"What's the matter with you?" Ann Dee asked impatiently plopping down on the bed.

"Nothing, there's nothing wrong. Why do you ask?"

"You just don't seem like your cheery self," Ann Dee said looking at her suspiciously.

Katie mustered a smile and threw a pillow at her friend. "I'm fine, see? Let's go eat. I'm starving."

"Okay, but we have to talk about Berlin. The trip is next week!"

"Yeah, yeah, yeah," Katie said pushing her friend out the door.

A week later, Katie was sound asleep in her room in Neckargemünd. She opened her eyes that particular Monday morning and looked sleepily at her alarm clock.

"Oh, no!" she gasped grabbing the clock and shaking it. The alarm began to ring with a shrill tone.

"Why didn't you go off two hours ago?" she wailed as she threw on her clothes and ran down the stairs with her coat and backpack. After hailing a taxi, she fidgeted in the backseat until they arrived in Heidelberg. Quickly paying the young Turkish man, she flew around the corner to the bus stop where they were supposed to leave for Berlin. The street was deserted and no bus was in sight. As she stood looking around feeling a little bewildered, a woman walked out of the Tabak store and said matter-of-factly, *"Der Bus ist schon weg. Sie haben ihn verpasst."*[97]

Katie looked at her in surprise and then checked her watch. What was she thinking? Of course, it was already gone. She walked down the street and found a café. Slumping in the corner of the room, she ordered tea and started thinking. *What am I going to do? Should I use my Eurorail pass and go to Berlin?*

She pulled out her compact mirror and looked at her disheveled hair. Wiping a tear that squeezed itself out of her eye, she suddenly got an idea. *What if I go and see— No, that wouldn't be right. I can't do that... But he can't come and see you. You know, Iron Curtain and everything... So? It will look like I'm chasing him. Aren't you? Well, maybe...*

She paid the waitress and stood up to leave. She knew where she was headed. Several hours later, Katie was calling to Trnava from a payphone.

"Tante Marta, ich bin im Wien. Darf ich zu Euch kommen heute?"[98]

Soon she found herself again in familiar surroundings and sighed with relief as Marta led her to her room. She was afraid that she was imposing on her relatives, but they always made her feel welcome.

---

97 The bus is gone. You missed it.

98 Aunt Marta, I am in Vienna. Can I come to see you today?

Marta squeezed her arm and patted as she left her alone. Karol was dispatched to the dormitory, and it wasn't long before he returned with Pavol at his side.

"What are you doing here?" he asked with surprise and kissing her on both cheeks.

"I was supposed to go to Berlin, but I missed the bus. I thought I would spend my holiday here – with you?"

"Good, good," he said looking a little confused. "Well, let see... I have a class to teach this morning, but then I am free."

He left abruptly, and Katie began to wonder if she had made the right decision. Marta poured her some tea and pushed a plate of food in front of her. "Essen, Katka – essen!"

Early that afternoon, Pavol came back and asked her to go for a walk. She quickly grabbed her coat and scarf and they set off carefully on the icy sidewalk. They walked along in silence until Katie said, "Is everything all right? Are you angry that I came?"

"No, no," he said distractedly pulling her closer to him. "It's just that, well, I am having some problems at work and I just wasn't expecting you. That's all."

He looked at her thoughtfully. "No, I am glad you came. It's very good." He began telling her about his difficulties finishing his dissertation and his boss's daily persecution.

"So, they fired you? Because you said you believe in God?"

"I wasn't that brave. I just told them each person should make their own decision."

"Wow, I can't believe things like that really happen."

"Unfortunately, they do in this country. Listen, I have an idea. Would you like to go to a retreat with me? It's about two hours from here. We must travel by train and soon."

"Yes, but I'll have to ask Marta and Karol. They feel kind of responsible for me and I don't want to upset them," she answered quickly.

He smiled reassuringly. "I'll speak to them."

Pavol talked and talked to Mara and Karol as they listened quietly. Marta finally nodded but looked worriedly at Katie as she helped her on with her coat. "*Sei vorsichtig, Katka – sei vorsichtig.*"[99]

Katie felt happy as she set off with Pavol for the train station. She liked walking beside him, and he seemed to stand straighter with her on

---

99 Be careful, Katie – be careful.

his arm. They boarded the train and as they sat down, he pulled her close and asked, "*Neni Ti zima?*"

"What does that mean?" she asked surprised that he was speaking Slovak to her.

"Aren't you cold?" he said smugly squeezing her hand.

"Not with that big bear coat of yours," she said laughing.

"You need to learn Slovak now," he said nodding his head knowingly.

Katie smiled and they whispered to each other so the other passengers would not notice them speaking English.

Soon, the train was chugging through the mountains, and Katie could not see any houses in the dim moonlight. Finally, it came to a stop and Pavol stood up. "We are here!"

"Here? There's nothing here!" Katie said peering through the dirty window.

Without a word, Pavol grabbed her hand and escorted her out of the train. The train pulled away and the two young people were left standing in a snowy field beside the railroad tracks.

"There's not even a station here," Katie said looking around wonderingly. The stars were bright and twinkling above.

"I know," he said winking at her. "I hope you have thick boots on!"

He started trudging in the snow and looked back at her.

"Yes, I do, thank God. That's one thing I have learned since coming to Europe," Katie said following after him.

They walked several meters in the snow until they finally came to a quiet road that led up into the mountains. Pavol pointed up the climbing road, and Katie took a deep breath.

"Pavol, where are you taking me?"

"Are all American girls so… how do you say, impatient?"

"We just like to know where we are going!"

"You will see."

After walking for what seemed like miles to Katie, a small sleepy village appeared with a cloud of smoke hanging over the roofs. Katie could smell coal burning. As they walked through the quiet streets, they came to a very dark house. Pavol motioned for her to go through an iron gate and, quickly looking over his shoulder, he slipped in behind her. He rang the bell, and they waited. Soon the door slowly opened, and a young girl peered up at them.

"Ahoj! You made it." She grabbed their hands, pulling them inside.

Katie blinked in the bright lights of the warm hallway. The young girl took their coats and led them to another door. As she opened it, Katie's mouth fell open with surprise. At least seventy people were squeezed into a large living room. Most of the people were her age, but there were a few older adults standing in the corner and behind the chairs. A very tall young priest stood in the middle of the room and came rushing towards them with open arms. He embraced Pavol and then turned to meet Katie. He said in broken English, "I am Milan, hello!" and shook her hand warmly.

Pavol took her to a seat and the other ladies came up shyly to offer some refreshment. Katie politely declined and sat back to observe her surroundings. Milan returned to his post in the middle of the room and began talking passionately to the group. Pavol tried to translate what he was saying, but soon gave up as Milan began speaking more rapidly. Katie didn't need any translation and could see by the enraptured look in people's eyes that this man was their shepherd, and he was feeding his sheep with the word of God. A peace came over her, and before she knew it, she had dozed off.

Then she felt Pavol gently shaking her. "Katka, wake up! We are going to eat now."

Milan was standing in front of her smiling and offering to help her up. As the men and women cleared the room to bring in tables, Milan asked her questions through Pavol. He was delighted to hear that she was a believer and didn't seem to care that she wasn't Catholic.

"In my country now, it is only important that you believe," Pavol explained. "We have all come together as believers." As the evening came to a close, they sang songs and Katie recognized some of the tunes from her coffeehouse days when she gathered with other young Christians.

She began singing along in English, and both Milan and Pavol glanced at each other. Milan nodded in delight, and Pavol squeezed her hand. Milan then offered to drive them back to Trnava, but he had one request. Would the young American girl drive? He was feeling very sleepy.

Pavol was surprised by his question and turned towards her. "Do you drive?"

"Yes, I do," she said firmly.

"Are you sure?" he asked again worriedly.

"Don't worry! I have been driving since I was sixteen!"

"And how old are you now?"

"Just give me the keys."

As she started the car and blew on her hands, Pavol looked at her with newfound admiration.

"Do all of the women in your country know how to drive?" he asked as Milan settled into the front seat beside her.

"Yep, they do," she replied putting the car in first gear. "Here we go!"

There was a slight jerk, and the car pulled away from the house. Soon, Milan was snoring quietly and Pavol whispered in her ear, "So, how did you like it?"

"I was amazed that so many people were crowded into that living room. Where were all their cars parked?"

"Most of them walked there. We are very careful to arrive at different times so that the police do not notice. Then we keep the curtains drawn so the light will not shine on the streets."

"Incredible. Would you get in trouble for meeting like this?"

"Of course. We are not allowed to meet privately like this. We could all be arrested!"

"Arrested?" Katie gulped.

"Do not worry. You were perfectly safe," Pavol said patting her arm chuckling.

"So, where does Milan live? Does he live in Trnava?"

"No, he has a parish in Banska Bela, but he will probably sleep at the rectory tonight with the other priests. He was sent to Banska Bela because it is far away in the mountains, and the authorities think he will stay out of trouble up there."

"Does he?"

"No," Pavol replied his eyes twinkling.

Katie slept late the next morning, and Marta looked questioningly at her as she sat down at the table. Katie tried to explain what had happened the night before, and Marta listened with great interest.

In broken German, she said to Katie, "Pavol is a good man. I heard him speaking in front of the church; he preaches like a protestant! He encouraged those of us who still believe. But he needs to be more careful. They are watching him."

She got up with difficulty and patted Katie on the head. "He must be careful."

That afternoon, Pavol came again to the gate and rang the bell. This time, Katie did not have any difficulties with the key.

"How would you like to go to a ball?" he asked as they walked towards the house.

"A ball? Like Cinderella?" she asked in wonder.

"Who is Cinderella?"

"Never mind."

"What does 'never mind' mean?"

"It means, go on with what you were saying," Katie replied in exasperation.

"My oldest brother Martin is coming to pick us up. He is the director of the Agrokomplex in Nitra, and he has two tickets for the ball. Would you like to go?"

"Definitely!"

Pavol looked puzzled but took her answer as an affirmative one.

That evening he returned with flowers in his hands. Katie stood in the hallway in her beige chiffon dress and high-heeled sandals. Pavol looked at her in disbelief.

"You are going to freeze," he said looking her up and down.

"This is the only dress I have," Katie said looking down at her short-sleeved dress. It was rather thin and billowy.

"This is not Texas," he said staring at her sandals.

"I'll be fine," she said pulling on her coat and nudging him out the door as she waved goodbye to Marta and Karol. As they trudged and sloshed through the snow towards Pavol's dorm, Katie began wondering if this might have been a terrible mistake. While she was contemplating how very foolish and cold she felt, a black car suddenly pulled up beside them.

"Ah, this is my brother," Pavol said. A driver stepped out of the car and opened the back door. A middle-aged man also got out of the car and stared at them both unsmilingly.

"Martin," Pavol said shaking his brother's hand. He introduced Katie, but Martin only stared at her intensely and did not say one word. He got silently back in the car and waited for them to get in.

After a few moments, Katie whispered to Pavol, "What does your brother do again?"

"My brother is the main director of the Agrokomplex in Nitra," Pavol said quietly to Katie as they squeezed in the back of the car.

"What is an 'Agrokomplex'?" she asked trying to straighten out her coat.

"It's a huge agricultural compound. He oversees the livestock production, dairy production, wine production, and even horses," Pavol said with a little pride in his voice. "He flies to Moscow periodically and meets with all of the big politicians there like Brezhnev and Gromyko."

Katie looked in silence at Pavol's brother. His face was pleasant but expressionless. She turned towards Pavol. "Wow, that's very impressive."

"Well, the only problem is that he is also a member of the communist party, so he doesn't go to church anymore," he said sadly.

"He's a communist? Your brother is a communist?" Katie asked in surprise.

"Yes. Why are you so surprised? There are many communists here. Even your cousin Karol is a member of the party. How do you think people survive here?"

"But you are not," she said defensively.

"No, I'm not, but I have a lot of troubles for that reason."

They sat in silence the rest of the trip. As they entered the building where the dance was, Pavol's brother looked at her sternly.

"He thinks you are an American spy," Pavol whispered in her ear, gleefully rubbing his hands together.

"What? A spy? Me?"

Pavol pulled her into the ballroom where the air was filled with chatter and fragrant dishes set on the table. They joined Martin at his special table and ate their meal in silence, but soon the band started playing and couples started onto the floor. Women stared at Katie in her sandals and summer dress, but before she could feel too self-conscious, Pavol grabbed her hand and led her to the dance floor. She soon forgot their looks and stares as everything else faded away. They danced all evening, almost furiously, until they collapsed exhausted on the settee in the hall.

"Have you had enough?" Pavol said as he laid his head on the back of the couch.

"I think so. I am getting pretty tired. What time is it?" she asked wearily leaning her head against the wall and wiping a bead of sweat off her forehead.

"It's about 2 a.m."

"Oh, Pavol, Marta and Karol are going to be freaking out that I'm not home yet!"

"Freaking out?"

"Worried – you know, scared that something bad happened."

"I talked to them. I told them you would spend the night at my brother's house tonight."

Katie didn't really relish the idea of going home with an unfriendly communist director who thought she was a spy, but she was too tired to protest. They drove silently again to Pavol's village where Pavol's brother had a large comfortable looking house. As Martin reluctantly opened the heavy iron gate to his garden, a large dog began barking and growling.

"*Ticho! Ticho!*"[100] Martin admonished as a big German Shepherd appeared around the corner. Katie started back in fear, and Pavol didn't look too comfortable himself. His brother led them up the stairs and a short, strong-looking woman with piercing eyes appeared. She glanced sharply at Pavol and Katie, and then took Katie quickly up another flight of stairs to a clean spacious bedroom. She pulled back the comforter and motioned towards the bed. Pavol left quickly after saying goodnight, and Katie sunk wearily on the bed. Without undressing, she soon fell asleep with her head on the soft feather pillow.

Bam, bam!

Katie opened her eyes wearily. Someone was knocking on the door. She could see a shadow through the frosted glass on the door.

"Katka, wake up!"

She heard Pavol's voice and went to the door. He was grinning broadly and said, "Come on! We have to eat breakfast. I must take you home!"

Katie picked up her purse and took a fleeting glance around the room. As she walked down the stairs, Pavol's sister-in-law appeared with a towel and soap. She gestured towards the bathroom. Taking the hint, she went in to wash her face and hands and smooth down her unruly curls.

As she sat down to a steaming breakfast of coffee, salami, and rolls, Pavol continued grinning at her. Not yet in the mood for jokes, Katie glanced up at him and said, "So, what are you laughing at now?"

He took another bite of his roll and said, "You."

"Me?"

"Yes, when I came to wake you up this morning, I heard someone in your room snoring like a train," he burst out laughing. "I don't know if I can be with a woman who snores like that. I almost turned around and ran away!"

"Well, maybe you should," Katie said wryly as she buttered her roll.

"Do all American women snore?"

"Yes, we all drive cars, ride horses, ask a lot of questions, and snore like trains. So just shut up," she said as she took a bite of her food.

Feeling refreshed after breakfast, they said their thanks to Pavol's sister-in-law Dalena and went outside to meet Martin again who was going to drive them himself in his white Skoda. He dropped them off at Pavol's dormitory, and Pavol walked with Katie to Marta and Karol's

---

100 Quiet! Quiet!

house. After a few moments of silence, Pavol suddenly asked her, "Katy, have you ever slept with anyone?"

Katie looked at him in surprise. "What are you talking about?"

"You know, sleep with a man… you know," he said anxiously.

"You mean… sex?"

"Shhh! Yes, that's what I mean."

"No."

"Really?"

"No, really."

This ended the conversation for a while and they talked about the party, his brother, and other things. After they arrived at Marta and Karol's home, he followed her to her room upstairs.

"Katie, sorry, but please tell me the truth. You have never slept with another man?"

"Look, Pavol, I told you – no!"

This conversation repeated itself several times during the course of the day until Katie feeling exasperated turned to him and said jokingly, "Okay, okay – I slept with a man once." It had never happened, but she was hoping this would shut him up.

Looking crestfallen, Pavol stood there silently. Then he said, "Well, I have to go. I have some work to do."

"But I am leaving tomorrow!"

"I know, but… I must go."

He looked at her sadly, kissed her once on the cheek, and left. Katie felt strangely empty inside. Marta looked at her curiously as she came down the stairs and asked, "Pavol? Go?"

"Ja, ja," Katie replied blankly. "He left."

Katie's Finnish Angel

The English Channel was choppy as the sturdy ferry bounced across the waves. Katie peered through the spray-misted window at the billowing clouds and clear blue sky. Sometimes faster ships hydroplaned by, leaving the ferry in their wake; however, she didn't mind going a little slower. She needed time to think. She had not heard from Pavol since she had gotten back to Germany, and she felt a little uneasy about the way things had ended. She thought back to Christmas and the beautiful evening they had outside in the snow in Orava. *Was he just feeding me a bunch of lines,* she wondered. Sighing she turned back to Ann Dee who was studying her *Let's Go Europe* manual.

"What's wrong?" Ann Dee asked without looking up.

"Nothing," Katie said sitting up straight and looking out over the empty dining hall on board the boat. Normally, the hall would be full of tourists, but this time of year, she and Ann Dee were almost the only passengers on the boat. The waiter brought over their fish and chips, and Ann Dee put down her book.

"You're still thinking about him, aren't you?" Ann Dee said as she dribbled vinegar across her plate.

"I just can't help thinking about him," Katie admitted moodily. "I don't know what I did or said wrong."

"Just forget him now," Ann Dee said impatiently. "We have to decide what we are going to do when we get to Dover. Do you want to go straight to London or head somewhere else? This is our break between semesters, and we have to make the most of it!"

Katie absentmindedly twirled her fries in the ketchup on her plate.

"Katie! Are you listening to me?" Ann Dee exclaimed.

"Yeah, yeah! London! Sounds perfect!"

Ann Dee sat back and looked at her through narrow eyes. Grumbling something about being stood up in Berlin, she turned back to her book as Katie's eyes wandered back to the window.

The next several days were spent touring the English countryside. The many flocks of sheep grazing in lush green pastures looked exactly like scenes out of a Jane Austen novel. Normally, this would have delighted her, but she felt distracted and couldn't focus on her surroundings.

Then they traveled to London, saw the sights, and later headed north to Scotland. Fortunately, Ann Dee knew exactly what she wanted to see and how to get there, so Katie blindly followed her lead. It seemed like, wherever she went, she was reminded of Pavol. The church was named St. Paul's, the tour guide was named Paul, a news anchor on TV was named Paul. In addition, there was a neighboring church called St. Catherine's! Ann Dee patiently tolerated her friend's absentmindedness, but one afternoon as they strolled through a village looking for a place to have tea, she couldn't take it anymore.

"Look, you have to resolve this. The best thing to do is go and see him. Communicate! That's what I have been trying to do with you this entire trip, but only half of you is listening!"

"I'm sorry, Ann Dee. I promise, from now on, I'll put him out of my mind." Katie held up two fingers. "Scout's honor!"

"Katie, I'm serious," Ann Dee said more gently. "I really think you need to see him face to face and set things right. If he didn't mean all those things he said over Christmas, well, you need to find that out. But if he did, you don't want to lose that, do you?"

Katie just gazed at Ann Dee and then shook her head.

"Now let's go and have a 'spot of tea' and then I'll go back to the hostel and help you pack! All right?" Ann Dee said mockingly in her best British accent.

The next evening, Katie was headed for Vienna on the *Franz Josef Express*.

"I'm a man-chaser, that's what I am. A man-chaser. I can just hear what people are going to say: 'Poor Katie, she can't get a guy, so she has to go all the way to CZECHOSLOVAKIA to find one'," she muttered to herself. "How pathetic. But I'm not chasing him! It's just he can't come to see me, so I have to go to him, right?" She argued with herself for the next five minutes when suddenly she noticed an elderly lady sitting across from her eyeing her curiously. Katie smiled politely and turned to look at the setting sun over the fields. *Oh, Lord, help me*, she prayed silently.

At five a.m., the train slowly pulled into Vienna's Westbahnhof. Katie sleepily opened her eyes and yawned. With her neck stiff from leaning on the window all night, she pulled her bags down from the rack and stumbled off the train. Still yawning, she headed for the bathroom and paid her *groschen* to the plump cleaning lady who guarded the stalls. The woman handed her a few sheets of toilet paper.

"Only in Europe do you have to pay to use the public restroom," she grumbled as she set her bags down. "At least it's clean..." The chubby cleaning lady snorted and led her to one of the stalls where she unlocked the door.

After washing her hands and face under the careful surveillance of the restroom attendant, Katie went to see if there were any trains going to Bratislava. She felt a little uneasy as she walked through the dark hallways which were unusually empty except for a few Turkish newspaper boys who blatantly stared at her. Shifting her heavy backpack, she finally found the timetable and scanned its contents for departures and arrivals.

"May I be of service?" said a deep voice behind her. Katie whirled around to see a blond-haired man with a beard addressing her.

"How did you know I spoke English?" Katie asked without thinking.

He rolled his eyes and shrugged, "Lucky guess! What are you looking for? Maybe I can help you find it."

Feeling a little hesitant about talking to strangers, Katie pointed at the timetable on the wall and said, "I'm trying to see if there are any trains that go to Bratislava. I know the bus goes, but I thought maybe I could get there by rail..." Her voice trailed off as the man started laughing.

"There hasn't been a train crossing that border for ages! Don't you Americans learn anything in school? You should know that!" He picked up her bag, took her by the arm, and guided her towards the exit. Katie stumbled beside him feeling unsure and a little annoyed as he continued talking. "A young lady like yourself really should not be in a place like this all alone. It isn't safe. Now, let's go have breakfast, and we'll plan the day."

Plan the day? Every warning her mother had ever given her was sounding alarms off in her head, so she started protesting, "Uh, look, I don't think that's a good idea. I really can't... I mean..." Not paying attention to her, he walked away carrying her bag.

"Now, do you already have your visa? Of course you don't. That will be the first thing we'll need to take care of." He looked at her staring at him with open mouth and held out his hand smilingly. "Forgive me, I forgot to introduce myself. My name is Aleks; I'm from Finland." He grasped her hand and gave it a hearty shake.

Katie found herself smiling in spite of herself. He had an odd appearance as he wore a multi-colored knitted ski cap with a little fuzzy ball on top. Blond curls peeked out from under the cap and piercing blue eyes seemed to penetrate her thoughts. He looked a little like a lumberjack in that flannel shirt, Katie mused as they turned into a cafe.

"This place has the best American breakfast!" he said confidently.

The waitress seemed to be well acquainted with him as she brought the food and smiled at Katie. She set a big plate of fried eggs, bacon, and toast in front of her. Katie did not realize how hungry she was until she smelled the tantalizing fragrance of sizzling bacon.

"Wow, this does look good. How did you ever find this place?" Katie said as she hungrily eyed the food, forgetting that she was supposed to be on her guard.

Looking very smug, he nodded and said, "Well, I am a businessman and I travel all over the world. I know the best places to eat anywhere!" Then he proceeded to talk non-stop about his travels to Eastern Europe and the Middle East. "See this passport? I can get into places that you can only dream of as an American!"

Boy, he's cocky, she thought as she sipped the tall glass of fresh-squeezed orange juice. *He sure doesn't look like a businessman.* Aleks proceeded to tell her that Hungarian and Finnish had the same language roots, and he did not have any trouble communicating with those clients he served in Budapest. Katie began to feel fatigued as he continued chatting non-stop, when suddenly he interrupted himself and asked, "All done? Let's go to the embassy now and get your visa. Come along!"

Katie pulled out her wallet to pay, but he waved his hand in disgust and pushed her to the door. "I'll be right there. Wait for me outside." Katie walked past the waitress who gave her a wink. She took a deep breath and looked up at the unusually clear blue sky. Soon, he came quickly out the door and ushered her towards the subway.

"We have to hurry as they are only opened until twelve o'clock. That's not much time to get your visa, but I'll think we'll make it!"

"Twelve?" Katie gulped her heart beating a little faster. She didn't really have enough money to pay for a hotel that night if they didn't manage everything.

"We'll manage! We always do," he smiled again, his intense blue eyes reassuring her.

We?

He continued talking, but Katie's attention span soon waned as they neared the embassy. True to his word, she did not need to worry. In less than thirty minutes, they had her visa and were out of the Czechoslovakian Embassy and heading back to the center of the city. As they walked down the *Mariahilfe Strasse*, he suddenly turned to her and said, "Katie, I have a meeting now and will have to leave you." He became very serious and then said, "You must be more careful in the future; you can't just wander alone around a big city like this. Now, I can leave you. It's safe. You know where the bus station is, so I would suggest you go and purchase your ticket as soon as possible. Goodbye."

And with that he disappeared. Literally.

"Where is he?" she said half out loud. She strained to see him through the crowds of people on the sidewalk, but she could not locate him anywhere. *Where did he go? He certainly wasn't dressed for a business meeting. What a funny guy! Oh, well,* she told herself, *you had better listen to him and buy that ticket.*

Later that afternoon, Katie patiently stood in line waiting to board the bus to Bratislava. As she handed her bags to the driver, she turned around and saw Aleks near the bus. He had a serious look on his face. Even more surprising was the red rose in his hand.

"Things are going to change soon. I just came to say goodbye. I wish you all the best and hope everything works out well for you and your... friend. Remember, love is like this rose sometimes: it has a few thorns and can be very painful, but nothing is more beautiful. Just be careful!" Katie was startled to see a tear rolling down his cheek.

He bent over and kissed her softly on the cheek and quickly ran off through the bus lot. Katie watched him as he disappeared into the crowd. He was gone. Katie felt a strange feeling in the pit of her stomach as if she had just said farewell to a very old friend.

"Who was that guy?" she said aloud as she settled into her seat. "And how did he know I had a boyfriend? I didn't tell him anything about Pavol."

She sat slowly down in her seat next to an elderly woman who was watching her carefully. As she carefully turned the rose in her hand to admire the beautiful bloom, the older woman leaned over slightly and asked her, "*Glauben Sie an Schutzengeln?*"

Katie just stared at her trying to decipher what she just said: do I believe in guardian angels?

Gasping, she turned towards the window scanning the sea of faces. He wasn't there.

The woman nodded mysteriously and settled back in her seat as the bus pulled out of the lot. Katie continued staring at the pedestrians in the street but their faces turned into a blur as the bus picked up speed.

"Wow," she said for the second time that day. "I have a Finnish guardian angel! Who knew?" She settled back in her seat with a smug smile on her face.

Misunderstandings

Katie had been in Trnava now for two days and still no sign of Pavol. Marta had not mentioned his name, but finally she could not handle it anymore and brought up the subject at breakfast.

"*Warum kommt Pavol nicht?*" she asked carefully as Katie blew on her hot tea.

"*Ich weiss es nicht,*" Katie said staring at her plate. *I don't know why he isn't coming*, she wailed inside. Suddenly the tears began to spill out onto the tablecloth.

Marta immediately stood up and pulled Katie to her side, hugging her tightly. After she had her cry, Marta took out a handkerchief and gently wiped her face saying, "*Nicht weinen, Moja Mila. Nicht weinen!*" Don't cry!

Katie tried to get a hold of herself for the next few minutes and explained her confusion in broken German. Marta looked thoughtfully at her and started asking her questions about old boyfriends. Taken a little aback by her cousin's sudden interest in her past dating life, Katie tried to answer her kind inquiries honestly. Then Marta shrugged and said, "*Ach ja, wenn ein Madchen schlaeft mit einem Bub, das ist nicht das Ende.*"

Startled, Katie looked at the nonchalant expression on her cousin's face and blurted out, "*Schlaeft? Mit einem Bub?*" *She thinks I have been sleeping around!* Katie winced. *And what does she mean, 'That is not the end'?*

"*Ja, ja,*" Marta continued waving her hand in the air. "*Es passiert manchmal – das ist nichts.*" she said beginning to look a little uncomfortable as Katie stared at her with open mouth. *It happens sometimes?*

"*Man muss nur beten und das nie weiter machen,*" she added nodding and shaking her finger wisely at Katie. One should just pray and not do it again!

"*Aber das habe ich nicht!*" Katie said emphatically. The puzzled look on Marta's face made her want to giggle, but quickly composing herself she tried to look grave.

"*Nein? Nie?*" Marta asked in surprise looking somewhat relieved.

"*Nein!*" Katie repeated bursting out in laughter.

"*Du bist eine Jungfrau? Aber der Pavol sagt...*" Marta stopped suddenly.

"*Was hat der Pavol gesagt?*" Katie stopped laughing and asked suspiciously, "*Was?*" What did Pavol say?

"*Nichts,*" Marta said standing quickly up and scooping up the food to return to the pantry. "*Gar nichts!*" Nothing! Nothing at all!

Katie was left alone on the divan to wonder about the strange conversation that had just taken place.

That afternoon, Marta began teaching her how to make an apple strudel when the bell rang. Katie's heart began to beat faster hoping it was you-know-who, but it was not Pavol; it was Marta's nephew. Marta introduced him to her. "*Mein Bruder's Sohn-sein Name ist Vili.*"

"Vili?" Katie asked in surprised. "*Aber Dein Bruder und Dein Sohn heissen auch Vili!*" Vili? Aren't your brother and son named Vili, too?

Marta smiled and shrugged, "*Ach, ja! Ein schoener Name!*"

She clapped her fat hands together and a puff of flour made a cloud in her face. Vili smiled broadly and shook his cousin's hands kissing her on both cheeks.

He was taller than the rest, stout, and had slick dark hair with a moustache. His eyes were friendly albeit a bit apprehensive. He had come at his aunt's invitation, and Katie enjoyed watching the two of them stretch and pull the strudel dough out until it was thin as tissue paper. Then they laughed and chatted as they painted melted butter on the dough and spread out the thin slices of apples. Marta let Katie sprinkle cinnamon and sugar over the top and then they rolled the dough up, pinched the ends, and lifted it on a greased baking sheet.

Soon the heavenly scent of baking apples drifted through the house. Marta made coffee and tea for them as they sat around the table enjoying the warmth of the kitchen. Vili did not speak any German, so Marta tried her best to translate, but after a while she gave up and just continued joking with her nephew in Slovak. Katie didn't mind being excluded from the conversation and just savored the wonderful fragrance of the baking pastry. She looked out the window at the gray sky and bare trees. A little wave of despondency washed over her as she thought about Pavol.

Marta noticed the look on Katie's face and patted her on the arm. "*Ich bin sehr froh – Du bist hier,*" she smiled showing her missing teeth. I am happy you are here. She pointed at Katie while looking at Vili. "*Sie ist meine Tochter!*" She patted her heart and repeated, "*Meine Tochter.*" She is my daughter! My daughter.

Katie gave her a hug and Marta stroked her hair. Looking up at the clock she said suddenly, "*Er kommt, Katka! Ne boj sa... er kommt.*" He's coming, Katie, don't worry.

Katie's heart skipped a beat but she didn't dare ask whom Marta was referring to. Soon the strudel was ready and Marta pulled it out of the oven to cool. They could not wait to sample it even though Marta insisted it wasn't healthy eating pastries that were still hot. However, she relented and cut each one a generous slice. The warm juice from the tart apples oozed out on the plate and the delicate, flaky pastry melted in her mouth. For the next few minutes, you could only hear murmurs of appreciation and pleasure as they relished their dessert. Suddenly, Katie heard the front door open and boots stomping on the ground.

"*Karolko, si doma?*" Marta called out. Karol soon appeared in the door of the kitchen with rosy red cheeks. He looked like a mischievous elf with a white shock of hair hanging in the middle of his forehead.

"*Pozrie!*" He pulled Pavol out from behind him and pushed him inside the kitchen. Pavol looked a little embarrassed but pleased to see them all. Katie smiled brightly at him, but her smile faded as his eyes avoided hers. He simply nodded at her in greeting. Taking note, Marta quickly introduced him to her nephew. Pavol's face became serious as he shook Vili's hand, but soon they were talking in a friendly manner.

Katie stood up and helped her aunt clear the table and bring clean plates and cups for their guests. Pavol continued to talk without noticing her, so feeling a little miffed, she sat down in the corner of the room not sure what to do. She saw her little pocket Bible on the table, so she opened it up and began flipping through the verses. "Be not afraid, for I am with you always..." "Trust in the Lord with all your heart..." She sighed and shut the small book. Pavol glanced at her for the first time and their eyes met. His blue eyes were intense; they seemed to be searching for something in her face. For the first time, she saw longing in his eyes and a hunger.

Vili stood up and announced that he must go, so Marta packed up a large piece of the strudel for him to take home to his family. Pavol also stood up politely and said his goodbyes, but he didn't leave when Vili left. He turned abruptly towards Katie and said rather gruffly, "Would you like to see my office where I work?" She paused not sure what she should do, but something inside her urged her on, so she nodded and went to get her coat. Karol and Marta looked at each other and quickly took the dishes to the sink.

They walked towards the center of town, the snow crunching under their feet. No one said a word, and Katie was starting to feel desperate. She looked at Pavol, but he seemed to be preoccupied and troubled. Suddenly, he asked her, "How long have you known Marta's nephew?"

Surprised at the question, she replied, "Not long at all. I just met him this morning for the first time. He seems very nice."

Pavol nodded and was quiet for a few more moments. Then he said quietly, "He's a lawyer – a judge actually. A big communist. My priest friends have told me stories about some of his cases." He paused again and then continued, "But to tell you the truth, I don't think it was entirely his fault; he was just frightened to do the right thing."

Katie asked, "What kind of cases?"

Pavol replied, "There was a murder. A priest was killed but they never found the killers. We all knew that the communists did not like that priest because he was very outspoken. Now he's gone. Anyway, the case came before your cousin, but he let the suspect go."

Katie walked along in silence letting these words sink in. "Marta said that he struggles with horrible headaches and can't seem to get rid of them."

Pavol nodded understandingly and then spoke, "It isn't easy here to follow your career and have a good, good... how do you say? Conscience? Very difficult thing..." His voice trailed off and he sunk back in his moody thoughts.

Soon, they arrived at a building and Pavol held the door open for her. He then led her to an office that had a desk, a big picture window and a sofa. They sat down on the sofa and he pulled her closer to him. He brought her face close to his and kissed her warmly and intensely.

"Katka, I'm sorry. I misunderstood." He kissed her again and then sat back. "I don't want to judge anyone or blame someone for a choice they made. I have made many myself that I wish I could go back and change." He looked intently at her eyes. "But I always wanted someone who had waited for me because, well, I have also been waiting. When you told me that you were with someone else, it, well, it ruined my dreams. I was so angry with God because I thought He brought you to me as a gift. I told God, why did you give me a scorpion when I asked for a fish? Why did you give me a stone when I asked for bread? Forgive me – I know this sounds terrible, but I believed He would bring me a girl who had also waited."

"Is that why I haven't seen or heard from you for so long?" She pulled back.

"Yes," he said simply shrugging. "Yes. What more can I tell you?" He leaned in closer. "I don't like games. Please tell me the truth once and for all."

Katie felt extremely annoyed and couldn't say anything for a few minutes, but other emotions took over, so she told him her story stumbling and blushing as she spoke. She finally finished by saying, "I just told you that I slept with someone because I was tired of you asking so many times! I didn't know it was so important to you. I was just joking!"

Pavol folded his hands and looked down at the floor. "I do not want to play God and judge someone – especially if they have asked for forgiveness. Who am I?" He looked up at her eagerly. "But I was always convinced that if I waited, God would bring me someone who also waited! I was sure of it! Katie, I want you, but I could not make love to you knowing that I was not the first."

Katie's face grew hot and she began to tremble. "I had a friend once who called me 'a sucker' because I believed the same thing," she said slowly. "I also believed right at that moment that God would lead me to that someone." She looked at him earnestly. "Is that you?"

Pavol smiled and said, "I don't know what a sucker is, but yes, I hope it is me." He squeezed her hand. "I hope so very much."

The Proposal

Katie was sitting on a bed in Pavol's dorm room the day before she had to go back to Germany. The bare white walls and stark furniture felt strangely comforting. He was reclining on the other twin bed in the corner with a book, but his attention was on her. He was asking questions about America, her home, and her friends. Then suddenly changing the subject, he started talking about their life together.

"We could live with my parents until I find another job. There are two extra rooms in our house," he mused aloud. "My brother might be able to help me find something. I could even work for the co-op in my village. You can teach a few private English lessons... maybe you could even play the organ at church!"

Katie let him talk for a few minutes, but then quietly interrupted him by saying, "We? Live with your parents? Teach English lessons? What are you talking about exactly?"

Pavol looked astonished and sputtered out, "I'm talking about you and me, our life together!"

Katie smiled sweetly back and replied, "You know, you haven't really asked me to marry you yet."

Pavol snorted and said, "Yes, I have. I think that's clear – one day!

Katie retorted, "Believe me, I would remember if you had asked me. It hasn't happened – not yet!"

Pavol was silent for a few minutes and then put his hands behind his head. Leaning back against the pillows, he stared at her. Then he began to speak slowly and deliberately, "Katka, do you think you can go wherever I go? Can you follow me no matter what? It won't be easy, I promise you. Can you do that?" His face was serious and his tone a little skeptical.

Well, that's not exactly how I imagined it. He didn't even get down on one knee. Was that even a proposal? She looked out the window at the buildings across the street – big boxy socialist buildings with red flags flying above the doors. *Could I handle living here?* she reflected. *I mean*

246

actually live here? A communist country? What about my parents? What will they say?

Doubts tugged at her heart, but then she thought about what would happen if she simply walked away. Pavol already felt like a big part of her life, and the thought of losing him brought on a heavy surge of sadness. She turned towards him and saw his blue eyes studying her intently, trying to guess her thoughts. He looked both anxious and amused. Giving a weak little smile, she nodded.

"Yes, yes, I'll try." She shrugged.

"Just try?"

"Okay, so I can do it. I hope."

Pavol's eyes twinkled as he turned back to his book.

The next week, Katie was back in Germany. As she unlocked the door to her apartment in Germany, she found a letter from her father in the mailbox. As her father rarely wrote her leaving that order of business to her mother, she wasted no time running upstairs to her room and tearing the letter open.

Dear Katie,

I hope you had a good trip to Slovakia and that Marta and Karol are well. Your mother and I are planning to come and visit you in May and bring your sister Margaret with us. She did not get to come and meet the relatives in Czechoslovakia on our last trip. Mike is going to take care of the girls for her while she is gone, so the three of us will fly to London, spend a few days there, and then travel down to Heidelberg to see you. Perhaps you can meet us in Cologne as we will need to get our visas from the Czechoslovakian consulate there. Your brother is in Spain now on a second honeymoon; they will meet us in Trnava.

Looking forward to seeing you.

Love,

Dad

P.S. I have already written Marta and Karol that we are coming on such and such date...

Katie wasted no time in answering it. Her letter was filled with plans of showing them around Heidelberg and introducing them to all her friends, but she felt a little nervous when she thought about them meeting Pavol in Slovakia. *What in the world are they going to think? That I've lost it! Oh well, whatever will be, will be.*

Pushing those thoughts aside, she grabbed her letter and ran to the post office.

May arrived in full glory. The trees were in full bloom and the air had become sweet and pleasant. The Neckar River sparkled in the sun, and Katie thought she had never seen such a dazzling spring. The train ride to Cologne seemed as if it would never end, but finally they pulled up into the train station under the shadow of the huge gothic cathedral. She had not seen her parents since last summer, and she wondered if she would look different to them. As was her custom, she went inside the cathedral and knelt in prayer for a few minutes before setting out for the Czechoslovak consulate. As she walked down the broad sidewalks in the residential area, she saw the outline of a woman in jeans sitting on the steps under the Czechoslovakian flag. As Katie got closer, she cried out, "Margaret!"

Running towards each other, the two sisters embraced.

"I can't believe you are here! Look at you! I love your hair!" Cathy exclaimed.

Margaret had trimmed her long mane shoulder length and looked quite stylish in her brown blazer.

"Hey, Miss Europe!" Margaret replied hugging her sister. "I can't believe my baby sister has been living here all by herself in this gorgeous country! It's so good to see you!"

"Where are Mom and Dad?" Katie asked as she sat down by her sister on the steps.

"They're inside finishing up the paperwork. I just came out to watch for you. You had better go inside and take care of your own stuff… Wow, you are positively glowing. What's going on with you?"

After a joyful reunion inside, Katie managed to get her visa and the four of them walked back to the train station.

"How did you get here so fast?" Katie asked. "I thought I would beat you here!"

"We got a ride from this nice young man we met in the hotel in London," Katie's mother proclaimed triumphantly. "He is actually a Wycliffe Bible translator who lives in Belgium, and we started talking…" Paula spent the next twenty minutes giving her all the details of another God-given encounter. "So, then he offered to drive us to Cologne, and here we are! Isn't that just the Lord!"

"Yes, he was incredibly nice," Margaret added. "It was so much easier traveling by car with all these bags."

"It would not have been so bad if you and your mother didn't buy out every antique store in London," John said dryly looking at his watch. "I'm hungry! Can we eat something around here?" He looked like a beast of burden with bags and suitcases draped over his body.

"We'll help you, Daddy," Katie said laughingly as she and Margaret lifted the heavy backpack off his shoulders.

After a delicious lunch of succulent grilled chicken, chips, and salad, they boarded the train to Heidelberg. Margaret's eyes were glued to the Rhein River as the train flew down the tracks.

"It's so beautiful! The scenery is fantastic here, and the lighting is just perfect," she murmured taking in all the sights.

The next few days were busy as they toured the Heidelberg Castle, hiked in the mountains, and had lunch with the Brandls. Ursel appreciated Margaret's admiration of her organic cooking skills and how she ground grain for her bread and porridge. They seemed to understand each other immediately.

"It's so fresh – and absolutely delicious!" Katie's sister exclaimed as she bit into one of Ursel's whole-grained rolls. Ursel nodded her head in satisfaction. Later their hostess took them out into the large garden where they sipped coffee, tasted the first strawberries of the season, and chatted.

"Thank you so much for taking care of Katie for us," Paula said gratefully as they got up to leave. "She has told us so much about you and how much you have helped her this year. I hope you know that you are always welcome in our home."

"*Nichts zu danken!*" Ursel said cheerfully. "We have been happy to have Katie with us here. She has really improved her German and taught us a few things as well! It's been a pleasure!" Then Ursel presented her mother with a beautiful large handmade piece of pottery to take home.

"Oh, no," John groaned quietly in Katie's ear. "One more thing to carry!"

"Shhh, Daddy! She'll hear you!"

The rest of their time in Heidelberg went smoothly with the exception of the visit to the elderly sisters' home on the hill.

Frau Mueller, as the Grand Dame of the home, felt it was her polite duty to invite Katie's parents to tea, but after they had sat in the parlor looking at the old photographs of her late husband, Frau Mueller seemed to be overcome with memories and suddenly burst out with an accusation. "*Sie, Amerikaneren,*" she said pointing at Katie's father, "*haben unsere wunderschoene Staedte und Gebauden bombardiert und vernichtet! Wie haetten Sie das so machen koennen?*"

Katie's parents and sister who had been enjoying their cake and tea looked up in surprise and waited for Katie to translate.

Katie stammered, "Uh, well, she said that you, uh, Americans bombed and destroyed our beautiful cities and buildings. She also said, how could you do such a thing?"

Katie's father set his teacup on the coffee table, trying to control the anger in his voice. "Madam, I would just like to remind you that it was your country who started that damn war in the first place!"

Frau Mueller looked at Katie questioningly, but Katie decided it was wiser not to give a direct translation of what her father said and quickly said in German, "War is a terrible tragedy for everyone."

Frau Mueller's eyes filled up with tears and nodded. They soon said their goodbyes, but Katie's father was still shaking his head and mumbling as they walked back down the hill.

The next day, they rented a car, packed it tightly with all their luggage, and headed south through Bavaria and Austria. They oohed and aahed over the majestic Alps, the neat white houses with flowerboxes full of red geraniums, and onion domed churches dotting the pristine landscape. This time, John had all his papers in order as they crossed the border, so the guards waved them disinterestedly along.

Their reunion in Trnava was a joyful one, and Margaret soon felt like one of the cherished family members in Marta and Karol's home. She met all the cousins, enjoyed the bountiful food, and soon impressed them all with her quick ability to learn both German and Slovak phrases. After the first evening was over, Margaret whispered in Katie's ear as they sat at the table drinking Karol's homemade wine, "Oh, how I wish I could have studied here like you. I would have been so, well, so happy here." Katie didn't know what to say at first, feeling a little awkward that her sister felt she had missed out.

"It's okay," Margaret said quickly sensing her feelings. "I chose my own way and don't have any regrets, but I can't help it. It's just I have gotten a taste of it now. I hope I can bring my girls here one day."

The day finally arrived for her family to meet Pavol. He showed up after breakfast smiling, but Katie could tell he was not completely at ease when she took his hand; his palms were sweaty. Wiping her hand on a napkin, she introduced him to everyone. He seemed relieved to see her mother's friendly face again, and Margaret's congenial manner and openness soon reassured him; he quickly fell into conversation with her.

Later Margaret came up to her younger sister in the kitchen and whispered with a smirk on her face, "These European men are quite charming, aren't they?" Katie responded by popping her on the butt with a dishtowel.

The next couple of days flew by as they toured the city and visited Modra, the home of John's mother. Pavol, trying to make himself as agreeable as possible, was busy translating, listening patiently to Paula's Christian testimony, and answering John and Margaret's more academic questions although he often turned to Katie for help with his English. He offended Marta by not eating enough, but was forgiven when he told her about his stomach troubles and migraines.

During the course of the visit, Katie noticed that Karol kept talking quietly to Pavol in a corner of the room. She saw the expression on Pavol's face becoming increasingly agitated. After several minutes, he actually seemed to lose his patience and snapped at Karol. Looking rather surprised, Karol became silent. *What was that all about?* Katie wondered.

That evening, her brother Rick arrived with his wife Janelle, and the family party became even merrier. Pavol was doing his best to converse and entertain them on his guitar with Slovak folk music, but his face looked fatigued. Finally, the clock struck midnight and he stood up. "Thank you for this nice evening," he said in English and then in Slovak to Marta and Karol, "but I have to go home now and take care of a little business. I hope to see you in a couple of days." Karol looked at him knowingly and nodded at him.

As they walked through the garden towards the irongate, Katie unlocked it easily and asked wistfully, "Do you really have to go?"

He smiled reassuringly at her and said, "I have to talk to my Godfather, Jan, about... well, about some important matters. I'll be back soon." He pulled her into his arms, held her tightly for a minute, and then he was gone.

The next couple of days were spent visiting relatives and introducing Margaret to her new relatives and of course, eating, eating, and eating. Mrs. Holcik readily came along to help translate in Pavol's absence, but Marta did not always appreciate her eagerness.

"She's spreading gossip all over town about us," Marta confided in Katie. "Everyone in town knows everything about you and your family now, but what can we do about it? Nothing! I know she does not mean anything bad, but I hope you learn Slovak soon!"

One afternoon, they were all gathererd around the table just finishing another one of Marta's sumptuous lunches when the bell rang. Karol looked out the window and then said very mysteriously, "Ah-hah!" and began rubbing his hands together in satisfaction. Grabbing the gate key, he quickly ran out the door and soon herded Pavol into the middle of the dining room. Karol's face was beaming.

Pavol was dressed in his best pinstriped suit carrying a small bouquet of different colored carnations and a few lacy asparagus ferns. He looked rather pale and beads of sweat appeared on his forehead. Standing in front of them and scanning their faces as if he were looking for a cue, he stepped towards her parents and said nervously in his best English, "Mr. and Mrs. Boszko, I come… to ask your permission. I would like to ask for your daughter's hand… in marriage!" Taking a deep breath, he stiffly thrust the flowers towards Paula who took them in stunned surprise. The room was deadly silent. No one moved. Katie thought her heart was going to pound out of her chest. Looking as if he were close to passing out, Pavol managed to stammer, "Do you… do you agree?"

Paula, not usually at a loss for words, gulped and stuttered out, "Uh, well, uh… I mean, I guess… well, yes, you… you have our permission," but then she looked at her husband horrified at what she had just said. John didn't know what to do either, but feeling sorry for Pavol who was standing there awkwardly in the middle of the room, stood up slowly and held out his hand to shake it.

Pavol's face broke into a relieved smile and vigorously shook his hand. Margaret and Richard began hugging them both while Janelle started to cry saying over and over, "Isn't that the sweetest thing you've ever seen?" Marta and Karol stood quietly in the back of the room not understanding the words but taking everything in.

Pavol immediately loosened his tie and took off his jacket revealing big perspiration marks under his armpits.

"Do you want to go for a short walk?" he begged Katie tugging her hand. Katie looked at her parents who nodded at her. They smiled, but Katie noticed their foreheads were lined with worry.

Walking quickly over to them, she hugged them both. "I love you."

Her mother clung to her neck whispering a bit desperately, "I just sold my youngest daughter for a few carnations! What have I done?" Katie began laughing and crying at the same time as Pavol watched them slightly bewildered.

"Go, go," her father shooed her away. "He's waiting for you."

Pavol held out his hand to her and without hesitation she grasped it.

"Let's go," he said hurrying her out the door.

Marta called out to her as they walked out the door, *"Wir werden heute abend feiern wenn Ihr zurueckkommt! Komm bald!"* We are going to celebrate this evening when you come back. Come soon!

As Pavol walked out the gate with Katie still holding his hand, he put his arm around her waist and pulled her close. Breathing a big sigh, he said, "Well, that's done, thank God."

Katie laughed and said, "Was is that bad?"

"Pretty bad," Pavol said wiping his brow. "But the results were good. Now, my family wants to meet your family."

This time, Katie felt butterflies in her stomach and swallowed nervously. "Your family?"

Pavol nodded grimly and said, "Yes, they are expecting us tomorrow – everyone!"

That evening, Katie explained to her family the plans for the next day while Pavol talked with Marta and Karol.

"How in the world are we all going to get there?" Paula asked Pavol.

"My brother and brother-in-law are coming with two cars. I think we will all fit," Pavol told her reassuringly. Paula and John looked at each other.

"Cool!" Margaret exclaimed. "I can't wait to see more of Slovakia!"

Pavol smiled gratefully and began to describe his village with enthusiasm. "The air is so fresh there and we have a beautiful little river running next to our village. The trees are just beautiful now; they look like brides dressed in white. I hope you will like it very much."

Margaret looked at Katie and raised her eyebrows. "Brides, huh?"

The next morning, Pavol's brother Ondrej and his brother-in-law Jan pulled up in front of Marta's house. Pavol jumped out of one of the cars and began ringing the bell.

"Are you sure they are expecting us?" Ondrej said looking apprehensively at the big irongate. He had never met any Americans before.

"Of course," Pavol replied exasperatedly. "I told you everything has been arranged. Look, here comes her cousin now."

Marta was huffing and puffing as she hurried towards the gate. Behind her came the entire family, so introductions took place in the garden. Ondrej's eyes sparkled as he met the ladies and smiled charmingly. Jan was very jovial and shook the other John's hand warmly. Soon, they were on the road and headed towards Čerešňa. The green landscape gradually became more rolling and low mountains became visible on the horizon.

"Those are the Tribec Mountains," Pavol pointed out the window. "I did all of my dissertation's research there. I spent days walking across those mountains and gathering data."

"What kind of data were you gathering?" John asked curiously.

"I was collecting soil samples from various locations..." Pavol began explaining. They continued to discuss his research until they finally pulled up in front of Pavol's house.

The gate swung open and Pavol's little elderly mother Zuzana stood there beckoning them in. She was dressed in her best navy blue polka dotted dress and her fine, white hair was combed carefully back in a bun. Pavol's father Jozef came up behind her dressed in his Sunday suit. Pavol soon made all of the introductions. His parents took everything in stride, but Katie could not help but smile when she saw her tall full-figured American mother standing next to Pavol's tiny Slovak mother.

Zuzana seemed to be amused by her American counterpart with her colorful clothes, make-up, and jewelry. All of the Americans towered over the Slovaks, which prompted Pavol's father to ask, "What do they feed those people over there?" Pavol grimaced a little and invited everyone into the sitting room where a large table was set up with elegant dishes and glassware.

"Oh, it looks so nice," Paula clapped her hands appreciatively. Zuzana graciously offered a chair and poured her guests a shot of Becherovka, herbal bitters. As they stood in a circle around the table, Zuzana raised her glass and said, *Vitaj u nas a Na zdravia!* Welcome and to your health!" They all swallowed the spicy clear liquor down and felt the burning liquid sear their throats.

"Wow," Richard smacked his lips. "That's good stuff!" Zuzana seemed to understand and quickly poured another round. Soon they were sitting around the table and dining on the first course of homemade chicken soup and noodles.

"I love this soup," John said. "Why can't we make soup like this at home? Maybe it's because all of the vegetables are so fresh."

"They are from our garden," Pavol said. "I will show it to you when we finish. We do not use any chemicals, so the taste is much better. Katie told me you have a garden in Texas, too."

"Yes, well, I try, but I can't grow anything as tasty as this," John said lifting another spoonful of goodness to his mouth.

"Please tell your mother that she is an excellent cook," Paula said. "And please tell her..." Pavol stayed busy the rest of the meal translating for his parents and Katie's family. His father, Jozef, seemed to take a special liking to Katie's sister Margaret.

"Tell her that I am going to divorce my wife and I will marry her," he said nudging Pavol and pointing a bony finger at Margaret. "She looks like a good peasant woman who can work hard. Look at her hands! They're not soft like your Katka's hands! And she's very pretty, too!"

"Apa, I can't tell her that," Pavol protested but Jozef kept urging him.

"Oh, just tell them," Zuzana said laughing heartily. "What would a pretty young thing like that want with an old man like you?"

Pavol reluctantly translated his father's statements and the whole table burst into laughter.

"You know," Margaret said looking around the room, "I think I would have liked living in a village like this and working in the garden and fields. Maybe this is what I have been searching for all my life!" Pavol translated and his father raised his glass to her and winked.

After lunch, they toured the garden behind the house admiring the lush vegetables and flowering fruit trees.

"Boy, these trees are loaded with blooms. You are going to have a bumper crop this summer," John said wistfully as he looked up at the plum, cherry, peach, and apricot trees. "I'm lucky if I get two or three peaches off my little tree back in West Texas."

"Tell him he must come back," Zuzana responded after her son translated.

John nodded eagerly. "I'd like that, thank you! *Dakujem!*"

"*Prosim!*" Zuzana said laughing.

Then Jozef took command and ushered everyone out through the gate.

"Where are we going?" Katie asked Pavol.

"We are going to my oldest brother's house. Apa, why are you going that way?" Pavol yelled at his father, switching to Slovak in mid-sentence. Jozef didn't turn around but headed towards the river.

"I guess he wants to show you our river," Pavol shrugged following his elderly father. While they walked down the street, curious neighbors appeared at their gates and greeted them. Pavol looked a little embarrassed but greeted them as they walked by.

"Rick!" Margaret said suddenly poking her brother's arm. "Look over there in that garden."

Richard stopped and looked at the plants his sister was pointing at in excitement. "Hey, it's marijuana! They grow marijuana!"

Pavol's parents stopped and looked at what the young people were pointing at and said, "That's to keep the potato bugs away, that's what it's good for, and making rope – nothing else." Pavol translated for them.

"I'll bet that's not all they use it for," Ricky said knowingly. Paula glared at her son as they continued walking.

As they neared the river, the fragrance of chamomile filled the air. Looking down, there was a carpet of the little white and yellow flowers all along the riverbank. Janelle, Margaret, and Katie began picking the tiny blossoms slowing the party down.

"Let's go," Pavol pleaded as they filled their hands. "We can pick more on the way back. My brother is waiting for us!"

As they walked along the river through the long grass, Katie looked at the hazy, blue mountains behind the fields. *This is so different from where I grew up*, she mused.

They soon approached a gate that opened up into a large garden full of sprouting corn stalks. Katie recognized Pavol's eldest brother Martin standing there holding the leash of the very large dog, who was strangely silent. His wife, Dalina, was herding a large flock of honking geese into the barn with a switch. Both looked more relaxed and friendly than when they were together earlier that year. After quickly meeting everyone, Martin led them up a dirt path towards his house and then up the stairs on the outside of the house to a large room.

"Please, sit down," he said in a heavy Slovak accent. Pavol looked surprised that his brother was able to speak a few words in English, but quickly pulled out a chair for his future mother-in-law.

Everyone was soon seated around a dark walnut table, more schnaps was poured, and polite toasting took place before another grandiose meal appeared on the table. The afternoon flew by, and both Pavol and Katie were stunned at how well the two families seemed to hit it off with each other.

"Here's your brother, a big communist director, and my father, a staunch conservative American, having a friendly conversation," Katie remarked to Pavol. Pavol smiled broadly and nodded his head happily. At four o'clock, they stood up to leave as they still had one more place to visit.

"What's the plan now?" Katie asked as they descended the stairs.

"We're going to visit my sister Helena, Jan's wife, in Topolcany. It's only ten miles from here. Apa!" Pavol cried out suddenly in exasperation.

Jozef Sr. was relieving himself in the corner of the courtyard. Zuzana muttered something under her breath shaking her head, but Katie's family politely turned the other way to admire a large apple tree growing near the house.

"When you gotta go, you gotta go," Rick whispered into Margaret's ear.

Summer in the Village

"You know, Katie, I think you made a really good choice," her brother Rick said as he gazed out the window of their hotel room in Vienna. "He is intelligent, he is about the right age, and I think he will adapt well."

"He is good-looking, too, which always helps," Janelle added walking over to her husband. "I have never seen such blue eyes – so full of passion!"

"Any other comments?" Katie asked amused at her family's remarks.

"Well, I think he is a very nice young man," Paula said, "but I'm worried. I don't want you living in Czechoslovakia and under a communist government! But if he does come to America, what is he ever going to do? How is he going to find a job?"

"Let's just take one step at a time," John said. "Hopefully, he can find something in his field, but he needs to improve his English first." In spite of his reassuring words, his eyes looked worried.

"And just remember, Katie," Margaret said with her eyes twinkling, "you can always come and live with us on the mesa! We'll set up an extra army tent. There's plenty of room!"

"Hey, we might take you up on that! I love New Mexico!"

The rest of the week passed quickly and soon Katie had to bid farewell to her family and return to Heidelberg to finish out the semester. Pavol had invited her to return to Czechoslovakia as soon as she could and spend the month of July with him and his parents. Now that they were engaged, it was permissible for her to stay under the roof of her fiancé.

"I can't believe you are getting married," Samantha said as they walked through the *Hauptstrasse* of Heidelberg the last day of classes.

"Sometimes it doesn't seem real to me either," Katie admitted. "It feels like I'm living in some kind of dream!"

"When is the wedding?" Samantha asked curiously.

"Hopefully in December. We are planning to get married after Christmas. I have to go home in August and fulfill my obligations at school as well as my speaking engagements with the Rotary Club, but then I will fly back to Slovakia the end of the fall semester."

"Wow," Samantha said her eyes shining. "I wonder when my turn is coming?"

"Probably sooner than you think," Katie replied. "Haven't you noticed the way Jorge has been looking at you lately?"

"Oh, stop it! He is only a friend! Anyway, I am going to miss you," Samantha said reaching up to hug Katie as they parted.

"I'm going to miss you, too," Katie said tears filling her eyes.

The following weekend was spent packing her things and lugging boxes of books to the post office. Finally, the day of her departure arrived. She looked wistfully around at the cozy little room where she had spent so many eventful months.

"*Aufwiedersehen, Fraulein Boszko,*" Herr Wagner said as she handed him the key. "I wish you all the best and much happiness in the future."

"*Vielen Dank,*" Katie said gratefully shaking his hand. "I enjoyed it so much here. Thank you for everything you have done. I will never forget it."

She loaded her bags in the awaiting taxi, leaned forward and said, "*Hauptbahnhof, bitte!*"

***

"What time are you leaving?" Zuzana asked her youngest son as he finished his breakfast.

"She should be arriving in Bratislava around lunchtime, so I have to go right now," Pavol said taking a last gulp of his cocoa.

"Do you think she will be happy here? We live very simply," Zuzana said worriedly as she looked around their little kitchen.

"I don't know," Pavol said honestly. "I hope so. It may not be easy for her." He stood up and gave her a squeeze. "But how can she not love it like I do?"

Zuzana nodded and turned back to the stove.

She was amazed at all that had happened the last few months. She had no idea her son had fallen in love with the tall American girl she had met at Christmas. Then one evening in May, he announced to both his parents that he was going to get married. It wasn't easy at her age to receive such a shock, but she soon recovered and meditated on the match. At first, she felt a great disappointment that her dream of Pavol becoming a priest was not going to be fulfilled, but in reality she had given up on it a long time ago. Katie seemed like a sweet looking girl with all those curls. But would she make a good wife for her Palo? She wasn't sure how stable these American girls were.

"You are certainly full of surprises," Zuzana said to the Lord as she looked up at the crucifix over the door. "I never know what is going to happen next!"

***

"The next stop is ours," Pavol said squeezing Katie's hand as they sat quietly on the train together. "Here it is! Let's go!" Grabbing her bags and struggling down the aisle, they got out of the train.

"Let me take one," Katie insisted as Pavol tried to pick up all her luggage.

"Janko!" Pavol yelled at his friend who was passing by with a wheelbarrow. "Can you help me here?"

Janko Hudec waved and quickly ran to them.

"*Dobry Den!*" he said with a big smile on his face bowing a little in front of Katie. "*Jak se mas?*" He began taking the bags and loading them on the cart.

"*Dobre!*" Katie replied smiling gratefully.

"Thank God you are here, Janko," Pavol said in Slovak wiping his brow. "I didn't know how I was going to get all this home. Do all women carry around so many things?"

"All of them, my friend," Jan said winking at him. "You had better get used to it! Grab that handle!" Together they pushed the wheelbarrow with Katie strolling behind.

Tall cherry trees lined the street and plump golden cherries hung enticingly within reach. Katie could not resist pulling a few big ones off and popping them in her mouth.

"We're here!" Pavol announced as they walked into the kitchen. Zuzana and Jozef stood up quickly and greeted them both warmly.

"*Vitaj, Katka!* Welcome, Katka," Zuzana said cupping Katie's face in her hands. "You are most welcome."

"*Dakujem,*" Katie stammered out as she bent over to embrace her tiny future mother-in-law. "*Dakujem velmi pekne!*"

"Oh, she already speaks Slovak! Look at that!" Zuzana exclaimed happily.

"Well, not yet, but I hope you will help her, Mama," Pavol said as he took the bags to the room.

Katie sat down at the table and Zuzana brought her a plate of homemade cheese kolaches and offered them to her. Not one to be shy, Katie readily took one and bit into it.

"Mmmm, I love these," Katie said hungrily as she scarfed it down. "May I have another?"

Pavol and his mother looked at each other as Katie helped herself to a second delicious pastry.

"Well, she has a good appetite," Zuzana said chuckling.

Living in a little village suited Katie more than she thought. Breakfast consisted of homemade cottage cheese, fresh farm eggs, and delicious hot chocolate – well, it tasted like hot chocolate – the socialist version of it called *Granko*. The days were spent taking long walks through the village and fields, swimming in the river and lakes as well as picking berries and wild plums in the woods. At night, she rested in the front room under a crisp clean comforter. Gentle breezes lulled her to sleep as the lace curtains quietly danced in the open windows. Moonlight streamed through the windows while an occasional pesky mosquito would sing in her ear.

"I can understand why you call this paradise," Katie said one day as they floated lazily down the river in a canoe. "You must have had so much fun growing up here."

Pavol smiled broadly and said, "You cannot imagine how beautiful it was. We were constantly sneaking out of the house and running to the river to swim. Then we did everything we could to make ourselves dry so our mothers would not find out, but they always knew somehow."

"Then what happened?" Katie asked curiously.

"*Fazku!*" Pavol said smiling broadly and sweeping his hand across his face in a slapping motion. "But it didn't stop us from doing it again."

Katie yawned and leaned back in the boat to rest when suddenly she felt a splash of water on her face. "Hey!" she cried sitting up suddenly.

Pavol sat holding his paddle looking innocently at her. "What?" he asked feigning surprise. "What's the matter? Oh, did you get wet? It must have been a jumping fish."

Katie grinned as she leaned over the boat and splashed him back with a scoop of her hand.

"Now you will be sorry," he smiled wickedly as he wiped the water off his face.

As they paddled back to the shore behind his brother's house, they were both dripping and smiling from their afternoon in the canoe. Katie helped Pavol drag the boat up the side of the bank and carry it to the barn where they deposited it.

"Let's see if my brother is home yet," Pavol said grabbing her hand as they walked through the garden. "I want to ask him about my papers."

As they walked in the entryway and slipped of their shoes, Dalina met them at the door.

"Where were you?" she demanded glaring at Pavol and Katie. "And why are you all wet?"

"We took the canoe and had some fun on the river," Pavol said shrugging as he walked past her into the kitchen and grabbed an apple.

"You took our boat without asking?" she said angrily, her voice rising.

"It's my brother's boat. He doesn't care, so why should you?" Pavol said nonchalantly biting into the apple.

Dalina's face turned red as she began pushing them hurriedly out the front door.

"Get out!" she said yelling, throwing their shoes behind them. "Get out! Who do you think you are? Don't come back until you learn some manners!"

Pavol shot his sister-in-law a piercing look and turned away shaking his head.

Startled, Katie asked, "What just happened here?" She bent down to pick up her shoes slipping them back on.

"I'll tell you later," Pavol said as they walked out the front gate. Grabbing her hand, he started pulling her towards the fields.

"Where are we going?" Katie said panting after a few minutes.

"Do all the girls in your country always ask so many questions?" Pavol said as they plopped down in a grassy meadow behind the cornfields.

"We just like to be informed," Katie said, "and—"

A kiss interrupted her lecture and soon all questions were forgotten as the big fiery ball in the sky began to set behind the mountains.

The next morning, Katie was awoken by the front door banging. She was surprised to see Dalina running into the front hallway of the house and hanging a bag on the door. She ran quickly back out the door. Katie peeked out of the window and saw her riding furiously away on her bicycle towards the brick factory.

Curious to see what was in the bag, she peeked inside. It was full of rolls and pastries.

"Yumm," Katie murmured as she took the bag into the kitchen. Pavol was sitting at the table with his mother. His father was whittling a piece of wood in his usual spot by the stove.

"Look what I found," Katie said depositing the bag on the table.

Zuzana peered inside and chuckled. She said something to Pavol as she stood up to get a knife.

"What did she say?" Katie asked curiously.

"She said that my sister-in-law is feeling sorry for throwing us out yesterday, so this is her way of apologizing."

"Don't people just ever say 'sorry'?

"No. Actions are better, don't you think?"

"I guess so." Katie bit into one of the cheese filled pastries. "Mmmm, maybe you're right."

To Be or Not to Be?

"Katka, wake up!"

Katie sleepily opened one eye and tried to focus on the figure bending over her. Slowly, Pavol's handsome face came into focus.

"What's going on?" she said groggily. "What time is it?"

"It's nine, but there is something very important that I need to talk to you about," he said with a more serious look on his face. "Just get dressed and have breakfast. My mother has already prepared it for you."

He left the room with a quick kiss on her cheek, and Katie threw back the feather comforter. Sitting for a moment on the side of the bed, she looked around at the room. Large wardrobes and old-fashioned pieces of furniture filled the room with its stenciled pink and white plaster walls. Sunlight streamed through the lace curtains. Yawning, she stood up and padded off to the kitchen where homemade cottage cheese, thick slices of sourdough bread, and a soft-boiled egg in a dainty eggcup awaited her.

After swallowing the last delicious bite, Pavol took her by the hand and led her outside into the garden. He pulled her into the cornfield where the stalks already stood high above their heads.

"Let's sit down here. We need to discuss something," Pavol began rather hesitantly. "It has to do with our faith and the Catholic Church."

Katie sat down on the furrows between the corn stalks and looked up at the blue sky. She said, "This is an unusual place to have such a serious conversation." She tried to smile, but stopped as she saw how earnestly he was looking at her.

"I have wanted to talk to you about this for a long time…" His voice trailed off and he began wringing his hands. "I should have done it a long time ago." Swallowing hard, he said, "I think it is very important that we both worship together, in the same church, and one day, when we have children, they need to grow up to be, uh, well, t-t-to be Catholic."

Katie stiffened, pulled back her hand, and looked at him with wide eyes.

Not surprised by her reaction, he gently reached for her hand again and asked, "Does that disturb you?"

Katie's mind started racing and she could feel her heart pounding. *Is he asking me to become Catholic? Why would he do that?*

She stuttered out an answer, feeling confused. "Well, yes – it does! I always thought we understood each other about these things, but I guess we haven't really talked about it yet. Not concretely."

Standing up, she looked down at him. "I love the Lord, as you do, but, but I don't want to be part of a big organized institution like, like the Catholic Church!" she burst out. "Can't we just go on like we are?"

Pavol shook his head slowly but firmly. "No, no, it would not be good. It would be much better if we were both members of the same church!"

Katie began to feel angry. "And you're just now telling me this? Don't you think it's a little late to be discussing this? I thought you told me that it did not matter in this country – that 'we are all just believers'!"

Pavol looked at her pleadingly. "Katie, I am sorry; you are right! We should have talked about this much earlier. But please try to understand – I have been attending Mass every day of my life. I grew up in this Catholic village and learned all I know from a very devout Catholic mother. Can't you see? It's who I am!"

Katie stared at him dumbfounded, the tears beginning to flow.

"Besides," Pavol said looking at his hands, "what would my family and friends at church say if I, Pavol Tesar, married a woman who was not Catholic?"

That did it. Katie jumped up and ran into the house slamming the door behind her. Throwing herself on the couch, great sobs began to wrack her body.

"I can't do this," she said aloud gasping for breath. "I can't join THAT church!"

Hearing her weeping, Zuzana opened the door with concern. "Katka, what's the matter? Are you sick?"

"Leave her, Mama," Pavol said coming behind her and pulling her out of the room. "I upset her."

"What did you do to her?" Zuzana said looking at him with alarm.

Shaking his head, he shut the door behind them.

"What's going on? Did you two have a fight?" Zuzana demanded in a loud whisper.

"I'll explain it to you in the kitchen. She needs to be alone right now to think things through," Pavol said tiredly.

Several minutes passed, perhaps an hour, before Katie pulled herself up into a sitting position and stared at the crucifix on the wall.

Okay, just breathe, she told herself. *Stop overreacting. Stay calm.*

She remembered what some people back home used to say about the Catholic Church. *They called it the great Harlot of Babylon and Jezebel! Those people pray to Mary and worship saints!*

She began to vehemently shake her head and said aloud, "I just can't marry him! This is simply not going to work! And how dare he wait so long to tell me!"

Suddenly a sheepish feeling came over her when she realized she hadn't really brought the subject up herself. She just assumed everything was okay the way it was.

"You did it, Boszko!" she said aloud. "Way to go! That's it. It's over!"

This last thought hit her with a sudden reality. She sat still on the bed and thought for a moment. What would her life be now without Pavol? A wave of loneliness and emptiness washed over her. "But I love him. I need him," she murmured.

"What am I going to do, Lord?" She cried lifting up her arms towards heaven, "What am I going to do?" She spent the next hour pouring out her worries and fears before the One who is always ready to listen.

Pavol went outside and helped his father chop wood. Neither one said a word to each other but worked silently together for the rest of the morning. After he put away the last armload of wood, he looked up at the door and saw Katie standing on the steps and leaning on the railing. She gave him a weak smile. Heartened, he sprang up the steps and gave her a hug.

"Katka, I am sorry for not talking about this before. I know it came as a shock to you. I am very sorry. It's my fault," Pavol said stroking her hair and looking at her face. "Wow, your eyes are so green!"

"They always get like that after I have a good cry. Look, I'm sorry for being such a drama queen," she said looking down at the ground.

"A what?" Pavol asked looking bewildered.

"Being so upset... You know, getting so hysterical," she replied glancing up at his face.

"Oh," he said waiting for her to continue.

"Well, I guess He is there, too," she said shrugging.

"Who? Where?"

"God. In your church – the Catholic Church," she said looking at him with a look of wonder. "You know, I had this distinct feeling as I was praying that He was in the room with me, and, well, it was like He was just patting me on the back."

Cathy walked down the steps and sat down as she continued, "He told me, Pavol, that it's going to be all right. You know, I felt like a little girl whose father was telling her not to be afraid."

Pavol looked up at the sky in relief and clapped his hands. "*Daka, Bohu!* Come on, we have to catch the bus to Topolcany!"

"Where are we going?" Katie said sniffing and wiping her eyes.

"We have an appointment with the Dekan at the church this afternoon," Pavol said. "Go get your shoes on!"

"But I am a mess," Katie said running into the hallway and peering in the mirror.

"It doesn't matter – you look fine! Hurry!"

As they arrived at the rectory offices in Topolcany, Pavol smiled reassuringly at her.

"I want to talk to the Dekan and ask him what you have to do to join the Church," Pavol said squeezing her hand.

Katie looked nervously at the door as Pavol rang the bell. "Aren't we rushing things a little bit? I mean, there's no hurry, is there?" she ventured to say.

An elderly lady opened the door and greeted them. Pavol explained his business to her in Slovak, and she ushered them into a large room with a large wooden table and a magnificent painting of Mary and the baby Jesus. Seating them, she walked quickly out and soon returned with a tray that had a bottle of juice and mineral water on it. Katie felt a bit comforted as the Slovak women poured her a drink and patted her on the shoulder.

"*Američanka?*" she asked wonderingly. "How did you two ever meet?"

"It's a long story, *Teta,*" Pavol said smiling at her, "but I can tell you it's an amazing one."

Pleased, the elderly woman nodded knowingly and shuffled out of the room. Soon, the Dekan came in and smiled broadly when he saw Pavol.

"So, this is your fiancée!" he said warmly shaking Pavol and Katie's hands.

Pavol explained their situation and Katie's plan to join the church. The elderly priest talked with them, and Pavol translated for her. He explained that she would need to attend classes when she returned home to America and that when she came back to Slovakia at Christmas, they would allow

266

her to enter the Catholic Church. He said Pavol could be her sponsor and mentor her in the process. Katie asked a few questions, and Pavol did his best to explain. When he finished, he brought out a beautiful crystal bottle of schnaps and said, "We must toast your engagement and upcoming nuptials!" Pouring the thick brown liquid into elegant crystal shot glasses, he said, *"Na zdravia!"*

After they left the priest's office, Pavol and Katie walked silently through the streets and out into the countryside. The birds flew above the soft green fields and wispy clouds dotted the light blue sky. Katie wondered at the sense of peace she felt. *Lord, you surprise me,* she chuckled silently as she looked up. The wind blew gently against her face.

"Oh, no!" Pavol gasped suddenly.

Shaken out of her reverie, Katie stared at him asking, "What's wrong now for goodness sake?"

"Now that you are joining our Church, maybe you will want to become a nun!" Pavol said looking at her worriedly. "Then what will I do? I won't be able to marry you!"

Katie began to laugh until she cried. "I don't think I'm that Catholic yet," she stammered.

Now that the most important question was settled, it was time to start the official paperwork of getting married. Since they did not have a phone in Hrusovany, Pavol began running from office to office in Bratislava to see what they had to do to get married in December. It did not seem like a good idea to wait until next summer.

Time was short, and they did not want to delay their married life together. Katie accompanied Pavol on many of these administrative visits. A few of the clerks were disbelieving that an American girl wanted to come to their country and get married. They became suspicious that Pavol was just trying to use the situation and flee the country.

Some of the office clerks were afraid of what their bosses would say and hurriedly referred them to another office in Bratislava. After yet another push out the door and directions to a different office, they finally ended up in front of the secret police's door and were harshly scolded that no one was even allowed to enter that building, and how dare they try to talk to them! They quickly ran down the stairs and out into the street.

Pavol held Katie's hand as they slowly walked through the streets of the Old Town. A light rain began to fall.

"Are you hungry?" Pavol asked glumly peering through the window of a delicatessen.

"You know I'm always hungry," Katie said trying to sound cheerful.

Pavol ordered a pudding for himself and brought Katie her Russian eggs.

"*Na pit?*" the young waitress asked impatiently.

"What do you want to drink, Katka?"

"Just water," Katie shrugged.

"You know, in my country, water is only for sick people," Pavol smiled dryly.

"I like water," Katie said shrugging her shoulders.

"Two waters, please," Pavol said to the young girl.

Looking surprised and rolling her eyes, the waitress brought out two bottles of mineral water.

"No, no, no – not the bubbles," Pavol began to protest in Slovak.

"It's okay, Pavol! I actually like it."

"*Dobre, dobre,*" Pavol said waving his hand.

Smacking the bottles and glasses down on the table, the waitress stomped off in a huff.

"The service is so friendly in this country," Katie remarked as she sipped her water.

"Is it better in yours?" Pavol asked absentmindedly.

"Hey, in America, the customer is always right – no matter what!" Katie said as she bit into the potato salad underneath the hard boiled egg covered in hollandaise sauce.

Pavol shook his head in disbelief and muttered, "I can't imagine. You always have to be afraid here that someone is going to… how do you say? Bite your head off?"

Katie stared at him sympathetically. He looked so tired and worn from all of their office visits. She leaned towards him and said gently, "So, what are we going to do now?"

Pavol looked at her and a glint of defiance shone in his eyes. "Well, my home district has not been very helpful, and we haven't made much progress here in Bratislava. What do you think? Where would you like to get married?"

Katie sat still for a moment and then said slowly, "You know, we met in Trnava, and all of my dad's relatives do live there."

Encouraged by the thought, Pavol sat up and exclaimed, "Yes! I have many priest friends in Trnava who could help us! Let's go visit Father Jan tomorrow! He might have some good advice for us!"

The next day, Pavol and Katie hopped out of the bus in Trnava and made their way to the rectory and rang the bell.

"Pavol, my friend!" a young, dark-haired man exclaimed as he opened the door. "We haven't seen you for several months! Where have you been?" He ushered them energetically through the courtyard and up into his apartment.

Pavol quickly introduced Katie to Father Jan and a look of incredulity spread across the young priest's face. He took her hand and shook it warmly. In halting English, he said, "Nice to meet you!"

Katie smiled appreciatively at him.

They sat down at a little table and Father Jan quickly brought open-face sandwiches and wine for their refreshment. Pavol began to talk about their troubles they were having trying to arrange their marriage. Father Jan listened intently glancing over at Katie now and then. Finally, Pavol finished his story by telling him that he had lost his job and would soon be unemployed. A serious look spread across the priest's face and he tapped his fingers thoughtfully on the table.

Slapping his hands on his lap, he looked up at Pavol and said, "Go and talk to the state office here. I know the woman who works there, and I think she will help you get your papers in order. Anyway, you should get married here! When your fiancée returns from America, we will bring her into the church and celebrate your wedding! But which church did you have in mind? You know we have several beautiful ones in Trnava. This used to be called 'Little Roma', you know. Please, tell her that!"

Pavol translated for Katie and a delighted smile spread across her face.

"I have always dreamed of a wedding in a beautiful European cathedral!" She clasped her hands.

"So, let's go! Let's take a tour right now! The weather is lovely outside," Father Jan said standing up.

They walked first to one of the churches and peered inside.

"What do you think?" Pavol asked Katie. Father Jan looked at her in anticipation.

"It's lovely, but don't you think it's a little dark?"

"Yes!" Pavol said emphatically as he led them out.

"What did she say?" Father Jan asked.

"Not this one – it's too dark. What about the Cathedral of St. John the Baptist?"

Father Jan looked a little taken aback. "Palo, it's not used anymore. It's more like a museum. The government won't allow us to serve Mass there. Only on very special occasions!"

"Let's go and look at it. I always liked that one the best."

As Pavol and Katie waited for Father Jan to get the key from the rectory's office, they admired the outside of the church and the plaza surrounding it. Father Jan pushed the huge key into the lock and pushed against the heavy door.

"Oy, oy, oy, this is a heavy one!" he moaned.

Pavol flung his body against it and the door swung open. Katie slowly entered behind them stepping onto the cool marble floors. Looking around in awe, she gasped, "Ohhh, Pavol. It is just, just... exquisite!"

Father Jan proudly gestured towards the barrel-vaulted ceilings and paintings as well as the chapels on the side decorated in gold and walls richly adorned in Baroque ornamentation. In broken English, he said to Katie, "Italian masters! Nicolas Esterhazy ordered it in 1629!"

Leading them towards the front of the church, he pointed at the massive wooden altar below the paintings depicting the story of John the Baptist and the baptism of Jesus. Katie gazed at the intricately carved figures decorating the altar.

Turning to Pavol, she said breathlessly, "It's magnificent! Would it... I mean, could we...?"

Pavol looked questioningly at Father Jan, who shrugged helplessly.

"Well, it still belongs to the dioceses. Technically..." his voice trailed off.

"Thank you, Father, thank you," Pavol said grabbing his hand and shaking it vigorously. Turning to Katie, he began to speak excitedly in English.

Father Jan stared at the happy young couple and mused. Finally, he tore his gaze away and looked up at the altar. "This isn't going to be easy, Father," he muttered. "Not going to be easy."

Back to America

The train began to pick up speed as Katie stared at the passing Czech villages and towns. She had just said her last goodbye to Pavol at the *Hlavna Stanica* in Czechoslovakia's capital city. Pavol had gone with her from Bratislava to Prague on the overnight train. They had been alone most of the night in their compartment, holding each other close and trying to remain cheerful. The only interruption came from the conductor who periodically came to check their passports, tickets, and make sure they were not doing anything improper.

She could not stop the tears from coming as they hugged and kissed one last time.

"Do not worry, Katka," he said softly as he stroked her hair and held her close. "We will be together soon. Very soon."

As the train pulled out, she watched him grow smaller and smaller on the platform. It seemed strange that he was not allowed to travel with her to Germany, but the Iron Curtain, like a big heavy iron gate, was slamming shut behind her. Tears blurred her vision, but she whisked them quickly away and tried to focus on objects outside. She glanced down at the gold band that she wore on her left hand, indicating that she was now engaged. The soft yellow metal seemed to glow in the morning sun.

The flight the next day was long, but finally she arrived in Texas. She was relieved to see her mother and father eagerly waving at her near the gate. A hot gust of dry air smacked her in the face as she stepped out of the airplane.

"Mom! Dad!" She fell into her eager parents' arms kissing and hugging them both. "Oh, it's so good to see you!"

"How was your flight? Did you have any problems? How was Pavol when you left him?"

They drove home and Katie relaxed on the couch as her mother brought her a big glass of diet coke.

"Oh, finally, lots of ice," Katie murmured contentedly as she sipped the cold drink.

"So, let's hear it. Tell us everything," Paula said eagerly settling in next to her husband John.

"Well, I want to tell you all about my summer in Pavol's village and his family, but first I want to tell you about last night at the airport hotel! The weirdest things happened in the restaurant; it was like a movie! You won't believe this…"

Katie began to relate how depressed she was feeling all alone in the Frankfurt Airport hotel, but she still felt hungry and thought if she ate something, it might make her feel better, so she went down to the restaurant in the lobby.

"You know me! I'm always hungry," Katie chuckled.

"Weren't you scared to be wandering around by yourself?" her mother asked worriedly.

"Mom, you can't just hide yourself away all the time! Anyway, just listen to what happened…" Katie continued.

She had wandered into the airport café, and even though it was crowded with travelers, she was able to find an empty table near the window. An elegantly dressed woman with a blonde chignon sat at the next table talking with a gentleman who had slicked back hair and wore several expensive looking rings. Two large men in black suits and dark glasses were seated next to the woman and man as they carried on a low conversation in Spanish.

The view out the big plate glass window was perfect for watching the airplanes land and take-off. As Katie watched the 747 Jumbo Jets take off in the air, a short dark man with a thin mustache asked if he could share her table. Surprised and awoken from her reverie, she quickly shook her head no. He walked away looking a little disgruntled, hovering near the door glaring at her and then casting furtive glances at the table full of people next to her. Katie felt a little apprehensive, but she tried to ignore him and eat her sandwich, but all at once she was aware that Mr. Mustachio was suddenly standing behind her pretending to look out the window at the airport.

What the heck? I think, this guy is trying to steal my purse, Katie thought, grabbing her leather bag off the back of her chair and putting it on her lap. The strange man continued to ease closer to the table next to her, trying his best to squeeze behind her chair. Suddenly, he leaned over, grabbed the briefcase that was next to the rich gentleman's chair, and tossed it to another man who was waiting at the door of the restaurant.

They both quickly dashed out of the dining room with the two bodyguards in hot pursuit.

Shocked, Katie sat up straight in her chair and gaped at the scene. The next thing she heard was a thudding sound down in the lobby of the hotel and a man's shrill cry. She sat frozen to her chair as she watched the two large bodyguards in black drag the limp little man and his accomplice back into the restaurant. Everyone in the dining area sat deadly still. Flipping off his sunglasses, one of the bodyguards popped the briefcase open to check if its contents were still intact. Katie gasped as she had never seen so much money in one place before. Stacks of dollar bills were neatly bundled in the briefcase. The owner of the briefcase murmured something angrily in Spanish, snapped the briefcase shut, and they all left quickly together. Katie sat stunned in her chair and then asked the flustered waitress, *"Entschuldigung? Die Rechnung?"* She paid her bill and ran to her hotel room where she deftly locked the door and the deadbolt.

"Oh, my Lord, I would have been scared to death!" her mother exclaimed patting her heart.

"Thank God, nothing worse happened," her father added seriously. "All kinds of characters in these airports. I think your mother is right – your guardian angels have their work cut out for them taking care of you!"

"Yeah, I felt like I was in the middle of one of those detective shows! Pretty exciting, huh!"

Her father snorted and returned to his newspaper. "At least you are home now safe and sound."

At eleven p.m., her father yawned and said, "Okay, ladies. You can continue this conversation without me. I have to get up in the morning and go to work. Don't stay up too late!"

"So, do you have peace about your decision to join the Catholic Church?" her mother asked tentatively after her husband made his escape.

"Yes, I do," Katie said smiling and shrugging a little. "I believe the Lord is directing us."

"Well, that's the main thing. You know I think your relationship with Jesus is more important than some religion, but maybe the Lord is going to use you there. You cannot put God in a box! Now, how long can you stay at home before you have to go back to school?"

"I have to be in Lubbock by next Monday as the teaching assistants are having a meeting with Herr Alexander and Dr. Goebel. The semester starts the week after that."

"Well, at least we have almost a week to spend together," Paula said hugging her daughter. "I think we need to do some shopping at the mall tomorrow! After you wake up and recover from your jet lag, of course!"

The week passed pleasantly by, but soon it was time to load up the blue Malibu and move her things back to Lubbock. She was renting a furnished studio apartment near campus and was going to live alone this semester. After her parents helped her unload her things in the apartment, they had lunch together and Katie kissed them goodbye. She felt a strange tugging at her heart as she thought about the months ahead on her own. *I guess I had better get busy and then time will pass quickly*, she thought to herself.

The next day in Lubbock, she rode her bicycle across campus towards the Foreign Language building. As she walked down the hall in the German department, she heard a loud, booming voice behind her. "Well, she's back!"

Katie spun around and saw her German professor, Dr. Goebel, beaming at her. He always reminded her of Rex Harrison in *My Fair Lady*.

"*Jawohl, Herr Professor!*" she said brightly. "You can't get rid of me!"

"*Und wie war es?*" he asked her trying hard to look serious.

"*Ganz toll, muss ich sagen!*" Katie said bursting into laughter giving him a big hug.

"It's good to see you. And what's this I hear? You're getting married? It's not true, is it?"

Katie shrugged her shoulders and replied, "What can I say? It's true! I'm getting married in December."

"This December? My, my, my! That's quite soon. Well, I have to be off to another meeting, but we'll talk later. See you this afternoon!" He turned and walked quickly down the hall.

Katie settled back into her office and checked her schedule. It was going to be a busy semester with classes to take and working part-time in the language laboratory, but she was looking forward to keeping her mind occupied. She missed Pavol so much, but writing letters helped her feel closer to him. In addition, she was starting her first class that day to learn about Catholicism. The classes were called the Rite of Christian Initiation and were going to be at the little Spanish style church near campus, St. Elizabeth's.

After working a few hours on her Introductory German class lesson plan, Katie checked her watch and gasped, "Oh, man! It's almost six o'clock! I've gotta go. I'm gonna be late!"

Gathering up her books, she flew out of the building and jumped on her bike. As she turned down the street where the campus church stood on the corner, she was struck by the beautiful architecture. It was not a grand cathedral like she had seen in Rome and other European cities, but it looked more like the small mission churches she had seen in New Mexico with its arched doorways and red tiled roof. She walked hesitantly towards the offices and knocked on the door.

"Come in," a voice sang out. Katie stepped in in and saw a plump woman with long black hair and dark eyes.

"I'm here for the RCIA class?" Katie asked a little nervously.

"Oh, welcome!" the woman exclaimed looking up from her typewriter. "Deacon Sid's class is just down the hall on the left."

Katie thanked her and made her way to the classroom. A strange sense of peace surrounded her, as she passed statues and pictures of saints in the corridor. When she opened the door, she saw a bearded man in his thirties sitting at the head of a table surrounded by six other people.

"Hello, hello!" he said jovially gesturing towards a chair. "Have a seat! We were just introducing ourselves!"

Katie took her seat and soon the class was having a lively discussion about the history of the Catholic Church and the Church Fathers.

"But what about Mary? Where does she fit in?" she asked towards the end of the lesson.

"What about her?" Deacon Sid retorted, his eyes twinkling.

"Well, in the Lutheran church we talked about her being the mother of Christ, but why do Catholics ask her to pray for them? Isn't that wrong? Aren't we only supposed to pray to Jesus or our Father in heaven?"

"This seems to be the biggest obstacle for Protestants when they are considering the Catholic Church. Look, do you ever ask your own mother to pray for you? Or do you ask your friends to say a prayer for you when you have an exam or something difficult to overcome?"

"Well, uh, yes."

"It's the same thing. She is not equal to God. She is not a god. But she is the mother of our Lord Jesus Christ and the mother of us all, so that makes her a very special lady. We ask her to pray for us and she has pretty good connections, let me tell you."

"But she isn't alive. I mean, she isn't on this earth anymore!"

"Oh, she's alive. She may not be on this earth anymore, but she is definitely alive and plays a very important role. Haven't you ever heard of the communion of saints? We believe that all the saints in heaven are alive and praying for us. They're rooting for us to make it in our Christian lives and finish the race!"

Katie was quiet as she mulled this over in her mind. She liked the idea of having a group of cheerleaders in heaven.

"Sometimes, it does seem like people are worshipping Mary or the Saints when they bow in front of statues or bring flowers. No one expects you to do that. You should not do something you are uncomfortable doing. However, some people express their faith in that manner."

"And why do people pray the Rosary?" Katie asked. "What is it exactly?"

"The Rosary is a type of prayer that leads us into meditation. It consists of five decades and each decade is dedicated to a different aspect of Jesus' life in this world. The first decade is called the 'Joyful Mysteries' and as we pray, we think about the events surrounding Christ's birth such as the Archangel Gabriel announcing the good news to Mary or His birth in a stable in Bethlehem. Here's a little book you can take home and look at it. Let me know if you have any questions. All right, any other questions before we close tonight? No? Okay, let's bow our heads in a closing prayer. In the name of the Father, the Son, and the Holy Spirit..."

Katie stepped outside after the class and took a deep breath. She opened the little booklet Deacon Sid had given her and looked at the pictures of the Virgin Mary cradling the baby Jesus in the manger. She sensed that special peace again that she had experienced earlier. Humming under her breath, she headed home.

Preparations

The fall months flew by and December quickly arrived. The young couple who had been separated by miles of ocean and land could not believe that their wedding date was already upon them. Pavol was busy finishing his dissertation as well as arranging the wedding in Trnava while his American fiancée was finishing her finals and wrapping up the semester at Texas Tech in Lubbock, Texas.

"But is he a romantic?" Dr. Goebel mused as he stopped by Katie's office in the Foreign Language building where she was packing up her books.

Her eyes sparkled as she turned and nodded, "Oh, yes, definitely!"

"Good," said Dr. Goebel briskly. "I would not have it any other way. Let me know if you need anything else before you go. Seriously."

Katie stood up and wiped her hands looking around her small office.

"I think I'm good," she grinned gratefully at her boss. "I'll be flying out this weekend, and then I'll be staying with Pavol and his parents until he can arrange his papers to leave the country. I'm fixing to call the embassy about my visa."

"Fixing to? Fixing to?" Dr. Goebel laughed.

"Okay, okay. I'm *about* to call the embassy about my visa. Is that better?" Katie said wryly as she piled more books into an empty box.

"You Texans and your dialects," Dr. Goebel chuckled. "And you are planning to finish your Master's Degree next year? You're coming back in the fall, correct?"

"Yes, God willing, if everything goes as planned."

"Well, keep me posted. We are anxious to meet him!"

"Thanks! I'll be in touch," Katie promised, sighing a little.

"Katie, is something wrong?" Dr. Goebel remarked quietly noticing her change of demeanor.

"It's just, well, I guess reality is hitting me a little," she said grimly. "I went to the department of geography here on campus and talked to the chair about Pavol."

"And?"

"He said that there are very few jobs in the field of geography, and that it would be better if Pavol stayed home and tried to work there."

"Oh, I see," Dr. Goebel muttered stroking his chin.

"I mean, how can he say that?" Katie exclaimed, frustration lacing her voice. "Doesn't he know that is not even possible? Pavol lost his job because of his religious views! He can't even work there as a professor anymore."

"It's not going to be easy, Katie," Dr. Goebel said patting her on the shoulder, "but I know your faith and Pavol's faith as well will see you through. By the way, how is his English?"

"He's taking lessons with Mrs. Holcik. She is an American lady who lives in Trnava. He learns quickly, but he needs more time. His German isn't bad though!"

"Yes, I remember meeting her when we visited your aunt and uncle summer before last. We'll just have to see what we can do to help him when you get back." Checking his watch, he suddenly started, "Oh, I've got to run to a meeting, but *alles Gute und schoene Reise!*" Dr. Goebel leaned over and gave her a hug before hurrying out of her office.

"*Vielen Dank,*" Katie waved at him.

***

"So, do you have everything ready, Synchek moj?" Zuzana stroked her youngest son's hair as he sat down wearily at the table.

"I hope so," Pavol sighed. "I hate all these details. I stopped by the police office this morning, and they said that I will have to bring Katka immediately after our wedding to register her. Strba, the main one, said that she will only be able to stay in the country six months, and no longer."

"Six months! She has to leave in six months?" Zuzana felt her heart stop for a minute. If Katie had to leave in six months, would her son be leaving, too?

Guessing her thoughts, Pavol said gently, "Mama, what am I going to do here? I don't want to leave you and Apa, but I don't have a job. I must find something!"

278

"You could work at the co-op," Zuzana suggested weakly, "or maybe Martin could find you a job at the Agrokomplex."

Pavol was silent for a moment and then said, "I'm not sure she can handle living here. She is used to a very different way of life. We will have to pray. If I decide to stay here, Katka will have to leave in any case and go back to America to apply for Czechoslovakian residency. It might take months or maybe more than a year before they give her permission."

Zuzana sat down beside her son and gripped his hand, murmuring a quiet prayer that only he could hear. He squeezed her hand and said, "Don't worry, Mama. Things will work out – for the best."

"Yes, my son, God's will be done. We will see... but couldn't you have just found a nice Slovak girl from our village? Do you have to always make things so complicated?"

Pavol smiled weakly at her, shrugging as he walked out the door.

***

Katie boarded the plane; she had her bridal garment bag in one hand, and a guitar case in the other.

That was a very special day when her mother and her mother's best friend drove up to Lubbock to go shopping for her dress. They drove to Hemphill Well's department store and the store assistant asked her what she was looking for.

"Well, I have always loved the Spanish style of dresses with lots of lace, and oh, I need to have long sleeves – it's going to be cold there! And if it could have a long train! I love cathedral trains!"

The girl smiled and said she would be right back. The first dress she tried on was a classical wedding dress with an ivory tone. Katie admired the cut of the dress and the lace, but when she put it on, her reflection looked pale and tired.

"Nope, not this one," Katie shook her head.

The next dress she tried on had a blue tint and was more of a ballgown.

"I don't think this is me either," Katie said looking at herself critically in the mirror.

"I liked the first one, Katie! You looked like a movie star in that one," Lura Lee, her mother's friend, exclaimed.

"I don't think ivory goes with your skin tone," her mother said flatly.

Lura Lee looked at Katie's mother but pursed her lips together.

The shop assistant knocked on the door and brought in another dress. "Why don't you try this one on. We just got it in yesterday!" she said excitedly. "It has the lace but I'm afraid only a chapel length train. I hope you still like it."

Katie stepped into the dress as the shop assistant helped fasten the back. She turned to look in the mirror and gasped.

"Oh, my," she gulped.

Katie's mother and Lura Lee were silent. Then her mother said, "Oh, Katie, you're beautiful. You're positively glowing! I think this is it!"

Lura Lee slowly nodded her head in agreement, a broad smile sweeping her face.

The stewardess took Katie's guitar to a closet in the front of the airplane and then directed her to a window seat. Pulling the overhead compartment down, Katie gently loaded her gown, trying not to crumple it. She plopped down by the window and peered outside at the Dallas landscape. The sky was clear and blue – no clouds in sight. She felt her heart racing a little as the engines started and the airplane slowly pulled away from the gate.

"Dear Lord, it's really happening. I'm on my way."

"What's in the bag, honey? I noticed you were being really careful about it." A little elderly lady with big earrings buckled herself in the seat next to her.

Katie smiled and simply answered, "My wedding dress."

"Oh, how exciting! So, what does it look like? Is it one of these modern strapless gowns like my granddaughter wore at her wedding?"

"No, it's quite classical really – lots of lace, a chapel length train, and long sleeves."

"And forgive me for being so nosy, but where are you getting married?"

"In Czechoslovakia," Katie began. "My fiancé is there..."

***

"Where is she?" Pavol mumbled straining to see through the snow. He rubbed his hands to get the circulation back.

"You know, you should wear gloves," Jana said as she huddled next to him outside at the bus station.

"You know I never wear gloves; besides, I always lose them," he replied impatiently.

"Yes, I know. So, what time is she supposed to come?" Jana asked again a little wearily.

"She said that she would arrive at six thirty a.m. at the train station in Vienna and then would catch the seven thirty bus to Bratislava. She should be here by now! What time is it now?"

Jane pushed up her coat sleeve and peered under her heavy gloves to check her watch.

"It's almost nine o'clock. Maybe they got delayed," she said trying to sound convincing.

Pavol suddenly stopped pacing and looked Jana frantically in the eye. "You don't think she's changed her mind, do you? Maybe she isn't even coming!"

"Palko, calm down. Everything is all right. Don't worry! Look, I have to meet Albert at home now, but come with Katka whenever you can. You know I want to help you with the wedding arrangements." Jana leaned over and kissed Pavol lightly on both cheeks. "Call me! Ciao!"

Pavol nodded nervously and waved as Jana walked away looking back at him over her shoulder.

"So, where IS she?" His voice trailed off as he saw a big bus lumber around the corner. Relief filled him as he saw Katie's face beaming at him from behind the frosted, grimy window.

His heart started beating faster as he saw her descend out of the bus. She waved at him, and he ran over to her scooping her up in his arms. She laughed as he spun her around in his big bear coat much to the amusement of the other passengers. Then he sat her gently down on the pavement and pulled her even closer.

"Katka, you are finally here. You are here – with me!" he whispered kissing her.

"Yup! You're stuck with me now!" Breathing in his scent, she returned his kiss and then pulled his hand playfully. "Come on, we have to get my stuff."

They walked over to the bus where the driver was unlocking the baggage compartment doors to unload the suitcases. Katie pointed at her garment bag, blue Samsonite suitcase, and black guitar case. "There they are!"

Pavol grabbed them up, staggering a little under the weight of the suitcase, and motioned towards the bus station. "Let's go inside and drink something hot. Our bus to Trnava leaves in about forty-five minutes. Did you have a good trip? Are you very tired?"

Just as she opened her mouth to answer, Katie's boot skidded on a patch of ice.

"Whoops! I think I need better boots. These are a little slick on the bottom. Well, I had a very interesting trip, and yes, I'm a bit tired, but I have a lot to tell you."

Pavol pulled Katie inside while juggling her luggage in the other hand. He found a small table in the corner and pulled back the chair for her. Gently setting her things down, he said, "I'll be right back with the tea or do you want cocoa? Are you hungry?"

"Oh, yes! I didn't eat breakfast this morning – hot chocolate would be great," she said feeling the jet lag descend upon her.

Pavol came back with a tray full of open-faced sandwiches and two cups of steaming hot chocolate. Katie helped him unload everything on the table.

"Mmmm, this looks so good. I have missed this good bread," she said putting a sandwich on her plate.

"Let's say a prayer of thanksgiving," Pavol said reaching for her hands across the table. Katie reluctantly relinquished her bread as they both crossed themselves and bowed their heads.

"Hey, you crossed yourself!" he exclaimed.

"I'm learning," she said smiling and bowing her head.

"Dear Heavenly Father, thank you. Thank you for bringing Katie here. Thank you that she is with me. Thank you for this food you have given us. Please bless us. Amen."

Katie looked up and smiled appreciatively. "Thank you for being here. You know I was worried that maybe you had changed your mind and would not even be here waiting for me!"

Pavol smiled incredulously replying, "The same thought crossed my mind, too. What happened? Why was the bus so late?"

Katie grinned and began to take off her coat and scarf. "It's kind of a long story. You know, everything went smoothly yesterday. I made all my flight connections, and I got to the Frankfurt Airport right on time."

She took a sip of her drink before continuing, "Then I found the shuttle train that goes directly to the main train station, so I hopped on it with all of my bags and caught the *Franz Josef* overnight express train to Vienna – just like I always do, right? But then the conductor told me there had been a change in the timetable and due to some work being done on the railroad, we would not get to Vienna until seven twenty in the morning!"

"I thought you were supposed to get there at six thirty!" Pavol said looking surprised.

"So did I, but it didn't happen that way. So, as a result, I missed the seven thirty bus to Bratislava!"

"But you were on the bus this morning," Pavol said puzzled as he took a bite out of his sandwich.

Katie's eyes twinkled. "Well, the Lord works in mysterious ways."

Pavol took a sip of his tea and asked, "What does 'mysterious' mean?"

"It simply means we do not understand everything the Lord is doing in our lives."

"Ahhh."

"Anyway, I got out of the train station, and took a taxi to the Vienna bus station to see if I could still make it. The traffic was not too bad, and the driver drove like crazy trying to get me there on time."

"Like crazy? Oh, you mean he drove really fast."

"Right. So, when I got there, they told us that the bus had just left. I started to cry, and the driver felt so badly about missing my connection that he offered to drive me to the border. He said he could overtake the bus, and I could board it there."

Pavol sat back in his chair amazed. "All the way to the border? But wasn't it very expensive? That's over fifty kilometers!"

"Well, that was the thing. I told him I could only pay him twenty U.S. dollars, and he said that would be fine."

As she continued her story, she remembered with a shiver how the taxi driver wove in and out through the icy streets at high speed. Katie sat in the back clutching her seat as he skidded around the corners. Finally, they were out of the city and on the highway.

"*Sehen Sie, Fraulein! Da vorne! Dort ist der Autobus!*" The taxi driver pointed at the Austrian bus on the highway. Katie peered over his shoulder and saw the bus headed for the Austrian/Czechoslovakian border.

"I'm going to pass him now!" the driver said gleefully as he accelerated even more. Katie peered up at all of the passengers staring down in disbelief as the Viennese taxi sped past.

Soon, they left the bus behind and headed east on the lonely highway. As they passed the gray, seemingly barren villages and small townships, Katie could see the guard stations and barbed wire fences on the horizon.

"Look, Fraulein, I cannot drive past the Austrian border, so you will have to walk across. Will you be okay?" The driver looked back at her with a trace of concern in his face.

"Yes, yes, thank you so much," Katie exclaimed pulling out the twenty dollars she had in her wallet. Thrusting it towards him, she said apologetically, "I'm so sorry that I don't have more."

The taxi pulled up in front of the Austrian guards who stared at them curiously. He put up his hand to refuse her money and then laid it on his heart saying, "It's my wedding present for you."

Then he quickly jumped out of the car, unloaded her luggage, and started the engine. Katie stood blinking in the snow with the wind swirling around her as the taxi drove off, its wheels spinning in the snow.

She turned around, and the Austrian guard asked her curtly, "Pass?"

"Moment." She bent over her purse and pulled out her passport. After studying it for a moment and then looking at her luggage, the tall blonde guard asked her in English, "Why are you traveling to the Tschechoslowakei?"

"*Ich werde heiraten*[101]," Katie replied in German.

The guards looked at each other in surprise and then began to smile. "*Eine Hochzeit? Dort drueben? Sind Sie verruckt?*"[102]

"*Vielleicht!*"[103] Katie laughed back.

Chuckling, the guard gave her back the passport and helped her balance the suitcase in one hand and the guitar case in the other. He carefully draped her wedding dress over her right arm.

Then he said in an apologetic tone, "I'm sorry you have to walk alone, but we are not allowed to cross over with you. Otherwise, I would help you." Then gently shaking his finger in her face he admonished her, "*Seien Sie vorsichtig!*"[104]

Katie took a moment to balance the things in her arms, took a deep breath, and started marching through the snow in the direction of the Iron Curtain. Burly guards in green uniforms, furry hats, and red stars waited there for her with their German Shepherds and guns. They gaped at her as

---

101 I am going to marry
102 A wedding? Over there? Are you crazy?
103 Perhaps!
104 Be careful!

she slogged across the open snowy space between the two countries. Slipping and sliding, she tried not to lose her grip on her bags or her wedding dress. It was one of the longest walks she had ever taken.

As she trudged up to the border, one of the dogs started barking at her but she bravely walked past and set her things down on the long wooden table next to the guards. She held out her passport and visa to the nearest one. He took it in silence and then motioned for her to open her bags. She quietly unlocked her suitcase and stood back as they looked through the garments and presents she had brought along. Then she unzipped the garment bag and pulled out her bridal gown. The guards gasped as they saw it shimmering brighter than the snow on the ground. One of the guards mumbled something to her in Slovak, but upon seeing her blank expression, he asked her suspiciously in German pointing at the glittery dress, *"Was machen Sie hier damit? Werden Sie es verkaufen?"*[105]

Katie vigorously shook her head saying, *"Nein, nein! Das Kleid ist für meine Hochzeit!"*[106]

"Ihre Hochzeit? Hierher? In der Slowakei?" The guards asked her in disbelief.

"Ja, ja!"

Their stony faces cracked and they began to laugh and relax. As they were zipping up the bag and carefully handing it back to her, the Austrian bus rumbled up to the border.

"Entschuldigung! Ich muss einsteigen!"[107] Katie cried out, grabbing her garment bag and running to the bus. The Czechoslovakian guards were still grinning slightly and shaking their heads, as they carried her suitcase and guitar behind her to the astonished bus driver.

"So, after I talked to the driver and loaded my things on the bus, I exchanged money and here I am!" Katie said with satisfaction to Pavol who was holding her hand as she finished her story.

Pavol stared at her dumbfounded, unable to say a word. Finally, he cleared his throat and said, "Our guards must have been very surprised when they saw you walking across the border like that," Pavol said in wonder.

"I think they were, but you know they were very nice to me after that," Katie said sipping her drink. "They're just people after all."

---

105 What are you going to do with this? Are you going to sell it?

106 No, no! This dress is for my wedding!

107 Excuse me! I have to board the bus!

Pavol began chuckling as he took a bite of his sandwich. Feeling tired, Katie asked him, "Now what's so funny?"

"I can see that life is not going to be boring with you, Katka!"

Suddenly, a loudspeaker blasted, "Trnava Autobus – Stanica 7!"

"That's our bus," Pavol said standing up and grabbing her bags. He looked at her steadily for a moment and asked, "Are you ready? To begin this new chapter of our lives?"

"Yes, I am ready," Katie said without hesitation. "We've come this far – no turning back!"

Wedding No. 1

Katie was trying hard to focus as the Mayor of Trnava stood before her, his monotone voice droning on and on; the glint of a large gold medallion around his neck was distracting her. A slender young girl with long brown hair stood off to the side holding a pink carnation, waiting for her chance to recite a few lines of poetry. The tall blonde woman who had helped them arrange this state wedding looked very elegant in her black dress. She smiled reassuringly at Katie when she caught her eye. Pavol stood gravely next to her in his pinstriped suit with his hands hanging stiffly by his side. He had grown a beard during her absence and looked like a distinguished professor. Her cousin Karol Lauko, Jr. was behind her as her witness, and Pavol's brother-in-law and godfather, Jan, stood behind him. A few guests like Stan from Orava and his girlfriend Beata were sitting in the audience as well as some of her Trnava relatives.

It was the seventeenth of December, and they were going through the motions of their "State Wedding." They were still going to have their church wedding on December thirtieth in the Cathedral, but it would not be technically legal without this first wedding ceremony. Katie wore a navy blue suit with a white ruffled blouse; she had purposefully chosen flats as she didn't want to tower over Pavol during the ceremony.

Finally, the mayor stopped, closing the big red book he was holding; this was the signal for the young girl to begin her performance. With her eyes shut, the poetess opened her mouth and swayed a little as she uttered the lines of verse. It all suddenly seemed a little ridiculous to Katie, and she had to stifle a smile with a cough. Pavol gave her a sidewise look of concern, and she quickly became more somber. Then the music started playing; they turned quickly around, and marched mechanically down the red carpet towards the door. The mayor and the assistant accompanied them and escorted them to a room where everyone signed papers, and then toasted one another with champagne. Pavol paid the young girl for her work, and she quickly disappeared. As they came out of the room, their

287

friends and relatives were waiting for them ready to shake their hands and kiss them with their congratulations.

"Well, in the eyes of the state, we are officially married now," Pavol said grabbing her hand as they got into the backseat of his brother-in-law's little red Renault. "You are... how do you Americans say it? You are really stuck with me now!"

Katie laughed as she kissed him and said, "Right! Do not pass go! Do not collect two hundred dollars?"

"What?" Peter asked in confusion.

They sped down the road towards Marta and Karol's house. Marta exuberantly greeted everyone at the door and ushered them quickly into the dining room where a sumptuous spread of finger foods awaited them. After lunch, Katie went upstairs to pack her suitcase. Pavol followed her up the stairs and sat on the bed while she arranged her things.

"When are your parents coming?" Pavol asked fingering the strings on the new guitar she had bought him.

"They are flying to Prague right after Christmas. I think the tickets are a little cheaper then."

"It's too bad they could not come for Christmas and spend it with my family in the village."

"Well, you know Marta and Karol would have been hurt if they had gone to your family for the holiday and not to them," Katie sighed as she folded her jeans. "Anyway, they will come on the twenty-sixth, and we will meet them at the airport in Prague. Then my father booked a flight for us from Prague to Bratislava. It will be much faster than taking the train."

Pavol sat up a little straighter turning a bit pale. "You mean we are going t-t-to f-f-fly from Prague?"

Katie looked up from her packing at him and studied his face. "Yes, is that okay with you?"

"Of course, it's just, well, I have never flown before," Pavol said hastily trying to gain his composure.

"Piece of cake," Katie said resuming her packing.

"Piece of cake?"

"Easy! It will be easy for you! Don't worry!"

After lunch, Pavol's brother-in-law packed Katie's luggage into the car, and they drove to Čerešňa.

"I hope you won't mind sleeping in the front room. I normally sleep there, but I will stay in my father's room until our church wedding," Pavol

288

said, looking a little sheepishly at her as he sat with his arm around her in the backseat.

"I know," she smiled at him, resting her head on his shoulder. "That's fine."

The next few days was filled with Christmas preparations in Pavol's house. Martin had obtained a beautiful live Christmas tree through his connections, much to Zuzana's delight, so they pulled out the ornaments and began setting it up.

"You shouldn't set it up until Christmas Eve," Zuzana scolded her youngest son.

"Mama, we have so much to do right now," Pavol answered. "Be glad we are doing it now!"

Surprised, Zuzana went back to the stove and started vigorously stirring something in the pan.

"Is something wrong?" Katie asked as she hung a silver-wrapped chocolate on the tree.

"My mother thinks we are decorating the tree too early, but we have so much to do right now!" Pavol sighed. "I should not have spoken to her like that."

"I know this is hard for you, arranging the wedding all by yourself," Katie said looking at him earnestly. "I'm sorry I can't help you more."

"You are here and that's more than enough," he said smiling wearily.

Christmas Eve came and the house was full of the sweet fragrance of kolaches that Pavol's mother had been baking all day. Pavol's sister Helena and his other two sister-in-laws also dropped off cartons full of Christmas cookies and biscuits.

"Aren't your brothers and sisters coming over tonight?" Katie asked wonderingly.

"No, everyone celebrates with their own families at home," Pavol replied as he munched on one of the star-shaped honey cookies.

"Why?"

"Everyone has their own traditions," he said smiling, stuffing a cooking into her mouth.

"In America, we drive or fly for miles, just to be home at Christmas with everyone," Katie sputtered, her mouth completely full.

"Really? Well, we usually visit our other relatives and friends on the first and second Christmas days."

"You have a second Christmas day?"

"Yes, do you not have the same custom in your country?"

"Well, no, not exactly. I mean the British have 'Boxing Day' but we don't have anything like that in the States…"

"That's very strange," Pavol said disinterestedly as he kissed her and pulled her close.

That evening, they set the table in the living room with a beautifully embroidered tablecloth. Zuzana lit a red tapered candle in the centerpiece and then set the plates and soup bowls around. Katie followed with the tableware. The tree glowed in front of the window and the icicles sparkled in their light.

Then Jozef, Zuzana, their son and future daughter-in-law gathered around the table and began to pray. Katie could not understand everything, but she understood enough to recognize the Lord's Prayer. Afterwards, Zuzana poured little shots of alcohol into delicate glasses for toasting. She recited a few words in Slovak and then everyone drank.

"What did she say?" Katie whispered to Pavol.

"It's a traditional wish she makes every Christmas Eve. In English, it sounds something like this: *On our Lord Jesus' birthday, I wish you from God, good health, happiness and many blessings.*"

"Oh, that's beautiful," Katie breathed.

The first course was a delicious wild mushroom soup followed by fried carp and hot potato salad.

"I am so stuffed," Katie groaned pushing herself away from the table.

"It's not over yet!" Pavol said as he disappeared into the pantry. He came out again bearing a plate full of thin white wafers with honey and offered them to Katie.

"Take it," Pavol advised her. "It is very good."

Katie examined the wafer that was as thin as paper; it was imprinted with Christmas bells and stars.

"Marta and Karol had these last Christmas, too. This actually looks a bit like the communion host," she remarked as she took a nibble.

"You are exactly right!" Pavol said pleased. "Here, dip it in honey."

After the meal, Zuzana took up four walnuts and said in Slovak, "My dear little house, I have nothing but these nuts to offer you." Then she threw each one to the far corner of the house.

Katie looked at Pavol again questioningly but he just shrugged and said, "Another tradition."

After the dinner, they retreated to the kitchen where they began singing Christmas songs. Pavol played on the guitar while Katie sang traditional American tunes and then she hummed along as he and his parents sang the Slovak *koledy*. She did not even notice when Zuzana quietly slipped out of the room. She actually began to doze when suddenly she heard the tinkling of a bell.

"What's that?" she asked in surprise.

With big smiles, Pavol and his father led her back into the front room. Under the Christmas tree, there were presents wrapped in plain but colorful paper. Pavol's mother stood back in the corner of the room in the shadows.

"Katka, this is for you," Pavol said. He watched her carefully as she opened the box and found a beautiful pair of garnet earrings.

"Oh, they're gorgeous!" she exclaimed, looking up. Pavol's eyes met hers and they locked for a moment.

"*Tu maš*," Zuzana said, nudging another package into her hands. She beamed as Katie carefully unpacked the little box and found a colorfully painted cup, rimmed in gold.

"*Dakujem*," Katie said as she hugged her mother-in-law.

"Well, it is time to get ready for Midnight Mass," Pavol said after they finished unwrapping the rest of the gifts, which consisted of deodorant and shaving lotion. Katie was surprised at the simplicity of their celebration yet she recognized a warmth and a richness that she had never experienced before.

"Dress warmly," Zuzana admonished them as they began pulling on their coats and boots.

As they trudged through the snow, neighbors greeted them and joined in the procession towards church.

St. Elizabeth's was packed with people, young and old. The smallest ones sat in the front benches excitedly whispering to one another and showing off their new toys. Katie admired the tall Christmas trees sparkling behind the altar. Candles burned brightly and a large number of "*ministrants*" or altar boys proceeded in carrying the cross. A nativity scene with Mary, Joseph, and Jesus was set up at the base of the altar. The organ swelled and people's voices joined in an enthusiastic rendition of *Ticha Noc,* the Slovak version of Silent Night. Katie began to feel a bit sleepy as the Mass finally came to its conclusion.

Pavol held her close as they marched back home, their breath hanging in the air like smoke.

"Are you cold, Katka? *Zima*?" Pavol asked as she snuggled against his bear coat. A thick blanket of fog hung over the village, but she could still see colorful Christmas tree lights glistening in each house as they passed by.

"Just right. It has been a beautiful Christmas. Truly."

Pavol smiled, giving her a big squeeze and a kiss. "Yes. For me, too."

Wedding No. 2

Albert pulled his car in front of the photography shop on Main Street in Trnava. Katie peered out the window as Jana quickly jumped out of the car and opened the small car door for her. They both carried in her dress and shoes. A short-haired lady ushered them into the dressing room looking a little intense as she gave Jana some instructions.

Katie felt strangely calm as she watched Jana carefully unzip the hanging bag and pull out her beautiful white dress, oohing and aahing at the workmanship. Katie stepped into it gingerly and eased it slowly up on her body. They were supposed to take the "official wedding pictures" before the church ceremony, which Katie thought was a little odd since the groom was not supposed to see the bride until she walked down the aisle, but when in Rome, do as the Romans do…

"Okay, I think I am ready," she said under her breath as she checked her makeup and hair in a small compact mirror. Jana helped her on with the veil fussing around her like a mother hen.

"*Ach, Katka, Du siehst wunderschoen aus!*" Jana breathed as she stepped back to admire her.

Katie peeked at herself in the full-length mirror and gasped. She saw a sparkling snow-white princess that she could not recognize. Just then, Albert and Pavol poked their heads around the corner asking impatiently if they were finally ready. Jane pulled back the curtain and revealed Katie in her wedding dress. Her veil flowed over her shoulders and her dark curls framed her face as she walked slowly across the room towards the men. The men both froze, and Katie noted with some satisfaction how their mouths dropped open.

"And where is the bouquet?" the photographer asked brusquely, breaking the spell that had fallen upon them. Pavol and Katie looked at each other questioningly.

"I didn't even think about the flowers," Pavol groaned.

"Don't worry," the photographer quickly replied in gentler tones. "We will manage."

"I'm sorry, Katka! I know you wanted flowers."

"Never mind," she answered smiling.

The photographer spent the next twenty minutes carefully posing them and arranging the train of Katie's dress. After the shots were taken, Albert brought the car around; Pavol helped her in the back seat as her dress billowed around her. They were silent as they drove back to Marta and Karol's house to await the rest of the family.

Her father's cousin had outdone herself preparing sandwiches, hors d'oeuvres, and drinks for the wedding party, but nobody had much desire to eat even though their hostess strongly urged them to at least taste something.

"*Essen, Katka! Essen!*" her corpulent cousin pleaded with her.

Pavol's friends slowly arrived and clapped him on the back, shaking his hand. Pavol seemed relieved to see familiar faces, and they entered the parlor laughing and talking where Katie sat peacefully with Jana, her Lady-in-Waiting. Her mother walked in and patted her daughter on the shoulder. "It won't be long now," she whispered into her ear. Katie's heart skipped a beat, looking up at the clock.

Finally, it was time to drive to the church. The sun was already setting outside, causing the snow to glisten in the garden. As the bride and groom stood up together in the parlor, Pavol asked their parents to come forward and give them their blessing. With tears in their eyes, his two elderly parents reached up and shakily placed their hands on their heads murmuring a blessing in Slovak. The American parents also reached up and placed their hands on the young couple's shoulders. Moved, Katie's eyes began to well up, but she fought back the tears.

"I don't want to spoil my mascara!" she said laughingly to her mother as she sniffed and carefully wiped her eyes with the tissue Jana handed her.

Soon they were in the cathedral and their families took their places in the long wooden pews around the altar. Katie and her father stood at the back of the church while Pavol walked down the aisle to take his place. Jana rushed over and placed a bouquet of flowers into her arms.

Surprised, Katie nodded and smiled gratefully at her. The entire church was completely packed with people sitting and standing in the aisles and the back of the church. Word had gotten out that the church would be celebrating a Mass, and that there was going to be a wedding with an American bride and a Slovak groom! This was something that everyone had to see. As the children sang in the choir, the priest beckoned for them to move forward.

Katie hesitated for a moment and took a deep breath. Her father squeezed her arm, and they proceeded down the aisle. The good citizens of Trnava strained to get a good look at this Western bride, quickly assessing her bridal gown.

As they neared the altar, John gave his daughter's hand to Pavol who looked very handsome in his tuxedo. Her father took a step back to stand alongside Jan, Pavol's brother-in-law. The Mass began with the sign of the cross as the children finished up their song.

The church was freezing inside, and Katie was very happy that Jana had loaned her a white fur stole to wrap around her shoulders. Shivering, she suppressed a cough. Pavol stared straight ahead, looking very serious. While the lectors stepped forward to read the scriptures in Slovak, Katie tried to take in all the images of the ceremony: the ornate wooden altar that loomed before them, the priests and altar boys moving gracefully around it, her parents and in-laws sitting quietly on the side, and her breath hanging frozen in the air. She felt like everything was moving in slow motion and the priest's voice sounded far away.

Then the priest gestured towards her father. John stood up stiffly, moving forward to read. He cleared his throat and began reading in English the scripture passage about Isaac and Rebekah.

After meeting Rebekah and going to her brother Laban's house, Abraham's trusted servant told her he would like to hurry back to his master's home. Would she go with him? Rebekah's family tried to persuade them to stay longer, but the servant insisted that he must return home as soon as possible. Then Rebekah's family turned to her and asked her, "Will you go with this man?"

As John read this particular passage, his voice began to shake. He hesitated for a minute and then continued to read Rebekah's answer, "I will!" A tear trickled down his face. Everyone in the church sat mesmerized but started murmuring as her father stepped down from the podium.

"Now, is the time," Pavol whispered to her, "to make our promises to each other."

As the priest read the vows in Slovak, Pavol quietly translated for Katie. She made her promise to Pavol and then he made his to hers. Slipping the rings on their fingers, the priest blessed their union.

The next order of Mass was the Eucharist and Katie received her first Holy Communion. Shutting her eyes, she felt a great joy sweep over her. Then the priest gave the final blessing, and the young couple kissed for the first time as man and wife.

Everyone applauded as they exited the church while the children were singing loudly from the balcony. As the new couple stood outside in the snow, people poured out behind them and formed a huge circle around the plaza in front of the church. Crossing their arms, everyone joined hands, and began to sing, "Auld Lang Syne" in Slovak. As young and old sang, they swayed to the melody and big smiles broke out across each person's face.

The evening sky was unusually clear and full of stars. Then Pavol and Katie's families lined up and began congratulating the pair with kisses, hugs, and tears. Strangers and friends followed them, heartily shaking their hands and even kissing them. A few bold people asked Katie if she would consider selling her dress, but she laughingly shook her head and just shrugged as they walked away disappointedly.

Albert pulled up in front of the church and beckoned for them to jump in the car. Pavol held the car door open for her as she struggled to get in the backseat of the car with her long train.

"Watch out for my dress," she cried panicking.

Pavol just smiled as he shoved in next to her and took her hand. With a jerk, Albert sped off and headed towards the hotel where the reception would be held. They stepped through the big glass doors and headed towards a large banquet room. Tables were set up in a big U formation and a small band was set up in the corner of the room in front of a dance floor. Beautiful crystal glass graced the table settings of flowered plates and bowls. Everyone slowly filed in taking their places. Pavol and Katie sat at the head table flanked by their parents on either side.

"Oh, look at these wine goblets," Katie exclaimed delightedly as she picked up the gold-rimmed glass. "Our names are painted here, and, oh, look! Today's date is there, too!"

Pavol examined his wine glass admiring the delicate flowers and ornaments that encircled their names. "My sister's daughter Maria must have done this," he said. "She's very good at this sort of thing."

Katie glanced over at Pavol's niece and saw her smiling at them. She raised her glass towards her and mouthed the word, "*Dakujem!*" She nodded happily at her.

Then the waiters began serving courses of savory soup with rolls and chewy bread, which was soon followed by large schnitzels and delicate little bowls of cucumber salad. Platters of layered cakes and desserts followed. Pavol's father Jozef smacked his lips delightedly and leaned in eagerly to taste the fare.

While they were eating, Katie was startled to hear the strains of violin music behind her. Turning around, a young blonde boy stood grinning as he tuned his instrument. Then, he began swaying and playing a romantic melody, focusing all of his attention on the bride. Katie blushed and Pavol leaned back in his chair grinning. However, the young violinist soon switched his melody to a livelier tune, and everyone began clapping and singing. The room became alive with joy, and the band took this as their cue to start playing.

Pavol stood up, bowed and held out his hand to his bride. Leading her to the dance floor, they began to waltz to the music. Soon, couples joined them on the floor and even Katie's mother started dancing with Marta's husband Karol. Katie looked over at her father and saw that he was holding his head in his hands.

"What's the matter with Daddy?" Katie whispered to her mother after the dance was over.

"He has a headache," her mother said smiling wryly. "You know, Katie, it's hard on fathers to give up their little girls, but don't worry. He'll be all right."

As they sat down at their place, Katie leaned over and kissed her father on the cheek. "Are you okay, Daddy?" she asked.

He smiled wearily at her and patted her hand. "Finally, a real wedding – a real church wedding. This is what I have been waiting for." He kissed her on the cheek and sighed.

The rest of the evening was a blur of laughing, singing, and dancing. Katie felt tired but exhilarated at the same time. All her life, she had dreamed of a wedding like this, and she thanked God silently for fulfilling her wishes. The scripture came to her mind, *Delight yourself in the Lord, and He will give you the desires of your heart*. "It's so true, Lord! Thank you!" she murmured contentedly as she held her husband's hand on the dance floor.

Finally, after hours of dancing and more courses of food, the tired couple said their last goodbyes to their family and friends. Jana helped Katie with her coat and then kissed her on both cheeks goodnight. Katie squeezed her hand gratefully and said, *"Danke, Janka – vielen, vielen dank!"* Jana just smiled and stroked her cheek before hurrying out the door.

"Where are we going?" Katie asked as Pavol led her through the hall and out into the quiet dark streets.

"We have a reservation in a hotel room nearby," he said as they began walking in the cold night air.

A group of his village friends were still standing at the corner smoking and waving at them. Pavol stopped and exchanged a few words with them. They chatted and then he beckoned for them to come, but they began laughing, vigorously shaking their heads. Pavol shrugged laughing, too, and then proceeded with his wife towards the hotel.

"I am so, how do you say? Exhausted!" Pavol exclaimed as he unlocked the door to their room. "I never knew that planning a wedding was such hard work. I need a good rest."

"Well, you did a great job. I could not have done it better myself," Katie said kissing him impulsively.

Pavol smiled gratefully at her as he unlocked the door.

Katie followed him into the room which was clean but very plain and simple with a large bed in the corner. As she set down her bags, she turned around and looked at her husband who had just shut and locked the door with a flourish. She breathed in quickly when she saw his expression.

Sparks seemed to be emitting from his eyes, and strangely enough, he didn't look very tired at all. Swooping her up in his arms, he began kissing her until she was laughing and gasping for air.

As he set her carefully down, she said smiling, "I thought you said you were too tired!"

"I think there will be time to rest later," he said in a husky voice, his accent a little thicker than usual. "Much later."

One Last Note

Katie looked over at her husband as she reclined on the sofa bed in the front room in his parent's house. He was busy looking through papers and sorting out what was important and what was not. They would be leaving at the beginning of June for Texas and there had been a great deal of bureaucratic hurdles to overcome. Zuzana was sweeping the steps outside humming a tune to herself while Jozef was outside chopping wood for the stove. Even though it was mid-spring, the snow still lay thick over the garden and the courtyard this year.

She felt a stirring in her stomach that could not be identified. It felt like the wings of a butterfly fluttering inside her. Her eyes became wide and she said, "I feel it!"

"Feel what?" Pavol asked absentmindedly as he stared at the document in front of him.

"The baby! I feel the baby!"

He looked up at her smiling, his blue eyes twinkling, and said, "Really? It's too early, isn't it? Maybe it is only your, how do you say, imagination."

Katie shook her head and leaned back against the cushions, shutting her eyes. This was definitely not her imagination although everything seemed like a dream. Good things were in store! *Eye has not seen nor ear heard the things that God has prepared for those who love Him!*